Vile Affections

Vile Affections

CAITLÍN R. KIERNAN

Subterranean Press • 2021

See pages 339-340 for individual story copyrights.

First Edition

ISBN
978-1-64524-043-3

Subterranean Press
PO Box 190106
Burton, MI 48519

subterraneanpress.com
www.caitlinrkiernan.com
greygirlbeast.livejournal.com
Twitter: @auntbeast

Manufactured in the United States of America

For Ramey Channell, my "Aunt Pat,"
who so often encouraged my childhood
curiosity and enthusiasm.

In memory of thirteen brilliant minds, each of whom helped me to tease truth from the great mysteries of the world. Mentors, scientists, educators, and friends, they are missed.

Dr. Dale A. Russell (1937–2019)
Dr. Richard Estes (1932–1990)
Dr. James L. Dobie (1935–2018)
Dr. Elizabeth L. Nicholls (1946–2004)
Daniel W. Varner (1949–2012)
Dr. Donald Baird (1926–2011)
Dr. James C. Hall (1945–2016)
Dr. Samuel Wayne Shannon (1951–2020)
Dr. Douglas E. Jones (1930–2010)
Dr. W. Donald Fattig (1936–2016)
Dr. Dail W. Mullins (1944–2016)
Dr. Erle G. Kauffman (1933–2016)
G. Dent Williams (1941–2017)

For this cause God gave them up unto vile affections: for even their women did change the natural use into that which is against nature…

Romans 1:26

Do I contradict myself?
Very well then I contradict myself,
(I am large, I contain multitudes.)

Walt Whitman,
"Song to Myself" (Stanza 51)

Table of Contents

Introduction

Years ago, I actually enjoyed talking about my writing, whether it be in person or through interviews or when writing introductions for my books. But as the years became decades and the books piled up, I found I had reached a point where talking about my own work had become an exhausting – and I suspect pompous – chore, something I had *ceased* to enjoy. Indeed, I came to loathe doing it. I can actually put my finger on the very *day* when I came to this realization – October 8th 2010. I was trying to write the introduction for *Two Worlds and In Between: The Best of Caitlín R. Kiernan: Volume 1* (that title; pomposity abounds). Four years later, when it came time to do the introduction for *Volume 2,* I just couldn't bring myself to even try, and I handed the job off to S.T. Joshi. And now, seven years after *that,* I have pretty much stopped doing conventions entirely, I avoid interviews, and I hardly ever stoop to more than rambling acknowledgements and mercifully laconic story notes.

But I have just managed (and it feels like just *barely* managed) to survive the strangest year of my strange life – we have, *all* of us, survived a very strange and terrible year, even those who somehow do not realize this fact. So I thought, just for shits and giggles, just to give Oblivion the middle finger, maybe a short introduction to these stories is in order, since they include the last few I managed to produce before, and immediately after, the coming of COVID-19, before my fourteen months of a self isolation so complete I let entire months pass me by without stepping foot outside the house. Indeed, I feel I've spent the past year locked in pages of a Kurt Vonnegut, Jr. novel that William Gibson was frantically trying to rewrite. And, if I may be so selfish as to say, there seemed an awful personal irony at work. For years, I'd struggled with homesickness, wanting to leave the cold Rhode Island winters behind me and go home to Alabama, at least for a time, and also to return to work as a paleontologist, and what happens when I've finally managed to do *both* those things and life is actually looking kinda swell? A Grand Guignol of chaos and plague, civil unrest and attempted coup the likes I had hoped I would never live to see, that's what, the darkest days visited on this country since – well, in quite a long while. You lot can argue over since exactly when. It likely comes down to very elaborate and subjective notions of darkness.

But any way you slice it, kittens, 2020 was somethings special.

Oh, and never mind the long spell of writer's block that sprawled from roughly the end of May until mid December 2020. In all the twenty-eight or so years of my career as a fiction writer, I had never once experienced anything like it. Not merely one of my occasional dry spells, when I might have two or three rough months. This was a complete and total silence at the keyboard. I just *stopped* writing, entirely and altogether. It was terrifying. The spigot was shut off, and I had begun to think, well, that is that. And then suddenly, thank fuck, it wasn't, and I am glad to report that since December 15th, when I began writing again, I have finished eleven short stories. Some people believe that calamity and fear are good at greasing the creative wheels, and I'm here to tell you, that clearly ain't exactly a universal constant.

But I *have* survived, along with those I care about, along with you and you and you. I have persisted stubbornly into a world that will never again be precisely the world it was before last March. And I *am* working again. I look back at the tangled nightmare of 2020 and I remember something wise that Harlan Ellison was fond of saying (though I do not know if he originated the sentiment) – The trick isn't becoming a writer. The trick is *staying* a writer.

The last year tested my ability to *stay* a writer as nothing had ever tested it before.

Fuck you, 2020.

That said…

There is no single thread uniting the twenty-two stories that comprise *Vile Affections*. They tend to be soft spoken, like most of my recent work. There's a little science fiction, a little fantasy, a whole lot of whatever it is I'm usually doing that *isn't* "horror." Also, most of these stories deal, in one way or another, with matters of the heart, and pretty much always in ways that some folks will find to deviate from the true north of respectable humanity. Hence the collection's title. Yeah, I'm being ironic. But…frankly there's nothing I find more tiresome than the author telling you what you're about to read, so I'll get out of the way now.

Welcome back.

Caitlín R. Kiernan
20 May 2021
Birmingham, Alabama

Virginia Story

I'm somewhere well south and west of Roanoke, and I admit that I haven't been paying attention to the road signs. Driving since before dawn, since Baldwin County, Alabama, and here it is almost midnight now, and the wheels on the wet interstate sound like sleep. The rubber-on-asphalt drone is as surely a siren as any mermaid ever was, as any winged maiden luring sailors to their doom with pretty songs of paradise and pussy. I rub my eyes, rubbing back the sleep demons, and squint at oncoming headlights and reflective highway signs and at the pitchy Appalachian night. I turn the radio up a little louder, wondering when and how the rock station out of Knoxville became a country music station out of Richmond. I fish the last can of Red Bull from the cooler, pop the top, and grimace at the syrupy taste like carbonated SweeTarts. I'm thinking about maybe taking the next exit and getting a motel room when I see the tall girl walking along in the breakdown lane. She doesn't strike me as a hitchhiker, because she doesn't appear to be making any effort to get anyone to stop for her. She's just walking, head down, arms crossed. I pull over, anyway, because maybe she ran out of gas or had a flat or a broken fan belt or a leaky, busted radiator. Maybe she doesn't have a phone to call for a tow truck, or maybe her phone ran out of juice, or she can't get a signal. I pull over a little ways ahead of her, let the engine idle, and wait for her to catch up to me. After a moment or two she appears in the rearview mirror, painted red and bloody in the brake lights. She pauses and stares at the car, and I think, just for a second, that she's going to back away, that she might even bolt. But then she steps around the rear fender and raps on the passenger-side window with her knuckles, and I turn the radio down again, reach over and roll down the glass. Her hair's wet, so I know that she's been walking since sometime before the rain stopped, even if I can't clearly recall how long ago that was. An hour, half an hour? I ask if she needs a ride, and she frowns and glances back the way she's come, as if there's anything to see but darkness and the headlights of oncoming traffic. "Yeah," she says. "I guess I do, don't I?" She wants to know if I'm going as far as Harrisonburg, and I tell her that I'm going a lot farther than that, all the way to New York. "I only need to get to Harrisonburg," she says. "I don't need to go to New York." I tell her I can drop her off, no problem. She opens the door, but then hesitates, still gazing back down the wide asphalt ribbon of I-81. It's a rainy October night in the mountains, but she's only wearing a T-shirt and a hoodie and jeans. I ask her if she isn't cold, if she isn't half frozen, and she shrugs and turns to face me again. The girl stares at me for what likely only seems like a long time before she slowly shakes her head and answers no, no she's fine, but thanks for stopping and am I sure it's no bother, taking her to Harrisonburg. "It's right there on the way," I reply, and she gets into the car. She brings the smell of the rain with her, and the smell of cigarettes and sweat. She fastens her seat belt, and that's when I realize that she isn't wearing any shoes, and that's also when I see that she's missing two fingers off her left hand, the middle and ring fingers. I switch on the heater, and she pulls the door shut and locks it.

"I'm really not all that cold," she says, but then holds her hands up to the heat vent and rubs them together for warmth. Her remaining eight fingers are long and slender. Her nails are short and painted some dark color, a very deep shade of red or maybe black or dark blue. Maybe purple. It's impossible to tell in the soft green glow from the dashboard. I check the rearview mirror again, then put the car into gear and pull back out onto the interstate. "I'm Hannah," she tells me. I reply, "Nice to meet you, Hannah. I'm Margaret, but people usually call me Meg," and then I wonder immediately why I didn't simply tell her to call me Meg in the first place, why I bothered with Margaret at all. "Where you from, Meg?" she asks, and I ask if she means where was I born or where do I live, and she says that if they're different places, she guesses she means the latter. "I was born in Mobile," I tell her, "but I live in Manhattan. I've lived there almost nine years now." She asks if I was visiting home, if that's where I'm on my way back from, and I say yeah, it is. "I've never been to New York," she says. "I've never been to Mobile, either. Hell, most times it seems I've hardly been outta Wythe County, Virginia." Hannah stops rubbing her hands together and sits back, watching the night rushing past outside the car. She tells me she's sorry if she's getting the upholstery wet, and I tell her not to worry about it, and that if I had anything at all to give her to dry off with, I would. "I'm fine," she says. "The rain doesn't bother me, not usually." I tell her that my coat's in the backseat, if she's cold, and she repeats that she isn't. That she's fine, really. "Did you break down back there?" I ask, and she says no, she was just walking. I start to say something about her being barefoot, barefoot without a coat in October in the rain, but instead I say, "You weren't planning on walking all the way to Harrisonburg, I hope," and she says no, no she didn't guess that she had planned on that. "I have a sister," she says, "in Harrisonburg. I haven't seen her in a while." And then Hannah asks me what I do in

New York City. I tell her that I teach at City College. She asks what I teach, and I tell her I'm an English lit professor. "So poems and Shakespeare and stuff," she says and almost smiles. "You don't want to hear about all that," I tell her, mostly because I don't want to talk about all that. I don't want to explain to her that I'm only adjunct faculty, and that I'll almost certainly be out of work in another six months or so, and then who knows what the fuck happens next, how maybe I'll be moving back to Mobile. How maybe I'll be waiting tables. "I wasn't ever any good at school," she tells me. "But I do like poetry." And then, despite myself, I say, "I don't teach poetry. I teach literary theory. The history of literary theory, actually." She says oh, well, she doesn't know anything about that, and I tell her it's okay, neither does anyone else. "What's it like, New York City?" she asks. I don't reply right away. There's a semi truck coming up fast behind me, and I wait until it has roared and rumbled past my car and is a good fifty yards ahead of us before I answer her. I hate those trucks. I have since before I learned to drive. Few things make me more nervous than being passed by a semi, especially on a rainy night, especially on wet roads. "It's very crowded," I say, finally. "And expensive. And loud." Hannah says that she's never actually been to a big city, but that she's never wanted to, either. "I'd miss the mountains," she says. "I'd miss the trees." She asks if I like living in New York, and I tell her no, not really, so she asks why I moved there, all the way from Mobile, Alabama. "Well, when I was in high school, I thought I had to move away, far away, or I'd never amount to anything. And Manhattan seemed like exactly the sort of faraway place that one moves away to in order to amount to something. Manhattan or Boston or Chicago. Someplace like that. But I should have settled for Atlanta. If nothing else, I'd have saved a small fortune on gas." She asks if I ever think about going back home for good, and I tell her yeah, I think about that a lot, more and more it seems. She starts telling me about how she used to believe that she wanted to be a veterinarian, because her grandfather had been a veterinarian, the sort that looks after farm animals – cows and horses and pigs and such. I listen and try to guess how old she is, but I'm lousy at that sort of thing. She could be as young as nineteen or twenty, or she could be a lot older. There's something worn about her face that seems at odds with her eyes and her voice. "Problem is," she says, "I never really got along with animals, especially not with horses. I like them, but they don't much care for me. So, that kinda got in the way. And I wasn't any good at math or science neither, and apparently you need math and science to be a vet, so there was that, too." It's started raining again, and I switch on the windshield wipers. I glance at the clock and see that it's a quarter past twelve and I wonder how long it's going to take to make Harrisonburg, how much the rain will slow me down if it gets bad again. I'm already regretting picking the girl up. If I hadn't, I could have stopped somewhere and slept for a while, had a hot shower and breakfast, instead of enduring two or three hours of awkward small talk with a stranger. Should'a, could'a, would'a. I'm trying to think of something else to say, considering turning the radio back on, when Hannah says, "I don't mind you're a lesbian, by the way. I want you to know that." For a moment, I'm a little too flustered to reply, and before I can get unflustered, she adds, "I saw your bumper sticker when you stopped for me back there. The rainbow bumper sticker, I mean. And I want you to know it doesn't matter to me, and that I didn't vote for him. I didn't vote for her, either. But I didn't vote for him. Just about everyone else I know did, but not me. Truth is, I didn't vote for anyone. I probably should have, but I didn't." And I'm still trying to think what to say, when Hannah asks, "Do you have a girlfriend in New York City?" Not anymore, I tell her. We pass a sign that lets me know it's another seventy-two miles to Roanoke, and I begin wondering if maybe I could convincingly fake engine trouble, get off at the next exit with a motel, and let Hannah find someone else to drive her to Harrisonburg. "I don't mean to pry," she says, and then she brushes a few stray strands of damp hair from her eyes with the hand that has only three fingers. "I know it's hard, being different. I ain't queer, but I know what that's like. Anyway, I didn't mean to make you uncomfortable. People say I talk too much. People say I ask too many questions." I tell her not to worry about it, and that if I minded people knowing that I'm a lesbian, I probably wouldn't have put the sticker on my car. That's not what I'm thinking, but that's what I tell her. "I went to school with a gay girl," Hannah says. "Everyone said it was because she was too fat and none of the boys would want to go with her, and so she might as well like girls. But I know that was just folks being hateful. It amazes me how hateful folks can be. Sometimes, I think it's like in the Bible, when Lot couldn't find even ten good men in all of Sodom. Sometimes, I think that if I tried I couldn't find ten good people in the whole damn world, much less in Wythe County." I don't know what to say to that, so I wind up saying something insipid like how maybe people aren't as bad as you think, at least not all of them, maybe not even most of them – something like that – and Hannah gives me a tired, sort of pitying glance. It's the way you'd look at a kid who's still got a lot of suffering to do before they finally learn just how hard the world can be, and it makes me feel foolish, and it makes me wish all over again that I hadn't picked her up. She turns her head and stares out the windshield at the cold rain peppering the glass and the metronomic sweep of the wipers. "It's actually a pretty fucked up story, Lot and Sodom and all," she says, sort of (but not quite) changing the subject. I ask if she means because of Lot's wife being turned into a pillar of salt, and she says no, not that. Well, sure that, but not only because of that. "I mean how when the men of Sodom come to Lot's door and demand that he turn over the three strangers – the three angels who have come to warn him that God's going to destroy the city – how Lot offers up his two girls to try and make them go away. Lot knows perfectly well that the men at his door want to rape the strangers, and he's saying, no, you can't have them, but you *can* have my two virgin daughters and do with them whatever you please. And *this,* mind you, is the one good man that God could find in all of Sodom and all of Gomorrah." I tell her that I'd never heard that part of it, and I half wonder if maybe she's making it up, but she tells me, "It's right there in the Book of Genesis. Anyone can see for themselves, but you won't hear it too often in the Sunday school lessons." And then she adds, with a faint air of authority, "I had an uncle who was a Pentecostal preacher, an uncle on my daddy's side." And who am I to argue. I haven't picked up a Bible since high school, and that was more years ago than I like to think about. "So, did Lot give the men his daughters?" I ask, and Hannah says no, no he didn't. "The angels blinded the men at Lot's door. And that was the end of that." Then she asks if I have a cigarette, and I tell her no, I don't smoke. "I know I should give it up," she says. "I know I never should have started to begin with, and I should give it up. I swear, it feels like just about everything I enjoy is bound to kill me, sooner or later." She folds down the sun visor and stares at her face reflected dimly in the little mirror. I start to tell her she can switch on the interior lights, so she can see better, when she sighs loudly and folds the visor up again. Hannah sits back and watches the rain. "I know you want to ask about my fingers," she says. "It's okay. You really don't need to pretend like you don't, like you aren't sitting there thinking about them, like you haven't even noticed they're missing." And she holds out her left hand, but I keep my eyes on the road. "To tell you the truth," I say, "I didn't figure it was any of my business." I can hear a faint tremble in my voice, but I'm not sure if that's because I'm embarrassed that Hannah has dared to call out my morbid curiosity, that she's perceptive enough to see it, or if it's because I'm angry that she's acting so presumptuous. "Hardly anyone ever comes right out and asks, but everyone wants to know," she says. "It's only natural, ain't it, wanting to know what happened when you see something like somebody missing two fingers?" The rain's coming down hard enough now that, even set on high, the wipers are having a hard time keeping up, and the water drums loudly on the windshield and the roof of the car. I know that if it doesn't slack off soon, I'll have to pull over again and wait it out, and I silently curse the sky and the night and whatever misguided bit of charity made me stop for the woman sitting next to me. "It's not like I'm ashamed of my hand," she says. "I hope that's not what you think, that I'm ashamed of it." I tell her no, that's not what I was thinking. That's not what I was thinking at all, and I sound defensive and hate myself for sounding defensive. "I just didn't think it was any of my business," I say again, and it comes out even less convincing than the first time I said it. "No, Meg, that's not it. You're just worried what I'd think of you if you were to ask, worried maybe it would make me uncomfortable and so I'd think less of you for having noticed my hand and for sitting there turning it over and over in your head, trying to imagine what it was took my fingers off. I know that's what it is, so you don't have to pretend. I don't think less of you. It's only human." I glance at her and see that she's watching me now and that she's still holding up her left hand. And I should just own up to my curiosity and agree with her, admit that she's right and that I'm no different from anyone else. But, for whatever reason, I don't want to give in and give her that satisfaction. And maybe she's right and it is because I want to believe I'm somehow above such things, that I'm too sensitive or conscientious or enlightened or what the fuck ever to have such a base reaction to another person's misfortune. Maybe it's exactly that. "I don't mind telling you," she says, and she lowers her arm, letting the diminished hand rest in her lap. And I want to say, *Honest to fuck, I'm a lot more worried about running off the road in this rain or getting sideswiped by a tractor-trailer truck than I am worried whatever it was happened to your hand.* But I don't. Instead, I tell her, "When I was a kid, I had a cousin lost a finger fixing a lawnmower." I'm not sure why. Maybe since it seems she's determined to tell me how she lost her fingers, me telling her about my cousin and the lawnmower amounts to some sort of fair trade. Tit for tat, an eye for an eye, a finger for finger. I don't know. "Is that so?" she asks me, at least pretending to sound interested, and I nod and watch the road. "I guess he was lucky," I say, "that he didn't lose his whole hand." And Hannah says, "Some people are like that, just born lucky." Then she's quiet for a while, watching the rain and the dark, and I'm almost ready to believe that she's decided not to tell me how she lost her fingers after all, when she says, "I dropped out of school after tenth grade and married this guy who'd just come back from Iraq. Jimmy. Jim. Jim Byrd. I'd known him before he was deployed. We'd been friends a long time, and when he came back, well…he came back like a lot of guys come back. And I suppose I had it in my head how I was going to take care of him, save him, do something good with my life by being there for him after what he'd gone through. I was young. I still believed people could do that, save other people. I guess I was idealistic." We pass a sign that informs me there's still seventy-five miles left to go until Roanoke, and right after the mileage sign there's a doe crumpled in the gravel and weeds at the side of the interstate. The way its head's bent back, the way its skull is resting between its shoulder blades, I know the deer's neck is broken. It jumped out into the traffic, someone hit it – probably one of the semis barreling along in the rain – and the impact broke the animal's neck. Its dead eyes are open wide, staring nowhere, waiting for a thoughtful crow or vulture to come along and peck them out. I try to put the sight out of my mind and concentrate on the road and Hannah's story. In the twelve hours or so since leaving Mobile, I've probably seen a dozen deer lying twisted and broken at the side of the road, at least a dozen, in various stages of dismemberment and decay. What's one more. "So it's not like he went to jail for it," Hannah says, "but he still couldn't hold down a job." I realize that I've missed something she's said, but I'm not about to ask her to repeat herself. "He got a pretty good job at the PepsiCo Gatorade plant, but that didn't last long at all. By then, he'd mostly traded the whisky for meth. He swore it helped with the nightmares, but I always knew that was bullshit. Meth and oxy and I don't know what the hell else all he was taking." Hannah pauses and wipes at the condensation that's formed on the passenger-side window, rubbing at it with the heel of her good hand, but not doing much more than smearing the water around and around. She gives up and wipes her wet hand on her jeans. "After he got fired, he saw someone at the VA about the nightmares," she says, "but all the goddamn doctor did was put him on more drugs that made him even crazier. I should have left him, I guess. My momma tried to get me to leave him, and I should have listened. But I've always been better at talking than listening. Maybe that's one reason I couldn't really help Jimmy. Maybe he needed someone to listen more than he needed anything. Anyway, it wasn't too long after all that, after him getting fired, that he started in dreaming about wolves. Whatever else he'd been dreaming about before, the desert and his buddies getting blown up and little kids with bombs strapped to their chests – you know, war shit – well, those dreams stopped and it was just the wolves from then on." Another semi passes us, even though I'm doing the speed limit. "Wolves?" I ask, without actually having intended to say anything at all, and "Yeah," Hannah replies. "Wolves in the sand. And not just regular wolves, he said, but werewolves. He said the wolves were really women who'd lost babies in the fighting, and at night they became wolves and hunted American soldiers." I say, "I don't even think there are wolves in Iraq," and Hannah shrugs and tells me she wouldn't know and, besides, it's not like bad dreams have to make sense. She says, "It got so that's all he would talk about, when he talked, which he was doing less and less. I tried to talk about, well, just about anything else, but he'd always start in again on the wolves in the sand. Jimmy said that even when he was awake he could hear them. He said that they didn't howl like real wolves do, that instead they prayed and sang Muslim holy songs and called out the names of the men they were hunting. He'd say, 'God gave the wolves our names. The wolves were the instruments of God's vengeance.' Crazy shit like that. But I didn't leave him. Jesus, where the fuck was I even gonna go? Move back in with my momma and stepfather? No thank you." Hannah stops talking long enough to cough and clear her throat, and I glance at the clock. It's almost a quarter past one. Hearing Hannah's story and seeing the dead deer, somehow the two have worked together to jog loose a memory of another rainy night, almost four years ago now, the night I saw a coyote in Central Park. It had never occurred to me that there could be coyotes in the park, or anywhere else in Manhattan. But there it was, regardless. I was taking a taxi back downtown from a dinner party in Harlem and the coyote dashed out in from of the cab somewhere along East Drive. It seemed painfully thin to me, and in the headlights, its eyes flashed red gold. The cabbie cursed in Hindi, honked his horn, and the animal immediately vanished into the trees and underbrush. There had been something in the coyote's mouth, something small and limp and torn. Beside me, Hannah yawns and rubs at her eyes, and then she says, "Fuck, I feel like I haven't slept in a week." And then she rubs her eyes again. I'm pretty sure that Hannah's eyes are blue, a very pale blue, but in the dimness of the car, it's hard to be sure. I want to say that she doesn't have to tell me any more. Sitting there, I feel like I've been forced somehow into the role of voyeur, and it's making me a little angry and embarrassed. I've always been a private person, rarely sharing more than I have to, sometimes to the detriment of relationships with friends and lovers and family members. I'm starting to resent the way that Hannah has made me a captive audience to her personal tragedies and those of the man she married. I want to change the subject, and I'm trying to figure out how to do that tactfully, when she stops rubbing her eyes and continues. "One night," she says, "Jimmy came home from – shit, I don't know where he got off to most days, and I didn't really want to know. I rarely bothered to ask. But he was high as a kite and scared half to death. I don't think I'd ever seen anyone half as scared as he was that night. He told me the wolves had found him, that they'd followed him home, that they were waiting outside the house, waiting until we went to sleep." Hannah looks down at her hands lying her lap, and then she covers her incomplete left hand with her whole right. "I was trying to get him to settle down, because he was starting to scare the shit out of me, too. I'd sort of gotten used to his being crazy and the things he'd say, but that night – it was a summer night, a night in July – he'd been so much worse than he'd ever been before. So, I'd been trying to get him to settle his ass down, but that only made things worse. He hit me. He'd never done that before. I always swore I'd never stay with any man who hit me, and I never had. He slapped me hard enough to knock one of my front teeth loose. He didn't knock it out, but he knocked it loose. I tripped over a chair and wound up on the kitchen floor, and I was sitting there on the linoleum, with my ears ringing, trying to clear my head, when he told me that he knew what I was, that he'd known all along." She pauses still looking down at her hands. She clears her throat again, then stares out the windshield at the rain. Despite myself, I ask her, "What did he mean by that, that he knew what you were?" And Hannah laughs. It's a soft, dry, papery sort of a laugh. Brittle. Thin. It makes me wish I had kept my mouth shut. It makes me wish all over again that I hadn't stopped to pick her up, that I'd minded my own business, rather than trying to play the Good Samaritan. "He said he knew how I was one of the werewolves. That's what he meant, Meg. And then he went into the bedroom and got one of his hunting knives and came back to the kitchen with it. I think I told him he was crazy and that I was going to call the police if he didn't stop. If he didn't settle down. But Jimmy said he knew what I was, and he said what's more he could prove it." I realize that the rain's slacked off a little, and I switch the wipers back onto low. "Prove it how?" I ask her, and she replies, "Jimmy said there was a way, because even when the werewolves were women they still wore their fur on the inside. He said if you cut one of them open when they were pretending to be a woman, that's how you could be sure the woman was really a wolf. That's why he'd gotten his hunting knife out. He said he'd start with my hands, if I wouldn't admit to it, if I wouldn't own up to being one of the monsters that had followed him all the way back from overseas to get even for all the murdered children." And that's when I finally tell her I don't want to hear any more. That's when I ask her to please stop. And she does, and she apologizes. She says, "I shouldn't ought to have started in on that. I know I shouldn't have. I hope I haven't upset you, not after you were good enough to stop and give me a ride." I tell her it's okay, that I'm not upset, but that I just don't want to hear any more. She asks if it's all right with me if she turns the radio on, and I say sure, go ahead. I don't mind. There's a Hank Williams, Jr. song on the country station out of Richmond, and she turns it up loud enough that I can't hear the rain anymore. After that, we don't really talk. I drive, and she listens to the radio. She dozes off somewhere after we pass the exit for Newbern, and I let her sleep. I glance at her, from time to time, wondering if the story I didn't let her finish is true or if it's nothing but a tale she's concocted to hide some far more ordinary explanation for what had happened to her hand. I wonder – if it *is* true – what happened to Jimmy, and why he didn't hurt her worse than he did. Maybe it was because he cut off those two fingers and saw there was only flesh and bone and blood, and he wasn't so out of his mind that it wasn't sufficient to stop him. I wonder if he's in prison or a mental hospital somewhere. But I decide it's easier not knowing for sure. I can live with the uncertainty, and, anyway, I suspect it's more likely Hannah lost her fingers in a car accident or to an infection from an untended cut or to just about anything but a husband who'd decided she was a vengeful Iraqi werewolf. It's just a little after one thirty a.m. when we make it to Harrisonburg. I leave the interstate and pull up to the pumps at a Shell station. Hannah wakes up when I cut the engine, and she sits staring out at the bright glare of the LED lights shining down from the gas station's canopy. She asks if this is Harrisonburg, and I tell her yeah, that we're there, and she gets out and stands by the front of the car while I fill the tank. It's long since stopped raining, but the night is cold and damp, and she stomps her feet and rubs her hands up and down her arms. She's starting to shiver. I return the nozzle to the pump, screw the cap back down tight, and then I ask her if she's going to be okay, if she needs me to take her somewhere in town before I get back on the highway. "Thanks, but I can find a phone and call my sister," she says. "My sister's expecting me." I ask if there's anything else she needs, and I know that I'm feeling guilty for not having let her finish her story, for having interrupted her and cut her off like I did. Hannah tells me she's fine, and she thanks me for the ride, and she says that it was nice to meet me. "If I ever make it up to New York City," she says, and she smiles sleepily. "Sure," I say. "I'd be glad to show you the sights." And then she turns and walks away, heading for the Shell's convenience store. She holds up her good right hand, shielding her eyes from the lights, and I think how I probably should have offered her my coat again. But I don't call her back. I wait until she's inside, and then I get back into my car and drive away. I make it a little ways past Wilkes-Barre, Pennsylvania before sunrise, before I'm finally forced to admit that I'm too tired to safely go any farther and decide to stop for breakfast. It's rainy again and foggy, and the overcast morning sky is the cold blue-grey color of mold. Exiting the interstate, an animal darts out in front of my car, and I very nearly hit it. It might have only been a dog. It's hard to be sure, and I have no idea if there are coyotes in northern Pennsylvania. I'm pretty sure there haven't been any wolves for a very long time. But its startled eyes are bright in the headlights, shining like the sun off copper, like twin dabs of molten gold.

VIRGINIA STORY

This story has at least two sources of inspiration. The first, several late night drives through the Appalachians, on our way to Birmingham from Providence and vice versa. If anything has the capacity to send my mind to strange places, it's the weird monotony of an interstate highway at two in the morning. Also, Neko Case's "Margaret vs. Pauline" (*Fox Confessor Brings the Flood,* 2006). "Virginia Story" was written between March 6th and March 17th, 2018. It's probably my last genuinely good Providence short story.

Theoretically Forbidden Morphologies (1988)

She calls herself by various names, according to whims and according to tidal charts, but tonight she call herself Perse, after one among the three thousand daughters of the union of Tethys and Oceanus. "My sister went and married that little bastard Poseidon," she says, leading me down a narrow concrete stairwell. She is nude, and I am only barefoot. We are bathed all in coruscating light rising up from some bright place below. There is no other light within the stairwell but this. She goes before me, and I follow, my right hand gripped in the long fingers of her left. My feet disturb thick grey strata of dust that has lain here undisturbed for an age, for a millennium, for all my life until tonight. I ask her where we're going, and she says that not knowing until we get there is half the battle. Or she says it's half the fun. I'm not sure which. I can hear her every syllable just fine, but something is lost in translation. Meaning is made more difficult to grasp than the comprehension of mere words. I can see the phenotype, but not the genome from when it was spawned. Look at it that way. I ask her how long we've been descending these stars, and Perse asks me what possible difference does it make? It seems like a very long time, I reply, and she laughs, and her laughs slam themselves against a jagged granite shore and break apart into sea spray and foam. The stairs are steep, and here and there are imprints pressed into the cement, casual fossils – a poplar leaf, the paw prints of a dog or cat, tread marks left by bicycle tires. "I asked if you were certain," she reminds me. "I warned you it was a long way down, and you said that didn't matter, so long as I didn't go so quickly that you were unable to keep pace." And I almost ask, *Is that what I'm doing? Am I keeping pace? Is that what this looks like to her?* I do not *actually* ask, though. I am pulled along in her wake, at best a tourist. If I protest too much, she might leave me to try and make my way back to the surface alone, and that way lies worse things than madness. I could get lost, and I would spend all of forever on these steps and never find my way back. I know that, and she knows that I know. So, I squeeze her hand a little more tightly. "It isn't much farther, I promise," says For Tonight I Am Perse. "But don't look down." I don't tell her how I've been looking down since all this began. It occurs to me how each of these concrete steps is not an actual, literal step, even if they do allow us to traverse actual, literal space. It occurs to me that each step is an aeon, or – no, that's not right. It occurs to me, rather, that each step is the variable distance between one species and all those that have arisen from that progenitor. We are walking down a family tree, you might say. We are backtracking evolution. And though I did not say that aloud, Perse says "More or less, if you gotta put a name on it." This stairwell is so narrow that my shoulders almost rub against the walls, and the ceiling seems to be growing lower and lower. There's a tiny, bright blossom of panic when I imagine it growing ever smaller and finally pinching out, leading us nowhere at all. *But then, where would the light be coming from?* Perse tells me I'm being too literal again, and then the waitress comes around and pours us both another cup of coffee. I pour cream into mine, and it swirls like a microcosm, like all the galaxy in a cup of Joe. Perse always takes hers black. She says that bitterness is good for the soul, a little bitterness or a lot. "You're sure you can find it again?" I ask her, and she asks, "You mean the doorway? Yeah, sure. It's not far from here. Most of those photographs were taken not far from here." I sip my coffee, and she talks about the first time she happened across the stairwell. That was only a couple months back, she tells me. She was at a gallery up in Harlem, and she saw the door in the wall, and painted on the door was something that she first mistook for a tree. Or for only a *mere* tree, she corrects herself. She talks about recapitulation theory, embryology, Lemuria, heterochrony, the writings of Ernst Haeckel, and that gallery with all its photographs, but in particular the door with the tree that was not merely a tree. She lights a cigarette and says "I can show you a series of embryos, early in their development – let's say a mouse, a pigeon, and a human being – and you could not *possibly* tell them apart." I gaze out the plate-glass window at the rainy night, the wet streets, the streetlights reflected on every surface. "This might not be the ideal night," I say. "No night will ever be the ideal night," she replies. "Ideal nights do not ever present themselves." Neither one of us says anything for a while after that. She smokes and drinks her black coffee. I watch the rain-slicked streets. Finally, she says, "I'll tell you something I have never told anyone else, if you promise to keep it to yourself." And I say, "How would I tell?" She says, "What I mean is, you can't ever use it in a story. That's what I mean. I'm not giving you material for a goddamn story, if I tell you this. It's personal, between the two of us." I say, "Yeah, fine, sure. I'll never share it with another living soul, whatever the hell it is." Then

Perse tells me she's not trying to be a shit about it, just she's seen how I tend to take what I hear and weave it into my stories. "Maybe you don't even do it consciously," she says, "but you do it." A delivery truck rumbles past the diner. There's a smiling cow painted on the side of it, and I check my watch. It's almost midnight. "I promised, didn't I? When have I ever lied to you," and she laughs and says, "Oh, don't you go and get me started. You've lied to me plenty." The air in the diner smells like cigarettes and frying eggs and coffee and ketchup. She sits back in her booth and stares at me in mine. "All right," she says. "I'll pretend I can trust you. I'll pretend I think of you like a sister who would never, ever betray that trust." I frown and start tearing a napkin into strips. "You pretend whatever the fuck you want. You tell me or you don't. Whichever, I don't really care." She exhales smoke and brushes the hair back from her eyes. "When I was a kid, when I was about fourteen, there was a traveling carnival set up in the vacant lot across from the subdivision where I lived, after we left Connecticut, before we moved *back* to Connecticut again. I'd never seen a carnival before. They had a merry-go-round, a Ferris wheel, striped canvas tents and games of chance, the whole shebang. My mother, who was the fretful sort, she told me not to go anywhere near it. 'You don't know what kind of people are associated with that sort of thing,' she said. 'Gypsies and perverts, that's what kind of people.' I swore I wouldn't go anywhere near the carnival, but I did anyway. How was I supposed to not? Jesus, you bait a hook and drop it over the side of a boat and ask the fish *not* to bite?" I tell her that I've never been to a carnival, and she says, yes, well, we aren't talking about you, now are we? "No, but I was just saying." She shakes her head and stubs out her cigarette, only half smoked. "Do you want to hear this or not." I really don't. Or, rather, I'm genuinely indifferent to the prospect. But if I say that aloud, she'll just get huffier than she is already. "Yeah," I lie, "I want to hear this." Perse watches me a long moment, like she's looking for any evidence that I might be lying. Her eyes are the only polygraph machine she'll ever need. And this, I think, is what it feels like to be a paramecium or a euglena or a rotifer beneath the lens of some asshole's compound microscope. This is how it feels. *This,* right here. Finally, she stares down at her coffee cup, instead of staring at me. "There was a chain-link fence separating the vacant lot where the carnival had set up from the subdivision where we lived. On one side of the fence, our side, you had the carefully manicured despair of brick split-level ranch houses and turf monoculture lawns. On the other side, the *other's* side of the fence, it was almost like a wilderness. Well, it's what we had instead of having a wilderness, that empty space in between our neighborhood and the next soulless subdivision over. We were forbidden to go there, so, you know, of course that's where everyone wanted to hang out. It was mostly tall grass, and a couple of oak trees. There was a lot of garbage people had dumped in the lot over the years, plywood and sheets of corrugated tin and corrugated plastic, empty metal barrels with warnings painted on them. Fuck only knows what they'd once held. Boys would go there with their air rifles and murder squadrons of soft-drink bottles and old mayonnaise jars. Kids went there to smoke cigarettes and weed and to have sex back behind the live oaks. It was that sort of place, the place we went to fucking escape suburbia. And that October, it's where the carnival set up." I ask how old she was, and she tells me she was fifteen, and then she wants to know what difference that makes. "It doesn't," I say, though I suspect that it does. She says, "My parents talked about getting up a petition to have the police run the carnival people off. They didn't, they only talked about it. My parents were the sort who were all activism until they actually had to act. The carnival set up loudspeakers, and at night they played rock music and recordings of calliopes and accordions and weird shit like that. At night, it was a sea of lights, like a rainbow had lain down in that vacant lot to die. I waited a couple of nights, and then I climbed over the fence." And I listen while she talks about the rides and about cotton candy and about the greasy, broken-down men and women who ran the attractions. But I know this is all preamble. Not because I've heard the story before. I haven't. But because of the way she's speaking, the way she's delivering the tale, building suspense, front-loading tension, sowing foreshadowing. Whatever the fuck ever. I've been with her long enough now to recognize these things. By and by, she arrives at the reason she's brought up a carnival she disobeyed her parents a decade ago to visit, back then when she was still only a teenager desperately looking for a tonic to her white middle-class desperation. It will even tie in with the door from the photograph from the gallery show up in Harlem. I know that. I take that for granted. "Off at one end of the carnival," she says, "there was a row of tents set up, and out front there were these enormous canvas banners. They had pictures painted on them. Horrible, lurid images. It was the freakshow. An actual, genuine goddamn freakshow. It cost a whole dollar to get in, and you were led past this procession of really pretty ordinary freaks. A bearded woman, a tattooed woman, this guy who'd pound nails into his face, the taxidermied corpse of a two-headed calf. Something that claimed to be a hermaphrodite, a pair of twins who claimed to be Siamese twins who'd been separated at birth, then sewn themselves back together. It was really all kinds of sad and funny and mostly fake – mostly obviously fake – but we were just the sort of mean little shits who paid our dollars just to snicker at these people and make fun of them. Even if it was fake, we pretended it wasn't, because where's the fun in mocking a counterfeit freak? But then there was something at the end of it all, in the very last of those tents." And Perse stops talking, and she looks out the window at the wet streets, and I watch her reflection in the glass. She lights another cigarette. I drink my coffee. *Or* right then, she looks a lot younger than she is. Right then, she looks the age she is, instead of the ten years older she's always trying to affect. Right then, the shadows in her eyes, they make me want to tell her I don't need to hear the rest. But now my interest has been piqued, and at the bottom of it all, Perse and I are exactly the same sort of selfish cunts. "What was it?" I ask, prodding, pushing her ahead. "What was what?" she asks, like she's not going to finish the story, and I feel a small flash of anger down in my gut. "In the last tent. What was it you paid a dollar to see in the last tent?" She shakes her head. "Actually, they made us pay extra for the last tent. An extra fifty cents. On the banner out front was – well, if you wanted to make a monster out of a mermaid, it was like that. Only, it really wasn't like that at all. That canvas banner out front claimed we would be seeing the daughter of Scylla and Charybdis, and I think I must have been the only one of us who had any idea who Scylla and Charybdis were, because – I don't know why. I just do. And I asked the carnival guy, the barker, whatever he was, how Scylla and Charybdis could have a daughter, when the both of them were female. Son of a bitch doesn't miss a beat. He starts in lecturing us about parthenogenesis and shit, explaining about all these species of lizards and snakes and amphibians and sharks, all these *lower* vertebrates, mind you, that are capable of breeding and maintaining healthy populations and genetic diversity without males. He told us how there are no records of parthenogenesis in mammals, and so this meant that when Scylla and Charybdis had been cursed by the gods, what they'd become, it was clearly no longer mammalian. He said, 'They'd been cast back down the evolutionary ladder.' Or some shit to that effect." And I ask, right on cue, because I know my lines, "So, did you pay the fifty cents extra." She laughs and smoke spills from her nostrils. "Well, yeah," she says. "What the fuck do you think? You think we were just gonna turn around and go home after hearing that line of BS? Whatever was in that last tent, it had to be at least worth the four bits, even if was just a con. Shit, man, everything's a fucking con, but if we played along at least we'd be able to tell the carnival guy how full of shit he was." I take another swallow of my coffee. It's still too bitter for my liking, so I add another pink packet of Sweet'N Low and stir until the powder has dissolved in my cup. "What did you see?" I ask her, and she looks away from the window just long enough for me to catch the wariness in her china-blue eyes. "I won't tell you that," she says. "I could, but I don't want to. You haven't paid the price of admission." This is pure Perse (or whatever name she happens to be wearing on whatever night, take your pick). These are the games she plays, although, I do not believe that to her they are games. I believe to her this is acceptable, normal human conduct. She switches off the lamp on the little table beside the bed that we've shared for six months now, and she says she doesn't want to sleep, and I ask her if she wants to fuck, and she says no, she doesn't want to do that, either. She's playing a gallery opening up in Harlem tomorrow night, just Perse and her violin, and I assume she's got the jitters. For someone with her musical pedigree, she gets the jitters an awful lot. She gets the jitters more often than she doesn't. "I was just thinking about something that happened when I was a kid," she says. I ask her what, and she says she won't tell me that, but, instead, she'll tell me about a dream she's been having. Maybe other couples talk about their dreams, but it isn't something that Perse and I do. I've tried, because I know how bad her nightmares can be. She wakes up at two a.m. or four a.m., sweating and breathless, and then she's up the rest of the night. She paces from room to room like a cat who's lost her kittens. She chain smokes and watches TV and plays her violin. I lie in bed and listen, trying to get back to sleep. I might as well, because I know well enough she'd only rebuff any attempt I make to get her to talk about whatever it is she's dreamed. I usually manage the obligatory "Honey, you should come back to bed." Never much more than that. So, anyway, this night, she volunteers to tell me about a dream, I'm all ears. Only trying not to seem eager. I'm also wondering what's different, if I've *done* something different, if it's something I could do differently on purpose. "If you don't mind listening," she says. "I don't," I reply. "You're a voyeur," she tells me, and then she sits up and lights a cigarette. She switches the lamp back on again, and my eyes sting. She looks at the clock, and then she looks at the bedroom window and the night outside, the night laying over the city outside. "When I was a little kid," she says, "I almost drowned." I've already heard this story, and for a second, I think she's changed her mind, and she's not going to talk about the dream, after all. "That's what you were dreaming about?" I ask, and she says no, but she was dreaming about water. "I was someplace surrounded by deep green pools. I think it was inside a cave, but it wasn't dark, because there was light rising up from the water. It was like swimming pool lights. You know what I mean?" And I tell her yes, I know what she means. "The light shining up through the water played across the roof of the cavern, rippling, shifting. I think there's a word for when light shining through water does that, but I can't remember it." She takes a drag on her cigarette and blows smoke rings at the ceiling. "Coruscating," I suggest, and she shrugs. "Maybe. Anyway, in my dream, there are these walkways or trails between the pools of water. When you look over into the pools you can see all sorts of things swimming around down there. Alligators and gars, enormous black eels and catfish, huge snapping turtles crawling along the bottom. Everything in the water just glides silently along, and there are all these plants down there, too, some sort of aquatic grass or kelp or something, swaying in the current. I look up, and there's no sky, just that shifting light coming up from the water, and it's sort of like light from a movie projector, which is why I think I might be inside a cave. There are no stars. There's no moon." I ask Perse if she's ever been inside a cave, and she says no, no, she never has. I ask her if there were any sharks in the pools, and she says no, it was freshwater, not salt, and then I say well, there couldn't have been any kelp, either, and besides, there are sharks that live in freshwater. She tells me to shut up and stop being such a fucking nerd if I want to hear about the dream, so I do. "The ground wasn't muddy. It was more like walking along the edge of a swimming pool. I was barefoot, and the ground beneath my feet felt like concrete. There was no one else there with me, except the things that lived in the water. I walked and I walked, and the more I walked, the more afraid I became of the water, the more I began to worry about losing my footing and falling in. The ground wasn't muddy, but it was slippery in places, and when I wondered why that was, I imagined things crawling out of the water. I began to be afraid that I'd come across one of the alligators lying across the trail, blocking my path. Or one of the snapping turtles, and then I'd have to turn around and walk all the way back to wherever it was I'd come from. I looked into the water again, and this time I realized that the bottom was littered with all sorts of animal bones, and with human bones, too. So, now I knew for certain what would happen if I fell in, right?" Then she gets quiet and just sits there smoking and blowing smoke rings and staring at the window. "And then what?" I ask. "And then what…*what?*" she replies. I say, "What happened?" She frowns and tells me that's when she woke up. "Fine," I say, and roll over, turning away from the light of the lamp, wanting to go back to sleep. "If you don't want to tell me, don't tell me." And she says, "I would tell you, if there were anything else left to tell. I woke up and lay here in the dark and started thinking about when I was a kid and

I almost drowned." I remind her that she'd said she wasn't going to talk about that. "I'm not," she says, "but that's what happened next, after I woke up." I tell her that I have never almost drowned. I admit that I have never learned to swim. I also admit that I have a fear of water, which is something I've never told her. "Aquaphobia," she says. "Unwarranted, persistant, and irrational fear. But it's not actually water you're afraid of. It's actually that you're afraid of drowning, which is ironic given how we spend the first nine months of our lives as aquatic organisms, given that our evolutionary ancestors were fish, and way back before the fish they were other things that lived in the sea." Then she holds up her left hand, the palm side turned towards me, and spreads the fingers far apart. I notice for the first time that her middle finger on that hand is shorter than the fingers on either side of it. "Doesn't that mean you're a werewolf?" I ask. "Doesn't what mean I'm a werewolf?" she wants to know. "That your index finger is longer than your middle finger," I reply. "For that matter, so is the finger to the right of your middle finger. I don't know what that means." She says it doesn't mean anything, just that not everyone's built the same way, that's all. "Why are you afraid of water?" she asks, still gazing at her splayed fingers. "I don't know. I don't have any idea. I just am," but she tells me, "Nobody just *is* anything. There's always a reason. There's something that happened that made you afraid of water. A traumatic event, or maybe when you were a kid your mother or father or a great aunt told you over and over and over that water was dangerous, and so you grew up believing it." I say, "Water *is* dangerous," and she replies, "Naturellement. Mais je suis fait d'eau." I tell her that I don't speak French, even though I probably speak French at least as well as she does. Perse asks me, "Je suis d'eau, je suis d'air, et je suis d'électricité. Qui suis-je?" I don't answer, no matter how elementary the riddle might be, no matter how obvious the answer. Instead, I reach out and touch that short middle finger. "Ma main est une main de poisson," she says, and then she sets her cigarette between my lips and laughs. "Maybe that's what scares you," says Perse. "Maybe what scares you is knowing that you are descended from a fish, and you're scared of going back the other way, slipping back down the evolutionary ladder, so to speak. Like the Little Mermaid in Hans Christian Andersen's fairy tale." I take the cigarette from my mouth, and Perse rotates her wrist so that the back of her hand, not the palm, is facing me, so that she's staring at her own palm. "Would you come and visit me at the aquarium?" I ask her. "You could bring me gifts of anchovies and plankton." But her mood has suddenly shifted, as it does, and there's no joking or playfulness remaining in her face. I would say that there is a shadow cast over her face, as if she's standing beneath storm clouds, hidden from the sun. Perse makes all her own weather. "Go back three hundred million years, or one hundred and fifty million generations," she says, "and my mother was a lobe-finned fish. I read that somewhere. A paleontologist from the Natural History Museum in London said that, I think. One hundred and fifty million generations. It's not as far back as all that." I ask her what a lobe-finned fish is, and she tells me coelacanths and lungfish are the only surviving lobe-finned fishes. "Along with all their descendants," she says. "Along with you and I. So, you see, mon amour mouillée, it's not only irrational, your fear of the water, it's an insult to your pedigree." I tell her that I'm tired. I tell her that I want to go to sleep now, that I have to be at work in a few hours. I take a drag on the cigarette, then give it back to her. I ask her to please turn off the light, and she does. "I thought you'd want to fuck," she says, and I say maybe tomorrow night. She reminds me about the gallery opening tomorrow night in Harlem, some pretentious hole on 7th Avenue called Backspace. I say what about after, and she says we'll see, if she's not too tired, if she's not out too late, if she's still in the mood. She might not be, after all. I might be passing up my one opportunity for the foreseeable future. "Be like that," I say and shut my eyes. When I open them again it's at least a week earlier, the day we left the city and took the train all the way east to eastern Connecticut, to Old Saybrook where Perse was born and grew up. She wasn't Perse back then, of course, or Clymene or Eurynome or Styx or any other of the Oceanids, she was just her mother's only daughter, always too pale, always too thin, never behaving as an only daughter should. Once, she told me, "The first time Mom found a copy of *Hustler* beneath my mattress, she cried for a week. All she'd ever wanted was a granddaughter, right?" We get off the train in Old Saybrook, and Perse knows a place where we can rent bicycles for the day. It's a bright early summer afternoon, not a cloud in the sky, the sun a white blazing eye, and there are tourists everywhere. "Where do they all come from?" I ask, and she says New Jersey. I suspect she's joking, but sometimes it's hard to tell with her. We ride our rented bikes through town, down Great Hammock Road and out across salt marsh inlets to a white strip of sand called Harvey's Beach, if the signs are to be believed. I ask who Harvey was, and she says she has no idea. The tide is out, and we find a little patch of beach that is, inexplicably, relatively tourist-free. "When I was a little girl," I say, "this is where I used to swim." I don't tell her that I can't swim. I don't tell her that I'm afraid of the water, that even now the sea is making me anxious. I keep that to myself, an embarrassing confession for another time. There are tide pools with tiny fish and snails and scuttling crabs. She takes off her sneakers and wades, but I hang back on dry land. After a few minutes, she comes and sits down beside me and shows me the handful of shells she's plucked from the pool: a spotted moon shell, a Scotch bonnet, a periwinkle, a dogwinkle. I laugh when she says "dogwinkle" and tell her it sounds like the name a Hanna-Barbera cartoon character or a fairy in *A Midsummer Night's Dream.* She tells me that I'm thinking of Dogberry in *Much Ado About Nothing.* She says that later, on the way back to the station, we'll ride past the house where she grew up and where her parents still live. When I ask, doesn't she want to stop and visit, she says not on your life, sister. "The last time I brought a girlfriend around my mother was the last time I'll ever bring a girlfriend around my mother." And then she tells me about the time when she was ten years old and she got caught in a rip current and almost drowned. "It carried me way the fuck out from shore," she says. "We learned in Girl Scouts what to do if that ever happened, that you swim parallel to the current, not against the rip. You try to swim back to shore, that's only going to exhaust you and make it that much more likely you'll drown. But I panicked. By the time a lifeguard got to me, I wasn't breathing. My lungs were full of water. That's what my father said, anyway. I honestly don't remember much about it. I remember being pulled out. I remember being afraid. I remember waking up on a stretcher in the back of an ambulance taking me to the hospital." Hearing this story, I feel cold, despite the bright summer sun. Hearing this story, I feel ice in my bowels. "And then..." she starts, then stops herself. "If I tell you this next part, you can't ever tell anyone, okay? I mean, no one. That means you can't ever use it one of your stories." I say sure, I wouldn't do that, and that maybe it would be best if she didn't tell me. I don't tell her that I don't *want* to hear it, not if it has anything to do with drowning. "I got my first period two nights later," she says, and I say how I've never heard of anyone who began menstruating that young. "I'm not saying you didn't," I add. "That's not what I mean." She says she didn't take it that way, and then she tells me how she woke with blood on her sheets and nightgown and panties, and not just blood, because there was also a little fish in the bed with her, still alive, gasping for air and flopping around in the bloodstain. She looks at me, like she's trying to see whether or not I think she's making it up. "I've never told anyone," says Perse. "I carried it in my hands to the toilet and I flushed it. I never told Mom or anyone else. Not until I told you, just now." She says that the fish was about three inches long, and that it didn't have any eyes. Then neither of us says anything else for a while. We sit there holding hands and listening to the low, susurrant waves rushing up the sand towards us, then withdrawing to the sea again. Overhead, seagulls wheel and scream, their sharp eyes searching the beach for picnic scraps and garbage, and I wish that we'd stayed in the city. "I have a gig next week at this gallery," she tells me. "Some photographer. I've never heard of him, but he photographs subway tunnels and sewers and, you know, places underground. You can come, if you're not busy. There'll probably be free wine." I say free gallery wine is the worst, and she tells me that beggars can't be choosers. "I'll think about it," I tell her, and in a little while we walk back to where we left our bicycles and head back to town and the train home. And now, tonight, after she led me through the streets and back alleys to a door with a tree painted on it, a tree stretching back through time one hundred and fifty million generations, three hundred million years, we descend the cement staircase, bathed in restless, coruscating light rising up from some bright place far, far below. I know what's waiting for us down there. I don't have to ask her. There will be deep green pools where alligators and gigantic eels and catfish swim through undulating forests of water plants. There will be no stars and no moon, and what passes for the sky will be so near that, if we stand on our tiptoes, we might be able to reach up and touch it. I could turn around, but I don't. I could beg her to turn around. She leads the way, and I follow, my right hand held tightly in her left, and I try not to think about her short middle finger. I try not to think about a blind fish on bloody bed linens. I just walk and wait for what comes next.

THEORETICALLY FORBIDDEN MORPHOLOGIES

This story was written in 2017. There's this *other* recurring dream that I have, of looking into deep, crystal-clear pools, watching fascinated as various species of enormous fish and reptiles, both extinct and extant, swim majestically past. It is always a very, very peaceful dream. Sometimes I am standing on a bridge that spans the pool. Sometimes it's very much like the cavern in this story. But the basic structure of the dream is always the same, and I'm fairly certain it leads straight back to the three years of my childhood spent in North Florida (1969-1972). My family frequently visited popular tourists magnets like Wakulla Springs, Weeki Wachee Springs, and Silver Springs State Park. Now, if you Google any of those you'll see the crystal pools from my dreams. Another important source of inspiration for this story is the late Dr. Jennifer A. Clack's *Gaining Ground: The Origin and Evolution of Tetrapods* (2002), a brilliant book I'd just read for the second or third time shortly before I did this story. "Theoretically Forbidden Morphologies" was written between September 20th and 25th.

©LOCKE 2021

The Line Between the Devil's Teeth (Murder Ballad No. 10)

I feel a pin prick at the nape of my neck, but hardly anything more than a pin prick. I may have winced, but now I honestly can't recall. It's an hour before dawn or an hour after midnight; it genuinely does not matter which, and I'm standing at the dormer window in the attic looking south out across the dunes towards the winter sea, and I only may have winced at a pain that was hardly more than a pin prick. There must be stars in that sky. There must be stars beyond counting up there, just as there were last night and every night before, back to the first night I slept in this house and back to the very beginning of time. But I can't see them. There are no clouds, and there must surely, certainly be stars, but the fact remains that I cannot see them. There's only the moon, three nights past full on this freezing December evening. The waning moon is a jealous, bloated thing, drooping in the heavens as if it has gorged itself on star flesh and starlight and soon will fall from the sky and lay bobbing in the ocean, a victim of its own unbridled appetites. I shut my eyes and try to remember if I winced.

The air in here smells like cobwebs and mildew and regret, and my breath fogs, which is the strangest sort of comfort to me. Beneath the cold white gleam of the moon, the dunes shimmer like parabolic mounds of granulated sugar heaped against the sourness of the sea and a sky filled with voids where devoured stars used to be. The dunes reach almost all the way to the house.

I lift my left hand and touch the spot on my neck where only a moment ago I felt the pin prick, the small and hungry pain, and my fingertips come away damp.

"Would you like to hear a story?" you ask me, and when I don't answer right away, you also ask, "If I told you a story about the moon, would that make it easier?" And your voice is a lot like the moonlight – hungry and cold and devoid of even the smallest trace of mercy.

"I'm tired of your stories," I reply. "If you want to know the truth, I'm sick to death of your stories."

"You're pouting," you say. "It's unattractive. It's futile, and it's unattractive."

I raise my sticky red fingertips to my mouth and lick them clean, feeling shame in that act and tasting the saltiness of my own personal interior seaway, for each and every living man and woman is no more and no less than the kingdom of Neptune made flesh and bone, given consciousness and the illusion of freewill. We are all of us emissaries and we are all of us castaways, tossed up on the dry shingle of the world three hundred and seventy-five million years ago and forever exiled from the womb and bosom of Mother Panthalassa. We are the forsaken children of Devonian heretics – *Tiktaalik, Ichthyostega, Panderichthys,* and a thousand other as yet unknown and unnamed stem-tetrapod progenitor gods. Behind me, you wipe your lips and smile your taunting razor smile at my thoughts, every single one of them laid as bare to you as if I were speaking them aloud. I imagine that your smile makes a sound like tearing paper – or maybe that's not my imagination at all. You kiss the wound you've made, counterfeiting tenderness, lapping at my skin with your sandpaper tongue, and somewhere in the room the albino boy with bat wings laughs and scratches at the attic floor.

"I could tell you the one about the *USS Revenge* and Oliver Hazard Perry," you say, speaking hardly above a whisper. "The ninth of January, 1811, and naval historians all say that the schooner became disoriented in a fog bank and tore out its bottom on a granite reef just offshore from Watch Hill Point. But you know better, and I know better. Or how about the collision of the *Larchmont* and the *Harry P. Knowlton,* the eleventh of February, 1911? One hundred and forty-three souls perished that night, only three miles from the Watch Hill Lighthouse, swallowed up by the wind and the snow and the sea. Would you like to know the last thing they heard? Would you like me to sing that song for you tonight?"

"I don't want anything from you," I say, but we both know that's a lie.

"Well, you can't stay locked away up here forever," you tell me. "It would be an awful waste, and I cannot abide wastefulness," and just for a moment I'm no longer standing in the attic gazing out across the dunes. Instead, I'm on the listing deck of a stormbound ship, no more than three miles out from shore, three miles out at the most. I know exactly where the lighthouse *should* be, but there's only a patch of deeper darkness waiting there, a throbbing, tenebrous void beckoning me forward. A lure, in point of fact. At my back, even over the wind in the rigging and the waves slamming against the hull, I can hear the bosun praying to St. Nicholas. There's another sound, as well, woven into the fabric of the nor'easter gale, high and sweet and deadly as nightshade, a sound that anyone who doesn't know better might easily mistake for a lullaby. It must be very much like what Odysseus heard, bound to the mast and his men's ears all stuffed shut with beeswax.

"I won't *listen,*" I say. "I won't *hear,*" and, for an answer, the sea heaves itself up, bearing the little ship towards the sky, spinning the bowsprit landward. A heartbeat, a dozen heartbeats, and we're over the crest and racing down the backside of the mighty swell. I lose my footing on the deck, the soles of my boots slipping on boards slick with ice and brine, slipping despite the shagreen nailed to the soles. As I fall, the storm tears itself apart around me, and I come down hard on my hands and knees in the attic of the house by the dunes, the house where I first heard you sing, the house where I might have died or surely soon enough will. I stare at the scars on the dusty floor and the scars on my wrists, waiting until all of this feels real again. I can still taste the sea, I think, then realize that it's only the taste of the blood I licked off my fingers. I look up, and you're right there standing over me, your eyes burning the same shade of pale as the bloated winter moon.

"You have to forget and let it all go," you say, and I ask, "Let all what go?" even though I know damn well what you mean. The asking is only deflection, a half-hearted defense mechanism, same as the sheets I've used to cover all the mirrors in the house, same as the way I force myself to swallow food I don't need and can no longer keep down. You reach out and offer me your hand, just like that night that you reached out and pulled me from the surf, where I was only trying to drown and be done with it, once and for all. But I was weak then, and my fear got the better of me. Faced with the absolute and undeniable fact of the end of myself, and so with the fact of the end of everything, I discovered that my resolve was a paper tiger, and I flinched. Tonight, however briefly, I'll pretend that I won't flinch, and so I don't accept your assistance. I don't take your hand. If I should ever decide to stand up again, I can manage it well enough all on my own.

"What is it you'd have me forget?" I ask a second time, playing dumber.

"The guilt," you reply, indulging me. "You have to let go of the guilt. It's no good to you here, not on this side. It's useless enough to the living, and to you it's worse than a millstone tied about your neck. You might think that you've nowhere left to fall, that this is the very bottom, but you'd be wrong, and guilt is the deadweight to drag you down so far that even I could never find you again. Do you really think it was curiosity queered things for Orpheus and Eurydice? No, my sweet, it was guilt. Now, stop being silly and take my hand."

I shut my eyes and hear a clanging bell buoy, rocking on the water out beyond the dunes. I don't take your hand.

"Fine," you sigh, all mock exasperation and annoyance and bother. "Go on ahead and crawl around down there like an insect if it pleases you. Wallow, if wallowing is the best you can do. I'll tell you a different story, instead. A different *sort* of story."

And hearing this, the albino boy with bat wings makes a high, ugly chittering noise. He was with you when you found me. He follows you about like your shadow, stitched into the lee of you, but if he has a name, I've never yet heard it. I have imagined that he's what I'll be someday, when you've stolen from me every last vestige of humanity that I have left to take, when I can no longer recall who I might have been the day before we met or the feel of the sun on my face. I suspect that he's only an indigestible bit of something you haul about behind you, because it gives you one sort of pleasure or another to see his ruin. Maybe you only came to me because he needs a sister.

"No," I say, opening my eyes again, opening my eyes and shaking my head. "I'm sorry. Please, tell me a story about the moon. Tell me a story about the moon and shipwrecks and drowning women." My voice has become that of a frightened woman, because suddenly I have become exactly that, because you're capable of far worse things than blizzards and icy decks and that foundering schooner bobbing about in Block Island Sound. I'm frightened because I've pushed you, even though I know better than to push you. Even though I knew there was nothing to gain, even if, strictly speaking, there was also nothing to lose. I glance about the attic, but now I can't see the boy with bat wings anywhere. He must have hidden himself in the clutter of old furniture and cardboard boxes, must have dug in amongst the newspaper bundles and dust. "I'm sorry," I say a second time, my eyes still searching the gloom for some evidence of what's become of the boy.

"Liar," you say, speaking hardly above a whisper. "No, you're not sorry, not in the least. You're a coward, that's all. You know that?"

"I do," I admit. "Of course I know that, and you knew that much from the start," and if nothing else in all the wide and time-haunted world is true, that much certainly fucking is. "It's not as if I ever claimed otherwise. Now, please, tell me a story about the moon. Tell me the one about the *USS Revenge* and Oliver Hazard Perry."

"No, I don't think so," you say, and you crouch down on the floor next to me and gently brush the hair back from my face. Your fingers are like frost on wrought iron. "Not tonight, darling. I'm afraid that ship has sailed." You laugh at your own joke, and your nails graze my left temple and my cheek, breaking the skin, drawing more blood. Somewhere in the attic, the albino boy with bat wings giggles happily to himself, delighted as a child pulling the legs off a spider. Then you tell me to look at you, and so I do as I'm told, because I'm frightened, and whatever stingy shred of resistance I'd scrounged and cobbled together since the last time you came sniffing around has all been spent, squandered on token refusals, and now there can be nothing for me but compliance. I obediently raise my head and look at you, looking *into* you, and I see that your irises are no longer the color of moonlight. If there's a word for the color they've turned, I don't know it; I doubt that it exists anywhere in all the languages of men.

"That's better," you say and smile for me. You lean in closer, your cat-rough tongue flicking out to lick at the fresh scratches on my face. Your breath washes over me, cold and clean as the sea, and I remember how surprised I was the first time we kissed and your mouth didn't smell like death, that your breath wasn't the breath of the grave. Abandon all preconceptions, ye who enter here. Forget the fairy tales and horror-movie clichés. What Bram Stoker didn't get right would fill a set of *World Book* encyclopedias.

You kiss me, and your tongue probes about and slides eagerly past my teeth. And I fall again, even though I'm still on my knees. This time there's no attic floor to rise up and catch me, and no slippery ship's deck, either. This time, you're letting me pick the destination, even if my choosing is purely unconscious. No matter how many times we've been through these motions, and no matter that I know exactly what's coming next, I'm caught entirely off my guard. I gasp, and you breathe yourself into me, bearing me down.

Time shatters. My *perception* of time shatters, and then it's made whole again. Easy as you please. Easy as falling off a log. Easy as cherry pie.

I'm standing barefoot in the sand, and it isn't winter anymore. Or it isn't winter yet. The air is warm, even though the sun's almost down, and tucked underneath all the smells of the sea, I catch the scent of dog roses. Behind me, the dunes are alive with them, pink and white blossoms speckling a wilderness of poison ivy, bayberry, and beachgrass. All that's left of the day is the thinnest fiery red-orange rind smeared out along the western horizon, bridging earth and ocean, tying together the end of a day and the beginning of a night. And here I am, caught in between, pressed like a dried flower between the pages of a book, standing in the sand and watching the tide go out. The sea at dusk is so calm that it's almost flat, and the little waves rushing up and breaking on the shore are hardly louder than a murmur. There are still a few noisy, complaining gulls wheeling about overhead, and a cormorant rushes past, sleek and skimming along only a foot or so above the water. Farther out, there are the crimson, green, and white running lights of shrimp boats, like Christmas coming in July, and farther out still, the old lighthouse at the northern tip of Block Island winks on and off, off and on. There is nothing whatsoever extraordinary about this scene. My apocalypse is the most mundane sort imaginable.

In the east, the moon is rising, and if it's not quite full tonight, then it will be tomorrow or the night after that. The full buck moon or the full thunder moon or whatever it was called by the people whose land this was in the long ages before white men came and took it all away and made the world safe for tourists and surfing and clam shacks.

And then I remember that it's a Thursday, and I remember, too, what this particular Thursday means. I look down and see the stone clutched in my right hand, a fist-sized chunk of granite I found washed up and half buried among the cobbles on this stretch of beach a mile or so north of Watch Hill Point. I'm holding onto it so tightly now that all the color has drained from my knuckles and my hand is beginning to go stiff and numb. The stone and my fingers are sticky and dark, and for a few precious seconds I try very hard to be confused by that stickiness, to fool myself into believing that I don't have any idea what's happening here, or, more precisely, what has happened, only a few short moments before. But the body is right there behind me, *her* body, lying facedown in the sand. The back of her skull has been caved in, and the way her arms are outstretched puts me in mind of a crucifixion. It always surprises me that I can smell her blood, even over the ocean and the dog roses and the acrid stink of my own sweat, but I can. Every time you leave me here, I smell the blood, the blood on the stone and the blood still oozing from her corpse and spattered across the sand and across the pebbles and the cobblestones, just as I must have smelled it on the actual night of the actual deed. I open my hand and gravity dutifully drags the murder weapon from my grasp.

Behind me, somewhere among the dunes, someone has begun to sing.

"Were you watching?" I ask you. "Were you watching the whole time. Did you see it all, start to finish?"

"I was watching," you reply. "I saw enough." And then you ask me, "Have you ever had to get rid of a body? I hope you're not just planning to leave it lying there, believing the tide and the crabs will do the work for you."

"It's not as if I planned this," I say, and that might be true, and that might be a lie.

"You could bury her, but a dog or a pack of coyotes would probably only come along and dig her up again. Skunks and raccoons and foxes, you have to think of those, too. But sure, you could give that a shot, burying her. Unless you didn't bring a shovel. Or a mattock. Or maybe a hoe. It would take you all night, to dig a hole deep enough and wide enough, but you could always give it a shot."

The song from the dunes sounds almost like a lullaby, and I gaze out across the water and the twilight wondering if the people in those fishing boats can hear it, too.

"There's little enough harm in trying," you continue, "unless, of course, it doesn't work out and you waste all that time digging a grave when you should be doing something else, instead. Something smarter. Something less obvious. Do you even know if you can lift her? A dead body is a surprisingly heavy thing, and you're not all that much larger than her. If you had to drag her all the way back to the car, what a sight that would be. And have you considered what you'll do should someone come along and catch you in the act?"

I'm already in the water up to my knees before it occurs to me that I've decided to drown myself, and I can't recollect taking however many steps I've taken away from dry land and the dead and crucified woman I've left lying back there with my neatly folded jeans and shirt and underwear, with my socks and shoes and with the bloodied chunk of granite.

"Do you even know why you did it?"

In the dunes, the singer's voice rises several octaves, and now it seems more like the call of some strange bird than anything from a human throat. It has, in fact, become almost painful to hear, but I don't cover my ears. Soon, the water will be deep enough to hide me safely away from the reach of the song. The sea sloshes about my hips now, freezing despite the season, neither welcoming me nor turning me away. I'm only going home, after all, only seeking redress for an ancient abandonment, offering myself as a sacrifice in apology for the faithless fishes that fled the sanctuaries of far warmer, more inviting Paleozoic waters, seeking their ill-advised terrestrial salvation. I take another step, and another after that, and something slimy and unseen wriggles quickly past my bare legs.

"There must have been a reason," you say, "though not necessarily one of which you are aware. That would compound the tragedy, wouldn't it, her tragedy and your current predicament, if you didn't even know the reason why you've done murder against that poor, poor woman? It would compound the waste, and you *know* how I feel about waste."

I don't remember walking into the water. I don't remember taking off my clothes.

"All evil enters the world by way of wasteful acts," I say, proud and prompt as any studious schoolgirl.

"Then you do know why you killed her?"

The sea buoys me up an inch or so, then gently, indifferently sets me down again, my feet once more touching bottom. I wonder if the people on the shrimp boats are watching, and it occurs to me that, if they are, all they'd see is one woman lying very still on the sand and another ignoring the ban on public nudity and skinny dipping under the cover of the approaching night. They might glance up from their nets, smile or shrug, then go right back to work. Or they might not even notice.

"She laughed at me," I say. I hadn't meant to tell you that. Not the first time I admitted the truth of it, and not this time, either. But what is intent and what is will, what is resolve but wishful fucking thinking, when I'm staring into your eyes that have turned a color normally hidden well out beyond the borders of the visible spectrum. An uneasy, shifting color to which I ought to be blind, but which I now can so plainly see.

I dare to look over my shoulder, just once, and the albino boy with bat wings has crept out of the dunes and the tangle of poison ivy and is hunched over her corpse, worrying at the crater in her skull.

"And that's all? She laughed at you?"

"Isn't that enough?"

Thirty, thirty-five, maybe forty feet from shore, the sand abruptly falls away beneath me, and I sink, the water folding me away like a funeral shroud, like an executioner's embrace. The salt stings my eyes and burns my nostrils and throat, and I leave a silvery trail of bubbles rushing back towards the surface. They remind me of the insubstantial, translucent bells of jellyfish. They remind me of spilled mercury. I breathe in the sea, and my lungs fill with ice and fire to freeze me and burn me away to ash. But at least I can no longer hear the song from the dunes.

"Why did she laugh at you?"

"Does it even matter?"

And you look taken aback (which I know you're not) and say, "I would imagine that your victim would think it matters, very much so, were she alive to care. Had you not so effectively and permanently silenced her. But, then, that was the point, wasn't it?"

"Is that all this is?" I want to know. "A cheap morality tale? A sordid pulp fiction wherein the killer gets her eternal comeuppance?"

"No, darling," you say. "This isn't that, at all."

Strands of kelp and ribbon weed seem to twine themselves about my feet and calves, ready to deliver me lifeless into the unloving arms of the waiting Atlantic abyss. And I'm ready to go. Indeed, I realize that I've *been* ready to go for a long time now. But then – then *you* intercede. You reach down and grasp me by the hair and haul me coughing and gagging and vomiting seawater back up into the cruel white light of the waxing moon. And you ask if I'd like to hear a story, and you sing to me and wrap me in your arms, pale and hard as if they'd been chiseled from Egyptian alabaster. I do not mistake you for death, not even for an instant. Anyone who has looked upon your face would know that you are nothing if not the opposite of death. Death is no mighty thing, and you *are* mighty. Death is nothing more profound than a piece of granite found lying on a beach, nothing more terrible than the consequences of a moment's rage or a lifetime's insecurities. Death is small and simple and inevitable, and you are nothing of the sort. No, whatever you are, it isn't anything like death.

For a time, we hang there in the sky, wedded, you and I, and then I open my eyes – which I'd not even realized were shut – and I'm on my knees in the attic of the house by the dunes. Anyone who did not know better might think that I'm kneeling before you in supplication. Moonlight spills in through the dormer windows and washes across the floor and over me. The boy with bat wings reemerges from his hiding place with, a mangled rat dangling limp from his jaws. I can hear the bell buoy again, tolling its lonely warnings against the songs of sirens. And I feel a pin prick at the nape of my neck, but it's hardly anything more than a pin prick, and your tongue laps at the sea leaking from the tiny breach you've made in me.

THE LINE BETWEEN THE DEVIL'S TEETH

I began this story on Halloween 2016, which was also, as it happens, the tenth anniversary of the first Death's Little Sister show way back in 1996. Of course, we were also in the home stretch of the disastrous 2016 Presidential election, the last few days before the rise of Der Trumpenfuer. Which is why I was unable to finish "The Line Between the Devil's Teeth" until November 18th.

King Laugh (Four Scenes)

1.

The water spilling from the showerhead is hot enough to scald and blister living skin, but here there is no living skin, only an ice so cold and pure that no heat can ever melt it. Your arms wound tight about my waist, your forehead resting heavy on my shoulder, heavy as marble, and my face upturned to receive the blessings of steam and the faint, splashing memory of warmth, a hollow baptism to scrub away the blood painting us sticky and red. We can never be warm, but at least we can be clean. Indeed, we stand as all the evidence the world would ever dare desire that death need not mean decay and the moldering earth and filth of the grave. We are a fine and recalcitrant sterility, you and I, not earth to earth, not dust to dust, but hoarding ourselves forever away against all the devouring inevitabilities of mere disintegration. "I guess we're sort of a fly in the ointment," you once said. "I guess we're entropy's rightful comeuppance." I open my mouth to receive communion and the heat bathes my teeth and rough tongue, fills my cheeks and then flows back out over my lips. I open my eyes and stare directly into the spray, as if I would look at the faces of gods whose mercies and favors are now denied us for whatever all time turns out to be. You kiss my throat. You lap at a tiny wound you've made there. You whisper to me, a fleeting dream of daylight and the sun and a field of flowers the yellow of butter. You're salt in the wound of me. You're insult to my injury. I never dream of the sunshine, and you seem to dream of nothing else, so it falls to you to torture me with something clearer than my fading memories of the colors of the day. I look down and kiss the top of your head, your tangled strawberry-blonde crown. You slip a finger inside me, seeking that greater interior chill, and I sigh and offer up no resistance whatsoever. *Here's your invitation, Pet. Cross the threshold of me.* I let you in, as always I have let you in, as I let you in the night I took your life. And though I cannot also *breathe* you in – because I haven't breathed in decades – I *smell* you, all the same. I smell your eagerness and longing, and I smell the hunger that no amount of murder will ever staunch by half, and I smell your absolute and utter devotion to me, even as I also smell the absolute and utter hatred you harbor for me. I smell shampoo and soap, lavender and rosemary and cucumbers, peppermint and sage, and I smell the wasted blood washed from our bodies and swirling down the drain on its way to the sewers of Manhattan and then to the sea. Your finger insinuates itself deeper, wriggling, taunting, insistent, my still heart's own Conqueror Worm; your eyeteeth prick at my neck, teasing that delicate sheet of flesh and muscle hiding my carotid artery and the river of stolen life flowing sluggishly through me. "You can't possibly *still* be hungry," I say, pantomiming ignorance of the most basic facts of our existence, of the single, all-consuming truth of us. "You're such a fucking glutton, Pet. You're such a little piggy." You giggle, and your thumb slowly massages my clit, and then you whisper, "One day, love, I will be the end of you. Just you wait and see. One day, love, I will be your undoing." Not the death of me, no – the *end* of me, my *undoing.* Fair enough. I'd surely have at least that coming, oblivion or whatever excuse for perdition has been prepared for demons who once were only women, who once were only the living waiting to die. "I don't doubt it for an instant," I whisper, half to myself, half to you. "I only wonder what's taking you so long." That earns me another giggle and a second finger in my cunt and your teeth widening the breach. "Don't be in such a goddamn hurry," you say. "It's coming, just like you." And I raise my head again, turning my face once more to the scalding water pounding us just as the waves of all the oceans of the world pound all the continents. *If only,* I think, *we were as soft as granite and could be so easily eroded, washed away grain by grain by grain, how much easier all this would be. If only it were as simple as that.* These thoughts tumble through my mind to mix with pain and pleasure, guilt and regret, famine and our curse's constant craving. You drink, and you fuck me, and you tear a hole in my throat that will take days to mend. (I don't say *to heal,* because the fact of the matter is that where we have gone nothing ever genuinely heals and every wound leaves behind something more disfiguring than any scar. A corporeal echo. An ugly smudge to mar the ice.) The hot water spatters your back and your thin shoulders and your ass, and you press me roughly back against the tiled shower stall. I feel that quarter second when the thought crosses your mind, when you wonder if I'd even try and stop you if you chose *this* moment, with me maybe caught half off my guard. *Isn't that why I'm here?* you think, loud as thunder, loud as the clamor of neglected machineries. *Isn't that why she's done this to me?* I shut my eyes, and I try very hard not to eavesdrop on your thoughts. I try to pretend that we are nothing more than lovers fucking in the shower. I pretend that I can hear a living heart beating in your chest. I pretend that I'm not hungry.

2.

Despite what you believe, and despite what you insist is true, it was not me who ran you off the road on a cold October night, years and years and years and years ago. For all I know, you simply fell asleep at the wheel. For all I know, it was a suicide. For all I know, you were too drunk to see straight. You certainly stank of booze, and you tasted of whiskey and cocaine, that first bitter taste I had of you. If anyone but you were responsible for the accident (if an accident it was), I can't say who the person might have been, only that it wasn't me. I am the one who came along and picked you up and stuck you back together again. I found a broken doll, and not knowing how to fix it, I fashioned *you* from its ruin. I never expected gratitude. I never expected anything much at all, except your company. That freezing night in the shadow of Storm King Mountain, I am the spider who came creeping down the rocks and through the dry, whispering brush to find the stink of gasoline and motor oil leaking from a cracked engine block and to find that crumpled scrap of flesh leaking blood and trapped beneath four thousand pounds of twisted steel and fiberglass and steelbelted havoc. I am only the shadow who came along and teased meat and bone from the wreckage, while the wide Hudson flowed by below us, deep and black and silent. I sat with you while you died. I held you. You looked up into my face and into the looming, star-specked dome of Heaven, and your eyes were the first thing I'd seen in longer than I could recall that had – as they say – taken my breath away. Bad joke. Sorry. Your startling grey eyes, grey as slate, grey as lead, grey as a fading photograph, and the unsteady amber ring traced around the bottomless twin abysses of your contracting pupils. I had looked into the eyes of ten thousand dying women, and never once had I looked into eyes like those.

The thought crossed my mind that you were something sent by God, finally, to gather me up, to snip a loose thread, to balance the scales. It crossed my mind how maybe those pupils would open up and swallow me whole and be done with it. And then the thought passed, and I cradled your cracked skull in my hands, and I told you it was almost done. I told you not to struggle, and that there was no shame in pain or fear or having pissed yourself. I watched the living light in those grey eyes fade down to a pinprick brilliance. So distracted was I by the unlikely beauty of those eyes, that I almost let you slip away. But then I kissed you and wrapped you up safe in the folds of holy, velvet darkness and whisked you away from that terrible spot where you'd died all but alone, with no living thing to witness your passing but a passing deer and the rattlesnakes huddled in their dens. I brought you home with me and washed away all the stains of your death. I dried the tears you were no longer capable of crying. Before the sun rose, I put you safely to bed, and then I lay beside you to guard against the nightmares I knew were pressing in and waiting to take you down, the cruel dreams of merciless judgment reserved only for souls who have robbed the ferryman of his coins.

"I know what happened," you say. "Even after everything you've done, I know what happened that night. Maybe you think I don't remember, but I do."

You get up and switch off the television, the movie that neither of us was watching anyway, and you light a cigarette and stand at the window, smoking, watching the city lights spread out below.

"I think it was an accident," I say. "You were drunk."

Smoke leaks from your nostrils and you shake your head. You glance back over your shoulder and stab at me with those grey eyes, and then you turn away again.

"I *might* have been drunk, but it wasn't a fucking accident," you say.

"What possible difference does it make, Pet? That was such an awfully long time ago. That was ages and ages ago."

"It makes a fucking difference," you reply. "I remember what really happened, and it makes a fucking difference." I can smell your anger and your spite and your abhorrence. My lips part, and I can taste your bitterness tainting the air lying like a stone on my dead tongue.

"Fine," I say. "Then tell me what it is you remember, if it will make you feel better."

I have lost track of how many times we've played this scene. You know your lines and I know mine.

"It won't help," you tell me. "It never does."

"Tell me anyway."

You take a drag on your cigarette and watch the traffic rushing past on the street below. I don't rush you. I can be patient. I have all the time that's left between now and sunrise, and that's still hours away.

"There was a woman standing in the road," you say, five or ten or fifteen minutes later. "I came around the curve at Target Point, coming down the mountain, coming up on the turnoff for West Point, and there she was in the headlights, standing in the middle of the road, stark fucking naked, with her back to me."

And I say, "Just exactly like you're standing here now, stark naked, with your back to me.

"You're mocking me again."

And I deny it. I deny that I have ever mocked you. "All right," I say. "There was a naked woman standing in the road."

"There wasn't time to stop. There wasn't even time to slow down. If I hadn't swerved, I would have hit her. I remember what it sounded like when I struck the guardrail. I remember falling."

"You were drunk," I say again. "You were drunk, and you were high. You were tired, and your eyes were playing tricks on you. Late at night, alone on the road, we imagine we see lots of things."

"It wasn't my imagination. I *know* what happened. I *know* what I saw." And then you drop the butt of your cigarette and grind it out against the floor with your bare left foot. You lean forward an inch or two, resting your forehead against the windowpane.

"It all happened so fast," I say, "you can't be sure. Maybe there was some sort of an animal in the road."

"It wasn't any sort of animal. It was something else."

"A woman," I say.

"Or something that wanted to look like a woman."

"You were drunk," I say, half to myself. "You were tired. It was dark," and I stand up and cross the room and turn the television on again. Humphrey Bogart and Tim Holt digging for gold in the Sierra Madre.

OK, I'm a liar. There isn't a Gila monster under there. Let's see you stick your hand in and get your goods out.

I go back to my place on the sofa and sit down again and stare at you silhouetted against the glass, instead of staring at the movie.

They never let go, do they, Howard, once they grab onto you? You cut 'em in two and the head'll still hang on until sundown, I hear.

"So, you never saw her face," I say, "the woman in the road."

"I saw her face," you tell me.

"But Pet, she was standing with her back to you. Isn't that's what you just said?"

You squeeze both your hands into fists, and now I can smell the blood your nails are drawing from the crescent wounds in your palms. "I saw her face. I saw it in the rearview mirror."

"Love, that doesn't make sense. You know that, right?"

"I know what I saw."

"You're upset," I say. "You should go to bed. Or you should come back and sit down and watch the movie with me. You're tired. I can hear how tired you are. I can hear it in your voice."

"I need to walk," you tell me. "I'm going out for a while," and I say to please be careful. I remind you how much time is left until sunrise, and you light another cigarette and go to the bedroom and find something to put on.

3.

There is much in this twilight of irony. Indeed, there are plenty enough times when my entire existence seems to have been rarified over the past century and a half (more time than that, if truth be told) into a rare and bitter distillate of irony. But it seems to me that the greatest irony of them all is that I no longer clearly recall the taste of any solid food, nor even the sensation of chewing and swallowing solid food. Not meat nor bread and certainly not any sort of fruit or vegetable, whether cooked or raw. And now add to this yet another irony – I'll call this a *meta*-irony, denoting the emergence of a *meta*-ironic state: my dreams are filled with the subject of eating. Yes, dead women dream, and this dead woman dreams all too frequently of food – or, to be more perspicuous, *this* dead woman dreams of her dead lover's obsession with all the things that *she* can no longer eat. That is, I dream of *your* preoccupation and all the many manic and neurotic ways since your death you have found and manufactured to cope with that preoccupation, none of which (of course) are equal to the task of dispelling the obsession, the need, the desire, the vestigial mortal animal appetite – as if the primary appetite that defines your new existence is not sufficient to burn down the mind of any sentient being. I close my eyes, and sleeping I revisit the inferno of your frustrations. I watch the dreadful parade of your futile attempts to satiate an insatiable craving, to scratch an itch always and forever beyond your reach, and some of these dreams are only a matter of revisiting something you've actually done, while, other times, my dreaming mind creates more terrible, more fabulous scenarios. *Your* dreams of tasting and swallowing and chewing and digesting and shitting as breathing men and women do, these dreams crowd – and frequently threaten to smother – all *my* other dreams. This is, I suppose, a sort of justice and only one of the several prices I pay for having committed the crime of your creation. The price I pay for the companionship of a creature at least somewhat like myself (and long ago I learned that mortal companionship is fleeting and in no way satisfying; food makes poor company).

Connected as we are, I only have to close my eyes, and I dream your hungry dreams of cakes and cookies, pies and casseroles, meat cooked until no trace of red remains. The crispness of a ripe apple or pear. The heat of curries and the sourness of pickled cucumbers. But all of it as no more than paste in my mouth, no more than flavorless ash, and I see in my dream of your disappointment that you don't taste it, either. "You've robbed me of every single thing I am," you say, as something sweet and sticky and creme-filled slips from your fingers and falls with an ugly plop to the floor at your feet. You stand staring petulantly down at it, and you say "You've taken it all, haven't you? You've robbed me of every single thing I love. You haven't left me even one thing I want." And since this is *your* dream and I am merely an *intruder,* a sort of succubal parasite along for the ride whether she likes it or not, I do not do you the disservice of arguing the point. "Do you remember mint?" you ask me. "Do you remember sage and rosemary, black pepper and cumin and turmeric? Do you remember vinegar? How about milk? Can you at *least* remember something as simple and as bland as the flavor of a glass of *milk?"* Each question more frantic than the question before. Each question more desperately in need of an answer, but I say nothing whatsoever.

I follow you down the narrow aisles of supermarkets, of corner bodegas, of greengrocers and past the refrigerated display cases piled high with their slaughterhouse delicacies. I watch while you fill shopping carts with all the things you can no longer enjoy. You take down a can of beef and barley soup from a shelf and you read the label aloud to me – beef, beef broth, hydrolyzed soy protein, modified food starch, sodium phosphates, onion powder, yeast extract, maltodextrin, celery, tomato paste, carrots, barley, peas, and on and on and on and on. Sometimes, the food dreams we share are nothing more *than* you reading me the ingredients on cans and boxes and bags. And me always patiently listening, indulging, not daring even to interrupt.

How very disappointed an Abraham Van Helsing or a Buffy Summers would be at such terribly mundane nightmares, obscene only in their humdrumness.

Sometimes, the market aisles become no more than dirt game trails, winding through forests, between underbrush and trees so tall their uppermost boughs are lost in cloud, and you're wearing a cap dyed the most indecent shade of crimson, and there's a picnic basket in your hand. It should be funny, it should be fucking hilarious, the sight of our anxieties reduced to fairy-tale caricatures. It isn't, but it ought to be. Cast as a monster in wolf's clothing, I follow behind you, *Le Petit Chaperon Rouge,* my lost little *Rotkäppchen*, and always, inevitably, you stop somewhere along the way to wherever it is that you're bound. Without fail, you never make it to Grandmother's house. You sit down beneath one of those towering trees or on a mossy boulder beside a stream and you open up the picnic basket and you gorge yourself on whatever has been packed inside. You eat until you've made yourself sick, and then I watch from my hiding place while you puke it all back up again, and I watch while you weep at the steaming mess you've made, because I am helpless to look away. Often I have wondered if you were ever to actually reach your scripted destination, if we'd find waiting for us there a house built of gingerbread and gum drops, and, too, I have thought what a fine, fine mark you'd make for a white witch of ice and snow, so easily might you be seduced by offerings of nothing more than hot cocoa and Turkish delight. I have burdened you with the nearest thing to immortality that a woman can ever hope to find, and – if your dreams are any measure – you would trade it all for sweetbreads or a can of lima beans.

"I wish to fuck that you would stay out of my head," you say, awake.

Awake, I reply, "I wish like hell I knew how."

4.

The shower, that night on Storm King, a fairy-tale path for a starving ghost. And now *this,* this thing that is only the *next* thing. It may all add up to something, but I have my doubts. You like to pretend that there's a judging, guiding hand in back of creation, even if it means eternal torment for the likes of us, Hell rather than simple oblivion. And I prefer the watch without the necessity of a watchmaker. So, for me, there is no pattern here. For me, it's all mere happenstance and white noise.

I come awake a little later than usual, half an hour past sunset, in the room where we sleep – this centrally located room without windows and with its four walls and ceiling and the floor all painted a flat matte black. I know at once that I'm alone. In fact, I likely knew that before I opened my eyes. Where you ought to be beside me, there's only an insomniac's tangle of bed clothes. It's been weeks now since you slept well, and so I think nothing of it, though I much prefer *not* waking up alone. I lie very still, gazing up through the darkness at the high ceiling, a full fourteen feet above me. At first I think that I'm only hearing voices on the television, the aimless chatter of reality TV mannequins or twenty-four-hour news channel talking heads or an old movie or something of the sort. I get up and slip on my robe before I switch on the lamp on the table beside the bed. There's a folded piece of paper lying there, a single sheet of lavender stationery folded over once. I pick it up and read what you've written. I have always envied you your penmanship, your tidy, artful cursive, and that's what I'm thinking about, even as my groggy brain tries to make sense of *what* you've written, these words you've left behind for me to find. I read the note once to myself, and then I read the note again aloud:

I saw her face, watching me from the rearview mirror. Just before I fell, I saw your face. I saw you, and you saw me.

I put the note back down where I found it, on the table beside the lamp, and I leave the black room, and (force of habit) lock the door behind me.

Down the short hallway and then downstairs, I find you in the space that the architects who remodeled this old building meant to serve as a dining room, but where we have never yet taken a meal. We haven't even bothered to furnish it, so there's only the shiny hardwood floor, the bare brick walls, electrical outlets and light fixtures and exposed pipes and heating ducts, the sort of austerity that people pay extra for in this new, confused millennium. And there is you, and you're naked save a pair of lemon-yellow panties, and there's a young dark-haired woman whom I have never seen before. She's naked, also, and she's sitting on the floor, pressed tightly into a corner as if she means to somehow melt into the masonry and escape. She's crying.

In fact, she's hysterical. Just a little more and she'll be in shock. And, finally, there is a child standing beside you, a little girl dressed in white, a white dress stained crimson. The child looks an awful lot like the woman in the corner, and it only takes me a few seconds to realize what it is that you've done here, what it is you've been waiting for me to wake up and come downstairs and see – because, of course, the tableau vivant has been crafted for my edification. I can smell the woman plainly enough, but where the scent of the child should be, there's almost nothing at all. From where I'm standing, her eyes look like polished garnets set in the face of a marble *sculpture* of a child. She's watching the woman in the corner, who is, of course, her mother. She's watching her the way that a cat who isn't actually hungry watches a mouse or a bird that it might decide to kill, just for the sport of killing.

The woman is sobbing something in Spanish. I don't speak Spanish, but, all the same, I can tell that she's praying.

The child starts to take a step towards her, but you hold her back.

"Not yet," you tell the girl. "Soon, but not just yet." And then you look at me, and your expression is a perfect, paradoxical alloy of love and hatred.

"How many people do you think saw them come in here?" I ask, and I reach into the pocket of my robe for a cigarette and my lighter, but the pocket's empty. "How long before someone starts looking for them?"

"You think I don't remember what happened that night on the mountain," you say, instead of answering my questions. "But I do. I remember exactly what happened."

"How long before someone out there notices these two are missing and calls the police?" I ask. "Her husband," I say and point at the praying woman. "Or *her* father," I add and point at the dead girl standing beside you.

"I want you to tell me it was you. I want you to admit it."

I turn away from you and watch the praying woman. She has a redbird tattooed on her left shoulder. There's a long scar on her right thigh. Her nails have been painted the color of ripe Damson plums.

"Or what?" I reply. "You'll make an even bigger mess than the one you've already made? You'll call the cops yourself?" I am surprised at how calm I sound. Annoyed, impatient, but calm. I suppose I've been expecting something like this for a while now. The woman on the floor stops praying and looks up at me. She smells like anything that knows it's about to die.

"Why me?" you want to know. "Why me in particular? Did you even have a reason? Or was I just the first person that came along."

"I dislike games," I say, and then I stoop down and take the woman's head in my hands and snap her neck. She doesn't even struggle. The child makes a faint, disappointed sort of sound. "I dislike games, Pet, and I dislike waste even more. You're smarter than this. You know better. I *taught* you better."

"What about the people who came looking for me?"

"No one came looking for you," I answer, standing again, turning to face you again. "No one at all. Which, I think, answers all your other questions, or at least all the ones I intend to answer tonight. And as for *her,"* and I point at the child, and the child stops staring at her mother's corpse and stares at me, instead. More than anything, the dead girl looks bored, which comes as no surprise whatsoever. "As for the kid, have the decency to finish what you started. I'm going back upstairs to take a shower."

"Maybe I *will* call the police," you say as I turn away. "Maybe that's exactly what I planned all along. Maybe I'll call them and tell them everything."

"No, Pet, you won't."

"You don't *know* that. You don't have any idea *what* I'll do."

"Fine, then. Do whatever you think is right," and I climb the steps and go to the upstairs bathroom and turn the shower on scalding hot. I stand beneath the spray and let the steaming water hammer at my face and breasts, my shoulders and belly and thighs, and in only a little while, you join me. Neither of us says anything about the child or her mother, and I help you wash the girl's blood from your hands and face and hair. Later, I'll make a phone call, and someone will come around to discreetly and expertly clean up the mess you've made, someone who gets paid enough to keep the secrets of monsters. You put your arms around my waist, and I kiss the top of your head. And you say, "One day, love, I will be the end of you. Just you wait and see. One day, I'll be your undoing."

"I know that," I reply. "I only wonder what's taking you so long."

"Patience..."

KING LAUGH (FOUR SCENES)

This story was written between November 23rd and 29th, 2017. On the 24th, I wrote in my online journal, *Once, I swore I'd never write another vampire story. It's a promise I keep breaking.* Inspiration? I don't know. I do know, though, that the whole thing began with that shower scene getting stuck in my head.

The Lady and the Tiger Redux

1.

I'm lying in bed, not sleeping but only half awake, half awake at best, listening to the cold winter rain and trying to remember what it was we were arguing about that day in the woods. The day you found the stone embedded in the trunk of an oak, that day hardly a week ago that now seems impossibly distant from this stormy night. I imagine the day as a painting hung on a gallery wall – *Two Women, with Trees* – serene, with only the faintest hint of any foreboding. I shut my eyes, only half wishing I could find my way back down to sleep. Sleep means dreams, and I'm not yet so far gone that I don't know how I'm better off avoiding those, if possible. I am quickly coming to realize there may never again be a time when dreams are safe for me. So I lie here, sweating despite the chill air filling up the bedroom, not sleeping, not quite awake, listening to the rain on the windows and roof and to the wind in the trees and to the noises that you're making in the bathroom. I close my eyes a little tighter, but it doesn't help. What I'm trying to recall, that argument from a week ago, it remains stubbornly just out of reach. You shut off the tap, and the rusted hot and cold knobs squeak like a sack of kicked mice. I open my eyes again and stare up at the ceiling. Outside, it's still dark. Inside, too. But there's a dim slice of white-yellow incandescent light from the only-mostly closed bathroom door, and that light shines out across the ceiling above the bed. I squint, as though the light is bright enough to hurt my eyes (it isn't) or as if squinting will somehow sharpen my memory (it doesn't). Above me, successive coats of white paint have chipped and peeled back to expose bare plaster. In the bathroom, you flush the toilet, and I can hear the sound of your bare feet on the checkerboard mosaic of pink-and-white ceramic tiles. It's a sort of whisper, that soft sound. I turn my head just enough that I can make out the time displayed in blocky glowing numerals on the digital clock sitting on the chifforobe all the way across the room, and I see that it's not yet even three a.m. I close my eyes again. I think maybe I'm getting a headache, all this straining to remember, this inability to sleep and unwillingness to be awake. It occurs to me that I should get up and take something before the pain gets bad, but I don't. The Tylenol and the aspirin are both in the bathroom medicine cabinet, and *you're* in the bathroom. And I cannot see you just now. Later, but not just now. So, I lie here with the darkness behind my eyelids, very clearly remembering our walk in the woods, even if I can't remember exactly why we were arguing. Dry brown leaves crunch loudly beneath our shoes. There's a crow cawing somewhere not too far off, and a pair of cardinals flit past overhead, darting between bare branches and pine needles and patches of blue sky. Here and there, weathered grey nubs of limestone protrude from the soil and detritus blanketing the forest floor. There's absolutely nothing whatsoever out of the ordinary about this crisp December afternoon. It's a Sunday, and you wanted to get out of the house and away from the city, so here we are, following a deer trail through the trees. It's warm enough that neither of us is wearing coats. You stop and glance back the way we've come. You're a little out of breath, and I almost say something about how you've been smoking too much and should cut back. I know better than to suggest you should quit. See, I can remember *that,* but I can't remember the damn argument. With your left hand, you shade your eyes and the fine wrinkles at the corners of your mouth are showing. I'm fairly certain I suggest that maybe we should head back. Up ahead, the trail gets steeper, and I'm honestly not sure if I'm game for the climb. I think I tell you that, but you only scowl and turn away and keep walking. In the bathroom, you're running water again, and I imagine you wiping steam from the mirrored medicine cabinet. I try to imagine the expression in the eyes of your reflection. And then I force myself to think only about that day in the woods, instead. The crow has gone quiet and the cardinals have disappeared, and suddenly there's a bad odor in the air, a familiar smell I can't immediately identify, but one that seems entirely out of place there on the mountain. Only later, when we're home again, when I'm loading the dishwasher after dinner, will I realize it's the distinctive acrid reek of a blown fluorescent tube. *That* smell. That *exact* smell. "Wait," I say. "Hold up," but you've already stopped and are standing there in front of me, staring at a tree. In the bathroom, you shut off the water again, and now there are small splashing sounds. I have the impression that I'm overhearing something very private, nothing meant for me, nothing meant for anyone. I have the impression that I'm eavesdropping. I try very hard only to listen only to the rain, but it doesn't work. "Did you hear that?" you ask me – the day in the woods, I mean, after I tell you to stop – and I say no, automatically, even though I'm not at all sure what I'm supposed to have heard. And then you crouch down in the dead leaves piled around the roots of the tree. I haven't yet seen what you're looking at. You haven't yet pointed it out to me. I ask if you smell anything, anything strange, anything out of place, but you don't answer. You're staring at the oak tree, and you raise your left hand, very slowly, the way a sleepwalker might or the subject of a hypnotism, and this is when I see what *you* see, exactly what it is about the tree that's caught your attention. A dark sphere, not much larger than a gumball, not much wider than my thumb, half embedded in the trunk. The sun catches it, just so, and the sphere seems to glint and shimmer in the light. It looks wet. "Don't touch it," I say, sounding more urgent than I'd intended, and you turn your head, gazing back at me over your shoulder. "Why?" you ask. "Do you know what it is?" And I tell you no, that I have no idea, but maybe it's best to leave it alone, whatever it might be. "Sometimes," you say, "I think you're afraid of everything. Sometimes, I wouldn't be surprised to find out you're afraid of your own shadow." And then you go back to staring at the thing in the tree instead of frowning at me. "It's almost like a glass marble," you say. "Like the marbles we played with as kids." I don't tell you that I never played marbles; I come nearer, right up behind you, and lean down to get a better view. You haven't touched it yet, but the tip of your left index finger is poised no more than an inch or so from the dark sphere. Up close, it's the unhealthy black-green color of an overripe avocado, a color that has always reminded me of infection. There is a series of fine concentric ridges in the bark surrounding the sphere, radiating out from the epicenter of it, like frozen ripple marks. And then – and *now* – not quite a week later, on this rainy winter night, I open my eyes and stare at the ceiling above our bed. At that stingy, unguarded sliver of light leaking from the bathroom. You flush the toilet again, and I get up and go to the kitchen to make a cup of tea. I don't know what else to do.

2.

"How old were you?" I ask, and you frown and stare out the diner window at the Atlanta streets and the cars rushing past, at pedestrians and storefronts and a big black dog sniffing at something in the gutter. "When she died, I mean?"

"Thirteen," you reply. "Maybe fourteen. I'm not sure. I'd just started high school, I think." You sip your coffee, and your hazel-green eyes seem unnaturally bright in the morning sun spilling in through the wide plate-glass window. This is *another* Sunday, a few weeks before you find the thing embedded in the tree. We're finishing breakfast, and a minute or two ago we were only talking about the weather. But when you saw the dog, you changed the subject.

You watch the dog, and you tell me, "At the top of the hill, back behind our house, there was a circle of standing stones. My mother used to claim that the Indians had built the circle, thousands of years ago, and that it was a place where they made human sacrifices to their heathen gods. That was just the sort of crazy shit my mother used to say. Mostly, me and my sister, we didn't take her seriously. She read the *Weekly World News* and believed in astrology and Atlantis and ghosts and that there'd once been Indians who made blood sacrifices up on the hill behind our house."

"You didn't believe her?"

You shrug and watch the black dog. "I don't know. When you're a kid, you believe a lot of things your parents say, whether they're making much sense or not. It's not like I knew anything much about what the Indians around there had and hadn't done. I knew there *had* been Indians in those woods. We'd find arrowheads in the fields, sometimes, and sometimes bits of pottery. Anyway, we tended to stay away from the place, probably because of the stories my mother told. Though, probably, it would have seemed creepy enough all on its own. It was a lonely place."

"Lonely?" I ask.

"Yeah," you reply. "Lonely, empty, desolate. You know. A place that feels like no one's been there in a thousand years. The kind of place where you always feel alone, even if you're not."

I don't understand what you mean, not really. But I nod and pretend that I do.

You say, "There were patterns carved into the rocks. Spirals, mostly. Momma told us they were mazes that trapped the souls of the people who'd been sacrificed inside the circle. She said the spiral designs were a sort of ghost trap, because the spirits the Indians had worshipped fed on souls and needed to keep them from slipping away too quickly. She said some of the ghosts were still stuck up there, going round and round inside those spirals, still trying to find their way out centuries after they'd died."

"My parents didn't tell ghost stories," I say. "They didn't even like us watching scary movies on TV."

You look down at your plate, at what's left of the scrambled eggs and link sausage, then push it away and go back to watching the dog.

"This was back in the seventies," you say. "It's not like we had the internet to look shit up, to find out whether or not the Indians in Chatooga County had actually practiced human sacrifice. And the only library was at school, and…well, it wasn't much of a library. There was a set of *World Book* encyclopedias from 1957. Anyway…" and you trail off and don't say anything else for fifteen or twenty or thirty seconds. I pick up the grease-stained check our waitress left on the table and read it over a couple of times.

Out on the sidewalk, people pass the diner, but no one besides you seems to notice the black dog. And it doesn't seem to notice any of them, either.

"Anyway," you say a second time, and I lay the check back down. "A couple of nights after Momma died, there was a bad electrical storm. My sister and my father were both asleep, but the thunder woke me up. I put on my robe and went out onto the back porch and watched the lightning. I don't think I'd ever seen lightning like I saw that night, arcing down out of the clouds and spreading out over the mountains like the crackling, white-hot fingers of those hungry Indian gods my mother had told us about. Once or twice, I was pretty sure it struck the top of the hill, up there at the stone circle, and I sat with my ears covered, thinking about my mother in the ground."

I glance out at the sidewalk again and see the black dog's gone. It seems like I ought to say something, but I have no idea what.

"I went up there the next morning," you tell me and rub your eyes. "That was the last time I ever did, though. You only need to see that sort of thing once." You don't elaborate, and before I can ask what it was you saw, you say you need to go to the restroom and slide out of the booth and leave me sitting there alone.

3.

Dreaming, entirely unaware that I am dreaming, I stand at a high, still place, surrounded by a ring of seven stones. The only sound is the screaming of cicadas. The ground beneath my feet has been seared black by a heat so great that wide patches of the sandy soil have been fused into sheets of brittle glass. I'm barefoot, and each time I take a step towards the center of the ring of stones, the earth crunches under my weight and cuts the soles of my feet. I don't like to think of my blood mixing with this seared ground, of myself leaking out to blend with the aftermath of the cataclysm that has burned away every trace of vegetation from the top of this hill. All around the high place, all around the hill, beneath a blazing summer sun, I look out over the canopy of a deep green forest, the shaggy upper stories of towering hickories and oaks, sycamores and pines hiding cool, restless shadows beneath their boughs. And I can sense how every molecule of every tree and shrub and weed shrinks away from this defiled place. Were it possible, I know they would all pull up their roots and slither and rustle and tumble far, far away from here, taking with them every other living thing, each insect and snake and squirrel and bird. I know this, as surely as I know how it was the careless touch of a god that is no god that burned the high place and turned the ground to glass. I know so many things I have no way of knowing. I know what traced the spirals into the seven stones that form the ring about me. I know the awful things that were done here long, long ago and by what agencies those atrocities wore thin the very fabric of creation in this place. If you know how, if you turn your head just so, you can see the stars and the gulfs between the stars and the shores of alien seas. In this dream, I know that trick, and I also know better than to risk even the briefest glimpses through those rifts in space and time, too keenly aware that in all those innumerable elsewheres there would be other eyes looking back towards me. I take another step, and the ground crunches again, and I wince at the pain. The air here smells like ammonia and blown fluorescent bulbs. I think how it ought to smell only of a forest fire, but there's not even the faintest whiff of the scorched earth. I pause and squint up at the noon sun, so brilliant and hot that I imagine it must be trying by its own heat to purify the hill and wipe away all traces of what's been done here. I shade my eyes and look south and east, where a muddy brown ribbon of a river winds through the forest, and you say, "That's the Oostanaula, and it flows into the Coosa and the Alabama rivers and all the way down into Mobile Bay and then out into the Gulf of Mexico. But you can't actually see the Oostanaula River from the top of this ridge. Not when you're awake." I turn back towards the center of the ring of stones, and you're standing there, naked, your skin smeared with soot, your blonde hair tangled and matted. "I don't need to see this," I say. I might be speaking to you, or I might be speaking to the lidless eye of the sun, or I might only be speaking to myself, trying to wake up. "Dreams have a way of playing havoc with geography," you tell me and I stare down at my bleeding feet, because it's easier than seeing you. Until now, I hadn't noticed how the scorched earth inside the ring of stones is littered with hundreds or thousands of tiny, charred bones, and I imagine all the various creatures caught in the fire that ruined this spot. A holocaust consuming all those many minute lives, creatures turned to so much ash between one heartbeat and the next, and I know that even a million times that many sacrifices would go no way whatsoever towards satiating the appetite of the thing that burned and poisoned this place. Entire worlds would burn, and it would still be hungry. "That was the night my mother died," you say. "That was the day we were walking in the woods, the day we argued over..." but you trail off, and when I look up again, you've vanished. All at once, the cicadas fall silent, and I close my eyes, because sometimes in dreams I've forced myself awake by shutting my eyes. But no such luck, not this time. I'll leave when all of it's done with me – the dream, the hill, the sun, those seven stones. I will be dismissed then and not before. I open my eyes, and nothing has changed. Simultaneously, I wish that you hadn't left me alone in this place *and* that I'd never seen you here. I take a deep breath of the stifling, acrid air, and it burns my throat and nostrils, and I finish my walk to the very center of the ring of stones and find there an eighth stone. It's almost perfectly round, and instead of the crude spirals etched into the other seven, there's a shallow triangular depression, set just off center, so sharply defined it might have been cut out with a laser. There's a hot breeze now, and all around me it makes little whirlwinds in the ashes. I lean closer to the eighth stone, not wanting to see, unable to do otherwise, because it has become *that* sort of dream. I might as well only be watching myself, witnessing events I'm helpless to prevent. In the triangular hole cut into the rock, there's a small, shimmering black sphere, no larger than a gumball or cat's eye marble, glistening wetly, and I know that I'm going to reach down and pick it up. It doesn't matter how much the thought of touching it repulses me. That doesn't matter, not at all.

4.

I try to pretend that *this* is also a dream. This *last* part. That I have come back from the kitchen after finishing a cup of chamomile tea I never drank and finally fallen to sleep again. Or even that I am still lying in bed staring wide awake at the ceiling and only *picturing* myself sitting here on the edge of the bathtub, watching you watch your reflection in the medicine cabinet mirror. If I could believe either of those things, it would be a mercy, but I know we have now both passed somewhere out beyond mercy. You lean forward and another of the black spheres slips past your lips and into the sink. There's a small wet heap of them there, damp with your saliva, damp with whatever secretions they sweat. They are each exactly the same size. They are each perfect. You wipe your mouth and then go back to staring at your reflection. Your skin has taken on an almost metallic sheen, washed with coruscating iridescence – blue, greens, deep and bloody shades of red, warm hints of gold and silver and copper – and I think of the carapace of a june bug, and I think of schools of fish darting about just beneath the surface of a bottomless pool. "I wish you hadn't touched it," I say, and you sigh and lick your lips and shrug. "I wish I'd been alone," you answer, and then, "I also wish you'd stayed out of my memories. You shouldn't have gone there. You shouldn't have seen what you saw." You look my way, but only indirectly, as if I were playing the gorgon here and you were playing Perseus and not the other way around. I ask, "When you were a kid, you went up there to the burned place, didn't you? After your mother died, you climbed the hill and saw what I saw, didn't you? That's how this happened, isn't it?" You don't reply. Your black eyes swim with color, light dancing on oil on water, and I recall a term from a long ago college physics lecture – *thin-film interference.* Your eyes are filled with rainbows, with the whirring wings of wasps and tropical birds and butterflies, with the photons of a million extrasolar suns. You spit another pearl into the sink. I have resisted thinking of them as pearls. I have resisted *allowing* myself to think of them as pearls. But I'm too tired now and my head aches too much and I cannot even recall why it frightened me to think of them that way, as pearls. A hard, nacreous mantle, silk smooth, to guard against some terrible irritant carried within you all these long years. "I wish you'd leave me alone," you say, hardly above a whisper. "I wish you wouldn't see me, not like this." And I tell you, "I don't think that I can do that." And I think, *I have to witness this, just as I saw you touch that thing embedded in the tree, just as I stood in the stone circle, I also have to witness this.* "Does that make it any easier?" you ask me. "I mean, pretending you have had no say in the matter, pretending you have somehow been robbed of free will?" I start to answer, but I'm distracted by the way your voice has changed, the brittleness there, like melted sand cooled to glass to shatter under clumsy footsteps. "You could walk away," you say. "You could walk away and forget and be done with this." That's almost absurd enough to make me laugh. But I don't. I'm beginning to wonder if I'll ever laugh at anything again. "I don't think it works that way," I say. "I don't think you can look upon the face of..." but I don't let myself finish the thought, not aloud. *I don't think you can look upon the face of a god, even a god that is not a god, and forget what you've seen.* It wouldn't be the truth, anyway. You aren't a god, even if what has scarred and twisted you may like to play at godhood. "Why did you even tell me about the night your mother died? About the lightning? If I wasn't meant to see any of this, why did you ever let me close to you?" And you reply that you're as weak as any woman, and you apologize, and you tell me how you wish it could have gone another way. I remember you watching the dog outside the diner snuffling at the gutter. I'd only thought that I'd imagined black pearls falling from its muzzle and rolling away across the concrete. In the mirror, your reflection ripples like heat off asphalt, like a highway blacktop mirage, and then it's still again. "Does it hurt?" I ask, and you say, "Not so much. Not so much anymore." I ask, "Would you tell me if it did?" Standing there before me, you could be a martyr. You could be a saint, as surely as you are anything else conceivable. There must be martyrs on other worlds, and it may follow that there must *also* be human women on *this* world who have been – by design or by accident – martyred for the sins of the children of far distant, alien Edens, surrogate Eves cast out of other Paradises. "It isn't anything like that," you say. And then you tell me that I should go back to bed. You clear your throat and spit another rotten black pearl into the sink. I wonder what you'll do when it's full. "Go back to bed," you say again. "You have work tomorrow. You need your rest." And I don't argue. I can lie in bed and pretend this is all a dream just as easily as I can do it sitting on the edge of the tub. So, I leave you there with the mirror and the checkerboard tile and the porcelain fixtures, and I go back to bed. But I pull the bathroom door shut behind me.

> *And so I leave it with all of you: Which came out of the opened door – the lady, or the tiger?*
>
> ~ Frank R. Stockton (1882)

> *The hall remains, it still contains a pair of doors, a choice.*
> *Behind one door, a muffled roar, behind the other, a voice.*
>
> ~ They Might Be Giants (2011)

THE LADY AND THE TIGER REDUX

There's an awful lot of H.P. Lovecraft in this one, especially "The Colour Out of Space." And there's a little bit of T.E.D. Klein's *The Ceremonies*. I freely admit to both. "The Lady and the Tiger Redux" was written between January 28th and February 4th, 2019.

A Chance of Frogs on Wednesday

Today the sky above the city is in no way different than it was yesterday, or a week ago, or last month, but when I glance up at the clouds hanging too low above the rooftops it seems somehow more threatful than usual and more pregnant with violence. It seems a greyer sort of grey, a broodier grey, as if it knows what I'm carrying in the rolled up brown paper bag clutched in my right hand. As if the sky is a thing that can care about what men do and why they do it. I don't like to think that it is any such thing, but I pride myself on never placing too much stock in what I do not actually know for a fact. And I don't know for a fact that the sky – or some brooding intelligence behind the sky – is not watching jealously, angrily, resentfully, as I make my way along deserted, trash-strewn St. Elder Street. Thinking these thoughts, I grip the bag a little more tightly, and I hold it closer to my chest. I try not to think on it too hard. And I try not to think about where I'm going, and I try not to think about…but it's like my father used to say: *Try not to think about a white bear, and the first thing you know you're gonna be staring one in the face.* He read that somewhere, he said. My father was a man who could read. My father was a man who had once traveled beyond the city, before the sky was always grey. It occurs to me that I should also try not to think about my father. But he is like a white bear, in that respect, and so is the paper bag, and the jar inside the paper bag, and the thing inside the jar. If it is in the nature of the sky to know the hearts and minds of men, it will see through me as easily as I see through a pane of window glass. That isn't a comforting thought, but, then again, so few thoughts ever are, not when you come right down to it. I arrive at the corner of St. Elder and Joshua, and I linger there, making an effort not to look up at the clouds, glancing instead behind me, because I thought I might have heard footsteps a moment ago. But there's no one and nothing back there. Well, nothing that can make footsteps. There's the burned-out, rusted shell of a city bus, and there's a dog carcass, and there's the black, gaping mouth where a manhole cover once decently hid the entrance to the sewers. A cold breeze stirs the air, and I turn up the collar of my coat against it, and I hug myself, and I stare at that round black void in the cracked pavement.

"You should hear the tales people tell about the underneath," says Lakota, on some day before this day, on some day when I have the good sense to stay indoors, some day when I have no cause to go wandering the avenues beneath the brooding sky.

"It's nothing I need to know," I tell her, and she shrugs and rolls a cigarette and keeps talking as if I'd asked her to please elaborate.

"The tales people tell about down there," she says, "they're enough to straighten your cunt hairs. Well, if you had a cunt." She snickers the way she does, and she lights her stinking cigarette, and she blows smoke at the water-stained ceiling of the apartment we share. It has a view of the river, the shit-brown and rotten river, and sometimes Lakota sits for hours at a time, just staring at all that water flowing past the western edge of the city and at whatever is hiding in the mists that blanket the shore beyond the river. But I'm digressing. I'm losing my train of thought.

"Rats," I say, "and darkness, and people who are too afraid not to huddle in filth, but I seriously doubt there's much else than that down there."

"That's not what I hear," Lakota smirks.

"Fine, then," I say, hoping that acquiescence will satisfy her and so she'll let the matter drop. "That's not what you've heard."

"Were you always such a coward?" she asks and taps ash on the floor.

"Probably," I reply, thinking how, if I were not a coward, I'd have sent her packing a long, long time ago.

"Are you even going to tell me what's in the bag?" she asks, and I blink and look up, startled, and I see that it wasn't Lakota who asked, and that I'm not sitting in the apartment. That I'm standing at the corner of St. Elder and Joshua streets, and there's an old, old man in a tattered, grimy wedding dress watching me. He's standing only a few feet away, squinting at me through a pair of wire-rimmed spectacles. Both the lenses are cracked. He's barefoot and missing so many toes I can't see how he walks without tipping over. He pushes the spectacles farther up the bridge of his nose and again he asks me what's inside the bag.

"Nothing that concerns you," I tell him.

He watches me silently for a moment, and then he says, "You don't know that. You might believe that you do, but you don't."

It occurs to me that the old man might be a thief, or that he might at least style himself a thief. That he might intend to take the bag away from me. But he looks as frail as a kite, and, though I might well be a coward, I'm not about to hand the bag over without a fight, which I'm fairly certain I'd win, should it come to that.

"You just go on about your business," I tell him.

"You *know* my business? Is *that* how it is?"

"I don't want to hurt you," I tell him, "but I will, if you make me."

The old man in the grimy wedding dress frowns, and he looks up at the sky, and then he looks at me again. His eyes are the color of piss.

"You're taking it to her," he says, not much louder than a whisper. If the day were not so still, I might not have heard him. "You're taking it to Locust Town, to the tower, to the pale lady."

And I think it may be that the sky knows everything there is to know, and that, from time to time, it mutters secrets into the ears of crazy old men with rotting feet and jaundiced, urine-colored eyes.

I tell him, "Mister, I'm not going to warn you a third time," trying to sound sure of myself. Trying to sound like someone who ladles out threats on a regular basis and someone who is willing to carry them out. I think about the carving knife tucked into the waistband of my jeans, concealed inside my coat, and I wonder if I actually have whatever it takes to kill someone. "This bag, I promise you it isn't anything that's worth you losing your life over."

"Well then," he sighs and smacks his lips and grinds his toothless gums, "you be on your way. Don't let the likes of me dissuade you, not if you mean to see it through. I never even should have spoken to you, and don't you think I don't know that perfectly goddamn well."

And then he limps away up St. Elder on what's left of his feet, and I watch him go, and then I stare again at the black hole leading down to the sewers.

Were you always such a coward?

I follow Joshua south past the ruins of museums and art galleries, tombs where the useless, wasted ghosts of culture crouch and watch me go by. I get as far as the intersection with Mimosa, and I have to make a detour, because there's a pileup blocking the way that

I'm not about to try to go over or under. A great jackstraw tangle of automobiles and one of those towering cranes that used to loom above the city like behemoth erector-set insects. If rusting steel could talk (and maybe I just don't know how to listen), the tale this wreck could tell, another awful vignette of pain and death and the fall of mankind down the gullet of this deep, deep well called Now, a pit to make open manholes seem as tame as kittens. I detour around the pileup, taking Mimosa east a block, but it's not long until I'm back on Joshua and walking south again. And it's also not long until I come upon the kid.

I've never been any good guessing people's ages, and I'm as bad with children as with adults. But she can't be much more than thirteen or fourteen years old, and she's naked, and most of her body has been tattooed. She's sitting in the middle of the street on a blue plastic milk crate, poking at a dead chihuahua with a mop handle. The mop end has been snapped off, so there's only the handle, and it has been whittled to a sharp point. Probably she's the one who killed the dog. Probably she means to eat it. I try not to be seen. I try not to attract her attention. I try to look like someone with purpose, going somewhere important, hoping the kid ignores me. But she doesn't. She stops poking at the dead chihuahua and aims the mop handle at me. She grins, and I see that her teeth have been filed so they look more like shark teeth than anything that should be in the mouth of a thirteen- or fourteen-year-old girl.

"Better three hours too soon than a minute too late," she says. Her voice is raw and gravelly. I look at the tattoos and think maybe hers is the voice of someone who has screamed for so long and so loudly that her vocal cords will never heal. I should keep walking, but I don't. I should pretend that I haven't seen her, haven't noticed that she's there, but I don't do that, either.

"Too swift arrives as slow as too tardy," says the girl.

"I have a knife," I tell her, keeping my eyes on the sharpened mop handle. "Just so you know. Just so you understand."

She closes her left eye, then opens it again. Her eyes are hazel green.

"Wisely and slow," she says, "they stumble that run fast."

"I wasn't planning on running," I tell her. "Not from you, and not from anyone else. I'm not lying about the knife. I'm not joking, kid."

"There is no evil angel but Love," she says. "Mercy but murders, pardoning those that kill." And only later on will I realize that she's quoting Shakespeare. I was honestly never much of a reader, and standing there on Joshua Street, beneath the mumbling clouds, all I know is that the kid's not making much sense.

"I don't have time for this," I tell her. "And I don't want you following after me, you understand? I don't have any food or anything else for you."

She cocks her head to one side, and with the mop handle she points at the paper bag in my hand. She says, "Let every man be master of his time."

"I'm going now," I tell her. And again I say, "Don't follow me."

"She knows you're coming?" asks the girl. And before I can answer, she says, "She doesn't see anyone who hasn't called ahead. Though she be but little, she is *fierce.*"

The girl gets to her feet, and for just a second it seems that her tattoos are moving, swirling like water going down a drain, like the eyes of hurricanes, like…but I'm nervous and it's only my imagination running away with me. That's what I tell myself. That's what it's better to believe. I open my coat and show her the handle of the carving knife sticking up out of my jeans.

"Don't fuck with me," I say, and she nods her head and sits back down again. If you believe what you hear on the wire, if I am to believe the stories that Lakota spins, there are cannibals lurking in every alleyway, and to me this girl looks as much like a cannibal as anyone ever could.

"My soul is in the sky," she says, and then she jabs the mop handle skyward.

"I'm going now," I tell her.

The kid nods, just once, and then she turns back to the dead chihuahua and pierces its distended belly with her spear. Maggots spill out and wriggle helplessly across the pavement. Whatever she does next I don't wait around to see. I close my coat and put my head down and I start walking again. My shoes are loud as jackhammers on the asphalt. My shoes are loud as thunder, and that thought makes me hold the bag closer to my chest. It also makes me want to fling it away and hurry back home. But I don't. I honestly do not think that I could, even if I tried. Instead, I follow Joshua south, putting as much distance between me and the tattooed girl as quickly as I can.

Around me, the crumbling canyon of the dead city abruptly gives way to the wasteland of tortured steel and the dunes of powdered masonry that people call Locust Town. Crushed flat by one of the gravitational anomalies of the late cataclysm, it's difficult to believe this place was ever a city at all. Where once were skyscrapers, now there are only the lean-tos and shanties of the most destitute and forsaken, those unfortunates prevented from venturing north by the guns on the pest guard. I feel eyes on me, the fearful, resentful eyes of the prisoners of Locust Town, but also the curious eyes of the guard, men and women watching my progress from their outposts, following me through the telescopic sights of their rifles. But no one tries to stop me. I suspect they have been ordered not to.

"Who were you before?" Lakota asks me, back on the night we first met, the night we found one another, for better or for worse.

"Who was I? I'm not sure what you mean."

"I mean," she said, "*what* were you? Everyone was something. What were you?"

I hesitated, and then I told her the truth. "An astronomer," I said. "I was an astronomer, before."

"Then you saw it coming," she says.

"No one saw it coming," I reply.

"I think you're lying," she says, looking away from me, looking out the window at the late night decently hiding the river from view.

"Why would I be lying? What does anyone have to gain from lying anymore?" And then, before she can answer me or press the question, I ask her, "What about you? What were you before?"

"It doesn't matter who I was," she tells me.

I have never asked if Lakota is her real name. It might be. I've never asked if she lived in the city before, or if she came as a refugee before the bridges were blown. I have always figured she'll tell me these things, if she wants me to know.

"What if the bitch won't see you?" Lakota asks me, only just last night. "What if you do this thing, and you go all that way, and you manage to get there in one piece, and then she won't even see you?"

"I think she will."

"It's foolhardy," she says, sounding angry and trying not to sound afraid, afraid of me never coming back, afraid of being left alone. "You sit here and you read your books and you don't listen to the stories people tell."

"I hear enough," I say.

"You might well hear, but you don't goddamn listen. If you did, you'd know better. If you did, you'd stay put. You wouldn't go."

After she found out what I meant to do, I had to keep the jar hidden from her so she wouldn't destroy the thing inside. To keep me from trying to reach Locust Town and the pale lady. I know Lakota well enough by now to know how far she'll go to have her way, especially if she's frightened. I'm not the only coward who sleeps beneath our roof.

The wind is blowing off the bay, and it raises a redbrick and concrete dust devil to dance across the road in front of me, like a warning dervish or an alarmed sentry. The air down here smells different from the air outside the crush zone. Down here, the air smells oddly of ozone and diesel and, more faintly and oddly, of roses. It's colder, too. My breath has begun to fog, and I wish that I'd worn an extra layer beneath my coat, an extra pair of socks, as well. *If wishes were horses, beggars would ride.* That's something Lakota is fond of saying, whenever the occasion arises. I shiver and hug myself and keep walking, because whatever she might think of me, I do listen to the stories people tell, and I have seen enough to believe enough to know that I'm risking everything, coming this far south. I've seen enough to know better than to linger.

Before much longer, the tower comes into view. Of course, I ought to have been able to see it even before I entered the borders of Locust Town. But light does funny things down here, light and geometry and even time. The scars of the crush run deeper than mere rubble, marking the very warp and weft of spacetime in subtle and unpredictable ways. Lakota wasn't wrong. It was foolhardy coming here. It was worse than foolhardy, but now I'm here. And there's the tower, like God's own middle finger pointing at that low and brooding sky. It's the only building that wasn't destroyed, and in this desolation it manages to seem both lonely and defiant.

"I heard," says Lakota, "that you can walk for hours and hours down there and still never get where you're going, even if you're only trying to walk a hundred yards. And I've heard that sometimes folks go in and when they come back out again, just the next day, they've aged ten or fifteen years. That is, if they come out. I've heard there's no horizon. I've heard there are electrical storms that split atoms and turn solid rock to soup."

"Me, too," I tell her.

"But you're going anyway," she says. "Even when any one of those stories might be true, you're still going."

"Yes. I'm going."

"And you won't even tell me why."

"You know why," I reply, and she lights one of her crummy cigarettes and smokes and glares at me through the smoke.

"You think she has answers," Lakota says. "Or maybe you think she can forgive you for not having the answers yourself."

"Maybe," I say. "Or maybe it's something else."

"You're telling me you don't even know?"

"I'm telling you I think it'll mean something to her. I just don't know what."

And Lakota glares at the jar sitting on the table between us, the jar and the thing inside the jar. The thing I scraped up off the roof of our building two weeks ago, after it fell mewling from the clouds.

"You don't even know if she's real. For all you know, she isn't."

"Then I guess I'll find out," I say.

"And if you don't come back –"

"You worry about that if it happens," I tell her, and she gives me a look so sharp that it could almost draw blood.

One of the low red-brown dunes is blocking the street, and I climb to the top of it. My footsteps create rivulets of sand that flow uphill, instead of backwards, away from me. The dune can't be more than eight or ten feet high, but it takes me at least half an hour to reach the crest of it. But finally I do, and I stop there, out of breath, heart pounding, my face slick with sweat, and I gaze out across whatever unpredictable distance remains between the tower and me. There's a heat shimmer now, rising up off the pavement, despite the cold. Maybe it isn't a heat haze at all; maybe there's something else creating the mirage. I know just enough to know that I will never know. I wipe sweat from my eyes and start down the far side of the dune. It only takes me a few seconds to reach the bottom. I'm not the least bit surprised.

"The Lightning-Struck Tower," says Lakota, the night before, but this time I ignore the memory of her and keep walking. My throat is painfully dry, and I'm wishing I'd filled a canteen from the cistern and brought it with me. I don't know why I didn't. If anyone were to ask me why I didn't, I wouldn't know what to tell them.

"Perhaps it's because you never expected to make it this far," says someone who isn't only a memory of a conversation with my roommate. I look up to see who (because I was staring at the toes of my shoes) and there's a young woman standing only a few feet in front of me. She's tall, and her hair is dirty blonde, and her eyes remind me of quicksilver. She's wearing a ragged black T-shirt and more ragged jeans, and the T-shirt is printed with the name of a band that broke up before I was born, back when the world was still the world and there was no suspicion that it would ever become anything else. The woman is barefoot, but she has all her toes. She's pale as asbestos.

"Are you her?" I ask, because it's the first thing that comes to mind, and because I'm thinking what a relief it would be if I don't actually have to try walk the rest of the way to the tower.

"No," she replies. "But I know who you mean." She smiles, and I'm relieved to see that her teeth haven't been filed to points. It's an easy, disarming smile. It's a smile that makes me want to smile back, but I don't.

"Do you work for her?" I ask.

"No one works for her," says the blonde young woman in the black T-shirt. "That isn't how it is. That isn't the way she wants it to be."

I realize that she's staring at the brown paper bag, and I glance down at it, too.

"I've come a long way," I say.

"I know," says the young woman. "Everyone who comes to her has traveled a long way. Every path that leads to her is long."

"And she didn't send you to try and stop me?"

The woman smiles again, raises an eyebrow, then looks over her shoulder at the stark tower silhouetted against the gloom. I realize that her breath isn't fogging in the cold the way that mine is, but I realize that could mean anything at all. Or nothing. She turns back to me and shakes her head. "No," she says. "No one has sent me to stop you. She is a great believer in freewill, and so the last thing she's going to do is try to stop you. Not if you mean really to reach her."

"I do," I say.

"You have an offering? Is that what's inside the sack?"

Is it? I wonder. *Is that what it is, an offering?* I certainly haven't been thinking of it that way.

"It's only..." I begin, then trail off, suddenly not at all sure what to say.

She says, "You don't have to tell me, not if you don't want to tell me. I don't need to know." And then she points at the brooding sky. It isn't any different here than it is above the rest of the city. The same grey clouds. The same sense that those clouds are nothing more than a convenient veil.

"You're the astronomer," the woman says, and I stop looking at the clouds and look at her, instead.

"How do you know that?" I ask, though, truthfully, it's something else that really doesn't surprise me. I think about the old man in the wedding dress and about the tattooed child, and I start to ask her about them, if they *also* don't work for the pale woman. But then I think better of it.

"Does it matter how I know? I mean, have you ever tried to keep it a secret from anyone?"

"No," I reply. "I never have."

"Well, there you go, then."

The ozone- and rose-scented wind whistles between the dunes and over the rubble. It stirs up another dust devil, a frantic dervish rushing along from nowhere to nowhere else. The wind ruffles my hair and tugs eagerly at my clothes, but it doesn't even seem to touch the blonde woman. She blinks her silver eyes and smiles.

"When I was a little girl," she says, "far away from here, I used to dream about the end of things. The end of everything, I mean. I used to have the terrible dreams, and it was like that Robert Frost poem, you know. Sometimes it was fire, and sometimes it was ice, and sometimes it was – well, I was an imaginative child. My sleeping mind seemed capable of devising an endless parade of devices for the world's demise. Some were quick and merciful. Some were slow, lingering deaths. But I never told anyone about those dreams. Not my mother, not my father, not my sisters or grandparents. I thought that maybe I was insane."

"Maybe you were," I say. I shouldn't have, but the words slip out before I can think better of them.

"Maybe," she agrees, and there's that disarming smile again. "But once I dreamed of you and your paper bag. Once I dreamed of a man who knew the names of all the stars in the sky, who knew how the universe began and what held it all together. I dreamed the world had ended, and he was standing on top of a tall building where he lived with a woman he didn't like. Then something fell from the sky, something awful, something broken, and he scooped it up and put it inside a pickle jar."

I clutch the bag more tightly, and I tell her, "I think you just made that up." I try hard to sound as if I mean what I'm saying, even though I don't. I only *want* to mean what I'm saying. Whatever inviolable laws might once have governed cause and effect, I'm fairly sure those were put to rest when the curtain fell. I feel certain that's one of the secrets the brooding, muttering sky believes it's keeping from the rest of us.

"Maybe so," says the blonde woman. "Maybe I did make it up, back when I was a little girl, and that's why you're here now, because I made it all up."

"You think that's how the world works?" I ask her, and she shrugs.

"There was another dream," she tells me.

"I ought to be going," I say, not wanting to hear any more from her, needing to be moving again, regaining momentum before I lose my nerve and tuck my tail between my legs and go running back to Lakota.

"You think possibly she's going somewhere?" asks the blonde woman. "You think you're on a clock?"

"What was your other dream?" I ask, half under my breath, because I don't have an answer to either of her questions, and I apparently don't have the nerve to walk on and leave her standing there. She isn't like the old man in the wedding dress or the tattooed child. Whatever she is, whatever the forces that made Locust Town have made of her, it's something possessed of more gravitas. Of more gravity.

"You're sure you want to hear?"

I stare at her a moment, and then I stare across the ruins at the patient, waiting tower. How many eyes are watching me from the lightless cavities of its windows? How long have they known that I was coming? And if the blonde woman was not sent to stop me, then why is she here? Until I die, I will ask questions, even if I know they have no answers. Being who I am, I have learned that I am helpless to do otherwise, no matter how futile the inquiries.

"All right," she says. "There was this other dream, like I said. And in this other dream I wasn't a kid anymore."

"Let me guess," I say. "You were standing here, talking with me."

"You or someone like you," she replies, and she doesn't scowl or furrow her brow or show any other sign that she's annoyed at the interruption. "But somehow, it wasn't a continuation of the *other* dream, the one of the man on the rooftop. Perhaps that's because there have been many people on many rooftops, salvaging what the sky doesn't want, gathering those things up and keeping them safe, the way the faithful used to build reliquaries for the finger bones of saints. But anyway."

"But anyway," I say, as if I have walked all this way to play her Echo.

"When we were done talking, me and whoever else it was I dreamed of, that person went to the tower alone. No one stood in their way. No one tried to turn them back. I watched them go, and then I sat down in the dust and I waited for them to come back, because I wanted very much to know whatever it was that they had learned. I waited until the sun went down and came back up again. It was a very long dream, but I sat there all the same, because I needed to know, same as the person who'd come so far to speak with the lady in the tower needed to know."

"Why didn't you go with them?" I ask her.

"Well, for one, I wasn't invited," she tells me, "and for another, the sky has never seen fit to speak to me. Though, probably those two things are one and the same. Probably, you're carrying your invitation to visit her right there in your brown paper bag, and if your invitation fell from the sky, well..." And she trails off and watches me expectantly, as if I'm supposed to know what comes next, as if I also remember her dreams.

"If you never come back," says Lakota, last night or the night before or the night before that, "does it even bother you that I'll be alone?"

"Aren't you alone now?" I ask her. "Haven't you told me how alone you feel? Haven't you told me that again and again, over and over and over? Haven't you even said that my being here sometimes only makes the loneliness worse, because I'm me and not somebody else?"

"I know I can't stop you from leaving," she says, and there's spite in her voice, and there's bitterness, and her eyes shimmer with tears that she's determined she won't cry, not for me and not for anyone else, not ever. "What you mean to do, you'll do it, no matter who gets hurt. Is that how you were before?"

And I tell her no, that's not how I was before, and she makes an ugly sound that's meant to be a laugh.

"You go on, then," she tells me. "By this time tomorrow night, I'll have someone else to take your place. Don't you think I won't. Don't you think for one split second that won't be easy as one, two, three." And she snaps her fingers, for emphasis.

"You'll do what you have to do," I tell her, and then I ask the blonde woman if the dream person she waited to come back ever did.

"I can't tell you," she says.

And I ask her, "You can't tell me because you aren't allowed? Or you can't tell me because you don't know?"

"I can't tell you," she says again. And then far up above us there's a muted, grinding noise, like metal against metal, the shattered machineries of Heaven complaining in their labors. The woman looks up, and then she looks at me again. "I can't tell you," she says a third time. "But I think we'll both know, soon enough."

The grinding sound stops, and oily, iridescent raindrops begin to fall, spattering the dust and spattering our skin.

"I should get going," I say, and the blonde woman with the mercurial eyes nods her head and says yes, I should. That it isn't polite to keep the pale lady waiting, even if she doesn't have any other place to be.

"Anyway, I'll be right here waiting, should you come back this way," says the blonde woman.

"You might want to get in out of the rain," I tell her, but she only smiles and squints up at the brooding grey clouds. And I leave her standing there. I put my head down, and I hug the paper bag to my chest, and I put one foot in front of the other. It doesn't take me long at all to reach the tower.

A CHANCE OF FROGS ON WEDNESDAY

This story was begun on June 3, 2018 in Providence and finished on June 28th, after the move back to Birmingham. It's the story I finished on the day that Harlan Ellison died. And the day after I finished it, I wrote of "A Chance of Frogs on Wednesday" in my online journal: *I suspect it's exactly the sort of story my detractors hate. It offers no answers, no resolutions. The mystery matters more than any imaginable solution.*

Which Describes a Looking-Glass and the Broken Fragments

1. *The Hunter and the Game*

On my left are the plains, stretching off forever, or so they would have me believe, and on my right the land drops steeply away to the sea, the flat violet sea, a sea the color of amethyst and without waves or even ripples to mar its glassy depths. Amethyst was my mother's birthstone. The plains have no particular color. Instead, they seem to be at once possessed somehow of all colors – iridescent, variegated, like the wings of a tropical beetle or the bioluminescent flesh of startled cuttlefish. Beneath the sunless sky, the plains shimmer and glint and coruscate. For all I know, they're alive. There's the soft rumble of distant thunder, and a while later there's the very faint spark of distant lightning. Beside me, the hedgehog makes an anxious sound, and I whisper something I mean to be comforting, but there's rarely any comforting the hedgehog. She would jump at her own shadow, if there were still a sun here to cast shadows. "I'm sure it isn't very much farther," I tell her, though I have no idea whether or not that's the truth. "I don't mean to the tower," I quickly add a moment later. "I only mean to the village." The hedgehog has promised to accompany me as far as the village, but not any farther than that. "I won't go to the tower," she reminds me. "I told you that from the very beginning," and the two parallel lines of rusty iron quills embedded in her skin, running from the base of her neck to the small of her back make a nervous, clicking sound. I needed a guide out past the Breaks, and even the hedgehog was more than I could afford. "All this land is hers," says the hedgehog, and with a single sweeping gesture she motions to the sea and the cliffs and the plains, without actually looking up. "The village is as much hers as the tower. Everywhere you look, *that* is her. Everything out this way is the *scar* of her." I don't feel like arguing. No, I mean to say, *I don't feel like clarifying what I'd meant.* I watch the line of low, crumbling cliffs, stone as black as graphite shot through with winking seams of the same iridescence that blankets the plains. Her reach is deep. For all I know, at this end of the world, she's reached down a thousand miles and poisoned the very heart of creation. That's exactly the sort of tale you hear, if you go off seeking stories of the Lady of the Tower, the Courtesan of Wolves, the Doll. That's the sort of thing the hedgehog says, if you get her talking, which I usually try not to do. I don't blame anyone for their fear, and most especially I cannot blame the hedgehog. She is *what* she is because she was careless and strayed too near once, years and years ago, before she *was* the hedgehog, and the Lady found a bit of sport with her. People can think what they will of skinners, but I am not a beast half so brave as the hedgehog, who has led me out across the plains even after what has been done to her. I asked her once if the quills hurt. For an answer, she said, "Kiss me," and she smiled an ugly smile and stared at the ground at her bare feet. There are dozens of needles driven into the bones of her face, hollow needles that drip yellow venom, which is how the Lady made certain no one would ever kiss the hedgehog again. "All this land is hers," the hedgehog tells me again; possibly she thinks I didn't hear her the first time. "This is her handprint. This is how she signs her name." And then the hedgehog tells me the story all over again – for the tenth or twentieth time – her tale of the mirror the Lady found embedded in stone in the lowest dungeons of the Tower, a mirror whose face did not reflect, but rather danced with its own color, like oil on water, like a rainbow shot down and gutted and flayed. The hedgehog has a grim way with words. Maybe that was another gift the Lady bestowed on her. The hedgehog, she says, "The longer the Lady stared into the mirror, and the more deeply she stared, the more angry she grew that she couldn't find her face in it. Finally, in a rage, she broke the mirror apart, shattering it against a wall," and here she pauses to pantomime the act. There's another rumble of thunder then, so far away it's only just audible, and the hedgehog winces at the sound. "That's where it came from," she says. "The color and the stillness and the blackness of the sky, and all the wrongness coiled up inside the Lady's soul. It spilled out of the mirror when she broke the glass. It was what the mirror had wanted all along, of course, because the mirror was really a prison. And what had been imprisoned there for all time, the Lady set it free." As far as I know, every word of this might be true. As far as I know, it's not. It might only be a metaphor, for something more mundane, or an analogy for something much, much more terrible. It isn't for me to judge which. "We should stop soon," I say. "We'll make the village tomorrow." And the hedgehog says no, we shouldn't stop just yet. She says there's a shelter a little farther along, an overhang in the cliffs, a shallow sort of cave, and resting there would be better than stopping here, out in the open. There are still animals that hunt out here, warped and starving things, and there are other warped things that sail above us, and there are still other things that sometimes wriggle out of the motionless sea. "It isn't very much farther," the hedgehog promises. "I'm sorry I brought you out here," I tell her, and she shrugs, and her quills rattle. "I didn't have to come," she tells me. "I had a choice."

2. *I'm Not Formed by Things That Are of Myself Alone*

I'm dreaming, and, as always, I know that I am dreaming. I'm dreaming of the day the cooper and his wife led me down a path lined with withered apple trees, back to the old well behind their leaning house. In my dream, it isn't raining, though it certainly was raining that day. In my dream, the cooper's wife is a pretty woman. "Our girl," the man says, "she's in here, like I told you," and then I help him lift the heavy iron lid off the well. The smell from the hole is indescribable. But it isn't the smell of decay or disease, which is what I'd been expecting and braced myself for. First, there's a musty odor, as one would expect from most any old well, even one that has been (like the cooper's) dry and neglected for many years. But behind that ordinary smell, there's an acrid, bitterly pungent reek, so strong that my eyes begin to tear up almost immediately. I think of the smells of vinegar and turpentine and sulfur and lye. I think of all those, and none are exactly right. This is something I've never smelled before. I force myself not to cover my nose and mouth. "You put her down there alive?" I ask the man. "Your own daughter? You left her to rot in the darkness at the bottom of an abandoned well?" Waking, I didn't ask him any of those things. Waking, I asked him other things, instead. "We didn't know what else was to be done with her," his wife says apologetically, and the cooper just stares mutely into the well. "When she took…" and the cooper's wife stops before she says *sick* or *ill* or anything so simple as that. She's quiet for a moment that stretches out longer in the dream than it did awake. "Madam Skinner, you haven't seen what we've seen," she finally says. "You didn't have to watch it eating her alive. You didn't have to hear her screams or the laughter or the *other* voices." The cooper, he says to his wife, "You don't need to explain yourself," and then to me, "Will you help or won't you?" I should say no, that this is beyond me, whatever this is. But that isn't what I do. What I *do* is lean a little ways out over the low stone and mortar wall encircling the old well and gaze into the darkness. And at first there's nothing, and then, seeming to rise up from so far away that I think this must be the deepest well in all creation, there's a shimmer, first violet, then red, the reddish green, then gold, this entire procession through the spectrum requiring only a few seconds. Then there's only the dark again. Then there's only me gazing down into it. "What has been done to you, girl?" I ask, hardly above a whisper, and the dark whispers back that it has a name, that even now it has a name. But whatever the name is in my dream, it isn't anything I recall now, and it isn't the name the cooper and his wife gave their daughter. In the dream, the name is a word that means *desolation* and *despair* and *hollowness,* all at the same time, and also *delight* and *relief.* I confess, I don't know that any such word exists in the waking world. But it does in my dream, and I speak it back to the cooper's daughter, there in her hole beyond the orchard. "Yes," she says, "that is my name. That is me. That is who I am now and will be for always," and the cooper's wife begins to explain that the apple trees were not so withered before they put the girl in the well. "The branches weren't gnarled, and the roots didn't clutch at the soil like they do now. And the fruit wasn't bitter. We grew the sweetest apples in the parish. Ask anyone if we didn't." Down in the well, the daughter says that they've put her in the hole because they're afraid of her, and because they're cowards who would see their own blood suffer, rather than try and save her. "Save you from what?" I ask, and there's that shimmer of color again, only this time there's also a rustling noise, as if something heavy is dragging itself through gravel and dry leaves. There's an unwholesomeness about the sound. Nothing I can put my finger on, not sleeping and not awake. It occurs to me that the colors are the same way, somehow unwholesome. I tell myself I ought to look away, but I don't. "Save me from the Lady in the tower," says the voice buried in the shimmer. "Save me from her touch. It's pulling me apart, bit by bit, rearranging me. Every day there is less of me and more of her." And here the cooper tells me again that if I'll do this thing, if I'll cross the river beyond the Breaks and then also cross the wastes to find the tower, that everything he has will be mine. "A few coins?" I ask him. "A dying farm with bitter fruit and starving pigs? A mad woman in a well?" He says, "If I had more, I would offer it all, Madam Skinner. Show some mercy, please." Down in the well, his daughter laughs at him, and it's the most awful sound I have ever heard or ever imagined hearing. It's the laughter that makes me tell him that I'll try. It's the laughter that damns me, and I suppose that was the point. The man and his wife fall to their knees, as if they would worship me, and I'm about to tell them to get up, when the dream ends, and it's now and not then. I'm back awake, back beneath the overhang in the rocks, the stingy excuse for shelter that was much too generously described to me as a cave. The hedgehog has my own blade against my throat. I hadn't meant to sleep, but I had. "They will be here soon," she says to me. "Who will be here soon?" I ask her, and the hedgehog replies, "The agents of the Lady. They're close now. Don't you put up a fight and make me need to cut you. They'll have you, either way." In the gloom, her eyes swim with the same oily iridescence that stains the plains, the same shimmer I saw shining up from the bottom of a well. "You hate her," I say, and a drop of venom from one of the needles in the hedgehog's face drips onto my cheek and burns like a bee sting.

The hedgehog replies, "I would have cause to hate her far more if I were to lead you to her front door. I would learn new ways to hate. If I had done that, she would have taught me whatever it is that waits for us out *beyond* hate. So, you just lay still and wait. As I said, they will be along soon now, her hounds." The way the steel of the knife is pressing into my throat, I can tell that her grip on it is sloppy. She's never done anything like this before. She's never had to. "If I could have found what I've come looking for," I tell the hedgehog, "I'd have shared it with you. I'd have made you whole again." She tells me that I'm a fool, and I don't disagree. A few seconds later, I'm holding the knife, and the hedgehog is dead, and her blood is spattered about the greasy, shaley ground. It shimmers exactly the way her eyes did. It shows me all the colors I saw at the bottom of a well.

3. *We are Not Responsible for Who We Come To Be*

I walk for days. And for days after that. Or it only seems this way. There's so little here to set day apart from night, night from day. There's the persistant assumption that one still surely follows the other. There's the expectation that the old order applies, even though it has been broken down in so many other ways. At what I take to be morning, there is in the east, out over the shimmering plains, a whitish glimmer I take to be sunrise. And long hours of walking later, there is to my west, out over the still and violet sea, a coppery red line, thin as a paper cut, and I take that to be sunset. This is all I have of time, beyond my footsteps and my heartbeats. But finally I do at last come to the village, to what remains of it, and I'm left wondering why I ever thought it would have survived. Necessity is the mother of self delusion. I needed it to be here, a convenient half-way point between the river and the Lady's tower, a place to stop and catch my breath and gain my bearings and summon the last requisite shreds of courage. But the world makes a folly of our needs, and all that greets me is ruin. I follow streets an inch deep with shimmering ashes, ashes that are lustrous even without sunlight or lamplight to shine back, because this ash is imbued with the poisonous light from a broken mirror that was really only a prison. I pass by empty house after empty house, their windows busted out, their roofs sagging. Some have actually burned, but not most of them. Doors and shutters stand open or are locked up tight or hang askew on their broken hinges. Every garden and hedgerow is dry and brittle; every leaf and twig crumples at the lightest touch. I find a water pump, but it spits up a greasy slime that seems almost alive with iridescence. I'll have to be a lot thirstier than I am to try and drink that, and my last canteen isn't yet dry. I sit down, finally, on a pile of fieldstones at the base of what once was a huge oak tree. I'm not sure what it has become, the tree. The trunk leaks color, and I'm careful not to touch it. I suspect the wood might wince if I did. I allow myself half a swallow of water, and I sit there and I stare at my feet instead of staring at the ruins. Sweat drips from my nose and chin and spatters the ash between my boots, little craters in the grey and the iridescent shimmer. I've not seen a single corpse. I've not seen so much as a bone or castoff article of clothing. And no animals, either, no dogs or cats or livestock. I count that as a mercy, in a place all but devoid of mercy. For days my goal was this village, first with the hedgehog and then alone. *Just get as far as that, then sort out the rest from there.* And now I am here, and I don't think there *is* any sorting out the rest. The far-off thunder rumbles a mocking sort of agreement. This always was a suicide march, I tell myself. I *admit* to myself. How could it ever have been anything more meaningful than that? I close my eyes, trying to decide if I have whatever is required to stand up and start moving again. I suspect there's a very good chance that I don't, better than even odds, I'd wager. It's not hard to believe I'm going to sit here beneath the limbs of this thing that used to be a tree until the color in the ash that I have been breathing in for all these days finally does to me what it has done to all the rest of them – the villagers, the girl in the well, the hedgehog, and the hundreds locked away in municipal and church sanitariums all up and down the Breaks. I realize that my sweat has begun to smell like that foul air trapped inside the well beyond the cooper's orchard, that acrid, sour stink. I close my eyes. I let my mind drift, back and away from this awful place, but even so, there's only regret waiting.

"You still blame yourself," she said to me, the night I told Immanuela I'd taken the job, the night before I packed my kit and left the city by the Jersey Road. "You know better, but you blame yourself anyway."

"This isn't about that," I said, and of course I knew that I was lying.

"You'll blame yourself for that child's death until the day *you* die, which, if you truly mean to do this thing, will be soon enough."

"I might make it back through," I told her. "A few have."

"Too few to mention," Immanuela replied, and then she got up from the table, taking the candle with her, and crossed the small bedroom to stand by the open window. There was a breeze blowing in off the harbor, and the air smelled clean. All these days later, I can only just almost remember what clean air smells like. I think maybe I am forgetting what *clean* even means.

"I've found a guide," I said, as if that was supposed to make Immanuela feel any better about my heading out into the wastes. "I'm buying a full month's furlough, so she can leave quarantine long enough to see me there and back, round trip. I haven't met her yet, but I'm told she was born in a fishing village over the river."

"It wasn't your fault," Immanuela said, looking out at the city and the night. "It wasn't anyone's fault. Children get sick and die. It's arrogant, thinking you had any more of a hand in it than you did. It's the worst sort of arrogance. It's paranoid. If you hadn't carried in that load of blankets, another skinner would have. It's not like you knew they were infected."

"I don't want to talk about this."

"It wasn't your fault," she said again. "You never meant that girl harm."

"No, I didn't," I said. "I didn't mean her harm. But I was responsible, all the same." And right then I was wishing I were better at keeping the impatience out of my voice, at hiding annoyance. "It doesn't matter what I did or didn't intend. And, anyway, this has nothing to do with that. Maybe you'd understand if you'd been there with me, if you'd seen what I saw down in that hole."

"I've seen plenty," Immanuela said, glancing briefly back over her shoulder towards me, then returning her gaze to the open window. "And I've seen plenty enough to know how you won't be coming back, and that there's nothing out there could ever help anyone, no matter how desperately you might *want* there to be. I've seen plenty enough now to know if somehow you *do* make it back, you'll spend the rest of your life – of what will *pass* for life – locked up in an asylum cell somewhere, screaming at the walls because no one can see what *you* can see."

"Well, I have to try," I said. "If you'd been with me, you'd understand."

"I don't know why you even bothered coming here tonight."

Then neither of us said anything else for a while. You stood at the window, your back to me, and I sat at the table and smoked and listened to the clock on the wall and to the murmur of night sounds down on the street. And *here,* and *now,* all alone in this ruined, shimmering village beneath a poisoned and poisonous tree, I open my eyes again and realize that I'm no *longer* alone.

4. *The Hunter Becomes the Game*

As prolegomenon, a caveat: All that is to come will seem, from one perspective, as a single, shifting episode. But seen from another perspective, those same moments – strung along the thread of space and time like pearls, moments as *nacreous* as pearls – will seem to comprise three distinctly independent episodes. It's only a casual trick of the mind, of course, a trick to which human beings are so very susceptible, this segregation of one moment from another, of one event from another, the illusory rendering of discontinuous episodes from the undivided, continuous river of existence, a partitioning of consciousness.

The First.

I am sitting alone on a heap of fieldstones, here beneath what once was only an oak, somewhere near the center of a dead fishing village not far from the shore of a violet sea. In all my life, I have never been even half so alone. It is an aloneness that seems inviolable, perfect, impenetrable. Absolutely profound. And then I'm *not* alone anymore. I look up, and there she is, the Lady of the Tower, the Courtesan of Wolves, the Doll, come down to me so that I would not have to summon the strength and the courage to try and cross however much of the wastes remained between myself and her. Come *down* to me, I know, because she understands I likely wouldn't have made it the rest of the way, and so she would have been robbed of whatever sport I might have to offer. I lift my head, and there she is, and immediately I realize that what's left of her is only the shimmer-dimmed recollection of the living, breathing woman who, in a fit of frustration and vanity, broke apart a mirror, thinking it nothing *more* than a mirror. I could conjure for you a dozen ways to describe her, but none of them would come very near to the truth of it, the truth of what I saw standing there before me, so close I might have reached out and touched it.

Touched *her,* I mean to say.

But anyway, think of a tailor and a pair of scissors, and think of a bolt of cloth so elaborately woven that it could faithfully represent the very fabric of creation. And now imagine that the tailor cuts from it the rough shape of a woman, then tosses away that piece, which, after all, is only a scrap, and all we are left with is a hole in the cloth, a hole in the *shape* of a woman. Yet there are colors trapped inside that hole, restless, stubborn threads of color that remember *who* used to occupy what now is merely empty space – *threads of color* – and though they are tangled and knotted and dreadfully frayed, they are both beautiful and terrible to behold.

"You shouldn't have come here," she says, and I sit up a little straighter. I wipe sweat from my face and lick at my dry lips.

"I was sent," I tell the Lady. "I was asked to come find you."

"You were hired," she says. "Isn't that somewhat more accurate?"

Her voice is all the same colors as the ash heaped at my feet.

"It is," I admit. "I was hired to find you and ask if you might show a piece of mercy for a girl in a well, a girl who only dreamed of you, but who dreaming was touched, all the same." And hearing this, the hole, the threads, the shadow before me, it all seems to take a step back, and it watches me in a way that nothing has ever watched me before. It's watching my soul.

She is watching my soul.

"And I strike you as the sort who grants mercy to careless girls?" asks the Lady.

"I can't say. But I was hired to come here and ask. Which is what I'm doing."

"It must have been a fair kingly sum to tempt you," she says. "It must have been an empire. This girl whom I touched in a dream, she must be a princess."

"No," I reply. "Only the daughter of a cooper."

"Then your own life must mean very little to you, skinner."

"I won't argue that point," I say, and the hole and the threads and the Lady laugh, and I'm surprised that it really isn't a cruel laugh. It's only a laugh.

"So, you ask me to forgive not one interloper, but two," the Lady says. "The one who trespassed on my sleep *and* yourself. And you believe I have within me as much mercy as all that, skinner?"

"I can't say," I tell her once again.

"But here you are, nonetheless, in spite of your ignorance, alone with me at the end of the world, when there was a woman back there who loved you and begged you not to go seeking after worse things than your death. What is one broken girl, this one filthy cooper's whelp, weighed against all the suffering I could show you? And all the long years I could draw that suffering out?"

"It seemed important," I tell her. "It seemed like something I had to do."

"Because of the blankets?" the Lady wants to know. "Because of blankets you did not know carried a pox?"

"Because of many things," I answer, not surprised that she knows about the blankets. "And also because of what I saw at the bottom of that well."

"Though," she says, "that sad sight must seem almost as nothing, now that you're here, now that you've seen so much more of the blight."

I start to answer her, but…

The Second.

I'm sitting on a leather sofa, and the leather is cool and supple and the color of cream. The floor is carpeted the same creamy shade of white, and the air is filled with cigarette and marijuana smoke and with the pounding cacophony of rap music. There are other people here with me, mostly women, women and pretty boys dressed like women, and some of them are dancing. Some of the people are only talking. One is watching a television so wide that it occupies almost an entire wall of the room. On the TV screen, there are men with guns, and there's blood, and there are cars speeding recklessly along narrow streets. Across the room from me are sliding glass doors, and someone has left them cracked an inch or two. It's snowing outside, and there's a tiny drift on the cream-colored carpet.

"Who the fuck left the doors open again?" I ask no one in particular, and no one bothers to answer. So, I get up and walk across the room to pull them shut myself. One of the pretty boys smiles as I pass, but no one else even seems to notice. I reach for the handles of the sliding doors and catch my reflection looking back at me from the glass. I look as tired as I feel. I'm wearing too much makeup and a tight black dress that hardly even comes to my knees. I'm barefoot. My hair is long and pale and hangs loose around my shoulders. I look at my hands, and the skin is smooth and soft and my fingernails have been painted the color of ground-fall apples in a withered orchard. Then a gust of freezing wind blows more snow into the room, and I yank the doors shut and lock them. It's late winter out there, late winter in Manhattan, and it's been snowing since just after sunset. I stare through my reflection at the snowy night. I am surrounded by the glowing spires of skyscrapers. It's a long way down to East 39th.

On the TV, something explodes.

I go back to my place on the leather sofa and try hard to ignore the television and the music, trying to remember why I ever thought this would be better than being alone, all these people, all this noise. Someone leans in close, then, someone who smells of rose perfume and smoke, and she passes me a small, square mirror. There are three parallel lines of powder on the glass, powder that glints and shimmers, iridescent with colors I don't know the names for, if they even have names.

"What the hell is this?" I ask.

"It's something new," says the girl who handed me the mirror. "Try it. Ain't no one gonna love it more than you, babe," and then she kisses my cheek.

"I have an early flight," I remind her.

"You know," she says, "it wouldn't be so bad if you stuck around a while this time. Whatever business you still got in Atlantic City, I'm sure it can wait a week or two."

"Maybe," I tell her. "I don't know who half these people are, did I mention that?" And I gesture at the crowded room.

"Just friends," she says. "Friends of friends. Etcetera. Now relax. It wasn't your fault, you know, what happened," and she smiles, then goes away, leaving me there with the mirror and the shimmering powder.

On the other side of the sliding glass doors, out in the storm, there's a hole in the world in the shape of a woman, and it's watching my soul.

The Third.

I stand at the edge of high black cliffs that drop away into the sea and into deep places hidden always in shadow, and the Lady, she stands somewhere close behind me. It comes to me that this is where the tower *was,* before she broke the mirror. Some of its foundations are still plainly visible, scattered here and there along the precipice, if you know what you're looking for.

"It fell," says the Lady. "It fell when I fell, or not long after. I *thought* that I would be carried away with it, but I wasn't." There's regret in her voice, coiled like an adder, and there's bitterness, too.

I start to ask her why I don't remember leaving the village, and then I realize it doesn't matter in the least. "This isn't what I thought I'd find," I tell her, instead, then wish I hadn't said anything at all. And now I can see a speck of greater darkness silhouetted against the sunless sky, suspended above the pit where once there used to be a tower. A speck no larger than a mote of dust, and I'm amazed that I can see it at all. "What is that?" I ask the Lady, pointing at the speck.

"The place where the mirror came from, and the place the tower's gone," she replies. "A doorway, maybe. A window, perhaps. Or nothing more than an old well with a cooper's daughter trapped inside."

Behind me, I hear footsteps in the gravel and the ash and the sand, the softest footsteps I ever have heard, and then the Lady of the Tower presses something small and hard into my left hand. Her touch is so cold that it burns, the way the plains beyond the Breaks have been burned, the way even the sea and sky here have been burned. I feel that cold, past flesh and bone, all the way to the core of my being, and yet somehow I am *not* burned. I open my hand and look to see what she's given me, because she hasn't said that I shouldn't, and find that it's a stoppered crystal vial. The crystal is as black as that speck of nothingness hanging in the void above the sea. There are designs worked into the crystal, and for some reason they make me think of snow.

"This is what you've come for," she says. "It isn't an antidote, because there is no antidote. But it *is* what you've come for, all the same."

"And you'll let me leave with it?" I ask her, closing my hand tightly around the crystal vial. "This isn't some deceit? You'll let me walk away from here and take this with me, back to..." But I let the thought go unfinished, because I realize that I'm alone, just as I realized back at the dead fishing village that I was no longer alone. "Okay," I say, turning from the pit and the motionless amethyst sea, turning to face the shimmering plains again. There's a distant flash of lightning, and I stand there, counting off the seconds until the rumble of thunder catches up to it.

WHICH DESCRIBES A LOOKING-GLASS AND THE BROKEN FRAGMENTS

For much of my writing career I have wanted to write an effective retelling of Hans Christian Andersen's "The Snow Queen," and it is something I have come at several times from several different directions. I don't think I've ever pulled it off, so I will likely keep trying. But it should be fairly obvious to anyone familiar with the fairy tale to see that's what I was trying to do here, albeit in a post-apocalyptic milieu. Maybe if Sergio Leone had decided to film "The Snow Queen" as a western. "Which Describes a Looking-Glass and the Broken Fragments" was written between April 2nd and 7th, 2019.

Metamorphosis C

1.

Trick to getting down so far as *she* is, it's not letting oneself be diverted and turned about by the beggars and the whores and the ballyhoo. And really, underneath the streets, it's all pretty much ballyhoo. It's all a come-on. A shuck and jive. Here in the darkness that stinks of sewage and spent engine oil and grease fires, rubber and dust and diesel, of a hundred filthy stalls frying up fuck-all knows what – anonymous meat on skewers, roots still unknown to botanists, black-market protogoop, and all of it sterilized and set ablaze with ginger and bleach and liberal handfuls of mutant hydroponic chilies. Down beneath the streets, what they call air is a toxic stew that singes the nostrils, clogs the lungs, and sears the eyes. You come down here without a filter, well, there's every kind of fool in the world, isn't there? But already I have digressed. What I mean to say, you come down here to find *her,* you have to stay focused. For however long it takes, you keep the buskers and catamites at arm's fucking length and pick your perilous, ill-advised way along narrow corridors and through holes punched in cinderblock and stone and mortar. Everything vies for your attention, and so you don't look. Follow me and keep your eyes on your feet, because there's gaping potholes and tiger traps, goddamn punji sticks and lots of other shit you do *not* want to step in down here (and I mean besides all the actual, literal shit, of which there's plenty enough, besides). You follow me, and you watch your step. Mind the gap, as they say over there. I'll do the looking elsewhere for both of us, and no, it's not that I'm immune to the barkers and titty-flashers, it's that I'm being paid to get you from Point A to Point Nemo, and if word gets around my charges have a tendency not to reach their intendeds, well, word gets around, natch. People talk. And I know the way not only by memory, from having been down this path twice half a dozen times now, but because I know the code scribbled on the walls in yellow chalk. I paid plenty and then some for the key to that cipher. Not that I *personally* have an interest in the things she has to say, all the crazy shit people go down to her to hear spoken. I'm no pilgrim, not no way, not nohow. I am nothing but a conductor. I am at best your Virgil, and what gets me wet isn't revelation, but commerce. So, you get distracted by that molly boy over there, or by missing evolutionary links fished up from Amazonian lagoons, or by, well, *whatever* and *what-have-you,* and then you step in an open access shaft and break your silly topsider neck, and that means debts do not get paid. There's easier and less perilous work, you know. I'll be lucky to see the far side of forty, between one thing and the other, but it is what it is. Beats wages. Beats selling off bits of myself for rations and a cardboard roof. Sure, it does. Watch your step and do *not* lean on the handrail. One day soon, those supports are gonna give way and – *boom* – this whole staircase is gonna go crashing into the pit, mark my words, a rending, twisting wrought-iron helix folding in on itself, and *when* that day comes, I'll be crossing any number of profitable excursions off my bill of fare, and it's slender enough as is. Anyway, you get the picture. And I talk too much, and I don't need anyone to tell me that. Hold that lantern higher, Miss Whoever You Are, and it's not much farther, now that we're through the bazaar and down the spiral, just a little ways farther along these narrow hallways carved from the native granite (I have been told) before America was America was this piss ditch, and watch out for rats. I've seen rats down here big as – well, let's not dwell on that. We take a left and a right and one more left, and *voilà, Mein Freund.* That wasn't so bad, now was it? However, before we proceed, and before you pay the child with the tin cup – that's her over there, the urchin girl that could pass for a ragpile – let's go over the rules one more time. It's not that I think you're *necessarily* stupid, it's just that I can't afford to discover how you are, in fact, a moron. And I bring the wrong person to see her, and I mean someone who doesn't take the etiquette to heart, who just blurts out what-the-fuck-ever, and I lose my privileges. So – listen – it's like this: You don't stare, but you also do not avert your eyes. You don't make any sudden moves. You don't cross your arms, run your fingers through your hair, or shift from foot to foot. You don't say a word, and I mean not a single goddamn word. You don't say so much as a syllable, you got that? Whatever she's gonna say, she doesn't need any prompting. And when she's done talking, when the tale's been told, you don't say thank you. You turn around and fucking leave that same precise way you came in. Me, I have to wait out here, so you're on your own, Little Miss Tourist, when you walk through that curtain and until you make the great egress thereafter. And you will *not* fuck it up, this audience, because I *will* leave your dumb ass to find your own way home, *capisci?* Remember those rats I mentioned? Remember the alligators and mite swarms that I didn't? I don't mean to be a frothing cunt on this score, it's just eggshells and thin ice and dynamite, you know? Good. Now, pay the child, and good luck. Hope you find what you're looking for, but I don't want to hear the whining if you don't.

2.

On the NERTA shuttle ferrying me from the slums and silver spires of Manhattan, northwards up the long grey gash of the Hudson towards the border and home, I sit and I make my notes and I try to remember what I saw and what was said and, most of all, I try to second guess the committee. I try to anticipate their curiosity and needs. First, they'll be standoffish and skeptical, that I haven't wasted their money, that *she* isn't just another urban legend, that I actually found what I went to find. But *then* the questions will begin. I recline my seat and watch the scenery rushing by outside. The train just passed the charred ruins of Poughkeepsie, and it'll be another five minutes before the diligent little red light above my seat winks out again, the all-clear to let us know we're past the hot zone. I shut my eyes and I try to think of absolutely nothing but the woman beneath the streets, the woman inside her injection-molded Perspex cube, her rasping, rheumy, tinny voice sifting through a ring of antique plasma speakers suspended above the cube. I did exactly as I was instructed by the guide. I didn't stare, but neither did I look away. So, I *saw* what there was *to* see. The sort of thing you read about, but only half believe, because it's easier that way. I would say what's left of her is more metal and plastic than meat and bone, but that's not strictly true. That's only a mistaken impression, like mistaking a walking stick insect for nothing more than an actual twig or an octopus for a lump of stones and coral. What the molecular assemblers have done to her, it's nothing so simple and straightforward as mere alchemical conversion, lead to gold, meat to chrome, whatever. It is so much stranger. That's not the sort of word the committee likes to hear – *stranger*. But they weren't there, and they never will be. They can only just begin to daydream. They can only fantasize about the revolutions to biomechanics if only acquisitions could get their mitts on someone like *her.* Every time they've tried to manufacture their own, the subject is dead before anything especially interesting happens. And no one knows why. That is, no one knows why the accidents and elects in the wild survive and the accidents and controls in the lab don't. Anyway, this isn't what I want to set down first. I'm good with morphology and metrics and stats. I can *describe* her as well as almost anyone. What I was not prepared for was the tale she told, though, of course, that *was* my cover story, that I was just another of the lost and wandering gone to seek the wisdom and prognostications of the Sibyl of Cobble Hill. I listened to every word. I stood on the yellow X painted on the ground, and she fixed me with those mercury ball-bearing eyes and she spoke from the cruddy old speakers, and her voice rained down like static:

There was a king who lived in a great castle at the top of a mountain, and all around his mountain was an ancient forest. It was a forest as old as the world. Before there were men in the world, there was the forest that girded the king's mountain. Every manner of tree grew there, and beneath the blue skies the forest was eternally every shade of green that ever was, because in the king's land there was never autumn nor was there winter. As men do, the king grew old, and as sometimes happens with old men, the king forgot the things he knew to be true when he was young. And those things which once had seemed good and right before became wrong in his sight. And the forest which it has always pleased him to look upon from his high windows and balconies took on an evil cast, and it haunted his dreams, and when he was awake he couldn't bring himself to gaze upon it anymore. Somehow, it had turned against him. He knew this, as surely as he feared death. And so he sent a thousand woodsmen to cut it down. His youngest daughter protested, and in his madness the old king condemned her. He had her sewn up alive into the belly of a dead sow and tossed into the river that flowed through the forest. "That is that," he thought, and watched with relief as his woodsmen felled mighty tree after towering, mighty tree. The king knew that it would take them a hundred years or more, and that he would certainly not live to see the work completed. But he took comfort knowing the work would be done in time. Soon, there were clear-cut miles between his mountain and the trees, a desert of amputated stumps and blackened, smoldering timber, immense pyres that glowed every night to help his dreams. The axes and saws and fires were a medicine for his terror and a balm for his dread. As for his daughter, she did not drown in her pig-belly coffin and was carried far from the castle to a deep still pool in a part of the forest that was ancient even as the forest counted time. Tiny fish chewed at the leather cords the king's executioners had used to sew the sow shut, and soon enough the princess was free. She swam to the shore and slept for a long time in the moss and bracken at the edge of the pool. And in her dreams, in her sorrow and pain and fury, she was changed by the forest. She woke to find that she had become a daughter of the trees and no longer the daughter of a man. Her body was transformed so that, when she grew still, she might easily pass for a sapling, nestled in the green shadows, reaching for the sunlight. Her skin became aspen bark and lichen, and there were hollows where her breasts had been and in them bees built hives and made honey that dripped from her wooden nipples. And in her womb the forest planted a thousand seeds that ripened and slipped from her sex to take root in the rich black soil. "You will be our vengeance," the forest told her. "We know as a human woman how you loved us, and we watched the cruelty done to you by your own father and our greatest enemy, and so you will be our vengeance. Your children will be an army, and when they are grown, they will cross the wasteland that now divides the castle's mountain from us, and they will bring the castle down, stone by stone by stone. When they are done, their roots will grind those stones to dust, and the winds will carry the dust away to the sea. All the king did will be forgotten. It will be as if he never was. And the forest will return." And the daughter of the forest who was no longer a princess listened, and the rustling of leaves and the creaking of limbs comforted her more than anything ever had. It was right and just that she had been chosen to be the vengeance of the great forest her mad king father had so injured. It was the greatest honor she ever could have received. And so she tended the aspen-skinned things that were her children, and she watched them grow, and she waited, because she was part of the forest now, and the forest had all the time it needed.

That's it. All that she said to me, or the gist of it, at least. The ragged girl scanned me for any sort of recording device, so all I have is memory. I open my eyes and watch the grey winter world outside the train slipping past, and I think about all the committee's questions, and I think about the tunnels, and I think that I will never again dream of anything but the living machine in her clear acrylic box, five hundred feet beneath a rotting city that once, half a millennium past, was as green and alive as any fairy-tale forest.

METAMORPHOSIS C

Yeah, I don't know. How about, for this one, you tell me? The story was written on April 27th and April 28th, 2019.

LOCKE
©2021

Day After Tomorrow, the Flood

1.

I've already been up for almost three hours when Jimmy comes into the kitchen, rubbing his eyes and looking like someone who's actually slept the night. Me, I've been sitting at the table, watching out the window, chain smoking and drinking coffee, watching while night turned into morning and the sun splashed gaudy daylight across the rooftops and treetops of Federal Hill. He stops rubbing his eyes and stares at me a moment. He squints and frowns, then takes down a cup from the cabinet and pours a cup of coffee for himself. I say good morning, and he doesn't reply. He opens the refrigerator and finds a mostly empty carton of milk, then he does to his black coffee what sunrise did to the night. He adds a couple of spoonfuls of sugar before sitting down across from me. He yawns and rubs his eyes again.

"You know, it's hardly still coffee once you're done with it," I say, and I motion towards his cup with my cigarette.

"Did you get any sleep at all?" he wants to know, and I tell him no, not much. He yawns and looks out the window. It's almost the middle of April and the trees are still bare as skeletons.

"I hope I didn't wake you," I tell him. "I try to be quiet."

"You didn't wake me," he says. "The garbage truck woke me," and I remember that it's Wednesday morning. I don't think it had even occurred to me yet to wonder what morning it was. Insomnia smears time into a timeless grey mess and all finer distinctions are lost. At least for me they are. I am left only with the grinding, imperturbable parade of daylight and darkness, and I suppose I ought to be grateful I'm left with that much.

"Jesus, Em, you should have taken something," Jimmy says. "That's why you have those pills. That's why you go to the trouble and expense of getting the prescription filled." He yawns again, takes a sip of his sweet, milky coffee, and then fishes a cigarette from my pack and lights it with my lighter.

"I don't like how they make me feel," I say, "and half the time, the damn things don't even work. Half the time they only make matters worse. I'd rather stumble through the day half awake than stumble through the day half awake with an Ambien hangover, thank you very much."

"Have you eaten anything?" he asks.

"I'm not hungry," I reply.

"When I'm done with my coffee," he says, "I'll make some eggs and bacon. If you're not going to sleep, you can at least eat. You're not a kid anymore, Em. You gotta at least try to take better care of yourself."

I take a drag on my cigarette and blow smoke at the window-pane. I shake my head and say, "A big dose of cholesterol, salt, and grease after a sleepless night, that's your idea of me taking better care of myself?"

"There's also oatmeal," he tells me, knowing damn well how much I hate oatmeal.

"I'll eat something later. I'll be sure not to skip lunch today."

"Was it the dreams?" he asks, as if it's ever anything else these days. "Did you even sleep enough to have a dream?"

"Yeah," I say, and he sighs and smokes and sips his coffee. I stare out the window at the sidewalk and the street and a man in a yellow T-shirt walking his shitty little dog. I think the dog is a Yorkshire Terrier, but I'm not sure. I'm not good with dogs. The man and the dog reach the end of the street and round the corner and are lost to sight.

"Are you going to keep your appointment with Dr. What'shername this week?" Jimmy asks. He knows my psychiatrist's name perfectly well, but my current shrink is my third in a year and a half, and so he pretends he can't keep them straight.

"Maybe," I say. "Probably." I know that there's a fifty-fifty chance I'll call and cancel the appointment, but I'm not going to tell Jimmy that. He doesn't know I cancelled the last one.

"I wish you would," he says. "I'm not going to pressure you, but I really wish that you would. You can't keep this up forever. Sooner or later, it's going to make you sick. Do you want to talk about it? I think I'm almost awake enough to listen."

"No," I say, "I don't want to talk about it." I can hear how I sound, as if I'm annoyed that he asked. I'm not annoyed. I'm just exhausted.

"But it was the city under the sea," he says, not asking because he knows the answer, not asking but expecting confirmation, regardless.

"Yes," I say, and I tap ash into the ashtray sitting on the table between us. It needs to be emptied. I don't think either of us has emptied it in days. "It's never anything else, is it? Sometimes I think that's the worst part of all, the sheer, unrelenting monotony of it."

"You should have taken a pill," he tells me again.

"You've never taken Ambien," I say.

"No, but –"

"Then shut up about it." That comes out harsher than I meant it to come out. Or maybe it's just that I'm losing my patience when I don't want to be losing my patience. Jimmy means well. I know that. I'm not so self-centered that I don't see how my insomnia is hard on him, too. It's not like I don't know he's started losing sleep over my losing sleep. But I have a headache and my stomach's sour and I've only managed one good night's sleep in the last week, and that's only if you count an hour here and there, a good night's sleep patched together from several different nights and also from nodding off for five or ten minutes at a time in the afternoon or early in the evening while we're watching TV.

"You have that thing at the museum today," I say, and he nods.

"If I didn't, I'd offer to stay home. You look like you could use the company."

"I'm fine," I say. "I'll be fine. I need to try and catch up on work."

Jimmy stubs out his cigarette in the ashtray, then gets up and goes to the refrigerator. He stands there for a moment with the door open, and waves of cold air wash over me and puddle on the floor.

"Shit or get off the pot," I say, glancing over my shoulder at him. "You stand there much longer and the milk's going to spoil."

"Shush," he says, taking out a carton of eggs and the butter. He sets them on the counter, then goes back for the bacon. "Sunnyside up or over easy?"

"I'm not hungry," I tell him a second time.

"I'll cook," he says, "you'll eat."

"Sunnyside up," I tell him, because there's no point arguing. I'll eat the bacon and pick at the eggs enough to make him think I've eaten some of them.

"Please keep the appointment," he says, and sure, I say. I will. I promise. And I watch the window and the undrowned world outside.

2.

Imagine you are a woman drowning. Imagine that the one you love stands above you, leaning down over you, one hand on your forehead and the other on your breastbone. The water is warm, and his hands are warm, and when you open your eyes and gaze back up through the shimmering, mercurial membrane dividing the kingdom of water from the kingdom of air, his face dances and you only recognize him because you have known him for so long. He isn't doing anything that you haven't begged him to do. You part your lips, and a stream of tiny jellyfish escape your mouth; at least, that's how the bubbles appear to your drowning eyes. Imagine that, and now also imagine that you stand at your bedroom window, looking out over the rooftops of the city, and the late summer afternoon is so still and silent that there is no sound of birds nor of insects nor of automobiles. There is only that stillness, like water in your ears, like the weight of waters closed in all about you. And standing there you realize that this cannot possibly be *your* bedroom, because you live in a dingy first-floor apartment and the only thing visible from *your* bedroom window is the house next door, pressing in so near it seems almost like you could lean out and touch its aluminum siding. Wherever you are, whoever's room this is, you can see all of Providence laid out below you and before you, and you can see the bridges and the river and the sharp line of the hurricane barrier and the leaden plain of Narragansett Bay beyond. You can see cargo ships and tugboats bobbing like toys on the water. And then a shadow falls over it all, like the shadow of the man kindly leaning over the tub, holding you down as you have asked him to hold you down. *Be my pocketful of cobbles. Be my millstone. Be the iron collar about my neck.* The shadow races across the land, turning a sunny July day to twilight, and the streetlights wink on, that sterile too-bright

LED glow like a swarm of phony electric fireflies. *I won't drown,* you told him the night before, the both of you lying awake, you mostly talking and him mostly only listening. You say, *I just want to know what it feels like, being so near to drowning. That's all that I'm talking about. That's all that I mean.* And he tells you again that he won't do it. He tells you again to keep the appointment with the psychiatrist. The water is warm, and his strong hands are warm, and the tub beneath you is cool, a pale enameled casket and you are a sleeping beauty grown rotten and old waiting on a prince errant. Your nostrils leak still smaller jellyfish, and you lean out the open window and watch the progress of that shadow as it flows across the rooftops and sluices down the avenues and splashes darkly in rainspouts and against curbstones. And here, right *here,* your wonder and amazement at the sight of it melts into fear, same as every time before, same as every incarnation of the dream over however many months it has come to you whenever you dare to fall asleep. Suddenly, you're afraid, which is only sensible. And you don't want to look up, to see what's casting so mighty a shadow, but you know that you will. You know this, because you *always* look up, every single time, and you have no cause to have faith that this time will be any different from all those other same dreams before. *What if he doesn't let me up?* you ask yourself, and you're surprised that the thought doesn't frighten you. *It will only be a great wave,* you think. *Only the mightiest wave that anyone has ever imagined, and all it can do is smash and drown and flood and in time withdraw. It will only be a wave to put Noah's deluge to shame, and the only thing I have to fear is drowning, and I don't fear drowning, because I have drowned. I know what drowning means. I know everything it holds in store for me. And the drowning of a city is not so very different from the drowning of a single woman.* He rolls over, turning his back to you, and you stare at the ceiling, at the water stains on the ceiling from your upstairs neighbor's leaking bathroom pipes. *I don't want to talk about it anymore tonight,* he says to you. *I'm not asking you to hurt me,* you say, so imagine saying that to someone whom you love. And you lean farther out the window, and now you can see that you're not alone in the city (which you had come to suspect, from the silence). There are people standing in the streets. Indeed, the streets are as packed with people as they are with the shadow of the wave. A sea of upturned faces, you think. A sea of eyes not so afraid of what's coming that they won't stand and stare into it and see what's bearing down on them. You think how shameful fear would be, and you think how shame is worse than drowning. You think how shame is worse than water rushing up your nose and down your throat when you finally couldn't hold the silver bells of jellyfish inside any longer, so you set them free and the water poured in and filled your lungs. Soon, you think, no one will have to hold me down, not ever again. Soon, I will never float again. Soon, I will become a cathedral for scuttling claws and barnacles and oysters and those were pearls that were before only my eyes. *When I raise my left hand,* you say – before he turns his back on you – *When I raise my left hand, then you'll know to let me up. It'll be like a safeword, a signal so that there's no danger of you accidentally hurting me.* And he replies that he wants you to please stop talking about this and please keep your appointment. *Don't be a coward,* you say, but you can't be sure who you said it to, because here you stand at the window and there you lie in bed and there in the tub of warm water with his strong hands on your breastbone and forehead. *I won't do it,* he says, *and I want you to stop asking me.* But isn't that exactly what he *is* doing? Isn't his weight bearing down on you, like the lightless force of the deep ocean places, all the proof you need that he must have changed his mind? He must have been persuaded. You must have made him understand. *Look up,* you hear yourself say. *Look up and face it. Be as brave as all these others. Be as strong.* And then the wail and woop of civil-defense sirens begin to shriek, shattering the calm and the silence pooled beneath the shadow, and in that moment you turn away. *Let me be a coward. Let me flinch, here at the end. Let me not look, but only hold me down until I give you the signal to let me up.* When he says no again, and when he wants to know how you can even ask him to do such an awful thing, you tell him there's no one else you can ask. If not him, then who? The sirens make you think of Odysseus and the ears of his oarsmen plugged with beeswax, and here you are bound to the mast, listening to the song and regretting your boldness. Here you are in shadow. Here you are lying in a bathtub of warm water. Now, imagine that you are a woman drowning.

3.

After dinner, but we're still sitting in the kitchen at the table, the table still cluttered with the remains of the meal, because neither I nor Jimmy has bothered to clear away the dirty plates and silverware and the scraps of food. We ate mostly in silence. We only rarely talk during meals. I have always found it unseemly, somehow, conversations all tangled up in the acts of chewing and swallowing, and so usually the meals we share are quiet. But when we're done and still sitting at the table, after I light a cigarette and Jimmy puts the cherry-red kettle on for coffee, then he asks me how the session with the psychiatrist went. I tell him I'd rather not talk about it, but then I also tell him that it went okay, that it wasn't the worst fifty-five minutes I've spent in that woman's dingy little office on College Hill. I tell him that this time she didn't say anything to piss me off and she didn't try to push any more drugs on me. She didn't even ask whether I was taking the Ambien.

"Then it was productive," he says, sitting down again.

"I wouldn't go that far," I reply. "It went okay. It went a lot better than last time, and a whole hell of a lot better than the time before last time."

"You talked about the dream?"

I almost lie and tell him that we did. There's nothing at all to prevent me from doing just that. It would be the easy way out. "No," I tell him. "We didn't talk about the dream." Jimmy frowns and smokes his cigarette and watches the kettle on the stove, the blue gas flames licking at the metal. "We talked about other things," I add.

"Okay," he says.

"It's not all about the dream," I tell him. "You know that, right?"

"I know the dream is why you can't sleep."

I start to ask him to pass me his pack of Camels, but then I remind myself that I've been smoking too much and I'm trying to cut back, so I don't. I stare at my hands, instead. There's a bruise on the back of my right hand, turning from the color of raspberry preserves to a fleshy yellow green, and I have no idea at all how I got it. That happens to me a lot, unexplained bruises. Maybe it's something that happens to lots of people. I honestly don't know. I often wonder at how very little I do know about other people.

"Well, it's not only about the dream," I tell him again.

He shrugs and blows smoke at the high kitchen ceiling and asks, "Did I ever tell you about the McCutcheon girl?"

"No," I say. "I don't think you ever did." I'm still staring at my bruise, imagining it's most likely that I whacked the back of my hand on a doorknob, probably in the night when I got out of bed to go to the bathroom and was only half awake. I've done that plenty enough times over the years we've lived here. Our apartment has antique octagonal crystal doorknobs, and they leave ugly bruises.

"She drowned when I was nine or ten years old," says Jimmy. "Her folks' place was just down the road from ours. They raised goats for the milk. Her mother made cheese from goat milk."

I grew up in Providence, but Jimmy grew up on a farm near Lincoln, a little ways north and west of Pawtuxet, a little ways south of Woonsocket. He still owns the land where his parents grew strawberries and corn and pumpkins, but I've never seen the place. He doesn't talk about it much, the same way I rarely talk about my own childhood. Neither of us are the sort given to fond reminiscences, for one reason or another.

"There's a huge old limestone quarry in Lincoln," he says. "It flooded years and years ago, before I was even born, and we used to ride our bikes down there in the summer and swim. The older kids went skinny dipping at the quarry and smoked weed and shit. You know, the stuff that older kids get up to in places like that. My parents didn't like me swimming there, but I did, anyway."

"It doesn't sound safe," I tell him. I force myself to stop staring at the bruise.

Jimmy shrugs again.

"I was a good, strong swimmer. But I can see why my mom and dad worried. The water's very deep in places, and the quarry walls are steep. You could get in trouble if you weren't a good swimmer."

"And she wasn't. The McCutcheon girl, I mean?"

"I honestly don't know," he says. "We weren't really close friends. My mom bought her mom's goat cheese, that's all. Maybe she was a fine swimmer, but something...I don't know. Perfectly good swimmers drown all the time."

I never learned to swim, and Jimmy knows that.

He takes another drag on his cigarette, and he says, "There were all kinds of stories about the quarry. Local folklore – or fakelore, to be more precise – the sorts of spook stories kids make up to scare each other. The sort of stuff that gets repeated over and over and over until no one knows who started it or if there ever was a grain of truth to the tales."

"Like what?" I ask.

"Like, for example, supposedly there was a monster in the quarry. Well, sometimes you heard it called a monster. Sometimes people said it was just a big fish. Someone even told me once it was a pet alligator from back in the sixties – when you could still buy baby alligators in pet stores – and it had been turned loose in the quarry, gotten really big over the decades, and occasionally it would eat swimmers."

"It would have frozen to death the very first winter," I say.

"Sure," says Jimmy. "Of course, but kids don't necessarily think about that sort of thing. Kids get a kick out of believing in alligators living in flooded limestone quarries. Wasn't it Mark Twain who said 'Never let the truth get in the way of a good story'?"

I glance at the window. There was still a little daylight when we started eating, but now it's dark and there are lights in the house next door.

"So, they said the McCutcheon girl was eaten by an alligator?" I ask Jimmy, and he laughs a dry, perfunctory laugh and shakes his head.

"Not that I ever heard. Maybe somebody said that, but all I ever heard was that she drowned. She went missing, and three or four days later her body turned up in the quarry. It made the news."

"No one actually saw her drown?" I ask him.

"No, but she was wearing her bathing suit."

"She was swimming there alone?"

"So far as I know. That wouldn't have been so strange. I swam there alone sometimes, if no one else wanted to go with me. Sure, it wasn't as safe, being by yourself, but kids don't always stop and think about what's safe. Anyway, if anyone was with her when she drowned, they never came forward and admitted to it. Her family sold their farm and moved away to Connecticut after that."

"Great fucking after-dinner conversation," I say.

"You're welcome," Jimmy replies, and then the kettle starts to whistle and he gets up and goes to the stove. I change my mind about the cigarette.

4.

The next day, crossing the olive-green Providence River and the silver-grey, iron-girder span of the Point Street Bridge, I see that someone has graffitied the eastern retaining wall. There are blocky white letters painted a full five feet high – WHERE WILL WE GO WHEN THE WATER RISES? I think of my dreams, and I think of the Hurricane of 1938, the terrible Yankee Clipper that swamped downtown beneath fifteen feet of flood water, and I think about the drowned McCutcheon girl. On the far side of the bridge, I pull over at the Shell station and convenience store, and I make into the restroom and lock the door behind me before I'm sick.

5.

At first, I am not certain that I am dreaming. It's like that sometimes, so solid can be the dream, and at times my waking reality can be hardly more substantial than cheesecloth. But I am in a high room, and there's a radio playing rock music, and I'm at the window, gazing out at the city, south towards the Point Street Bridge and the hurricane barrier and, beyond that, the bay, and beyond *that,* the sea, running all the way to Spain and Africa. Also, I am not alone, and that's a first. Someone stands behind me, but I don't dare turn to see their face. Not yet. Perhaps later on. *I must be dreaming,* I think, because that shadow has risen from the direction of the sea and hangs twilight over the day. So, however this dream is different from all those that have come before – all those I can recollect – it is in its most fundamental aspect still the same. The window is open, as it usually is, but the fresh air getting in does little to mask the fetid smell that seems to be coming from behind me. From the place where my unseen companion stands. It's the smell of rot and deep, wet places, of algae and weeds that grow only in stagnant ponds, of frogs and mud and water snakes. Of time and the passing of time. I ask for their name, still not turning to see them for myself. I think of Perseus' mirrored shield given to him by Athena. I think of Eurydice foolishly looking back. And Lot's wife. I think of her, too. But here I am confusing my apocalypses. As I have said, I ask for their name. And a woman replies. Her voice is muddy and strangled, and it hurts me somehow, hearing it.

"Ellie McCutcheon," she says. "You can call me Ellie McCutcheon."

And I should have known that, oughtn't I have?

"What do you know of waves?" I ask her.

"Is that what you believe is coming?"

"Isn't it?"

She doesn't reply, and so I force myself to cross the room to the windowsill and look out. I don't think I have ever before dreamt of standing in this particular building. It may be no real building. I mean, no building with a counterpart in the waking world. It must be somewhere near the Federal Court House and the Industrial National Banking Building – the "Superman Building," circa 1928. Walls of weathered marble and of concrete and of brick, and before the shadow, they may as well be tissue paper. I know the wave is hundreds of feet high at its crest, even though I have never actually laid eyes on the wave *itself,* not once in all these dreams, but only on the shadow of the wave. The *herald* of the wave. Somewhere, in one of Jimmy's books, I have read that the megatsunami created by the asteroid impact that took out the dinosaurs sixty-six million years ago would have towered three hundred and thirty feet high by the time it reached the shore. Maybe that's exactly what is approaching now, a wave to wash us all away that a new world can rise from the muck and the mire.

"I don't think so," says Ellie McCutcheon.

"You're dead," I tell her.

"It's a dream," she replies. "Have you never dreamed a dead woman alive?"

I can't say if I have. Possibly. Probably, but, regardless, I don't feel like answering the question, and so I don't. Instead, I ask her why she's here.

"It's your dream," she says. "You tell me, Em."

I don't ask how she knows my name.

Down on the street, people are making the sounds that panicking crowds make. What's coming, they've seen it, too. I wonder that not a single one of them tries to run, but then where would they ever run to that could hope to provide them sanctuary? Running would be futile, only delaying the inevitable. Better to stand and face the hammer fall.

The walls of this room are hidden behind peeling olive-green wallpaper and behind dozens and dozens of articles clipped from magazines and newspaper articles held in place with thumbtacks and pushpins. The clippings are yellow and brittle, and every one of them concerns the Great Hurricane of 1938. Flooded streets, men paddling flooded streets in boats, millions of trees uprooted like matchsticks by the storm surge, the land scoured raw.

Behind me, Ellie McCutcheon coughs – an ugly, phlegmy sound – and I wonder briefly if there's a word for being haunted by a ghost meant for someone else.

"Jimmy told me about you," I say.

"Do you love him?" she asks me.

"He told me how you drowned in that quarry up near Lincoln."

"He said that I drowned?" she asks.

"Didn't you?"

I want to turn and look at her, in equal measure to how much the thought of seeing her horrifies me – the spectre of a girl drowned thirty-seven or thirty-six years ago, when I was a child and Jimmy was a child and the drowned girl was only a child. There's a tall floor mirror to my left, framed in gold, and all I would have to do is turn my head a little ways to see her. I bite my lip and taste blood, and I marvel at how much it tastes like the sea.

On the radio a man intones, *There's always a siren, singing you to ship wreck.*

"When I was a kid," says Ellie McCutcheon, "I dreamed of a city in the sea."

Steer away from those rocks, we'd be a walking disaster.

"You know the city I mean," she says.

"If you weren't drowned," I say, "then what happened to you?"

"Oh, I drowned," she says. "But it was more complicated than that."

"You were alone and went in swimming," I say.

"Is that what he told you?"

I keep my eyes on the city outside the window, on the deepening twilight below the advancing wave, on the doomed populace of a doomed city.

Don't reach out, don't reach out…

"I wanted to see what you see when you dream of the city," the dead girl says.

"I try not to go there," I tell her. "Isn't this bad enough?"

I hear an awful wriggling sound, like eels out of water and flopping on the carpeted floor of the room. I hear a squelching sound, like feet struggling through deep mud.

Ellie McCutcheon recites Edgar Allen Poe: *No rays from the holy heaven come down/ On the long night-time of that town;/ But light from out the lurid sea…*

And then she says, "People have been dreaming about the city for a long, long time. People have been dreaming about the city since before we came down from the trees. It's as old as all that. It may even be as old as the sea."

"Then who built it?" I ask her.

She doesn't answer. She asks me, "What does it mean to you, the wave?"

"I think it's a prophecy," I reply, surprising myself with the truth.

"Then you are a prophet?" she wants to know, and I think that if I had the nerve to look at her, she would be smiling, a wicked, taunting smile.

I can hear the wave coming now, bearing down, probably already sweeping aside Newport and Jamestown as it races up the bay towards Providence. It sounds like all the freight trains that ever were. *Where will you go when the water rises?*

"Where were we to begin with, back at the start?" asks the dead girl. "There's your answer. You won't talk about the city in the sea."

I tell her no, that I won't, and then she goes away and leaves me to wait alone.

6.

The flooded quarry is hardly more than a ten-minute drive from Providence, north and west along Route 146, past Pawtucket and Central Falls and Lincoln. I take a shortcut from the highway to Wilbur Road, cutting across the gravel parking lot of the landscaping supply company that now owns the property, the grandsons of the men who operated the quarry before the pumps were finally shut off and the three deep pits were surrendered to eager groundwater. Jimmy called it a limestone quarry, and it's marked on maps as a limestone quarry, but the brilliant white crystalline stone is actually marble, Precambrian marble laid down in ancient seas, half a billion years ago or more. I park at the side of the road and walk a short distance to a bridge, where Wilbur Road crosses over an edge of the northernmost of the three pits. It's very late afternoon, almost twilight, and the air is cooling off after the heat of the day. Here, the quarry is ringed about with big trees and underbrush, with maples and oak and hickory, wild grapes and greenbriers. There are catbirds arguing somewhere close by, and there are whippoorwills, and also the constant hum of the traffic out on 146. A couple of high marble outcrops jut above the waterline and the woods to remind the world how this dark pool came to be, how and why men peeled away the skin of this place and left this scar behind to mark their industry. To my right, maybe fifty yards back from the road, the crumbling chimney of a brick-and-mortar lime kiln rises from the trees, another reminder. Only a moment ago, the air was still, but now a chilly breeze rustles the leaves and branches and spoils the still surface of the pool with tiny wavelets.

Resignedly beneath the sky/ The melancholy waters lie.

I stand on the bridge, both hands braced against the concrete guardrail, and stare down into the green-black water. I'd meant to come much earlier in the day, but work ran later than I'd expected. Standing here now, with night so near, I wish that I had waited until tomorrow. It would have been wiser, I think to myself. Women who are afraid of ghosts should only visit haunted places while the sun is shining high and bright in a clear blue sky. Women who are superstitious and who lie awake at night because they fear the revelations of their own dreams.

But here I am, I think. *All the same, here I am.*

From where I stand, it's maybe twenty feet down to the water. Maybe less.

Two nights ago, I dreamed of swimming here, even though I'd never visited the spot before today. Jimmy's story had been more than sufficient grist for my unconscious mind. The quarry and its surroundings aren't quite the same as I'd dreamt them, but near enough to compound the general eeriness of the fading day.

I asked Jimmy to come with me, but he'd begged off and said, "I don't know what you think you'll find up there. It's only a hole in the ground." He'd sounded vaguely irritated, and so I hadn't pressed the matter. I could go alone. I also didn't tell him that I'd searched the online archives of the *Providence Journal* for anything about the drowning of Ellie McCutcheon.

Jimmy frowned and said, "You're better off keeping appointments with your psychiatrist than wandering off legend tripping. I wish I'd never told you about any of that."

I don't argue, because I don't necessarily disagree.

But standing on the bridge, looking down at the pool, I do wish he were here.

In my dream, the quarry water had been so clear that you could see straight to the bottom, a hundred feet or more down, and the pool had been filled with the iridescent, shimmering bodies of fish – schools of bluegill and sunfish, perch and crappie, here and there a solitary carp, along with other species I didn't recognize. I'd sat on the shore and watched them darting about, and I'd seen crayfish and a couple of turtles, as well. Then I'd stripped off my T-shirt and jeans and underwear, taking care to neatly fold everything and place my clothes well back from the shore, beneath a large blueberry bush. When I dove in, I found that the water was as warm and welcoming as if I'd drawn it for a bath. I swam out to the center, and then I swam down and down and down until I reached the very bottom. I found the submerged hulks of a steam shovel and a dump truck, scabbed red with rust and partly overgrown with algae and aquatic weeds that swayed and billowed. There were huge mud-colored catfish, hiding in the ruined machinery, and they watched me with bulging eyes, their barbeled mouths opening and closing as if speaking in some secret, silent tongue.

I believe that the drowned girl saw me before I saw her. Like me, she was naked. The fish had taken her eyes and lips and worried at her flesh with their hungry lips. Her teeth shone like pearls. Even so changed, I recognized the face of the McCutcheon girl, thanks to a newspaper photograph. She held out a hand to me, and the catfish watched us, somehow seeming simultaneously expectant and indifferent.

It's not so bad down here, she said. *You'll see. It will be better with your company. And you won't have to worry about the floods anymore. Will you, won't you come and join the dance?*

I have rarely desired anything so much as I desired in that moment to reach out and take her hand. But then the dream had come apart and I'd awakened, gasping and cold from my own sweat, and lay staring up at the bedroom window and the night outside, listening to Jimmy sleeping beside me.

On Wilbur Road, I take a step back from the guardrail. The catbirds have fallen silent, but there are more whippoorwills now.

Low above the trees, there's a white sliver of moon, like a fingernail clipping. Way out in the middle of the pool, the dark water ripples suddenly, and I hear a faint splash, though I don't see anything that might have made the sound. I imagine that I hear laughter, too. I close my eyes and count to ten, and then I turn and walk quickly to my car and hurry back to the city.

7.

"But Ellie McCutcheon," says the psychiatrist, "she wasn't a part of this, not originally." And I reply that I don't see how that matters. She's a part of it now. I'm standing at the window of the psychiatrist's office, in an ugly, nondescript brick building just east of the Brown University campus, and I'm gazing out towards the bay, and the shadow is coming. I feel it in every cell, an unbearable premonition, a certainty born of having dreamt the same dream too many times now. Except this time I can't be certain that I am dreaming, and I think that maybe this is the day that all the other days and all the dreams and my visit to the Conklin Limestone Quarry have led me to at last. "It may be that you've latched onto that incident, the drowning, as a focal point for your anxiety," the psychiatrist says. "It's something concrete, something that happened outside your mind, to which your fears can attach themselves. Do you see what I mean?" I don't, but I say that I do. It's easier than arguing. Everything is easier than arguing. "Last time," she says, "last time we talked about where you think the fears of the flood began. Can we go back to that?" I tell her that we can, if that's what she thinks we ought to do. "It may be instructive," she says. So, I watch the world outside the window, and I talk about Sunday sermons at church in Foster, and I talk about Noah's Flood, and I talk about being a terrified seven-year-old girl.

The psychiatrist listens. I figured out early on that what I am paying her for isn't to offer me some solution, but only to sit patiently, listening to whatever it is I have to say. If I were someone else, I might have gone instead to a priest. At least then I wouldn't be paying for the privilege of confession. My prescription would be hail Marys and Our Fathers and a string of rosary beads, instead of Valium and sleeping pills I don't take because I don't want to sleep. Away to the south, above and beyond the trees, there is a darkness brewing, like an oily smudge against the sky. "Forty days and forty nights, right?" I ask, but she doesn't reply. That's fine; I hadn't really expected her to answer. "It was supposed to be a lesson in mercy," I say, "that God spared the righteous, and that he sent a rainbow as a promise that he would never again flood the world. I was supposed to take it that way, but all I saw was the earth opening up and belching forth as much water as would be needed to consume an entire planet. 'The fountains of the Great Deep burst apart and the floodgates of heaven broke open.' Genesis 6:9 through 9:17. And every drop of rain was commanded to pass first through the fires of Gehenna before it fell, to burn the skin of sinners, because, you know, drowning wasn't horrible enough." The psychiatrist wants to know if I still attend church, and I tell her no, not since I was a teenager, not since I realized I could stop going. She asks if I'm an atheist, and I hesitate a moment before I tell her whether or not I believe in God isn't something I'm in the mood to discuss. I must have sounded annoyed, because she apologizes for having interrupted, and then she tells me to please go on. "Until every mountaintop was covered to a depth of fifteen cubits. Until nothing but what had been given sanctuary in the ark remained alive and breathing." She asks me if I ever told my parents – or anyone else – that the Bible story frightened me, and I answer no. "I imagined there must be something wrong with me if I was afraid of what

I was hearing. If I were good and righteous, I'd have nothing to fear. Surely that's the way it worked, I thought." The oily smudge on the horizon looks more like a cloud now, a straight black cloud stretching east to west, west to east, rolling towards the city, rolling towards the continent. "My father had a book," I say, "a book on the Victorian geologists, and there was a chapter in it –" I pause here, and I very nearly ask her to come to the window and tell me what she sees. But I don't. I might not be dreaming, and she might look and see nothing whatsoever. So, I continue. I go on. "There were paintings, how different artists had interpreted the deluge. They were all monstrous, cruel things. Naked people clinging to rocks and to one another as the waters rose. People being swept away. Cataracts that reached up into the sky, before descending again to batter the earth and bury everything that had offended its creator. There was this one that I hated in particular, *Shade and Darkness – the Evening of the Deluge.*" The psychiatrist says that she's surprised how I recall the title, and I tell her I found the painting a few years ago in a library book, or else I wouldn't. I tell her that I actually have a copy of the book now, *Victorians and the Prehistoric,* that I ordered a used hardback off Amazon. "That probably seems awfully masochistic of me, doesn't it?" And she says, "Not necessarily. It can be healthy to confront your fears. That's why you're here, after all." I want to correct her: No. I'm here so that Jimmy will stop nagging me for a little while. That's why I'm here. Outside the window, the shadow advances, unstoppable, almighty, sweeping across the bay, twilight at noon, and behind it is the wave, the fountains of the Great Deep, roaring and all in flame. Only it isn't roaring. It isn't making any sound at all. The birds have gone quiet. There's not even any traffic noises. *You really have no notion how delightful it will be, when they take us up and throw us with the lobsters out to sea.* I turn and look back over my shoulder, and the psychiatrist has gone, and the room is empty. There isn't even any furniture, just four bare walls and ugly beige carpet on the floor. There's no door. I turn back to the window and look down at the street, at the sidewalk, and the drowned McCutcheon girl is standing there, gazing up at me with her eyeless face. So at least I'm not alone. I open the window (it isn't locked), and the air smells like the sea.

DAY AFTER TOMORROW, THE FLOOD

J.R.R. Tolkien wrote:

"This legend or myth or dim memory of some ancient history has always troubled me. In sleep I had the dreadful dream of the ineluctable Wave, either coming out of the quiet sea, or coming in towering over the green inlands. It still occurs occasionally, though now exorcized by writing about it. It always ends by surrender, and I awake gasping out of deep water. I used to draw it or write bad poems about it."

(JRRT, Letter 257)

It was this dream that served as the inspiration for the Downfall of Númenor by Eru Ilúvatar in S.A. 3319 (yeah, I'm a big Tolkien nerd). Over the years, I've had my own recurring version of what Tolkien called his "Atlantis-haunting" dream, and given it began in childhood, well before I first read Tolkien, must have its genesis somewhere other than his writing. So that's one source of inspiration for "Day After Tomorrow, the Flood," but see also Arcade Fire's "Black Wave/ Bad Vibrations" (*Neon Bible,* 2007). Oh, and the Conklin Limestone Quarry, that's an actual place, and on a shelf in my office I keep a chunk of marble I picked up there while I was writing this story. Finally, yet another source of inspiration for this story, the WHERE WILL WE GO WHEN THE WATER RISES? graffiti actually did appear on that retaining wall, just as described. "Day After Tomorrow, the Flood" was written between April 11th and April 28th, 2018; it's the last short story I finished in the house at 45 Oak Street in Providence.

The Last Thing You Should Do

The sun hangs in the sky like a molten coin, and you hold up your left hand and encircle it with thumb and index finger. *Such a small thing,* I think. And I think, *My, what big hands you have, to hold a star at bay.* You're telling me about a dream you had the night before, a dream in which the sun rose at midnight and burned the night away. You know how I don't like hearing your nightmares, but that has never yet dissuaded you from sharing them with me. You do it to watch the anxiety in my eyes. You do it to watch my discomfort. You do it because you learned a long time ago it's not possible to keep all that darkness caged up inside yourself. I think you would burn like a *black* star, if you were to try. I think nothing would be left but cinders. The afternoon sun shines through the window, through the keyhole of your encircling fingers, and you talk about sunshine at midnight, and about great clouds of crows, and you tell me how in the dream you knew that there was a bear that would come soon and devour the sun. The whole point of it having risen at midnight, you tell me, was to try and fool the bear, but the bear was too smart to be fooled, so it was coming, anyway.

“Something terrible had happened to the bear,” you say, and when I ask what, you say, “Her cubs had been shot by a hunter, and all she wanted to do was go to sleep and never wake up again. She wanted to hibernate forever, so she’d never have to think about her murdered cubs. If she killed the sun, it would always be winter, and she’d never have to be awake again.”

You break the circle, and the sun escapes.

“I was standing alone,” you tell me, “at the top of a mountain, looking out across a wide valley, and as the bear came, its shadow stretched across the land, and I knew that what I was seeing, it was the last sunset, even if it was happening at midnight.”

Down on the street, there are people talking, and out on the freeway, cars and trucks roar and rattle past, and all of it seems a thousand miles away. The room smells like sweat and dust, cigarette smoke and your rosewater perfume. You sit in your chair and watch the window, and I sit on the floor at watch you.

“When I was a little girl,” I say, “there was an eclipse, and my mother told me that people had once believed that an eclipse meant that a dragon was eating the sun. But she told me not to be afraid, because the dragon would spit it out again as soon as the sun burned its throat and stomach.”

You frown very slightly and take your eyes off the window long enough to aim the frown my way.

“I’ve never met your mother,” you say, lighting another cigarette. “For all I know, you made her up. For all I know, you never even had a mother. Maybe I invented you, to have someone to listen to my bad dreams, and when I’m done needing you…” You turn away and blow smoke at the window instead of finishing the sentence.

“You wouldn’t do that, would you?”

“I might,” you reply, “if you interrupt me again.”

"I'd miss you, if you did that. And you'd miss me the way that bear missed her cubs, if you made me go away."

"Don't you bet your life on it. I just might not."

In the afternoon sun, you hair looks like butterscotch and honey.

"She'd read it in a book somewhere," I tell you, "that thing about the eclipse and the dragon."

"Like I said, I never met the woman. I think you're making her up." You flick ash on the bare floorboards and shut your eyes. "I could make you go away, even easier than a giant bear could swallow the sun. You want to see?"

"You'd miss me."

"I might, but I also might not."

Neither of us says anything for a minute or two, and then I tell you I'm sorry, that I won't interrupt you again, that I want to hear the rest of the dream, even if I don't, even if that's one of the very last things I want.

"Did I mention the crows?" you ask me.

"You did."

"They were all leaving the world, before the beginning of the winter that would last forever. They knew a secret hiding place that would be safe from the snow and ice, and that's where they all were going, as fast as their wings would carry them. But none of the other animals knew the way. Only the crows. There were clouds of them, like a thunderstorm of crows. And the footsteps of the bear were the thunderclaps. I stood there on the mountain, wondering if I would see anything more of the bear than her shadow before she swallowed the sun and there was only darkness and cold forever and no one would ever see anything again."

"There would still be the moon," I say, breaking my promise.

You scowl and blow smoke rings at the window. A halfhearted wind rustles the drapes and only makes the room seem hotter. You say, "The moon has no light of its own," you say. "The only light that the moon has is reflected sunlight. So, if the sun were gone, if the bear *ate* the sun, then the moon wouldn't be dark, just like everything else. Did you even go to school?"

I want to reply, well, but there would still be starlight, but I keep my mouth shut.

"I don't think you did," you say, "but then, if I only just made you up a few hours ago, when would you have had the chance? It's all my fault. I should have imagined someone less ignorant. Next time, that's what I'll do."

"If you only just made me up, why do I remember being a child?"

"Because it seemed unreasonably cruel, inventing someone who'd never been a little girl and never had a mother and never heard stories about dragons eating the sun. I'm not a monster, you know. I've never seen any sense in being cruel simply for the sake of being cruel."

I don't disagree. I know better than to think there's anything to be gained by disagreeing with you. I sit on the floor near your chair and watch the sun and the wind rustling the drapes. We got them at Woolworth's for five dollars, the day after we moved in to this place. Or that's what I remember, which may or may not be the same thing.

You stub out the cigarette, not even half smoked.

"In my dream," you say, "the bear had a name, but I don't recall what it was. Maybe I never knew. If I did know, I've forgotten."

"Was I there with you?" I ask, and you stop staring at the window and stare thoughtfully at your bare feet, instead. Your toenails are painted pale violet.

"Why would you have been?" you ask me right back. "I only just had the dream last night, and I only just invented you this morning. I'm not precognizant."

I'm getting tired of this game, but I don't tell you that. Instead, I ask, "Was anyone else there with you on the mountain?"

I've learned it's better just to be patient. You bore easily. In fifteen minutes or half an hour, you won't even remember taunting me about whether or not I'm anything but a figment of your imagination, like sun-eating bears and the secret hiding place of the crows. You are nothing if not quick to lose interest.

"There were other people," you tell me, and there's something about the way that you say those words, it seems an almost reluctant admission, as though there is some shame in telling me that you were not watching the end of the world alone.

"Were they people you knew?" I ask.

"No. I don't think any of them were real people, though I did know them in the dream. But that isn't the same thing, is it?"

"No, I don't suppose that it is."

"I couldn't ever get a good look at their faces, even when I'd try. Even when I'd turn and look directly at them, it's like their faces were concealed behind veils or obscured by shadow, like the shadow spreading across the valley floor. I remember that there was an old woman, a very old woman. She had a rosary and she was praying. I kept telling her to shut up, that I didn't want to hear it, that if her god meant to save her, he'd already have done so by now. But she wouldn't listen. She just kept praying and fingering her beads. There was a child, too, and sometimes when I'd look it was a boy child, and other times when I'd look it was a girl."

"Maybe that was me," I say. "Maybe that was you just beginning to imagine me."

"I don't think so," you say. "I think it was just some kid who was never going to grow up because a giant bear was about to devour the sun. He, or she, was afraid and kept whispering to itself and every now and then it would cry. I wanted to tell it to shut up, but I didn't. I'm not cruel. I wouldn't have done that. I thought how the praying woman ought to comfort the child, how it would have least have been a more useful way to pass her final moments than praying for salvation from never-ending winter. But every time the mountain shook with the bear's footfalls, every thunderous step it took, she just prayed that much louder."

A drop of sweat runs down my cheek and falls to the floorboards.

"I think I'll get a Coke," I say. "Would you like a bottle of Coke? There's a lemon. I could slice it, and we could have Coke with lemon."

"I don't want anything to drink," you say, "and neither do you. I'm not done. If you were really paying attention, you'd know that. If you were really paying attention, I wouldn't have to tell you, now would I?"

My mouth is as dry as sand.

"No," I say. "I don't suppose you would."

You sigh and go back to watching the window.

"You know how I hate the cold," you say. "So, you surely must know how awful this dream was for me. It's hard for me to imagine what would have been worse than the thought the world would end in winter, a winter that would just go on and on and on in perpetual night, because some bear had decided to eat the sun, because some hunter had gone and shot her cubs."

"I know," I say, and I touch the splash of my sweat on the floor. I raise my finger to my tongue and taste the salt of me. It tastes as real as anything.

"In the dream, I thought how, before I finally froze to death, I would find the hunter. I promised myself that before I died, I would find him and see that he died first, if he wasn't dead already. I stood there, watching the shadow of the bear and waiting for the sun to vanish down the bear's throat and thinking of all the different ways I could kill the hunter very, very slowly. Who kills bear cubs, anyway? That's just hateful, isn't it?"

"It is," I agree. "This one time, I ran over a rabbit by accident. It dashed out into the road, in front of the car, and I didn't have time to swerve to miss it. So, I hit it."

"You never did any such thing," you remind me.

"Well, anyway, that's what I remember happening."

"That doesn't make it so."

"No, I know. What happened next?"

You lick your dry lips and sigh again. Then you say, "What happened next was the floor of the valley split open, because of the earthquakes the giant bear was causing. There were these great fucking fissures, and I could see they were so deep that they might reach all the way down to the center of the earth. They glowed orange and red, from the lava or magma or whatever was at the bottom of them. And it occurred to me that there must be hiding places underground, caverns that would stay warm for a long time after the sun was swallowed by the bear. Scientists say it will take billions of years for the molten core of the earth to get cold and hard, so I'd be safe. And there would be food, I thought. There would be mushrooms and blind fish and whatever else lives in caves. I just had to get down off the mountain to the edge of one of those cracks. I just had to hope that they didn't close up again before I could."

"It's an awful thought," I say.

"What is? What's an awful thought?" You don't look at me. You're still staring at your toes.

"Living in caves the rest of your life. Living alone in caves the rest of your life."

"I'm not afraid of the dark," you say. "And I'm not afraid of being alone. It's the cold that scares me. But you know that. I've told you that plenty enough times. I've told you how much I'm afraid of the cold."

"You have," I say. "But it still seems awful to me. I was in a cave once, Mammoth Cave up in Kentucky, and I didn't like it at all."

"Well, was it worse than freezing to death? Was it worse than being eaten by wolves because you were the last thing left alive for them to eat? Was it worse than dying of thirst because all the water in the world had turned to ice?"

It wasn't worse than any of those things, but I don't answer the question.

"Did you make it to the fissures?" I ask.

"I don't remember," you reply. "I woke up. I woke up, and it was still dark outside, and for a few minutes I was afraid it hadn't been a dream, not all of it, that a bear really had eaten the sun while I was asleep."

"But then the sun came up," I say.

"Yeah, but then the sun came up. Just like it always does. I wouldn't mind a Coke. Since you offered, I mean. A Coca-Cola with lemon. If it isn't too much trouble." You aren't staring at your feet any longer. Now you're watching the window again. There's a shadow in your eyes, I think. You look afraid, as if you're frightened *this* is the dream, and you'll wake up any moment now to find that you're alone deep underground, knowing that you'll never see the sun again, wishing you could at least dream of slicing open the belly of that monster bear to allow the sun to escape back into the sky.

You hold up your hand again and once more make a ring to hold the sky inside.

"Sure," I say. "I'll get it. I don't mind."

"I wouldn't do that, you know. I wouldn't make you go away."

"I know," I reply.

Then I get up and go to the kitchen, and you stay there in your chair and keep your eyes fixed on the window and the sun, so small it fits within the circle of your thumb and index finger.

THE LAST THING YOU SHOULD DO

I remember, about 1968, my mother telling me a story about how people had once believed that an eclipse meant a great beast had swallowed the sun. In her version it was a dragon that did the deed, not a giant bear, but same difference. "The Last Thing You Should Do" is one of those vignettes where I begin with a very simple premise and two characters and just let them talk. I get lost in these little conversations. This story was written in two days, May 11th and 12th, 2019, not long after I'd started working at the McWane Science Center.

The Tameness of Wolves

Here's the scene: In your bed by the window in your house at the edge of the fields that run on all the way to the pine forests and the swampland and the muddy river coiling like a water moccasin beyond it. In your bed, half wrapped in quilts made by your mother when you were still a child, because the night is cold, because the first chills of November have come, and there will be frost in the morning. In the morning, just after dawn, the ground will crunch softly underfoot. In your bed by the window, with its shabby draperies and cracked pane and the window screen with enough holes in the rusty steel wire to admit any half-interested swarm of mosquitoes. And you, portrait of insolence, portrait of my lover and my shadow's shadow as a young and ribsy beast, sitting not near me at the foot of the bed, but all the way at the other end, your back pressed against the headboard. Your hair is blacker than the Alabama prairie night, and your eyes seem blacker even than that. Your eyes might be holes mashed into creation by the thumbs of an angry god who was beginning to think better of having ever fashioned eyes from blindness. Your fingers so long and white, your skin like milk in the moonlight through the window, the moonlight I have until now neglected to mention. It fills the air with silver. It stains the fields with a light so pale it seems hardly any light at all, despite whatever dim revelations are granted by its grace. And you sit there with your back to the headboard and your legs pulled up almost flush against your small breasts, and you smoke cigarettes and talk about how before the Civil War your mother's-mother's family had owned most of a county in Tennessee.

"Which county?" I ask, keeping my eyes on the window.

"I can't remember," you say, and your voice makes me think of clouds that are not moving across the autumn sky. "Anyway, what difference does it make which county?"

"It doesn't make any difference at all," I say. "I was just curious."

You blow lungsful of smoke towards an unseen and even unimagined Heaven, adding to the tobacco fog already drifting above the bed and below the room's high ceiling and crown molding and flaking paint and water-stained plaster. The moonlight through the window makes restless silver threads of the smoke. I watch the smoke, and then I watch you, and then I go back to watching the fields. I wonder how many decades they have lain fallow, how long since anyone bothered to plow them. I wonder if you could tell me if I were to ask. I wonder, too, that the forest has not yet reclaimed them. Maybe that ground went bad a long time ago. Maybe nothing can grow there now but the thickets of briers and nettle and poison oak. Maybe there's a curse at work, and it's just that you've not ever gotten around to telling me about it.

"Have you ever done anything really bad?" you ask me, and I only almost look back over my shoulder. At the last moment, I stop myself. The view of the moon-washed field is safer by far.

"What do you mean by bad?"

"I mean bad," you reply. "I mean the sort of shit they told us we'd go to Hell for."

"You mean evil."

"Fine. I mean evil."

This is one of those games of yours that we've been playing as long as I've known you, since that first night you brought me home to your gone-shabby house and laid me down in this shabby bed and fucked me and breathed smoke at the ceiling. Your games have infinite permutations. Your games are never the same twice. And yet they never stray very far, circling always round the same obsessions: sins of the fathers, sins of the mothers, sins of the children and grandchildren and great grandchildren. All the careless and calculated hurt we do one to the other. You stand as proof there can be a crushing monotony, even in the presence of infinite variation, and that is one thing I have learned from loving you, just as I have learned that terror can be tedium.

"Have you ever done anything genuinely evil?" you want to know, and the way you put the question to me might just about fool me into thinking you've never asked me before tonight.

"Probably not," I reply.

"Not even the money you stole when you ran away from home, the money and your mother's jewelry? Not even that?"

I don't answer you. I'm not in the mood to answer you.

"Not even all those times you fucked your sister?"

"Can we just please not do this tonight?" I ask you, and out in the fields I think I might see something move. Something passing by the house on long legs. A deer, I tell myself, nothing but a deer. Around here, they're thick as pea soup and pig shit.

"Yeah, sure," you say. "We can not do anything you want. We can not do anything at all. We can just sit here and wait for the sun to come up again."

"We could sleep."

"No, we can't do that, either," and I don't argue, because I don't feel like arguing with you tonight, just as I don't feel like the confessional game.

The room smells like smoke and sex and raw meat and old pennies. Like dust and the wilting roses in the cut-glass vase on the unsteady little table beside the bed. Yellow roses. You brought them home with you three days ago, and you still have not told me where they came from. I have always thought roses smell like mold.

Whatever was moving around in the fields is gone now.

Or at least I can't see it anymore.

I glance at the dead girl on the floor, half hidden in shadows, half visible in moonlight. Her cut throat makes it seem as if she's smiling without using her mouth. I did that. I cut her throat, and I did it with such force, with such violence, that the knife severed her windpipe and went all the way to the bone. I look back at the window.

I pull the quilts a little more tightly about me. I can see my breath fog.

"I'll tell you a story," you say.

"Okay, tell me a story. I don't mind listening to a story."

"I didn't *ask* if you minded. I certainly didn't mean to imply you had some say in the matter."

But I do, dear heart. I could get up and get dressed and find the keys and drive away and never come back to you again.

"Sorry," I say, managing, mostly, not to sound sarcastic. "I misunderstood."

I could make an anonymous call to the police.

You light another cigarette off the smoldering butt of your last one, the cigarette it seems you lit only a moment ago, not long enough ago that it's already burned down to the filter. You light another cigarette, and I'm forcing myself to watch you again now, rather than the window, rather than the fields, rather than the broken shape on the floor. I want to get up and take that vase to the kitchen and put those wilted yellow roses in the garbage. Or open the back door and toss them out into the cold night. Your nostrils bleed smoke, and you push tangled black hair back from your face.

"But it has to be a true story," I say, almost whispering.

"Fuck that," you say. "Anyone can tell a true story."

"I don't care. It has to be a true story, whatever story you tell me now."

"Fine, fuck it, whatever. It has to be a true story. Fine."

I could tell them everything. I could lead them out across the fields...

Last week, I painted your fingernails and toenails the same color as the slash in the dead girl's throat. You've already chewed most the polish off both your thumbs and index fingers.

"I've never told you about the first one," you say.

"I've never cared to hear. I've never wanted to know."

"She looked a lot like you. She slept in my bed, too, until I got tired of feeling the heat of her body next to mine. I put a dog collar on her next, then, a heavy old leather collar from the barn that I'd found, and I chained her to the radiator. The collar had been one my grandfather used on his hounds. He bred bloodhounds and blue-tick hounds, and there's still a bunch of his shit out in the barn." You point at the radiator beneath the window. None of the radiators in the house work anymore. You've told me that they haven't worked since you were a kid, when the furnace stopped working and your drunkard father wouldn't pay to have it fixed. "In fact, she looked a *lot* like you. She had the same eyes. She had the same nervous look in her eyes."

And before I can think better of it, I say, "Maybe she was me. Maybe I'm only a ghost come back to haunt you. Maybe I'm that same girl, reincarnated."

You do that thing with your mouth. It's not a smile. It's not a grin or sneer or even a grimace, but it shows me your teeth, just the same. Sometimes, I think you made up the expression to suit your own special needs, having found no existing countenance that fit the bill. The mother of invention and all that. You are nothing if not resourceful.

You do that thing with your mouth, and you say, "Then one of these nights I'll have to do something about that, won't I? But as I was saying, *ghost,* I chained her to the radiator. The first few nights, she just thought it was part of the game, and she went along with it, pretty as you please. With all of it. You really *do* look an awful lot like her, *ghost.*"

I turn away. It's better to watch the window and the moon and the fallow, weedy fields. It's better to think about the muddy river and where it leads, winding two hundred miles through bayou and bald cypress, and how easy it would be to float slowly away from you and this rotten old house with its vase of wilted yellow roses.

"I might be any of them," I say. "I might be all of them, every single one."

"You might be," you reply. "But *that* story isn't *this* story. That's another story for another night, one when I don't feel like telling you *this* story." There's the slimmest rind of anger in your voice now, anger or only impatience (both equally dangerous) like a waxing or waning fingernail-clipping sliver of moon.

"How long until she finally figured it out?" I ask.

"She wasn't as smart as you. So, you can't be her, ghost. It took her three days. Three nights. You'd have caught on almost right away, wouldn't you?"

"Sure," I say and try not to shiver beneath the quilt. "I'm smart as a whip."

You laugh and smoke and I hear you do that thing with your mouth that isn't a smile. I think how the cold never seems to bother you. You sit there naked as the day you were born, as if it were a summer night, seeming not the least bit uncomfortable, so maybe you're the one of the two of us who's the ghost. Maybe all this time I've been sharing the company of a hungry phantom, a living ghost who drinks blood and eats tender, fresh kidneys and livers and still-beating hearts. One day soon, maybe you'll eat my heart, if you haven't done it already. I push these thoughts away. I can be plenty enough miserable without them, thank you very much.

"When the time came, what did you do to her?" I ask, not because I care, but just to have something to say.

"You're rushing me. You're jumping ahead."

"That's probably because I want to go to sleep," I tell you. "I might have mentioned that already. I'm cold, and I want to go to sleep."

"Fine, then. You just go right on ahead and waste the whole night sleeping, if that's what you want, if that's all you want. But not me, lover. And don't expect *me* to stand watch over your slumbering, supine fucking body, if you go to sleep before the sun comes up. I got better things to do, and you know that for a fact."

"I do," I say. "I know that for a fact. I'm just sleepy, that's all."

I hear you frown. I hear your disappointment with me.

"Fine, but you *want* to hear the story. It's right up your alley, I promise. Remember that girl from Shreveport, the blonde, how we did for her? Jesus, that one got you wet. You remember her? Well, I didn't want to tell you at the time, you were so pleased how it all went, *but*

and

also

You talk and I listen and I watch the fields.

The long-legged thing is back, and I'm no longer so sure that it's only a deer. It's moving away from the house, towards the line of trees, towards the swamp and the river. It occurs to me that its legs are so long it almost looks like something walking on stilts or like some gigantic insect. Maybe it lives in the swamp. Maybe it lives at the bottom of the river and only comes out on the first really cold night of every autumn, when there's bound to be a frost in the morning.

I listen to you, and the long-legged thing parts the silver moonlight like Moses parting the Red Sea. Before long, I can't see it anymore again, and sit here and shiver and wonder if I ever saw it at all.

I stop staring at the window and look at the dead girl again.

I tell myself again how I can leave, any time I please, how I could be two states over before you even figured out I was gone.

I've gotten very good at lying to myself. That's one of *my* games, the only one I never share with you.

but

but then

then I showed her what's what," you say. "Same as we did with the one from Shreveport. But I didn't want to spoil it for you. I didn't want you to know how it was something I'd already done before, how it was the same as my very first time."

"That was very kind of you," I say. I think my words are turning to shards of ice. The dead girl smiles at me with her cut throat. "That was very thoughtful."

"I wanted it to be special for you."

You stub out your cigarette in the ashtray by the vase of wilted yellow roses, and a last grey-white wisp of smoke coils lazily towards the ceiling. You ask me if I want to fuck now, and I consider how I could lie to myself about that, too, how I could say no, I *don't* want to fuck you, not tonight and not ever again. I could lie and say I just want to drive away and pretend that we never even met. I could wish you dead and buried with all the rest of them. This is what I'm thinking, right now, staring at the corpse on the bedroom floor, the girl with the smiling throat, trying to remember if either of us shut her eyes. If we did, they're open now, and the pale moonlight falls across her pale face same as it falls across the fields and the pines, the swampland and the river, our bed and you and me. Once upon a time, you told me that only the dead are really free, and I think okay, then the girl on the floor is free to see everything there is to see, because we couldn't be bothered to shut her eyes, and at last she sees and understands exactly what we really are, because – you told me – the dead can see through all masks, no matter how clever. And then you yank the quilt away, and you force me facedown onto the mattress, and I wait to feel your sharp teeth against the back of my neck.

THE TAMENESS OF WOLVES

This story was written on May 17th and 18th, 2019, almost immediately after finishing "The Last Thing You Should Do." I was reading William Faulkner's *Absolom! Absolom!* and that novel undoubtedly influenced the vignette, in both mood and setting. It's another little conversation. I'm actually very fond of this piece, and I can imagine expanding it into a longer work. It's one of those very rare stories that actually managed to unnerve me while I was writing it.

©Locke 2021

Iodine and Iron

1.

I am old now, or near enough, and thinking back upon very young things. I have all about me the false security of daylight, and from daylight I recall darkness. I recall the house where we lived as children, where we grew up and remained when our parents had finally gone, the great, rambling house in the woods, the house between the mountains. The house that lay always in shadow, where the summer never seemed to reach, but which seemed always caught up in bitter, wet Southern winters, no matter the season. I recall you, your painted face, your eyes like well water, just that cold and just that clear and just that deep. I recall the games that began only as games. Pretend that was only pretend, harmless and consoling, a balm for isolation, a medicine for our boredom and loneliness. You would deny that we ever were lonely, so long as we had one another's company, but I know better. I knew better then, and I know better now. Loneliness was as palpable to us as the stink of mildew and ash and dust pervading that house. Even now, I do not know what kept us there, as though we were bound to the spot. Sometimes, you told me you were sure that we'd die if we ever tried to leave, but I knew better, and you knew it was only a story you were spinning because we both were too afraid to leave. And now I sit in the sun, and now I remember you, and I remember a night when thunder and lightning raged across the mountains and wind roared through the hollows and whistled around the eaves of the house. We are together, as we were hardly ever apart for very long, in the room where we sleep, where we have slept all our short lives, or good as all our lives. I sit on the bed with my back against the headboard, my legs pulled up tight against my chest, my arms around my knees, my eyes shut. You move, and the box spring squeaks like a paper bag of angry mice. The rain against the window sounds hot, scalding, like frying meat, despite the cold and the damp. "Tell me again," I say, and you ask me to please open my eyes, and so I do. I open my eyes, and in the warm, unsteady glow of a kerosene lantern you smile back at me and your eyes don't seem quite so much like someplace I might slip and fall and drown. For an instant, you are only my brother, or my sister, whichever we have chosen to pretend you are on this night, whichever suits this consoling game meant to keep the storm at bay. For an instant, I'm almost not afraid, and this is any other night. But then that instant passes, and I want to close my eyes again, but I don't. "It's only wind," you tell me. "It's only thunder," as though either of us believes it's only the storm that frightens me. You smile, and your teeth are white and your lips are rouged red as poisonous berries. "It'll pass," you say, and then you kiss me, and you taste of whiskey and smoke and salt. "Come on, pillbug," you whisper, "open up and let me in." You know that I will. You know that in all the world, in all my twenty-two years, you're the one thing I haven't yet learned to deny. I open up. I take you in my arms and bury my face in your pale hair. "If it frightens you bad as all that," you whisper, "then I'll send it away. I can do that, you know? I can call it up, and I can send it away just as easy." *That's what it wants you to believe,* I think to myself, the words clanging like pots and pans and midnight thunder behind my eyes. *That's exactly what it wants you to believe.* You tell me, "It isn't here to hurt us, not me and not you. It only wants to watch, and I don't see the harm in that. I don't see the harm in letting it watch." I lift my head then and glance past you and past the foot of the bed to a corner of the room where darkness is pooled so thick it's hard to believe the sun has ever touched that spot. If I were to push you aside and get up and take the kerosene lantern from its place on the dressing table, if I were to walk as near to that corner as I dare with the lamp held out before me, I know the darkness would still remain exactly as it is now. Like the storm battering the house, like night smothering the mountain, the darkness is inviolable and absolute. It lies coiled there in that corner of the room, sticky as molasses, heavy as water grinding against the slimy bottom of the sea, blacker than pitch. I feel sick, looking directly at it, I feel dizzy and alone, even with your distracting hand right there between my legs, your fingers curled around my cock. You want to know if I still trust you, and I manage to answer, "Of course. Of course, I do." I shut my eyes again, and the darkness behind my eyelids is a thousand times brighter than the darkened corner. "Then don't be afraid. It won't come any closer than that. It knows the rules, and it knows not to break them." *And, after all, it's only something dreamed up for our game of pretend,* I silently lie. *I'm only scaring myself, only allowing you to scare me, because we're good at what we do.* "Yes," you say. "Yes, exactly. Because we're so very good at what we do." And I realize that I must have said that last part aloud. You kiss my cheek and then my throat and then the soft, sweating spot between my collar bones. You fold open the blade of your pocket knife, and you make the tiniest hole in me. I hardly notice the pain. That's another thing we've gotten very good at, through practice, through trial and error, all the expert ways that skin can be broken with the barest minimum of pain. You put the knife in my hand, and then you press your red lips to the wound and suckle. And I open my eyes again and watch the jealous, hungry darkness in the corner watching us.

2.

Late on a winter afternoon, late in January, I am the wolf and you are the girl who has wandered off the path. The girl who knew better, but has strayed. You're wearing a dress that was our mother's, that she sewed from cloth the color of goldenrod and daisy fleabane, and you have a red Christmas tablecloth tied about your shoulders for a cloak. I'm wearing our father's heavy coat with its fur collar and cuffs. You run on ahead, and I follow after, keeping my distance for now. We pick our way between the familiar trees, through the woods below the house, between the house and the creek winding its way along the very bottom of the hollow. The air in my nostrils smells cold and clean, of the clean decay of the forest floor, of beetles and fat grubs, mushrooms and rotting trees and of the leaves that fell in October and November. Before the game began, you said that you had something to show me, and I wanted to know what, but you said no, that's a secret. "Since when do secrets have a place in *this* game?" I asked, and you smiled and replied, "Since almost always." *Fine,* I said, out loud or to myself. *Fine, if that's the way you want to do this.* The woods slope away, down and down, a maze of oaks and maples, hickory and poplar and strangling creeper vines. Every now and then, I catch a crimson flash of the tablecloth, like a warning. *Stay away. You know how this story ends for the wolf.* And, every now and then, I hear you laughing, your laughter floating back to me between the trunks of the trees, through the wan daylight and the cold. I stop long enough to gaze up at what few scraps of the sky show through between the branches. It's later than I thought, not so very long from dusk. You dithered and hemmed and hawed about which dress you would wear, and so we started much later than I would have liked. You don't fear the woods after sunset, but I do. I wonder sometimes if there's anything in the whole wide world you do fear, except to be alone. Standing at the weedy edge of our yard, by the rusted hulk of a pickup truck perched on crumbling concrete blocks, you asked me, "If you were me, which road would you take? The Road of Pins or the Road of Needles?" That couldn't have been more than half an hour ago, but I have already forgotten my answer. I'm not sure it matters, though. The game today is not the game as usual. You've changed something. You've inserted into the script a secret, some surprise that I am being led towards. We might pretend I am a ravenous wolf pursuing a foolish girl through the forest, but today that conceit has been subverted, and it's all I can do to keep my mind on the game. Distracted and not looking where I put my feet, I step into the hole left by a stump that has long since rotted away and I almost twist my ankle. I fall and curse myself for not paying attention, for being clumsy, for making such a sorry excuse for a wolf. I get up and resume the chase. And soon I've reached the bottom of the hollow and the shallow, murmuring creek between its low, muddy banks, and usually this is where the wolf catches up to you. But not today. You've crossed a fallen log and are standing on the opposite shore, looking back at me, smiling, and you wink, then run on ahead again. In the shadows beneath the trees, in the fading day, the Christmas tablecloth is red as spilled blood, red as the blood from a wolf-gnawed throat. And I almost shout for you to wait up, almost remind you of the rules, that the pursuit ends at the creek. But only almost. Always, I hate to seem a coward, just as, always, you are putting me in situations that threaten to expose my cowardice. I glance at the sky again, then back the way we've come, and then I cross the fallen log. It's slick with moss; I almost lose my footing and, for an instant, think I'll wind up in the creek. I imagine you coming back to find me wet and shivering and ashamed. *Poor drowned thing,* you would say. *Poor soggy beast.* You'd help me out, and wrap me up in the tablecloth and only mock me in the subtlest ways. *Poor, poor silly wolf.* But now I'm across the log and pushing my way through a dense tangle of honeysuckle and briars, blackberry and supplejack, and we're heading up the steeper, far side of the hollow. I'm sweating now beneath the heavy coat, sweating despite the cold. All around me, the woods are quiet and still, as quiet as if we are the only living things here, as if there's no wind to stir the trees and no birds. I've come to a narrow deer trail, and you've left the prints of your bare feet pressed clearly into the mud, so there's no chance whatsoever that I could be uncertain which way you've gone. Somewhere up ahead, you're laughing again, but I know you're not laughing at me. It's always a part of the game, the girl so careless and so filled with childish delight that she cannot *help* but laugh, no matter who or what starving, ribsy thing might overhear. But it *feels* like you're laughing at me, and my face is suddenly flushed and hot. There's a bright rind of anger, and I think how I should just turn back for home. It would serve you right, changing the rules the way you have. Sooner or later, you'd realize I wasn't following you anymore. And maybe you'd even lose your way, because by then it might be dark. Maybe I'd have to come back and find you, and you'd be so grateful you'd cling to me and cry and tell me how sorry you are to have tricked me and promise how you'd never, ever do that again. I'd be grateful and forgive you. For a moment or two, I allow myself to think I could actually be so cruel as to do such a thing, just as I allow myself to believe you'd ever possibly get lost in these woods that we've known since we were small. And then I get back into character, and I play my part, and I follow the tracks you've left in the mud.

3.

The game has been forgotten. You've led me to a small clearing, and night has caught up with us. But you'd expected it to; you planned this, after all, and so you've come prepared. You've brought along a beeswax candle and a box of kitchen matches, hidden in a pocket of our mother's dress. So there is your little yellow-white candlelight before me, and overhead there is the blazing pinprick fire of however many stars are glaring down at us, indifferently watching, halfheartedly pondering what we'll do next. The moon hasn't risen yet, so the stars have the winter sky all to themselves. You hold your candle out before you, I can see it a little better, the crooked, listing clapboard shack at the center of the clearing in the woods. The walls have been decorated with the sharp tines of deer antlers, bleached white by the Alabama weather and by time, dozens and dozens – maybe hundreds – of interlocking antlers held securely in place with nails and wire. There's no door on the shack, just a rectangular hole in the curtain of antlers. There are no windows, either. "I found it a few days ago," you say. "I came looking for sassafras and watercress, and I found it. Isn't it marvelous?" And I wonder aloud how it is we never saw this place before, how we've walked in these woods all our lives and never stumbled across the shack, not so very far from our doorstep. "I don't know," you say. "But people miss things. No one always sees everything." And I very nearly say, *Or maybe it wasn't here until you came along to find it. Or maybe it was always here, but you couldn't find it until it was ready to* be *found.* You hold your candle up a little higher, cupping the flame with your hand so the wind won't snuff it out. “I think it must have belonged to moonshiners,” you say. I ask why you think that, and you tell me how you found busted jugs and barrels and a lot of copper coils out behind the shack. In the cold, our breath fogs. Every word is steam. “We should go home now,” I say. “It’s freezing. We can come back later. You can show it to me then.” But you’ve already walked over to the doorway and are peering into the shack. “I haven’t been inside yet,” you tell me. “I wanted to wait, so that we could see it together, whatever there is to see.” All around us, the forest is murmuring anxiously to itself in the secret languages of plants and animals, rocks and detritus and soil. I reach out and take your hand, tangling your fingers up in mine, meaning to pull you away from the shack and the antlers and the doorway. “Anything at all might be hiding in there,” I say. “Could be a bear, even. Maybe a mountain lion, for all we know.” You scowl at me and shake your head, and you say, “There aren’t any mountain lions left around here, and there sure as hell aren’t any bears.” Well, then there might be something else, I tell you. “We can come back in the daylight. What’s the hurry? It’ll still be here, won’t it? It isn’t going anywhere.” My heart is racing now, and I realize I’m afraid, really afraid, and I feel the too-familiar shame at the weight of my fear. I take a step or two or three backwards, putting distance between me and the shack, backing away towards the periphery of the clearing, the sanctuary of the trees to shield me from the watchful Milky Way. You tell me that I’m being silly, and then, before I can say anything more, you step across the threshold and the darkness in the shack swallows you whole.

4.

It was never a straight line, but always only a maze, a labyrinth that we haunted and that haunted us back, in turn. A circular haunting, a spiritual Möbius strip – our games, your shifting faces, the sex, stories we told and untold, picked apart and refashioned to suit our needs, the loneliness, the old shack in the woods, what we found when I followed you inside, and on and on and on and on. I could write this tale for a thousand more days and nights and still I would draw no nearer to a genuine ending and I would find no tidy resolution. Conclusion is arbitrary.

I could choose any night.

This one will do as well as any other.

This night there is no wind and no thunder and no rain. There's only the cold of a December night on the mountain. There's only the darkness and the light of the kerosene lantern. There are the smells and tastes of you. We're sitting together on the floor, on a threadbare rag rug that one of our grandmothers made before we were born, and I've been listening to you talk for what seems now like hours and hours, hardly ever interrupting. I never have much to say, and even less to say that ever seems important. This was the dining room, when our parents were alive, but now the only furniture remaining are a couple of chairs. We eat our meals in the kitchen, mostly. You've written some of your stories on the walls of this room – words tattooed on plaster in charcoal and ink and pencil lead. In one corner, there are a couple of floor boards that have rotted straight through, and the damp and cold seep up through the hole and surround us. Usually, there's a piece of plywood laid over the rotten spot to keep the chill out, but tonight you've slid it aside. And the cold is not the only thing you've invited in. That palpable, living darkness is here, too, clinging to a spot halfway up one wall. I watch it and imagine that it's devouring the words you've written there. I imagine it means to wipe the walls clean, taking away all the stories for itself. You kiss me on the throat and then your teeth nip at my earlobe. I'm wearing the coat with the fur collar and fur cuffs, and you're wearing nothing at all. It often seems you need nothing to keep you warm but sheer force of will. I'm watching the pool of blackness splashed across the wall. "We don't even know what it is," I say. "We don't even know where it came from." You kiss my neck again, and then you say, "It came from the shack. You were there. You saw." And I tell you no, that isn't what I meant. "It couldn't have always been there," I say. "It must have been somewhere else first. It must have come from someplace else." You ask, "Why?" And I don't have an answer. "Maybe," you say, "the shack was built around it. Maybe it's something that was never anywhere else until we came along and it followed us home. Maybe all this time it was waiting there for just the right two people to show up and set it free." I want to know if you really believe that's what we've done, set it free. "I think so," you reply. "I think it was trapped there. That's what all those antlers were for, some kind of a spell to keep it from getting away." A lot of your stories have witches in them. "I think a witch found it there in the woods and wanted to keep it all to herself, so she built the shack and stuck up those antlers." I ask when you decided it wasn't moonshiners who built the shack, and you shrug and tell me how possibly the broken jugs and the copper coils were just there to fool people. "Well, what about there being no door?" I ask. "Looks to me like it could have left any time it wanted to, since there wasn't any door." And you say that only goes to show how little I understand about witches and spells. You kiss my cheek, and then you get to your feet and stand there, staring down at me. In the light from the kerosene lantern, your naked skin is pale as milk and most of your face is lost in shadow, so I can't be sure of your expression, but it *feels* like you're smiling. "Make it leave," I whisper, but you shake your head, turning away from me and towards the blackness hanging there on the wall. You sigh and say, "You're always so afraid, pillbug. You miss so much, because you're scared of just about every damn interesting thing in the world." I want to protest, but I don't. "Watch this," you say, and you hold out your left arm, and suddenly concentric ripples appear and move across the blackness, beginning at the center and spreading slowly towards its edges, like the ripples from a stone dropped into a puddle of engine oil. "What's it doing?" I ask, and you reply, "Wait. You'll see." I tell you that I don't want to see, that I'm cold and I only want to go to bed. "I've had enough of this for one night," I say. *I've had enough of this forever,* I mean. And then I see that there are slender tendrils rising from the black thing, snaking away from the wall towards your outstretched hand. In a moment more, the tendrils of darkness have twined themselves about your slender wrist, and I might scream at that sight, if I were only a little less afraid. "It won't hurt me," you say. "It's never hurt me before. This is how we talk. This is how it shows me stuff." Then you half turn back towards me and reach down to take my hand, but I back away. "No," I tell you, then look on in horror as the blackness spreads slowly, steadily from your wrist around your hand and then begins to flow up your arm. If I were not the coward I am, I might get to my feet and try to wrestle you away from it, try to force it to release you. But I am a coward, and I don't. The blackness spreads along your shoulders and breasts, down your belly and across your face, no more substantial than a shadow, as impenetrable as stone. I sit and watch. For all I know, it's devouring you alive, but I make no move to try and stop it. It wraps you up completely, and you go down on your knees.

I sit there and watch until, just before dawn, it finally releases you and vanishes back into the hole in the floor. When I touch you, your skin is warm as if this were a summer afternoon. You look up at me and smile a sleepy, tired sort of smile. "I didn't mean to make you worry," you murmur, and I shush you and kiss your forehead. We go to bed, and, as the day leaks in through the curtains, I dream of the shack in the woods and of witches nailing deer antlers to the walls of our bedroom. I dream of you, and in my dreams you have been made as black and empty as the void between the stars.

IODINE AND IRON

Someday, maybe, someone will have nothing better to do than to catalog all the many times I've come at "Little Red Riding Hood" and all the many ways I've done it. There are other things here, of course. My childhood in the mountains of Shelby County, Alabama and the unexpected things you find wandering in the woods and the things that find you. This story was written between October 8th and 13th, 2018.

Untitled 44

"I don't like that one," you say, pointing to one of the framed photographs hung on the gallery wall. The gallery walls are the color of old bone.

"I didn't think you liked any of them."

"I mean I most especially don't like that one."

Imagine something in this space that was useful – a grocer, a pharmacy, a hardware store – in some only briefly vanished past time when this part of the city was still a living, breathing part of the whole, before the hollow gloss of gentrification, before this shoddy present day. Go ahead and imagine something like that, where there is now only this gallery, and you and I, and now only these people who buy six-figure lofts that once were department stores or warehouses or automotive repair shops, and who have come together on this hot Southern evening to sip mediocre wine from plastic cups and nibble at pale, sweating cheese. These grey people who mingle around us and stare at the grey walls and twitter among themselves like hungry grey birds.

I was young in this city, and I am not young anymore. I lived in this place, and I suspect now I would hardly even count as a decent sort of ghost. But I am standing here with you and with all the twittering grey birds, pretending to be one of them, and I'm telling you how once upon a time this redbrick building by the train tracks was a bakery that sold fresh bread and pastries, back when I was a kid. You politely nod as if you've heard me, as if you're *listening*. But I know better. I know you well enough to know your mind is somewhere else altogether, and in a moment you look away from the black-and-white photographs hung on the walls and tell me where that is, what you're thinking about *instead* of the photos and instead of all my useless, dull reminiscences of past useful places.

"I never got around to telling you about the dream," you say, and the way you say it, the words come together to sound as if you're admitting to something a lot worse.

"I figured you would," I reply, "in your own time, if it really mattered. If it was anything I really need to know. I decided maybe you'd just thought better of telling me."

That isn't the truth, though. The truth is I'd forgotten your having even mentioned the matter of a bad dream.

"No, I forgot, is all. I meant to tell you, and then there was that phone call from my mom, and you were running late and in a hurry to get to work, and I just forgot."

I finish my share of the mediocre wine, then look around for someplace to get rid of the cup, but there isn't a trashcan in sight, so I hold onto it. Maybe we're not meant to throw them away. Maybe we're meant to keep them as souvenirs.

Your long dishwater blonde hair is pulled back from your face, pulled back into a ponytail that reaches halfway down your back, and you narrow your green eyes and look past me at the plate-glass windows and the sidewalk and parked cars and the street beyond. Your expression is inscrutable, as it almost always is, unless you're in one of those increasingly rare moods when you *mean* for me to read you like an open book.

"I'd moved away and was living somewhere in New England," you say. "It was near the sea, but not actually by the sea. The air always smelled like the ocean, but I don't remember ever seeing the sea in my dream. I'd moved away, and it had been years and years since we'd seen each other, and all I wanted to do was come home. It was cold all the time, even in summer, and I wanted to come back here. But whenever I'd call to tell you, all I'd get is your answering machine."

I look back at the photographs. There are twenty of them, arranged on three walls.

"I haven't had an answering machine since, I'm not even sure. It's probably been close to twenty years now."

"I know that," you say, still staring out at the street. "But it was a dream, and dreams don't have to make sense or be up-to-date on current affairs or whether or not you still have an answering machine."

The whitewashed brick building across the way is empty and dark. By the streetlight, I can see a "For Lease" sign, and I wonder if *that* building envies *this* one, this one having been dutifully repurposed and all, having been made busy, if not actually useful again. Or maybe, I think, the empty building is relieved at having been passed over. Either way, in another two or three weeks the place will probably be home to an artisanal brew pub or a vegetarian dive bar or something else momentarily hip and unthinkably out of place in my memories of the city.

"Why would you have moved to New England?" I ask you.

"I don't know," you reply. "I didn't dream why I'd done it. I just had."

"That's a long way to go, just to want to come home again."

"I know that," you say again, almost whispering this time.

"And you hate winter so much."

"I know that, too."

"Is that what made it a nightmare?" I ask, turning back towards the photograph, wishing I could get a beer or have a cigarette to get the taste of the wine out of my mouth, thankful I'd at least steered clear of the sweaty cheese.

"No, I think it was mostly the wanting so badly to come back home that made it a nightmare. That and trying to call you, but you never answering."

"I was always pretty bad about ignoring the answering machine," I admit. "People used to ask why I even bothered to own one of the things."

Now you're looking at the black-and-white photographs again, too. Each one is some perfectly ordinary, mundane scene – a living room, urinals in a public restroom, a park bench, a stairwell, and so on – and in each one there's a shadow. Only ever one single shadow, and only ever an ill-defined, imperfect shadow, at that. It's impossible, in every instance, to know if I'm seeing the shadow of a woman or a man or an animal or some inanimate object, and the shadows seem thin and incomplete, like twilight or shadows during a partial eclipse of the sun. The photographer is someone from out on the West Coast, from Los Angeles or San Diego, I can't remember which, and I assume that all of the pictures were taken in California.

"In the dream," you say, "the television was always on."

"You don't even own a television."

"In the dream I did."

You take a step nearer the photograph that you've said you especially don't like. I stare at it a moment, but it doesn't seem any better or worse to me than all the rest – a dining room, and a dining table with an unfinished jigsaw puzzle. There are no pictures hung on the walls, but they've been papered with striped wallpaper. There are no chairs at the table, and there's an open window. In this photograph, the imperfect shadow falls across the table and the jigsaw puzzle.

"If you don't like it," I say, "you shouldn't keep looking at it."

There's a small white card stuck onto the wall next to the photograph, and printed on the card in a sans-serif typeface is *Untitled 44* and a date and a price. I assume the date records the day the photograph was taken. And I think, well, people who've bought six-figure loft apartments in converted department stores and warehouses, they can probably afford to pay that kind of money for art. As for us, we're only here because you wound up on a mailing list somehow and were curious and bored.

"In the dream, there was a room sort of like that one," you say.

"All the more reason," I reply.

"All the more reason what?"

And I say, "Well, all the more reason not to stand here examining the damn thing." Then I look at my watch, and I frown and look back at the photo hung on the wall. The unfinished puzzle, I realize, is exactly the same image as the photograph – a dining room and an open window and a jigsaw puzzle only two-thirds put together. And *that* jigsaw puzzle, it's the same image, too. "Okay," I tell you, "now I see it."

"See what?" you ask, and I say, "The thing with the puzzle."

"*Mise en abyme,*" you say, and I have to ask what that means.

"It means 'into the abyss.' It's an artistic technique, when a copy of an image is placed inside itself, in order to suggest an infinite regression." And before I ask, you add, "I took two semesters of art history in college. Every now and then, I remember something like that. Anyway, that's an example of *mise en abyme.*"

"Clearly you remember more from art history than I remember from my freshman year of French."

"Just bits and pieces," you say, "every now and then."

"Is that what bothers you about it, the infinite regression part?"

"I don't know," you reply and rub your eyes. "Maybe, but I don't think so. I mean, I only just noticed the trick with the puzzle. I think maybe it's something else."

"The shadow?"

"No, the shadow's a sorta cheap shot, like..." and you trail off. I think possibly you're not going to bother finishing the thought, which is fine by me, but then you say "...like a not especially good ghost story. Because it's so vague, I mean. Because it could be almost anything, the shadow's supposed to make us uneasy. We see the shadow, and our imaginations are supposed to fill in the blanks, and the way the photos are presented, the way they're framed, and with the inclusion of the *mise en abyme* technique, the photographer is trying to lead us someplace dark within ourselves. But I think they're overplaying their hand."

"You see all that?" I ask, and I check my watch again, as if maybe more than a minute or two might have passed. You shrug your shoulders, the way you have a habit of doing when you're trying to decide if you're tired of talking about something.

"There was a room like that in my dream," you say.

"You already mentioned that," I say, and then I add, hopefully, "We can leave now, if you're ready. We could get a drink someplace, or maybe just go on home."

"Not yet," you say, and the way you say it, just a little too quickly, a little too forcefully, you come off defensive and annoyed. "Soon, okay, but not yet."

"Did something happen there?" I ask.

"Did something happen where?"

"In that room in your dream, the dining room that looked like *that* dining room, did something happen?" Almost immediately I wish I hadn't asked the question, because it sounds like something a psychiatrist would ask, and neither one of us cares very much for psychiatry.

"I don't think so," you say. "I don't think so, but maybe. I'm trying to remember, but you keep talking and interrupting my train of thought."

I apologize, but I'm beginning to lose whatever slim rind of patience I had with the gallery and these photographs and all the twittering grey people. And you, too, for that matter. But it's not worth the fight we'll have later on if I keep pushing about why the picture bothers you or, worse yet, if I tell you that I want to leave now because it all bothers me and wish we'd gone to a movie, instead. So, you stand there and stare at the photograph of the dining room and the jigsaw puzzle and the open window, and I watch the other people in the gallery. There's a man and woman standing not far away, examining a photograph of a street corner, cracked sidewalk concrete, a fire hydrant, a curb with a "no parking" painted in it. And the obligatory shadow, of course. This shadow, I think it almost looks like a dog, like the shadow a large dog would cast, a Great Dane, maybe, or a Rottweiler. The man and woman are standing much nearer their photograph than you're standing to yours. He's wearing a porkpie hat and shiny black suit that fits a little too tightly. I look at his feet, and see that he's wearing white Converse Chucks, which figures. There's nothing at all remarkable about the way the woman's dressed, and I wonder if they're even a couple. Maybe they only just met five minutes ago. Maybe, I think, *he's* the asshole who took all these silly photographs and *she's* the owner of the gallery.

And then you say, "In my dream, though, there was a telephone."

I mostly stop watching the couple (who haven't caught on that I've been watching them), and try to turn my attention back to you. You're rubbing at your forehead now, like you do whenever you're getting a bad headache.

"A real telephone," you say, "not a cell phone or a smart phone or Skype or anything, and I was sitting in that chair – that same chair there – talking to you. I don't know if I'd called you or if you'd called me, but I was sitting at the table, and we were talking on the phone."

"Do you remember about what?" I ask, and the man in the pork-pie hat glances at me and smiles. His teeth are crooked.

"I wanted to come home, but you told me it wasn't the best time, that I should try and stick it out a while longer."

"Didn't you tell me earlier that every time you called you'd get my answering machine, that I never actually answered the phone myself?"

And you say, "I might have. I might not have remembered how you answered that one time, just before I woke up, I think. I told you how I didn't like the house where I was living, that it was a very old house, built just after the Civil War, and how at night I'd lie awake and listen to the sounds it made. It was a huge old house, cut up into three apartments, but no one lived there but me, and at night it made awful noises."

I reluctantly smile back at the man in the porkpie hat.

"Did I ever say why I thought it wasn't a good time for you to come back to Birmingham?" I ask.

"You said how I'd spent so much money moving north, and how I never follow through on things, but I could tell there was something else."

"I was just a dream," I say.

"I know," you reply.

And that's just a photograph, and it's only a coincidence that the room in the photograph looks like the room in your dream. A creepy coincidence, I'll grant you, but still only that, just a coincidence. Don't make more of it than it is.

I want to say all that, but I don't. Instead, I say, "Look, I really need a cigarette. I'm gonna step outside. But I'll be back in five minutes, all right?"

"Sure," you say.

"You don't mind?"

"I don't mind."

And so I leave you standing there, still rubbing your forehead and still staring at *Untitled 44,* the shadow in a dining room and the unfinished puzzle on the table, the recursive image within an image within an image, and I exit the gallery that used to be a bakery when I was a kid. The door eases shut very slowly behind me, and I trade air conditioning for the muggy August night. But sometimes it's better to sweat. There are streetlight shadows staining the sidewalk and on the asphalt and the redbrick and limestone façade of the gallery, my own shadow and the shadows of parked cars and parking meters. Nothing whatsoever out of the ordinary, only shadows, but I don't look at any of them too closely. I light a cigarette and keep my eyes on the tall buildings and lights of downtown, just over the Twenty-First Street Bridge, on the other side of the railroad tracks. I think how maybe, if I'm lucky, you'll have had enough of the photographs before I'm finished, and I won't have to go back inside.

UNTITLED 44

This piece was written between July 2nd and 3rd, 2019, so count it as the third consecutive "two-day tale" presented here. The actual location of the story can be found at the corner of 1st Avenue South and 21st Street South, on the east side of the street. Upon returning to

Birmingham after an absence of fifteen years – five in Atlanta, then ten in Providence – I've been in a state of mourning for a city that pretty much ceased to exist while I was away, and, more than anything else, that's what I'm trying to write about here. It's the shock of realizing that my homesickness was not only for a *place,* but for a *time* and how you can maybe get back to the place, but the time, that's gone forever.

The Surgeon's Photo (Murder Ballad No. 12)

At twilight, the lake is so black it may as well be a vast spill of India ink as however many tens of thousands or hundreds of thousands of gallons of mere water it might actually be. Looking out across the lake, flat and calm, flat as glass, just as it is black as ink, I think how it looks like a hungry, caged thing. Caught here in the narrow hollow between one sandstone ridge and the next, hemmed in by the tall trees, the lake is fed every minute of every day and every night by all the little trickling streams flowing down from high places and by subterranean springs and by rain whenever there is rain. The lake is always feeding, always drinking, and it still manages to look so awfully hungry and thirsty. I suspect I'm mixing metaphors right and left. I also suspect it hardly matters. I climb into the flat-bottom aluminum boat, untie the frayed nylon rope from the railroad spike that's serving as a cleat, and then use one of the oars to push away from the short, crooked pier. Near as I can tell, I'm alone out here this July evening.

Near as I can tell.

It isn't a very big lake, and it's as far out of the way as I could manage, all things considered, and on such short notice and all. But still, I've tried to be careful, but *also* still maybe there *are* other people and I just can't see them or I just haven't seen them yet. There are plenty enough spots a boat could tuck into and go unnoticed, weedy coves hidden behind curtains of pine and hickory, and way out here, I imagine folks tend to ignore local nighttime boating laws about running lights and such. But if there *is* anyone else on the water with me, night anglers patiently stalking largemouth bass or flathead catfish, I don't see any sign of them. So many more accessible lakes, if all you're after is fishing, lakes you don't have to spend forty-five minutes bouncing and swerving along rutted red-clay back roads just to reach. Then again, my grandfather always said not to sink my line where everyone else is busy sinking theirs. He always said the out-of-the-way spots are sometimes the best, *because* they're hard to reach.

I look down at the bundle in the bottom of the boat, at the reason I'm here, and I tell myself how I'm overthinking this thing.

"Those are the people who get caught," you said, "those people who worry and worry and worry, nervous as a cat. Being like that can get you caught just the same and just as quick as being careless will."

"Just seems like there are an awful lot of stupid mistakes we could make."

"Sure," you said, "but we're not gonna make 'em, because we're *not* stupid, and we're *not* gonna be careless, and so no one's ever gonna know a thing."

You're the one who pulled the trigger, and I'm the one who drove to the lake to sink the corpse in this black lake. I asked you to come with me, but you said no. You told me how you'd already done enough – probably more than your fair share, you said – and you were tired and needed to get some sleep. You said disposing of the corpse wasn't anything so complicated it required two people to get the job done, and, besides, two are more likely to attract attention than one, you said. I didn't want to go alone, but I didn't argue. I've spent years not arguing with you. No reason to stop now.

I dip the oars in as quietly as I can, making as little noise as possible, and the boat glides out across the flat-calm India-ink water towards the center of the lake. You told me it gets deep out there at the middle. You told me the middle would be the best place to drop the body over the side. I'd almost asked how you knew that, but then I decided I didn't want to know, not really. I just figured you'd read it in a book or found it on the internet. I wouldn't be the least bit surprised to learn there are entire websites devoted to the best ways of sinking dead bodies in lakes and rivers and in the ocean so that they won't come floating right back to the surface again, and I decided I'd rather believe you'd learned everything you knew *that* way instead of some *other* way.

It's full dark now and this lake and the mountain seem like the very reason that God invented blackness. Also, it's the first night of a new moon and there's not even a slimmest rind in the sky, just a dim, inconstant scatter of stars above me, just light that's traveled billions of light years only to amount to nothing much at all. I want very badly to switch on the Maglite I've brought with me, just in case, but I'm pretty sure that would be one of the several dozen stupid things that I'm trying not to do.

"You gotta make goddamn sure it's not gonna come bobbing right back up in a few days," you said, your hands already red to the wrists, the knife blade already slick with gore. "All the bacteria that live in the gut and the chest cavity, those don't die just because the person dies, so that's why it's not enough just to slice open the belly and puncture the lungs. You need to get all those guts out of there or you might as well just go on ahead and tie a string of empty Clorox bottles to the thing and let it float around for all to see. All those bacteria, they make carbon dioxide, hydrogen sulfide, methane, and so forth, which make the body bouyant, same as helium makes a balloon bouyant, and that's why they've got to come out."

"You think it was worth it?" I asked, and you stopped working and looked up at me, furrowing your brow, your expression puzzled like you had no idea what I was talking about or like you did, but what I'd said was just about the dumbest thing imaginable.

"It better fucking be," you said, finally.

"I never did anything like this before," I told you.

"You got it in your head maybe I have?" And I start to say, *Well, it sure sorta seems that way, what with you knowing how to get rid of the body, what with you kneeling there in the garage cool as a cucumber in an icebox chopping away like this was nothing more out of the ordinary than dressing a deer carcass. What with the way your hands didn't even shake when he said no way you'd squeeze that trigger.* But I don't, for more reasons than I even bother to count. I don't, mostly, because I don't want to piss you off and end up stuck in this mess alone. I'm not sure how that could possibly happen, given you're the one did the actual killing, but I've never been the luckiest woman and I prefer not to take my chances.

"No," I said. "That wasn't what I meant. That wasn't what I meant at all, really."

You stared at me for a while, then went back to work on the corpse.

"I just pick things up is all," you said. "I read and I see movies and TV shows and all that, and I pick things up, just like anyone else does."

And think how maybe that's true, but I also think how I've spent too much of my own life watching TV and movies and reading books, but it never would have occurred to me to gut a body before sinking it in a lake.

"What about the gun?" I asked.

"I'll get rid of the gun tomorrow. I'll strip it down and scatter the pieces. Don't you worry about the gun."

"I'm gonna worry," I said. "There's nothing I can do about that."

"Fine, then do your worrying about making sure no one ever finds *this,*" and you jabbed roughly at a thigh with your knife. Then you smiled for the first time since two or three hours before the killing. "Maybe you should just take it out to the Neely Henry Dam and toss it over the edge. I've heard stories there are giant catfish below that dam, way down deep at the bottom where the Coosa River comes pouring through the spillway. I've heard stories there are catfish down there big as Volkswagens. A catfish that big could swallow a body whole and wouldn't no one ever be the wiser."

"Catfish don't get that big," I said. "At least not any catfish I've ever heard of."

"You ever for five seconds stopped to consider maybe you don't know everything worth knowing?"

And then you told me some story your brother or father or someone else had told you about divers being sent down to check for cracks at the base of the Neely Henry Dam, years and years ago. You said whoever told you the story had said how the divers came right back up again, scared half to death and back because they'd seen those monster catfish right where the spillway empties out, like those fish were just laying in wait for anything tasty that might come tumbling out of the Coosa River and into the reservoir. You said both the divers' hair had turned white, that's how terrified they were.

"I just don't think catfish get that big," I said, but you ignored me and got up and went into the house, into the kitchen for a box of Hefty garbage bags.

"Out back there are some bricks," you said. "Go get four or five of them. Better make it five, just to be on the safe side. I'll put them inside where the guts were, then wrap the torso shut with duct tape. I figure that oughta do the job."

"Five bricks," I said, and my voice sounded thin and far away, and like maybe it was someone else talking and not me at all.

"Yeah, I think five should do. That's probably about all that will fit, anyway."

So, I went and got the bricks, and you put them in the body and wrapped it up in silver duct tape, just like you'd said. You added about two feet of rusty steel chain, just for good measure.

"I'll get rid of the intestines," you said. "And I'll wash up in here. You just worry about the body."

"What if it's too heavy," I said, beginning to wonder if I'd be able to wrestle the corpse out of the trunk and down to the pier and into the boat all on my own.

"You're a big girl," you told me. "I think you can probably manage."

"Yeah, but what if I can't."

"You'll find a way, I reckon. But I'm not going with you, so don't ask me again."

The boat glides smoothly across the India-ink lake, and the wooden oars splash softly every time I dip them into the water and pull them back out again. But the cicadas and frogs and the crickets on shore are making so much noise I figure no one would be able to hear the little splashes – if there's anyone around *to* hear, anyone to listen, and I still haven't seen any sign there is. I'm more than halfway out to the middle now, and as far as I can tell, I'm completely alone on the lake. I'm trying hard not to think about the bundle at my feet, the bundle that used to be a living, breathing human being, not just meat swaddled in Hefty bags and duct tape and filled up with bricks. I tell myself all I have to do is get it over the side without capsizing the boat, and after that I never, ever have to think of it again. But then I start worrying about what would happen if I *do* flip the boat over, about whether I'm a good enough swimmer to make it the hundred yards or so back to dry land, and I wonder how cold the water is, and about what all else might be there in the water with me. I can blame you for that last part, because the story of the giant catfish at the Neely Henry Dam wasn't the only tall tale you told while we were carving up the body. After you told me how to find this lake, you started in talking about how your granddad would bring you here to swim in the summer, even though it was way the hell out at the end of that dirt road. You and your sister would get in the back of his green Ford pickup and he'd drive the two of you out to this lake. But almost every time he'd warn you not to go too far out, because there was something that lived in the lake, he said. Something besides all the fish and turtles, the crawdads and cottonmouths. He didn't know exactly what it was, but it lived half buried in the deep mud and waterlogged stumps at the very bottom and hardly ever had to come up for air. He swore he'd even seen it once, way back before the Great Depression, when he was still a boy. He said it hadn't looked like all that much, just a big grey hump a foot or so high, its skin all wrinkled like an elephant's, no teeth or claws or tentacles or anything like that. Just the wrinkled hump floating in the lake. But all the same, you said *he'd* said, it was plenty bad enough that the sight of it made him never want to swim in the lake again.

"After that, after he told you that story, did you and your sister stop swimming there?" I asked.

You shook your head and laughed a dry, tired laugh and said, "Nope. But you can bet we stayed in the shallow water, close to the pier."

"So you believed him?"

"Well, sure. Kids will believe just about anything," you said, "at least half the time. When I got older, though, I figured it was just something he read somewhere, maybe in a book about Loch Ness or something. He was always reading." You paused to find a twist tie for the Hefty bag with all the intestines in it, then added, "Granddad was probably just about the most literate brick mason in St. Clair County."

"I think you just made all that up," I said.

"You go and think whatever you want. What you think is your own business, and right now we've got bigger troubles than what you do and don't believe."

You used four of the Hefty bags – one around the head and shoulders, one for the feet and lower legs, and the two cut open and wrapped around the middle – and then used just about a whole roll of duct tape to keep the four bags from coming apart again.

"I hope duct tape doesn't float," I said.

"Not when it's held down with a chain and five bricks, it don't," you told me, and then you used your knife to punch holes in the garbage bags, so there wouldn't be air trapped inside them with the corpse.

"Jesus, I need to wash my hands," you said, and then you held them up for me to see, as if I wouldn't have believed you otherwise. There was blood on your shirt and jeans, too, and all over the cement floor of the garage. There was a crimson smear turning scabby on your forehead where you'd wiped away sweat and a few strands of hair.

And I'm kneeling there, not even half as bloody as you, and I'm thinking how you've turned the body into a sort of gigantic cocoon or chrysalis, and I can't help but imagine the terrible sort of moth or butterfly that would grow in there.

You said, "Stop worrying. It won't be as heavy as you think."

"With all those bricks inside it," I said, "it's gonna be plenty heavy enough. If you went with me –"

"Well, I'm not and don't you dare fucking bring it up again." And now there's that cold fire flickering in your pale blue eyes, like just before you used the shotgun, and I look down at the thing on the floor, instead of looking at you. "I ought not be surprised at the way you're sitting there whining, but I am. I'm surprised, after all I've done, after I've done murder for you. After I've done almost everything but this one last part, I'd think you'd be able to suck it up and take a little fucking responsibility."

"It wasn't just for me," I said, so quietly that I was almost whispering. I could feel your eyes on me like ice.

"Is that what you think?" you asked, and before I could answer, you laughed that dry laugh and said, "I'm not the one who can't let sleeping dogs lie, who has to keep poking and poking and poking until shit comes to a head. Until someone gets a few ribs broken or their skull caved in or their belly blown wide open. I'm not the one who pushed and pushed until this whole situation finally went sideways. So I don't want to hear any more about going to the lake with you, because I'm not, and you need to shut up and let that fact settle in."

"I wasn't trying to piss you off," I said.

"You just don't fucking know when to stop pushing is all," you told me, and then you said you'd help me get the body into the trunk of my car, and you said how it would have been better if we'd used a garment bag instead of the four Hefty bags taped together like that, because there was a lot less chance a garment bag would rip open if I had to drag the body from the car down to the pier and the boat you told me I'd find waiting at the end of the pier.

"Coulda, woulda, shoulda," you said, and then you went back to staring at your bloody hands.

I wanted to ask how you *knew* the boat would be there, how you could possibly know for *sure* like you seemed to, after telling me you hadn't laid eyes on the lake in more than twenty-five years. But I knew you'd have told me what difference does it make *how* you knew, and, by the fucking way, that was *exactly* the sort of question kept getting me into trouble and when was I gonna learn to stop asking them?

I apologized, and you told me not to waste my breath *and* your time being sorry over shit, just to get up and let's get it over with. Meaning, of course, get your part over with, not mine. You said how it was already nearly four o'clock in the afternoon, and how I didn't want to be driving that dirt road for the first time in the dark.

I didn't tell you I didn't want to be driving it at all, ever. You knew that already.

So you lifted the feet and I lifted the shoulders, and after the way you'd eviscerated it, and even with the bricks and the steel chain shoved inside, I was surprised at how light the body was. I told myself this wouldn't be all that hard after all. I told myself to be cool and just take it all one thing at a time.

"Watch out for cops," you said, as if I needed to be told. "Don't speed, but don't drive too slow, either. Driving too slow is suspicious, especially when you get outside the city limits."

I dip the oars into the water and they make their little twin splashes, and I pull them out again. I think I must be almost to the middle now, but it's hard to be sure, without at least the moon to see by. I squint down at the bundle at my feet, as if squinting could manufacture more light or make more efficient use of what little light was available. I prod the Hefty bags with the toe of my left shoe.

"You brought this on yourself," I say. "You know that, right?"

And maybe the body answered me, but maybe it's just that dead people speak so very, very quietly that I could hear the reply over the noise of the insects and the frogs.

"We weren't hurting you," I say. "And I absolutely wasn't trying to take anything away from you, either. It wasn't ever like that. She wasn't going to leave you, though I want you to understand that if she ever had, it likely would have been the smartest thing she ever did."

And then there's a splash from somewhere off to my right. Not a little splash like the oars are making. This is a loud splash, a *big* splash, and a few seconds later the ripples from it are lapping and sloshing against the sides of the boat. And I sit there as still as still can be, and my heart is beating so fast and so hard I wouldn't be surprised if it's making more of a commotion than all the toads and spring peepers and bullfrogs and the bugs in the trees. I realize that I'm not breathing, and so I take a deep breath. I hold it a moment, waiting for whatever might happen next, and my mind is summoning pictures of your granddad's lake monster, of a something with thick, wrinkled hide like an elephant's back drifting along beside me. I pick up the Maglite, and I don't care anymore who else might be out on the lake tonight. Let them see me. Let them make of this whatever they will. Let them go home and tell everyone who'll listen, because the darkness is suddenly so heavy I'm not sure I can draw *another* breath. I switch on the flashlight, and I play it across the surface of the water, and there's nothing at all to see. Nothing whatsoever.

It takes me about five minutes, and afterwards I'm soaked in sweat, almost like I've been in swimming, but I get the body over the side and into the water. It hardly makes any sound at all when it slips beneath the surface, and it sinks like a stone.

"Now, you fucking stay put," I whisper, wiping sweat from my eyes and trying to catch my breath. "I hope it's lonely and cold down there, cold as hell, and you never see the sun ever again. Didn't neither one of us want to have to kill you, and I don't care if you spend all eternity thinking it was otherwise, so long as you've got no one to listen to you but the worms and turtles."

I play the Maglite out across the lake again, but there's still no wrinkled hump.

That was just her fucking with me, I think. *I know her, and I know damn well that was just her fucking with me, because maybe it made her feel better, telling me crazy stories when she's exhausted and scared and up to her tits in gore, and the very last thing she would ever do is let on that she's scared. So, this is me, floating around out here, feeling her fear for her.*

You said, "Just don't ever forget, I did this for you."

And I said I wouldn't, not ever.

I leave the Maglite burning, bright as a falling star, but I set it down on the seat beside me. And then I use the oars to turn the boat around and start rowing back towards the pier, back towards shore and the car and that rutted dirt road winding back down to the highway and town and the hollow safety of electric streetlights.

THE SURGEON'S PHOTO (MURDER BALLAD NO. 12)

Another story grounded in a real-world location. When I was a kid, growing up in Leeds and Dunnavant, Alabama, on hot summer days my Grandpa Ramey would load me and my sister into the back of his green Ford pickup and drive us out a long, long meandering red-dirt road that ran the crest of Sand Ridge to what he called Stump Lake. We'd swim and I'd catch salamanders and water snakes. Sometimes, usually on the way back, we'd stop at a tiny, overgrown Confederate cemetery. These days, maps call the lake Hillhouse Lake, and they call the dirt road Sand Ridge Road. But it'll always be Stump Lake to me. The story was written between July 5th and July 7th, 2019 and was originally titled "The End of All Flesh is Before Me."

Wisteria

"I guess that was the same summer I turned twenty-four," you say, because the second George Bush was already president, and I say, "Then it was the summer that I turned forty-something." You look at me the way you do when you'd prefer that whatever I've just said weren't true, even when you know perfectly well that it is, and you say, "As old as that? No, I don't think so." We're sitting on the back porch, and the sun's been down for almost a whole hour now. The summer night is electric with the shrill, buzzing throb of cicadas and with occasional flickers of heat lightning. You're in the swing, gliding to and fro on rusted, creaking chains, and I'm in the high-backed wooden chair I've brought out from the kitchen. We're drinking beer and smoking cigarettes. You bring me both, even though I claim to have given up smoking and alcohol years ago. Sometimes you even bring whiskey, nights like this, when it's too hot to stay indoors, when there's no point trying to read or watch TV, much less sleep, until long past midnight. You'll show up like clockwork, unsummoned, and you park in the weeds beneath the live oaks and pecan trees at the edge of the long dirt driveway leading to this house that was my mother's and her parents' before her. I once told you the history of this little house, how my grandfather bought it right after the war, but how, before that, it had been some sort of hillbilly whorehouse or honky-tonk, hidden way back here where not too many people would come snooping around, where they were likely to get shot, or at least shot at, if they did. "I think you're a lot younger than you even remember," you say, and I take a swallow of beer and shake my head. "I honestly don't know how the hell you figure that," I reply, "but I was taught that it's rude to argue with a compliment, no matter how baffling it might be. For that matter, I was taught it's rude to argue with company. So, anyway, the summer you turned twenty-four, that's the summer of the ghost story you owe me." You're sitting there in the swing, watching the moths and little brown beetles flitting about the porch light above the kitchen door, and you nod your head and say, "It is, or was, or whatever. I'd just moved here from Arkansas. I had an apartment in Birmingham. It was sort of a dump, but it was cheap enough I could afford it and was high enough up the side of the mountain that it had a nice view of the city and the valley. It had two bedrooms, so I could use one for painting, which was the major selling point." You pause to wipe the sweat from your face with the sleeve of your T-shirt. "Shit, I swear it's always twice as hot out here than back in town," you say, then sigh, then wipe your face again. "One day, I'm gonna show up with a window-unit AC in the backseat, and you can just deal with it." I set my empty bottle on the porch boards at my feet, and I say "Fine. And you can also pay the electric bill when it comes due. So, this apartment you had in Birmingham was haunted." You tell me no, that's not what you said, not exactly, that the only strange thing that ever happened was just this *one* thing, and it hardly seems fair to brand a place haunted over one strange experience. That's the word that you use, *experience*. "Anyway," you add, "I don't believe in ghosts." You open another bottle of beer and pass it to me, and I take it and think how if I were a younger woman, or how if maybe you were an older woman, maybe I wouldn't feel like such a letch, imagining you naked and in my bed, the way I inevitably find myself feeling on hot nights like this. "You don't believe in ghosts," I say, "but you said you saw one, so seeing isn't believing." You scowl and stare out at the night and the tops of the trees instead of the porch light and the bugs. "Keep it up, lady, and you're gonna ruin this before I even get started," you tell me. "When I said it was a ghost story, I was speaking in the broadest sense." And then you tell me to think of *ghost* as a metaphor for something that can't be explained, or that can't be explained for the time being. "That would make an awful lot of things ghost stories," I say, and you shrug and take a drag on your cigarette. You blow smoke rings at all that darkness and the cicadas and the peep toads. "It isn't enough that it's something that can't be readily explained away," you tell me. "That's a necessary condition, sure, but it isn't sufficient, not all on its own. The experience in question also has to elicit certain particular emotions, like dread or apprehension or fear. Some sort of unease, at any rate, at least in passing. You know that sudden cold shudder when people say someone just walked over your grave? It has to do that much, at least." I tell you I always heard how that shudder meant a *possum* had just walked over your grave, the place that would someday be your grave, and you call me a redneck and blow more smoke rings at the dark. "Okay," I say. "You don't mean literal ghosts. You don't mean the restless spirits of the dead come back to wander lost and forlorn. You just mean something that somehow spooked you or gave you the willies…or whatever. Are you gonna stop stalling and tell me what that was, in your not-haunted apartment, or am I going to turn sixty sitting here waiting to find out?" You tell me I'm surely an impatient woman if ever there were one, and I do not disagree. Patience has never been my long suit, never especially numbered among my virtues. If it were, well, I wouldn't be growing old alone out here in the woods, ten miles from anywhere that could pass for anywhere. I'd be somewhere else, instead, and I'd have amounted to something, the way I thought sure I would when I was young. "Anyway," you say again. That's a habit I might find annoying in someone I don't find so charming, your tendency to preface sentences with that word, *anyway,* whether it's actually warranted or not. "Anyway, what?" I ask. "Anyway, I'm fucking coming to it," you say, then drop the butt of your cigarette into a mostly empty beer bottle, then add, "if it hasn't already been built up too much." I say, "That would be your doing, not mine." You say, "Whichever," pause, then continue, "So, I had that cheap, roach-ridden apartment on the side of Red Mountain, tucked in right there underneath all those radio and TV transmission towers – which made the needle of my record player buzz like angry hornets, by the way. I swear, I went two years hardly able to play a record, but that's a different story. Or no story at all." And I say, "Anyway," and if you realize that I'm teasing you – and likely you do – you let it slide. You go on. "It was in late October or early November, either just before Halloween or right after, but I can't recall which." I almost say, *That's convenient,* but I don't. I light another cigarette and watch the heat lightning, wishing it would rain, knowing that it won't. It hasn't rained a drop in more than two weeks. "I'd paint at night," you tell me, "usually. Nights and Saturdays and Sundays, but this wasn't on the weekend. I remember that, because I had to be up early the next morning for work. I had a waitressing job, which almost was enough to keep the rent covered, so it's a good thing I was still getting regular checks from my dad back then. That night, the night it happened, the thing that you're going to have to count as a ghost story 'cause it's all I have that even comes close, I had just finished cleaning my brushes and was about to have a shower and get ready for bed. Then there was this noise outside. I don't exactly know how to describe it. At first I thought it was a car having trouble getting up the hill – see, the apartment building, the only parking we had was around back, and there was this insanely steep driveway – only when I looked out the window there weren't any headlights. There wasn't a car with its headlights off, either. The driveway was empty. And standing there, listening to the noise, I realized it really didn't sound like a car, anyway. Standing there, I wasn't sure why I ever thought it had. There ought to be a word for hearing a sound that doesn't sound like anything you've ever heard before, and so your mind tries to compare it to something familiar, but can't. At least, if there *is* a word for that, I don't know it." I tell you I don't, either. I'm trying to blow smoke rings, in imitation of yours, but I'm no good at it. Once, you told me it was because my tongue was shaped wrong, and I wanted to know what you could possibly know about the shape of my tongue. "That's what it was like," you say. "I realized it really *didn't* sound like anything I'd heard before, though it was sort of a mechanical noise, maybe. There was something hard about it, hard and hot, like grinding gears, maybe. Like an engine overheating, sorta. And it just kept getting louder and louder, and pretty soon, I kid you not, the windows had begun to vibrate from the noise. It got that loud. I looked up, thinking maybe it was a helicopter or an airplane of some kind passing really low overhead – though it had already gone on too long to be either of those. I looked up, but all I could see were the trees and the black silhouette of the mountain and all those transmission towers lined up on top and twinkling like Christmas trees." I ask if you went outside to see what was making the noise, and you glare at me and take another bottle of beer from the styrofoam cooler. "I'm coming to that part," you say. "Don't rush me." I say I wouldn't dare. I wouldn't dream of it, that, after all, we have all night. "Yes," you tell me, "I went outside. I put my shoes on and went out the back door. I'd thought there would be people from the other apartments – there were four that had back doors opening onto the parking area – who'd also heard the commotion and come out to see what was happening. But there wasn't. There was just me. And that sound, which was a lot louder outside than it had been inside. Right about then, that's when I started to be afraid. Or maybe it's then that it occurred to me that I was afraid. I suspect that I'd thought that once I went outside, the source of the noise would be obvious, and I'd be relieved and feel stupid for not having recognized some perfectly ordinary sound right away. But that's not what happened. If anything, it sounded stranger once I got outside. There was a sort of *churning* quality to the noise, and this really high-pitched buzzing, too, that was almost like hearing a second sound, buried behind or inside the first." I stop trying to blow smoke rings and say, "You know, this is starting to come across a lot more like a UFO sighting than a ghost story." You're sitting there staring at the bottle cap from your fresh beer, the bottle cap lying in your palm, and then you drop it into the cooler and it sinks in the ice and water. In the morning, after breakfast, I'll empty the cooler, pour the water from all that melted ice over the side of the porch into the weeds, but first I'll fish out the bottle caps and put them in the china bowl by the kitchen sink where I've been saving all your bottle caps for almost a year now. "No," you say, and I can tell you're a little annoyed at the interruption, "it *wasn't* like a UFO. It wasn't at all like that. There wasn't anything in the sky, for one thing. At least, I didn't see anything in the sky, even though I looked repeatedly. But I think I said that already." So, I apologize, and I promise I won't interrupt you again, and you sigh and sip at your beer and go on with your ghost story. "I was standing there behind the building, and all at once the sound just stopped and I could smell wisteria. You know, that musky, sweet smell of wisteria blossoms. Only, like I said, it was late October or early November, and wisteria blooms in the spring. But it was unmistakably the smell of wisteria. When I was a kid, the stuff grew wild back behind our house, and in the spring there would be all those heavy, drooping purple flowers, and on hot days the smell was almost suffocating. That's how it was that night. The smell was almost suffocating. I remember I actually covered my mouth and nose, the smell was so strong, like the whole mountainside was covered in wisteria flowers." You take a long swallow of beer, start to light another cigarette, then stop and stare at me a moment, then stare at the darkness. "Anyway, it was right after the noise stopped and I noticed the smell – not more than two or three minutes, at the most – that the wind started. At first, it was just this rustling in the trees out behind the apartment. There weren't any other buildings behind mine, just woods all the way up to the top of the mountain. Lots of pine trees and dogwoods and hickories and whatever. I used to walk back there a lot, before this happened. Afterwards, I never went walking back there again." And I ask, "Was there wisteria growing in those woods?" even though I'd promised not to say anything else until you'd finished. "No," you reply. "Lots of kudzu, and I guess kudzu flowers smell a little like wisteria. But kudzu blossoms late in the summer, in July and August, and so it couldn't have been kudzu, either. But like I was saying, this wind came roaring down the side of the mountain, like a goddamn freight train, and the first thing I thought of was a tornado, of course. Only, the sky was clear, you know? Not a cloud in it. There was just the smell of wisteria and that wind and all those trees, all those branches and dry autumn leaves, making an awful racket, like old bones and rattlesnakes, and you could even hear the trunks of the trees groaning. I turned to go back inside, because I was still thinking it must be a tornado, or something just as bad, and then it stopped, same as the noise had stopped." And you snap your fingers for emphasis. "Just like that. Just as suddenly as it had begun. And the smell was gone, too. It didn't fade away, the smell. It was just gone. The whole thing couldn't have lasted more than thirty or forty-five seconds, start to finish. I think I must have stood back there a long time, sweating and my heart racing, getting more and more freaked out by whatever had just happened. I mean, yeah, it was just the smell of wisteria and some bad wind, but…it was weird. I'm probably doing a shitty job of explaining just *how* fucking weird the whole thing was." I don't bother to agree with you. "And afterwards, there was this taste in my mouth. Like tinfoil. And I don't mean like aluminum foil, but actual old-fashioned *tin*foil. And I remember I stood there staring up at the trees and the transmission towers and the sky, and I kept spitting, trying to get that taste out of my mouth. Finally, I went next door and knocked, and when the girl who lived there – alone, like me – when she answered, I asked if she'd heard the wind or smelled anything strange, anything out of the ordinary. I think I asked if possibly she'd smelled flowers. I know I didn't actually come out and ask if she'd smelled wisteria, in particular. And I swear, she looked at me like I'd lost my mind. But she said no, she hadn't heard any wind, and she hadn't smelled anything unusual. Then she said good night and shut the door again. And after a couple more minutes, I went back inside, too. I locked my doors and turned on the television, not because I thought I'd find some explanation there, like maybe a weather alert about freak straight-line winds or something. I just wanted the company of the TV voices. I've never minded living alone. I've never minded how *quiet* it can be, living alone. You know that. But right then I minded it. Right then, quiet was about the last thing I wanted. I sat down and listened to whatever was on – I don't remember – not watching, just listening, but also listening to the night outside, waiting for that wind to start up again, waiting to smell wisteria again." You pause, then mutter something about how hot it is and laugh a nervous sort of laugh. You pull up the front of your shirt and wipe your sweaty face on it, showing me your pale, bare belly. "I fell asleep sitting right there in that chair," you say. "I fell asleep and woke up a little after dawn with my back aching and a crick in my neck, feeling silly about the whole affair, half suspecting I'd just dreamed it. The woman next door, she never once brought it up, and I was glad for that. I think I *wanted* to believe I'd only dreamed that smell and that wind. And to this day, wind makes me nervous and I cannot abide the smell of wisteria. But, anyhow, there you go. That's it, my ghost story, such as it is. That makes us even." Neither of us says anything else for a while. We sit there together on the porch, you in the creaking swing and me in my kitchen chair, and the cicadas buzz and throb and once or twice there are flashes of heat lightning, back towards town. Finally, I say you should spend the night and drive back in the morning, that I'll make up the sofa for you, and in the morning I'll make breakfast. I expect you to argue. I expect you tell me no, you're fine, or you'll be fine after one more beer, but you don't. You just nod your head and rub your eyes. "I guess it's kind of a sorry excuse for a ghost story, after all," you say. "I guess maybe I ought to have invented something for the occasion, something with moaning phantoms and ectoplasm and rattling shackles and what the hell ever." You light a cigarette and blow smoke rings at the night. "Nah," I say, "it was fine. Consider the debt paid in full. Hell, it'll probably give me nightmares. You just watch." And I don't say so, but I'm thinking about the wisteria vines growing in the tall old trees at the end of my driveway, the strangling vines and their drooping purple flowers, and I catch myself wondering what it would take to get rid of them. "You know how it's poisonous, right?" And when I ask *what's* poisonous, you say wisteria. You tell me, "It's a poisonous, invasive species, brought over from China or Korea or Japan, anyway someplace or another in Asia, back sometime in the nineteenth century. It isn't even supposed to be here." I tell you how I didn't know either one of those things, and then we both go back to just sitting there, drinking our beers and smoking and wishing it would rain.

WISTERIA

From December 1989 to April 1994 I lived in a tiny apartment on the side of Red Mountain (No. 5, 1619 16th Avenue South), which I used as the setting for this story. In fact, "Wisteria" is a fictionalized account of a *very* strange experience I had there one evening in the late summer or autumn of '93. As recounted in the *Little Damned Book of Days* chapbook (Subterranean Press, 2005), my life has been littered with more than its fair share of unexplained events, or so it seems to me, especially considering the staunchly rationalist and naturalist philosophies that have (usually) guided me since high school. "Wisteria" was written between July 23rd and August 7th, 2019.

Cherry Street Tango, Sweatbox Waltz

1.

The hotel room is hot as blue blazes, and it smells hot, and it also smells simultaneously of dust and mildew, both dry and damp. The room is, in fact, almost unbearably hot, and I sit on this sofa, alone in my private darkness and I sweat and listen to the radio. Usually, there's only music, jazz from a hundred years ago, discord and jangle and a thousand arrhythmic anti-harmonies on piano and clarinet and baritone saxophone that seem composed to mock my disorientation. But then I am a paranoid woman. It comes with the job, the paranoia. That is, either you bring it with you to the job or you pick it up soon afterwards – or you don't live very long. And sometimes you don't live very long anyway. So, the radio plays and I sit here listening to the jazz, sweating in someone else's silk bathrobe, cradled in frayed upholstery, alone in the darkness behind the bandages that cover my flash-burned eyes. I might have been sitting here for hours. I lose track of time, in between sleeping and being awake. But finally the music stops, as it periodically does, and a man with a heavy Hungarian accent comes on in its place, and he wants to know if I'm feeling any better than I felt the last time we talked. I tell him sure, I feel like a million bucks, and he reminds me how snark and sarcasm isn't going to cut it. His time is precious. On the other hand, my time, like my life, is disposable, expendable, no kind of rare dish, me, and I should therefore behave accordingly. Which is to say I should behave.

"Last name first," he says. "First name last."

I have lost count of how many times I've given my name to the man on the radio. I lick my dry lips, wishing for anything wet besides my own inner sea leaking out of me. "Sakellarios," I reply. "Elenore."

"Are you in pain tonight, Ms. Sakellarios?" the man with the Hungarian accent wants to know.

"Nothing has changed since the last time we talked," I say.

The radio crackles with a burst of static, and I wonder if that's all I'm going to get from him until next time. Sometimes it's just that short. Other times I think he's gonna yammer on forever. Anyway, this time the static fades and he's still here with me. Sweat runs down my face and drips onto my hands where they lie folded together in my lap.

"It's a dream-kill-dream world in here," says the man on the radio.

"Yeah, but ain't it always," I reply.

"I'd like to hear about the dog again," he says. "The dog on the beach." He sounds as if he's reading off a script, just like every time before. He sounds like he's reading cue cards.

"I've already told you about the dog, what, a dozen times over?"

"Indulge me," he says calmly, flatly, indifferently.

"How about you tell me how much longer I'm gonna be here, wherever here is?"

"Why?" asks the man on the radio. "Have you got somewhere else to be? Please, tell me about the dog."

I dig my nails into my palms and try not to think about the heat or the stinking room or how badly my eyes ache. It seems like they ache worse whenever I'm talking to the man on the radio, but always I tell myself how that's probably just a product of the aforementioned paranoia.

"I was seven years old," I tell the man on the radio.

"Last time you were eight," he reminds me.

"Well, *this* time I was seven. I was seven years old, and the tide was out, and I was dragging for scrap in the muck. My father ran a junkyard up in Queens."

"Last time," says the man, "his shop was in the Bronx."

"Fine," I say, "it was in the Bronx."

"If you would, please finish this sentence, Ms. Sakellarios: There is another shore, you know –"

I want a cigarette so bad it hurts, almost as much as my eyes hurt. "– upon the other side," I reply.

"Tell me about the dog, please, Elenore."

"I was seven years old, and I found the dog in the mud at low tide. It was dying when I found it. The sea lice had been at it. They were bad that year."

"So, had you killed the dog, it would have been an act of mercy," says the man with the Hungarian accent.

"If you want to think of it that way, fine."

"Why didn't you kill the dog?" he asks me. "It was suffering."

"It was dying anyway," I reply.

"If you would be so kind, please finish this sentence, Ms. Sakellarios: Then turn not pale, beloved snail –"

I swallow. My throat feels like a sandstorm. I cough and wipe sweat from my face onto the sleeve of the borrowed silk robe. It always seems hotter whenever I talk to the man on the radio, but that's also probably only my imagination.

"– then turn not pale, beloved snail," he says again.

"– but come and join the dance," I say, hardly louder than a whisper. I clear my throat and cough again.

"Are you in pain?" asks the man.

"My eyes ache," I tell him. "My eyes hurt, and I'm thirsty, and I need a fucking cigarette."

"You didn't kill the dog that was being eaten alive by the sea lice, did you, Elenore," he wants to know.

"Up till then, I'd never killed anything in my life."

"That day at low tide, did you kill the dog, Ms. Sakellarios?"

"Yeah, sure. I picked up a rock and bashed its brains in."

"Please complete this sentence: They are waiting on the shingle –"

"– will you come and join the dance?"

"When you were seven years old, or eight, did you kill the dog or didn't you?"

"I don't remember," I lie. It always feels good to lie to the man on the radio.

"In Trenton, were you paid to botch the hit? Or did your failure follow from mere incompetence?"

I want to stand up and leave the room. I've memorized the path from the room with the sofa to the room with a bed and a toilet and a sink. It isn't a long walk, not even for a blind woman. But I've not yet had the nerve to walk out on the man who speaks to me through the radio, and if wishes were horses, beggars wouldn't go around hungry, just like they say in the funnies.

"I *did* my job in Chinatown," I say, sounding more angry than it is wise to sound. "Before the grenade went off, I did my fucking job. Don't you try and tell me otherwise. I know better."

"Did the dog have a name?"

"How the shit would I know?"

"Most dogs do," says the man.

"Not strays. Not dogs no one has ever bothered to name."

"Why didn't you kill the dog, Elenore? It must have been in agony."

And I'm sitting there, sweating and smelling dust and mildew and my own stink, my own filth, and I'm wondering whether the man on the radio *is* a man or whether he's only tick-tock or AI. I'm sitting there in the darkness wrapped around my face, just wanting him to go away and let the music play again. I'm sitting there trying to remember if there really was a dog.

"There were a lot of strays along the waterfront," I say. "I knew an old man who shot dogs for the commodore, for the bounty money. Ten bucks a head. Twenty for a pregnant bitch."

"You haven't answered my question," notes the man, just as cool as a scoop of vanilla ice cream.

"My eyes hurt," I tell him.

"Rubbing doesn't help," he says, and then he asks me why I didn't take the shot in Trenton. He asks me why I froze.

"I took the shot," I reply. My hands have begun to tremble.

"It's a dream-kill-dream world in here," he says for the second time.

"Don't you know it, Mister," I reply. And then he's gone and the jazz returns. He's gone and I'm alone, and I lean back and try to think about anything at all but whether or not the dying, writhing dog is a real memory or something else. It's so hot that I can almost believe the world is ready to catch fire, and that would be a mercy, too.

2.

I'm on my second Scotch and soda, when Mercedes Bélanger strolls into the place. She's almost an hour late, but that's nothing much to make a fuss over. That is absolutely no sort of surprise, not to me and not to any other blackstrap who's ever had cause to deal with the Turk. His merry band of goons and gunsels are not known for their punctuality. But that's fine. I'm not in a hurry. I have just been sitting here getting very slightly drunk and watching the river burn. Out on the Delaware, a petro barge caught fire right after sunset, and the low-slung underbellies of the clouds glow like the roof of Hades. More likely than not, someone neglected to pay someone else this, that, or the other bribe, and so the barge was torched. Anyway, I am sitting there sipping my Scotch and thinking how if the fire keeps drifting downriver towards the ramshackle span of the Calhoun Street Bridge, it is gonna be a bitch getting back over to Levittown. Mercedes Bélanger, she spots me and comes weaving her way through the joint, just as slick as Cleopatra's asp, easy as the snake in Eden, between the tables and chairs and all the other gawkers watching the fire. Right at the last I let her know that I have seen her. Then I go back to watching the river. She sits down in the booth across from me and lights a cigarette, and she does not say one word about being late. A waiter flits over, and the Turk's woman orders tequila, and then the waiter flits away again.

"And, what's more, they don't even charge extra for the floor-show," she says, then blows a smoke ring that drifts lazily up towards the ceiling. Her accent sounds like South Philly, but fuck only knows. It could be a coverall. Everything about her might well be a cover, for all that I can tell, from her rust-colored hair to her shiny black shoes. Me, I have learned not to bother looking too close when dealing with the Turk. If he wants to play hide the Nazi with masking socks, that is more than his prerogative – just so long as I get paid my due. Just so long as he does not decide to cut corners by popping the folks who do his dirty work.

"You got the box?" I ask the woman sitting across from me.

"Well, ain't you all business," she smiles.

"Yeah, ain't I just."

"How long has it been burning?" she wants to know, and Mercedes Bélanger, she points at the window with her cigarette.

"Long enough that I am pretty sure no one is coming to put it out."

"The Turk, he don't do arson," she says, like maybe I have said he does.

"No, Ma'am," I say. "I am sure he has never in his life struck a match, save to light his fat cigars."

She sits back and she stares at me. Her eyes are lined in crimson smudge and filled up with flecks of gold and silver, and that right there is when I decide this one is exactly as she presents herself. Nobody would go to all the trouble and discomfort to mask and not hide those cheapskate implants.

She says, "I was told you don't know when it's best to keep your mouth shut. I see I was not misinformed."

"Do you have the box or don't you?" I ask the woman with artificial eyes.

"Is there a hurry up on this evening that no one told me about?" she wants to know.

I finish my drink, then go back to staring at the river.

"If I had known it was a courting," I say, "I would have brought you flowers. Hell, I would have brought you a box of chocolate bonbons."

Mercedes Bélanger points at the fire again. "Use to was round here," she says, "folks wasn't so sloppy they let shit like that go down. Use to was, everyone knew his place, and if a ship's toll needed paying, it got paid, and if a fire was burning, someone in a yellow hat showed up to put it out. Yeah, Ms. Sakellarios, I got the box, but my instructions are that we talk until half past ten, and so we still got fifteen minutes left to go. Think you can make do with that?"

"If those are the rules."

She grins and says, "I hear you were soldier, use to was. I hear it you did a couple tours down in Nuevo Léon, right after the uprising."

"I never got anywhere near Nuevo Léon," I tell her. "I did my stint down on the Yucatán, mostly."

"Oh, I see," she says. "Is that where you acquired your fascination with fires? 'Cause what I heard is you were a sprayer for the infantry, one of the blowtorch brigade, but if that ain't so, you should set me straight."

I take a quick hinge at her, a glance at those stark metallic eyes, and I'm about to say something – I do not recall just what – when the waiter flits over with her tequila. I order another Scotch and water and the waiter goes away again.

"I was a breaker, a translator," I tell Mercedes Bélanger, instead of whatever it was I'd meant to tell her before the waiter interrupted. "I'm good with code."

She raises an eyebrow, plucked thin as a razor's edge and she wants to know, "Then why is it you're running meat wagon for the likes of Constantin and not decrypting for the highest bidder?"

"I am not *that* good," I reply.

She takes a sip of her tequila. "Yeah, well, what's it the spielers out on the strand all say? The clutch of life, right? Ain't that something from the Bible?"

I tell her how she's asking the wrong person. This whole scene is beginning to wear on me, and I want to get the package and make my exit. Still, it isn't that I don't know what is and what is not in my best own sweet interest, and right here it *surely* is in my best interest to play along and trust that there's no way through this palaver but straight down the middle and that Mercedes Bélanger isn't up to something. I know her by reputation. She's the sort the Turk sends round when he is not taking chances. She is not the sort to offend with impatience.

I need the work, and I do not need the black star next to my name. So, I let her talk, and I sit there counting off the minutes in my head and I listen. Every again and now, I try to contribute something, and I watch the barge burn.

"Well, it's been a pleasure," she finally says, "more or less." She finishes off her tequila and mashes out the butt of her cigarette, and then she reaches into her handbag and takes out a shiny little brass cube just about the same size as a lump of sugar. "I trust you know what to do with this," she smiles, "a smart cookie like yourself." She slides the box across the table, and I make it vanish into my jacket.

I say, "Please relay my respects to Mr. Constantin, and let him know I said how much I appreciate the job, same as ever."

And she tells me, "Just don't fuck it up, lady."

Right then, the barge collides with the span of the bridge, and the resulting explosion rattles the tall plate-glass windows of the joint. There's a chorus of appreciative oohs and ahs from most of the other gawkers, and when I go to turn my attention back to Ms. Mercedes Bélanger, to assure her I do not make a habit of fucking it up, she is nowhere to be seen.

3.

In the moldy, dry room – in the sweltering room that is so much like a fire on a river – I sit smoking and listening to the man on the radio, the man with the Hungarian accent. Someone else is here with me now. I think that it is a woman, but I cannot be sure. They do not speak. They have not let me touch them, and my eyes are still hidden behind the bandages, and if they were not I still probably could not see my whoever-come-lately companion. But they brought me the cigarettes and a lighter and a bottle of cold water, and they linger somewhere nearby. The spicy, pungent smoke from the Javanese kreteks tastes like cloves and cumin, nutmeg and tobacco. I have to be careful not to burn my fingers, but I'm managing. A regular magician, I am.

"It was raining," says the man on the radio.

"Yeah, that's what I said, isn't it? First, it *wasn't* raining, and there wasn't a cloud in the sky. And then it *was* raining, so hard I thought I might drown every time I drew a goddamn breath. I was running across the catwalk in the fucking rain, trying not to drown, or lose my footing, because it was a hundred feet down to the street. I was also trying to stay far enough ahead of the dogs – the dogs that no one bothered to tell me to worry about – that they wouldn't be taking a plug out of my ass."

"The wolves," says the man on the radio.

"Wolves, dogs, whatever."

"Earlier, you told me that they were wolves."

I take a long drag on my cigarette. I hold the smoke in so long that my ears start to buzz. I exhale and wish the man would stop talking and let the jazz come back.

"Look, either way, I was not warned to expect them. They weren't on the manifest, not dogs and not wolves, and, for that matter, also not rain. None of that shit was in the box."

"You were running on the rooftop," says the man on the radio.

"Not on the rooftop. On the catwalk dangling fifteen feet *above* the rooftop. The goddamn dogs were down there on the rooftop."

"Not wolves, dogs."

"I figure, no matter which they were, they get their teeth in you, it's gonna hurt just about the same."

"You said the sky was clear," the man on the radio tells me.

"And then it was raining. I said that, too."

"Elenore, would you please complete this sentence?" he asks, and I take another long drag on my smoke. "What road are you taking? The Road of Needles or –"

"– the Road of Pins."

"Why then, I'll take the Path of Needles –" says the man on the radio.

"– and we'll see who gets there first," I reply.

"How many shots did you fire before you were hit?" the man wants to know.

"Like I have told you – however many times it's been now – five or six."

"And that was before the wolves showed up?"

"No, that was after, in the rain."

"The wolves or the dogs," says the man, his voice as flat as hammered shit.

"Isn't it just possible that whatever gleet coded that box Bélanger slipped me wasn't exactly so good with the quality control?"

And he says, "The possibilities are all but endless."

"And isn't it also possible, just maybe, it was tampered with and the stream corrupted on purpose, because maybe someone – and fuck if I would know *who*, so do not ask – wanted that whole scene to go sideways. Which would then be the *why* of all this Heisenbergish bushwa."

"The esteemed Mr. Constantin has many professional rivals," says the man with the Hungarian accent. Which could be him agreeing sabotage is a possibility, or it could be something else altogether. "Ms. Sakellarios, you had a clear view of the target when you fired?" he asks me next. Again.

"As clear as I could get, what with the rain and the yapping mutts, yeah. I knew it was the best I was likely going to get off, so I took the shot."

"The shots," says the man, correcting me. "You have said you discharged your firearm either five or six times."

I crush out the butt of my cigarette in the ashtray on the table in front of me. Or I miss and crush it out on the table. Six of one, half dozen the other way round.

"Please complete this sentence, Elenore," says the man on the radio. "The better to eat you with –"

"– my child."

"Now come –"

"– and lie beside me."

"And the grenade?" asks the man on the radio.

"That was right after."

"After the fifth or sixth shot."

"Yeah."

"It wasn't raining when the extraction team reached you. You are aware of that, aren't you, Elenore. In fact, the conditions were quite dry. There was not a cloud in the sky. The moon was like a wheel of cheddar, hung up against the velvet night."

"Yeah, I know. And there were no dogs. Or wolves."

"Indeed not," he says.

Then he doesn't say anything for a while, and whoever it is here with me passes me another lit cigarette. I resist the urge to grab hold of their arm. His arm. Her arm. *Its* arm. I smoke and I wait.

There's white noise, and then the man is talking again.

"Prior to this incident," he says, "your record was, for want of a better word, spotless. Which, of course, is why you were retained. Mr. Constantin had never before been given any cause to doubt your efficiency. But in light of the discrepancies at hand, concerns arise. I am certain, Ms. Sakellarios, that you understand our position in this matter. I am certain also that you sympathize. Your patience is appreciated."

And then there's more static and this time the man with the Hungarian accent goes away and the room fills up with music made by folks who died before my mother was born. And I sit smoking and sweating and wishing the person standing nearby would open their mouth and say anything at all. One stinking, stingy word would be as good as gold.

4.

Up a flight of stairs so narrow my elbows are bumping the brick walls, and I honestly have no idea what the poor son of a bitch I'm chasing has done to deserve the Turk sending someone like me to end his time among the living. It is not now and never shall be my place to ask those sorts of questions. I am a blackstrap, and I just do my fucking job. I'm taking the stairs two at a time, and then there's the open door leading out into the night, and I pause there just a moment at the threshold to get my bearings. It's a hot night in late January, the mercury pushing seventy Fahrenheit or better, and I'm dripping sweat onto the concrete at my feet. It stinks out there, like every food stall and overflowing dumpster and cut-rate whorehouse in Chinatown. I take a deep breath, breathing the night into me, making of it my ally. It tastes as bad as it smells. I can see that the door does not open out onto the roof proper, but rather it leads onto a rickety-looking catwalk, rusted iron even narrower than the stairwell. I curse and I check my weapon and then I step out to get this over and done with. The mook should be dead and getting stiff by now. He shouldn't have been able to give me the slip down on Cherry Street. And yet he did. My boots on the catwalk sound loud as hammers on tin. And right here it starts to rain pitchforks. Or it has been raining all along, and I just didn't realize through the mist-red haze of adrenaline behind my eyes. And the dogs start barking. It sounds like a whole goddamn kennel has been let loose on the roof beneath me. I wipe rain from my eyes and look down at them. Lips curled back to reveal fangs the yellow white of old piano keys, the bared canines of canines, if you will. I squint, trying to get a better view, because it occurs to me that maybe they are not mere dogs at all. On this side of the river, you get a lot of assholes packing test-tube exotics for guardian angels. I once busted in on a goddamn tiger, if you can believe that. Or even if you cannot. So, maybe they aren't just dogs. It occurs to me they might be wolves. But I am wasting time. They're down there; I'm up here. I have let myself get distracted, and now my mark is getting away. I take my eyes off the snarling, yapping pack beneath me and turn my attention once more again to the work at hand. To my surprise, the mook is standing not more than twenty yards away, just staring back at me. He looks like a goddamn drowned sewer rat, but then, most of a certain, I probably do too. I raise my gun and the laser draws a pretty crimson bead upon his forehead.

"You know this ain't personal," I say, shouting to be heard above the torrential fucking rain and above the hullabaloo of the barking dogs. "Hold still, fella, and let's make it easy. Let's make it fast."

The mook wipes his long, wet bangs from his eyes. He's a stylish-dressed breed, the sort of kid who spends more on clothes and baubles and pomade in a week than I spend on food and rent in six months. And I figure it might just be his taste for fancy duds that has him so far in dutch with the Turk that I'm about to squeeze the trigger and lay him low. The mook looks at me, and then he looks down at the raging cacophony of dogs.

Then he looks back at me again.

"You're Sakellarios, ain't you?" he wants to know, also having to shout to be heard. "Elenore Sakellarios? Yeah, I heard of you. You got glitter. Quelle surprise, that I should rate the likes of you."

"Yeah, you must have made quite an impression," I shout back, and I blink water from my eyes, and I think how, at this range, the blast is gonna rip the mook's head off. I am not taken back that he knows my name. You work dillinger long enough and with any degree of confidence, you get a reputation. You do it up right, you get T-shirts and fan clubs and goddamn trading cards. You get fortune cookies.

"Funny," says the fancy mook, "how secrets travel."

He smiles.

And me, I fire my gun, and that one shot is all the thunderclap that any rainstorm will ever need. It is loud as the voice of the Lord Jehovah Almighty. *Boom.* The shiny black Heckler and Koch .45 caliber rips a hole in the night, and *that* ought to be *that*, all she wrote, Mister, the last and definitive word on the subject. Or so you would think. But you would be wrong, for the mook is still standing right there, grinning at me, and the dogs are still barking their heads off, and I squeeze the trigger again. I know I did not miss, but I squeeze the trigger again. And however many times again after that. The kid does not move, and also his head does not come apart in a satisfying spray of blood and bone and teeth and atomized fucking brains. He just stands there, watching me.

And all those dogs – or whatever – have fallen silent as the tomb.

I see the grenade rolling along the catwalk towards me maybe two seconds before it pops and I'm blinded by the flash. That pineapple, it pukes up light like it has serious designs on going full-tilt supernova. And then I realize that I am down on my knees, even if I can't recollect the fall, and I also realize how it isn't raining anymore. I can hear the *whup-whup-whup* of the approaching extraction drone. And I'm wondering how and why I'm still drawing breath, why it is the mook has not followed through and done for me, even more so than I'm wondering how I could have conceivably blown the hit at twenty yards. Twenty yards and the fancy goddamn mook standing still as a marble statue.

The rotors blow like a hurricane, and all I can see is a hatful of nothing.

5.

Mercedes Bélanger cuffs my wrists before she takes off the bandages. I let her, because she says she has a gun. Also she pokes a lit cigarette between my lips, and I sit there, drowning in sweat and sucking back smoke, and only just then do I realize that it has been her in here with me all along. I might have known. She snips the gauze away, then gently lifts the cotton pads off my eyes. I blink and squint, but there is not a whole lot more than a watercolor blur of colors and shapes, truth be told. Still, I am not blind as a bat, which is what I'd expected.

"It'll get better," she tells me. "There wasn't any retinal or corneal damage, nothing long term. But you're gonna want to avoid bright lights for a bit."

Wrapped up in only the silk robe, I sit here in the stifling room that smells like dust and mildew. I'm looking at the dump for the first time, but I can't tell much more about my surroundings than I could with the bandages on. Mercedes Bélanger is facing me, sitting on the table, and jazz spills loud from the radio behind her. All the lights are down low, but it is sufficiently bright to sting my aching eyes, so I close them again.

"You've been here all along?" I ask, mumbling around the cigarette.

"Not all along, but mostly," she replies and takes the kretek from my mouth.

"So, what's this bushwa then?" I want to know. "You taking me away to the Turk to pay for my ineptitude? If that's it, lady, you could have left the damn bandages on."

"I ain't taking you much of nowhere, Ms. Sakellarios. You'll be on your own when those cuffs come off. Your part in this particular shell game is done, and maybe Constantin don't see it yet – 'cause he can be a short-sighted son of a bitch – but I figure you'll be useful again some day. I don't like waste. My dad, he once told me how, when all is said and done, every evil in the world boils down to a wasteful act."

"You're letting me walk?" I ask. "Don't you think your boss is gonna be a little more than just hot under the collar about that?"

"You let me worry about the Turk."

"Fine, but first you tell me how it is I didn't kill that fancy fella on the catwalk when I had him dead bang, and about the rain and the wolves, and –"

"Used to was," says Mercedes Bélanger, interrupting me, "you did a bitch a solid, and she didn't start right in demanding all the secrets of the goddamn universe tossed into the bargain. Used to was, she'd have shown a jot of gratitude."

I open my eyes, and it seems I can see just a little more than before I shut them.

"Yeah, well, be that as it might, I am not so accustomed to playing patsy in a grift, and most especially not when that grift involves stealing from men like Constantin Arat, so you'll just have to forgive my lack of gratitude. It was the box, wasn't it? You slipped me a ghost or three in the upload. For all I know, there wasn't only not any rain and not any dogs, there was not even any fancy fucking mook on a catwalk."

And right here Mercedes Bélanger, she taps the side of her nose with a forefinger. Or I think that's what she does. Maybe she's flipping me off and my eyes are still too scorched to know the difference.

"You'll get something for your troubles," she says.

"I just bet I will."

"How about let's get you outta here before the next transmission rolls round," and quicker than I can say yay or nay, she sticks the cigarette back between my lips. She helps me up off the sofa. She leads me from the room and down a long hallway and down enough flights of stairs that I lose count after four. But before too long we're outside. It's night, which is just as well. She puts a pair of cheaters on my face, sets them down on the bridge of my nose, then takes off the handcuffs. There's a car waiting at the curb. I smell hot asphalt and garbage and the fumes from the automobile's tailpipe.

"Just so we're clear, I'm not happy about this," I say, and she gives me a little shove towards my ride.

"Just so we're clear," she tells me, "I ain't overly concerned with any one blackstrap's dissatisfaction, not even when it's the dissatisfaction of the great Elenore Sakellarios. Got bigger fish to fry and all."

"And if you're wrong and the Turk comes round for my hide?"

"It comes to that," she says, "you'll know he took my hide first. But it ain't gonna come to that. I am a careful girl. Now git," and with that she turns about and marches away and the blur of her vanishes back into the streetlight blur of the tenement building looming before me. I stand there for a minute or two before the driver decides I've stood there long enough and honks his horn. So I get into the backseat, and he asks where I want to go, which comes as a surprise. I expected the Turk's lady would have gone and decided that for me.

"The airport," I say, but when the car pulls away from the curb, I take that back and instead I give him the address of a bordello and shooting gallery across the river in Jersey. Just now, I need to be high and I need to be fucked more than I need to get out of Philly. I have this wounded ego to soothe, I do. And a considerable need to stop puzzling over how one and one isn't making two. The driver tells me it's my funeral.

"Don't I just know it," I reply. "Don't I just."

CHERRY STREET TANGO, SWEATBOX WALTZ

There *is* an actual story behind this story. Short version: On March 29th, 2018, Joyce Carol Oates invited me to contribute a story to an anthology of original noir fiction titled *Cutting Edge.* As a longtime admirer of JCO, I was very flattered, and a few months later, between July 24th and 31st, I wrote "Cherry Street Tango, Sweat Box Waltz." JCO read the story and replied:

I am not sure that I quite understand it, however... I'd asked Johnny Temple, the series editor, to read it also, & he concurs that it is a well-written & engrossing story which has left him a bit baffled...[itemized list of various things she and Mr. Temple did not understand]... *in any case thanks for sending this. Johnny & I look forward to hearing from you & being enlightened.*

I agonized over this for a couple of weeks, and then I replied:

I apologize for taking so awfully long to reply. But I wanted to think this over before I did, and I have. I have pretty strong feelings about not explaining stories, and it's a policy that I believe has served me well for the past twenty-five years (or so). Add to that the fact that I tend toward the admittedly enigmatic, and that, in this case, I was playing with that element in noir that is more concerned with characterization and mood than resolution and clarity of plot (see, for example, The Big Sleep*).*

I very much appreciate having been invited to the anthology, but it's probably best, I think, if I withdraw "Cherry Street Tango, Sweatbox

Waltz." If I set about trying to clarify what wasn't, from the start, meant to be clear, I'd wind up with something that is less than my best work, and I know that from experience. Again, thank you.

And then I sold the story to Subterranean Press. But that line about looking forward to "being enlightened," it rubs me a little more wrong every time I remember it.

Mercy Brown

1.

"A *hair* vampire?" she says, looking back at me from the mirror on the medicine cabinet door, raising one eyebrow skeptically, her eyes blue as ice. "Are you serious? What does that even mean, a 'hair vampire'?"

"I'm still working on that part," I reply, and I light a cigarette, then look around for something in the bathroom that I can use as an ashtray, not finding anything and deciding my left hand will have to suffice.

"Jesus, that's one of those ideas that's so bad it might be brilliant," she says, then rinses her toothbrush beneath the tap before she sets it back into its appointed hole in the white ceramic toothbrush holder mounted on the wall. There are four holes in the ceramic fixture, but only one toothbrush.

"That or one of those ideas I should bury in a deep hole in a vacant lot."

"You ever heard of the rokurokubi?"

I say that I never have, and I take a long drag on my cigarette, then exhale towards the open window, but at least as much of the smoke stays in the bathroom with us as finds its way outside.

"I thought you'd quit," she says.

"I thought I had, too," I reply, and then she frowns and asks me to light one for her, so I do.

"When I die of cancer, they're sending you the bill," she says.

"So, what's the rokurokubi?" I ask, and she leans closer to the mirrored door of the medicine cabinet and stares at a blemish on her neck.

"Evil Japanese spirits," she tells me. "Women whose heads come loose from their bodies at night and fly around drinking people's blood. I read about them somewhere, but I can't remember where it was. Or when. I might still have been in college. Anyway, you have to admit, that's at least as silly as a hair vampire."

"You're going to be late for work," I say, glancing at the clock.

"I honestly don't think they much care anymore. I'm waiting to be fired and put out of my misery. Dad would be pissed, though."

I tap ash into my hand, and she taps ash into the sink. Her skin is only almost as pale as the white porcelain. She goes back to staring at the spot on her throat.

"Heads will roll," I say, and she smiles but doesn't laugh.

Outside, down on the sidewalk, a man's shouting at a barking dog.

"It's just a mole," I say, because it's starting to make me anxious the way she's still staring at that spot on her neck, and she takes the cigarette from between her pale lips and says, "That's what everyone thinks, until it's *not* just a mole."

"So, these rokurokubi," I say, "how do you kill them? What's their weakness?"

"Their weakness?"

"You know, like Count Dracula and cloves of garlic."

"Oh," she says, "her weakness. Hell if I know. Maybe she doesn't have one. Maybe the flying heads of Japan are impervious."

"You could destroy the body while the head's away," I suggest, and she laughs, probably because she's starting to suspect that I've taken the whole business too seriously, that I'm actually sitting there on her toilet seat trying to work out how you'd kill the rokurokubi, because she suspects I take everything too seriously. Like being late for work. Like losing a job, even when I know perfectly goddamn well how her daddy will be there to pay the bills.

"Sure," she says, "that might work. Then again, it might not. It might just piss her off, and then your goose would be cooked, wouldn't it?"

Down on the sidewalk, the man's stopped shouting and the dog's stopped barking.

"It's kind of messed up when you think about it," she says, and the smoke curls over her head like a ghostly question mark.

"When you think about what? What's kind of messed up?"

"How just about every culture in the world, probably every culture going back to the fucking Neanderthals, has some sort of vampire. How human beings are so obsessed with something sidling up next to them in the dark and drinking their blood."

"Did I ever tell you about the time I got a leech on my leg?" I ask, and she stops staring at the blemish and makes a disgusted face.

"No," she says, "and I would prefer if you did not. Some of us didn't grow up in the sticks, and we were spared such grotesque indignities as leeches and rabid possum attacks and what the hell ever else."

"I'm not even sure possums can get rabies," I say.

"Now you're just being pedantic."

"Serves you right, not wanting to hear about my leech. I was wading in a creek, and before I noticed it was on me – there's some sort of natural anesthetic in their saliva, I think, so you don't feel when they bite –"

"I said I don't want to hear this."

"– and before I noticed, the thing was swollen about as big as my thumb."

Then she says that if I won't shut the hell up about leeches, I can find some other fuck-buddy, because, after all, she's not that hard up, and, by the way, did I at least leave enough milk that she'll have some for her coffee? I tell her sure, I left enough milk, and I don't say anything else about leeches. Or ticks. Or fleas. Or hair vampires.

"Well, don't just mope around the apartment all day," she says. "If you can't write, go somewhere. Take a walk or go to a movie or something. You're getting morbid again."

I say I'll look at the paper and see what's playing, that a movie might be a good idea. If I can't write, that is, and lately there have been more days when I can't than there have been days when I can. I want to point out that, morbid or not, I wasn't the one who brought up flying, detachable, blood-sucking lady heads. I'm just a horny freelance between checks. I know which side my bread's buttered on. You betcha.

2.

It rains on Monday, and I lie here in bed listening to the raindrops spattering across the roof and windows, and it sounds so much to me like bacon frying that I would almost say the two sounds are indistinguishable. Every now and then there's thunder, but no lightning, just the storm dry heaving over the city, and me listening, and the apartment as still as it ever gets. You're at work. I'm not. I should be at the typewriter on the desk, here in this spare bedroom you're letting me use until I'm on my feet again, but I'm lying here in bed, instead. The rain sounds like cooking meat, but I've said that already. And I'm thinking about the last time I was in Philadelphia, one of those cities I find myself in, from time to time, even though I have no particular fondness for it. But, that last time, one thing or another had taken me to Philadelphia, it doesn't really matter what, and I looked up a friend there, someone I'd known in college but hadn't seen for years, and she asked had I ever been to the Mütter Museum at the College of Physicians, and I told her no, I never had. I told her that, in fact, I'd never even heard of the Mütter Museum, and she said I'd love it. She said it was right up my alley, unless I'd changed an awful lot in the decade and a half since college, and I said no, I didn't suppose that I had changed very much at all. Not really. I don't think any of us do, she told me, and I didn't argue. I know that, after a fashion, it's my job to understand people, not the same way it's the job of a psychiatrist or a psychologist, but it's part of my job, all the same. But knowing people is one of those parts of my job that I'm not very good at. Anyway, she said we should have lunch first, and later I'd understand why, so we met at a sandwich shop on Market Street, just a couple of blocks from the museum, and we ate and drank coffee and caught up, the way that friends who have become only close acquaintances do. She talked about her children and her husband, and we reminisced about school, and I talked about writing and the books and the things I did to pay the bills whenever the books weren't enough. I told her that it was a point of pride that I'd not yet resorted to prostitution or selling illegal drugs, and she laughed as if I were joking. I told myself I was. She picked up the check, and then I put more change in the parking meter, and we walked hand in hand to the Mütter, as though *this* were still *then* and she were still playing at and trying on a life and a sexuality that she'd shed shortly after graduation, easy as a snake sheds its skin. I don't hold that against her. I never have. Truthfully, at times I have been jealous that I was unable to do the same, but that's nothing I have ever told her. It's nothing that I would ever tell anyone. It doesn't take long to reach the black iron gates and the white marble columns and pediments of the museum, "College of Physicians" etched into the stone, a façade of sturdy Federal architecture to conceal the menagerie of horrors tucked inside. I won't go into all those particulars. I'm not in the mood. But it would be difficult to conceive of an affliction of the human body, whether congenital or inflicted by disease or injury, that was not represented among those jars of formaldehyde, the plaster casts and skeletons, the wax models and teratologies and row after row after row of human skulls, all of it kept safe behind glass, framed in garish Victorian splendor. It wasn't right up my alley, or if it was, I'm now pretending that it wasn't. But she led me from case to case, and I followed, dutiful as a hound, and I feigned interest (and not revulsion) while she talked enthusiastically about this or that or some other malformation. Siamese twins. A paper-thin bit of Albert Einstein's brain. A human embryo with two perfectly developed heads. Examples of hydrocephaly and microcephaly. And then we came to a case with odd bits of gold jewelry, and she explained to me how the stones set into the rings and pendants were actually bezoars, hardened masses of food and other substances that sometime form within the human intestinal tract, believed by some to have magical or medicinal properties. Beside the jewelry, a jar preserving a trichobezoar, an ugly tangle of half-digested hair taken from the gut of a young woman who suffered from "Rapunzel syndrome," trichophagia, and as if the trichobezoar weren't awful enough, there was a larger jar inside the same display case, a jar with something else inside, something larger and much more awful than the trichobezoar. That time I almost looked away, while she read the printed label aloud to me and said how she didn't recall this from any of her other trips to the Mütter. Occasionally they swap things out, she said. The thing in the jar was mostly hair, but there was also the lump of flesh that the hair was attached to. It made me think of a heart, even though it really didn't actually *look* much like a heart. It almost looked like a sea urchin, I thought, but still it reminded me of a heart. Unidentified growth removed from the base of the skull of a man in Timișoara, Romania in 1972, she read, and I stared at it, thinking of a pumping heart, sending oxygenated blood one way and deoxygenated blood another, but also thinking of something clinging to a rock at the bottom of the sea, all that hair drifting to and fro in the current, poisonous tendrils cast about to ensnare plankton and tiny, unsuspecting fish. Then we moved along to the next exhibit, the next assemblage of monstrosities, and look at that, she said, and isn't that remarkable, and isn't that just the most hideous thing ever?

3.

And *this* night, this night here that I am putting onto paper and rendering only sterile words by the clack, clack, clack of the antique keys of my sturdy German-made Olympia, *this* night *right* here I have left the window partway open, because on summer nights that apartment would become an oven. I have left the window open, and if my sorry, broken life is only a ghost story, told so many times the truth of things has been forgotten, if that's the truth, then this night is what I sometimes think of as the fulcrum in the void. Three apartments ago now, because I move around a lot, which is what happens when you neglect, on a regular basis, to bother paying the rent.

"I have a big box fan I'll bring over," she said, and I said sure, if you're really not using it. And then she said, "It must be a sauna in there. It must be an kiln."

Something like that, I replied.

"You could get a window unit," she said, "maybe something secondhand. I can't imagine that would set you back very much."

No, I said, but the electric bill might.

So, it's this night in August, this August 12th, to be precise, and I am lying on sweaty sheets, unable to sleep for the heat. I've just switched off the light, because it was also too hot to read and I kept dripping sweat on the pages. Don't ask what I was reading; I honestly do not remember. But I remember switching off the lamp beside the bed and having a cigarette and listening to the traffic down on Highland, and I remember hearing a train. I remember the *smell* of my sweat and thinking that I needed to make a trip to the laundry soon. I stubbed out the cigarette, only half smoked, and I shut my eyes, and I tried to sleep. I can hear a night bird, but nothing that I recognize, and I'm thinking how when I was a kid, when I was a boy, I could name just about every birdcall there was, at least the calls of the birds that live around here. And so I am lying there sweating and stinking of sweat and thinking about birdsongs I don't recognize, and the bedroom window is partway open, and – even though there's a screen on that window – something gets in, flowing not-quite silently over the sill. It made a sound like velvet drawn across bare skin, a soft sort of a sound that is almost not any sort of sound at all. And I remember turning my face towards the window, not startled, only curious and expecting some utterly prosaic explanation for whatever I'd heard. I am not by nature a superstitious person. I never have been. I have never been afraid of the dark. I have never jumped at shadows.

"Well," she said, "I'll bring the fan over tomorrow. I doubt it uses as much electricity as a window unit would."

I told her I didn't know whether it would or not.

"Maybe it'll be cooler tomorrow," she said, but then I say no, not if the weathermen are to be believed. If anything, it's going to be worse.

"I had an apartment like that," she said. "A few years back. I'd take long cold baths before bed, just about every night in the summer."

And what I almost said then, I barely manage to keep it to myself.

So what happened next, after the bird and after you heard that sound?

I really don't think the bird was a part of it, a part of whatever did or didn't happen that night. I think the bird was only a bird.

Was it an owl?

No, it wasn't an owl.

Well, the Greeks and the Romans, they believed in something called strixes, and the strixes were birds, or something like birds, like owls. They would attack babies in their cribs and drink their blood. They would disembowel infants.

That's fucking awful.

Ovid wrote about strixes attacking a baby. Petronius wrote about strixes, too.

Jesus, how do you know all this shit? Anyway, it wasn't an owl. It didn't sound anything like an owl. It was something else, not an owl.

"Well, I'll bring the fan over tomorrow evening, after work. I'll get some takeout, because Lord knows it's too hot to cook, and we'll drink beer and watch old movies. I think TCM is having some sort of film noir festival. You'll be done writing by the time I get off work, won't you? I don't want to interrupt. Just tell me what time, because I don't want to interrupt."

I tell her sure, I'll be done writing by the time she gets off work.

I'm not stalling. Somehow, it all fits together, if you look at the haunting from just the right angle. Somehow, it's all of a piece.

Or maybe I'm not *only* stalling.

And I'm a goddamn coward, but, then again, so are you.

...something gets in, flowing not-quite silently over the sill. It was a sound like velvet drawn slowly across bare skin. It was that sort of sound that is almost not any sort of sound at all. And I remember turning my face towards the window, not startled, only curious, and someone is standing there beside the window. In the room with me. I cannot see her clearly. The only light is the glow of the streetlight getting in through the window, and mostly I can only see her in silhouette. She is tall and thin and obviously female, or at least something that's doing a very good job of passing itself off as female. She isn't wearing any clothes, and her hair is so long that it comes all the way down to her ass. She stands there staring at me, still as stone, and I realize that I'm not the least bit afraid, and for a moment that seems more remarkable than whatever has slipped over the windowsill and into my stifling hot bedroom. My heart isn't racing. My mouth hasn't gone dry. The hairs on my arms and the back of my neck are not standing on end.

She takes one step towards the bed, and I start to sit up, but she tells me to be still.

Her voice is like the voice of a night bird.

Her voice is like broken glass.

And thunder.

"Are you death?" I ask, and as soon as the words have left my lips, I wish I'd kept them to myself.

"I don't have to be," she says, and then she says, "Why don't you wait and see?"

Her skin is as pale as milk, and her hair is as black as coal dust.

When her eyes catch the streetlight, they flash back a blue-green iridescence.

"Do you even have a name?" I ask.

"Why don't you wait and see?"

When did I start shifting tense. That's never a good sign. I mean, when I do it by accident like that. It always makes me think of Billy Pilgrim coming unstuck in time. But my memories of that night, they are both past and immediate and, in some sense, they seem almost like a presentiment, all at once.

"Why don't you wait and see?"

What scares you most of all? What scares you more than dying the most horrible death you can imagine, that's the sort of fear I mean. I don't mean what merely frightens you, the way that people are afraid of spiders or germs or failure. I mean something that absolutely fucking terrifies you, like Moses must have felt looking at that burning bush, like that. Maybe I mean awe. Maybe I mean wonder as much as terror, and maybe there really isn't any difference between those things.

What scares me most of all? I won't tell you that...

4.

Only a few days ago, after breakfast, and she's washing up, rinsing the frying pan and plates and placing them inside the dishwasher. I'm sitting at the table by the window (and there is so much to this about windows, I know), smoking and watching her. She made eggs and bacon and toast. She made me eat breakfast, because she knows how often I skip breakfast and lunch. She says I'm losing weight. She says I'm looking thin in the skin. I blow smoke at the ceiling and wonder if there's enough coffee for another cup. She rinses her hands, then shuts off the tap. The air smells like food and cigarettes and dishwashing detergent.

"I've read about the Mütter," she says. "I've never been there, but I've read about it. I've seen pictures. I don't think I'd enjoy the experience."

I balance my cigarette on the edge of a souvenir ashtray shaped like the state of Florida. There's a tiny ceramic alligator perched right about where Jacksonville would be.

"I can't say I did, but I didn't tell her that. I made like I was having a blast, ogling the dead and the maimed, the diseased and the stillborn. Anyway, it's where this whole business started. The hair vampire, I mean."

"You still haven't finished the story."

"No, and I'm starting to think that I won't. It might be one of those I stick in the filing cabinet and leave stuck in the filing cabinet. It's probably one of those I never should have started."

"I can't do that," she says.

"You can't do what," I ask her.

"I can't start something and not finish it. Even if I know I shouldn't have begun it to begin with. I wonder if psychiatrists have invented a phobia for that, for people with a morbid dread of not finishing things?"

"They've invented one for just about everything else."

"So," she says, shutting the door to the dishwasher, "that's the inspiration, the thing in the jar from Romania?" She turns a dial and the machine clatters and makes a loud, wet hissing sound, and she says how one day it's gonna blow up and take the whole damn kitchen with it.

"Have you told your landlord about it?" I ask.

"Only fifty or sixty times," she says. "I don't think fixing my dishwasher is high on his list of priorities."

"Then fuck him," I say, and she laughs and sits down and lights a cigarette of her own. And I say, "Yeah, it was the thing in the jar. And I started in wondering about hair and blood and mosquitoes –"

"Mosquitoes?"

"Think about it," I say. "The diameter of human hair varies from seventeen to one hundred and eighty-one micrometers in diameter. The proboscis of a mosquito, specifically the part called the internal tubular labrum, the part that draws blood when you get bitten, it's about forty to one hundred micrometers in diameter. And the diameter of a human red blood cell is only six point two to eight point two micrometers, with a maximum thickness of maybe one micrometer. If human hairs were hollow –"

"Which they're not."

"But if they *were,*" I say, "if they *were*...well, the average human head has about a hundred thousand hair follicles. Now, hungry mosquitoes can hold about three millionths of a liter of blood, which isn't very impressive, given our bodies hold about five liters. At the rate a mosquito drinks, speaking hypothetically, it would take about two thousand of them a day and a half to completely drain a human body dry. But the hairs on your head, well, that's like *ten* thousand mosquitoes worth of hair, *if* those hairs functioned as hollow proboscides –"

"I think you might be right about the file cabinet. Also, I think it's proboscises, *not* proboscides."

"Look it up," I say, and I tap grey ash at the alligator's feet. "But do you see what I'm getting at, whether it's a dumb idea or not."

"Oh, it's a dumb idea," she says. "It's most definitely a dumb idea."

"I've sold dumber."

"I'm not sure that's something I'd go around bragging about, dear."

5.

"It was a dream," you tell me, and I say no, it wasn't a dream, that I was wide awake, that I'm very sure I was awake, as sure as I'm awake right now and having this conversation, and you say, "Fine, so maybe it was sleep paralysis. Maybe you were waking up, but you couldn't move, because that's what happens during sleep paralysis," and then you start in talking about hallucinations, how people who suffer from sleep paralysis often imagine there's someone in the room with them who isn't, an intruder, someone who isn't supposed to be there. You say how, once upon a time, long ago, people probably would have thought of the intruder as an incubus and a succubus, but now we tend to imagine we're being abducted by little grey aliens from Zeta Reticuli. "I wasn't asleep," I say. "I wasn't even partway asleep, and I could move just fine. I was even able to talk just fine. So, it wasn't sleep paralysis." I realize that I'm starting to sound annoyed. From the look on your face, I might even be starting to sound a little angry, and you say, "Okay, have it your way. There was a woman in your room. She climbed in through the window, like in that Joe Cocker song." I say that in the Joe Cocker song it was a bathroom window, not a bedroom window, then add, "And, anyway, it was a Beatles song. Joe Cocker only covered it." You shrug and tell me you've never heard the Beatles version and that I'm being pedantic, just arguing to hear my own voice, and I say that doesn't change the facts, Ma'am.

What scares you most of all?

I used to think it was dying in a fire, being burned alive. Or being dead but still fully conscious and having to be aware while I was being embalmed and buried and everything.

But now it's something else? Now it's something even worse?

Isn't there always something worse?

Isn't there always?

And you say, "So I used this wire coat hanger that I'd straightened out, which now they say you're not ever supposed to do, because these days all the pipes are shitty PVC and not copper or iron or whatever pipes used to be made from before we started making everything out of fucking plastic. I stuck the wire down the drain and sorta fished about with it for maybe – I don't know – five minutes or so until I finally hooked the clog and could starting pulling it out. Jesus, *that* was nasty. Some of that hair had probably been stuck in there for years, catching toothpaste and little bits of food and dead skin and whatever, right? And turns out, the worst of it wasn't the stench of all that rotting hair. But the worst of it was how the damn sink still wouldn't drain, even after I got all the hair out. Well, all of it I could reach. I could only get the coat hanger in just so far, because of the S-bend or the P-trap or whatever plumbers call it. I think I washed my hands about a hundred times afterwards. I was a regular god-damn Lady Macbeth for the rest of the day."

6.

Silhouetted against the window, silhouetted by the streetlights, her pale skin seems almost luminescent. It reminds me of the moon. *Maybe it's supposed to,* I think. *Maybe that's exactly what it's supposed to do. Maybe she's something the moon sends down whenever it's hungry.*

The woman, the thing that might be a woman, takes a step nearer the bed, and I start to sit up, but then she tells me to be still, to lie there just exactly as I am, and I do as I'm told. I do as she's *told* me to do.

Her voice is like the voice of a night bird.

Her voice is like broken glass.

And thunder rolling across the face of the world.

I've said all these things before. I have spent night after night after night, day after day, saying these things, never coming any nearer to the truth of it, knowing that I never, ever will.

"What if I'm not afraid of you?" I ask her. "What if I'm not afraid of you at all."

"What if you're not?" she asks me, not quite an echo.

"Isn't that what you're for?"

"I don't have to be," she says.

"Then why are you here?"

"Why don't you wait and see?"

I smell flowers then. I think that I smell morning glories, but I can't be sure. The last time I smelled them was when I was a child, and there were morning glories in my mother's garden. The seeds of morning glories can be as potent a hallucinogen as LSD, if you eat enough of them. My mother only warned me they were poisonous.

The air smells like flowers, and I imagine that I can hear thunder.

"I want to know what you are," I say.

"Why do you assume that I would know?"

"Don't you?"

"Why don't you wait and see?"

She's very close to the bed now, very close to the foot of the bed, and she reaches out with her left hand and gently touches my belly, but that's impossible, unless her arms are much, much longer than they seem. Her hand is cold, but not yet *ice* cold. On these hot nights, I sleep above the covers because it's too hot to sleep beneath them, so all she had to do was reach out farther than she should have been able to reach and touch my bare skin. All she had to do is touch me, only she's still too far away. Her fingers trace a circle around my navel.

"Why, my dear, you're burning up," she says. "I always forget that part. I always forget that there's so much heat. Sometimes, I have even forgotten what warmth is."

"If I told you to leave, would you have to go?" I ask, and my voice doesn't sound even the least bit afraid.

"Is that what you want? For me to leave?"

I don't answer the question, because I honestly don't know the answer. Maybe that's exactly what I wanted when I first saw her standing by the open window, but it seems like that must have been hours and hours ago now. Her index finger draws a line through the sweat on my abdomen, all the way up to my breasts, and I can't help but suspect that she's looking for something. And I wonder if it's my heart, and I wonder if it's my soul, and I wonder if it's only the memory of something she's lost. Her cool finger is as good as any plough, splitting open the rough sod of me, digging invisible furrows in fallow meat, not like anyone was using it for anything, anyway, not like I haven't been sleepwalking through the years leading up to this sweltering August night. *Maybe she knows what I'm for,* I think. *Maybe she'll tell me, and so maybe, finally, I'll know, too.* It occurs to me that she can hear every word I'm thinking, and I'm surprised that I really don't care. After all, doesn't that make it all so much easier, that at last there's no need to talk or to type or to worry over correct syntax?

Maybe she knows what I'm for.

Why don't you wait and see?

Her hands are colder now.

I ought to shiver, but I don't. I only close my eyes.

She climbs on top of me, and the cold that wears her like a mask becomes a living presence, not a part of her, a being unto itself, and I can hear the whisper of snowfall and the splitting apart of ice on a frozen river and the almost imperceptible bone-deep rumble of a glacier grinding its slow path between mountains and down to the sea. I wonder what will be left of me when she's done, if there will be any more than the dust that a glacier makes of the hardest granite.

In the heart of a blizzard, a woman is lost and wandering alone.

Is that you?

I don't know anymore. It might have been almost anyone. It's an old and evil memory, and you shouldn't dwell on it. You shouldn't have even seen it.

The woman in the blizzard has long black hair, hair as black as coal, and the wind whips it into fantastical, impossible shapes.

Once, I saw something awful in a museum.

I know, she whispers somewhere deep inside my head, between the secret convolutions of my brain. I open my eyes again, and I gaze up at her face and all that hair, hair blown about her face by a wind that brings winter wherever she goes, a wind that is a dying woman's remembrance of the storm that lured her out into the snow, that got her so turned about she could never find her way home again. The storm that took her life. She leans down to kiss my lips, and I still smell morning glories. She leans down to kiss me, and I wonder how long it will take, and if there will be anything at all left when she's finished. I think these thoughts as black hair flows over and into me, searching and probing and piercing my skin like the needle mouths of hundreds and thousands of starving mosquitoes, seeking warmth, and – lost and alone and drifting through the cold, howling heart of a blizzard – any warmth at all will do.

MERCY BROWN

What I said earlier about me and vampire stories? Well, here's another one. The idea of a "hair vampire" occurred to me one night, and, try as I might, I could not drive it from my mind. It was simultaneously so horrible and so funny, I had to use it in a story. To my knowledge, it's nothing anyone has done before me. But I might be wrong. "Mercy Brown" was written between November 22nd and November 29th, 2019.

The Great Bloody and Bruised Veil of the World

Driving too fast, even if the roads are dry and even if the sky is clear and blue. Even if the sky is without even one single merciful cloud, razor blue, blistering blue, and the late spring Alabama sun good as summer shining down. Driving too fast, because I'm not sober, and I can at least pretend it's possible to run from myself, even if I'm right here next to me all the time. Hardly an hour now since the phone call. "Didn't you know? Jesus, I thought you knew. I thought… I thought…I thought…" And so now I am not sober and racing over the steep, winding mountain roads, roads too steep, curves too sharp, sharp as the blue of the sky. It crosses my mind that maybe I have not been this careless since high school, and certainly I have not been this careless since college. Oh, I *was* careless, once upon a time, before I had my hands slapped sufficiently and frequently enough by consequence to learn better. I was reckless, and now I am a reckless driver, running from herself along this two-lane black band laced between the tall green trees, between the pine and oak and maple and sycamore and between those places where Eisenhower-era road crews sliced cruelly into and straight through the bones of the mountain most of a century ago to expose banded brown and yellow and terra-cotta sandstone and oil-dark beds of shale. I rush past a small lake, and the water glimmers in the sun. The water looks hot, even though it's hardly May. The water looks like you could fry an egg on it. And suddenly all this wilderness seems wilder than I remember. Used to, I knew these roads and woods like the back of my hand. Like I know my mother's face. But I grew up and moved away, and I let the city convince me I was someone else, someone who'd never been born and raised in these low Appalachian foothills. I cleaned up nice. I told people I was from someplace else than here, that I was from Memphis, because that sounded good to me without seeming to stretch the truth *too* far. My knuckles are white, and in my hands the steering wheel feels like a weapon. "I swear, I thought you knew. I wouldn't have *said* anything if I hadn't." I spare half a glance at the speedometer, and it says I'm doing fifty miles an hour, and that hardly even seems possible. Not on these roads. I'm not that good a driver. I'm not that reckless. But there's the speedometer and the blur of the advancing, retreating landscape on the other side of the windshield. The smear of the world, all but the sky that cannot be smeared by mere speed. *I can slow down now. I can slow down and maybe pull over somewhere and try to clear my head.* I think that thought, but then I answer myself, *No, no I can't. I'm not even half that far away. I'm haven't gone even half that far, half that fast. Just shut up and drive. I'll tell you when to slow down.* "I'm sorry. I fucking swear I thought you knew." The sun off the road and off a glimmering, glittering lake and off the hood of the car. You could fry an egg. You could boil water. The wheels whine and burr on the asphalt beneath me, beneath this magic carpet of steel and chrome and rubber and glass, and for an instant or two

I'm back in the apartment, still holding the receiver, staring at the window and whatever was outside the window. I can still hear someone apologizing, because she *thought I knew.* "I didn't know," I tell her. "I guess I ought to have, but I didn't." And before she can say anything more I hang up, before the sister of my all-at-once ex-lover can apologize even one more time, have my keys in my hand and I'm out the door and down the steps and now I'm driving this back-road country highway where I might as well be the only driver on the face of the Earth. And I drag myself with me, and I drag that phone call with me, 'cause like the man said, no matter where you go, there you fucking are. Outside the car, the woods briefly give way to hilly, weedy pasture on both sides of the road, tall grass and the heavy white heads of Queen Anne's lace. Stranded there behind strands of rusted barbed wire there are five or six or seven obligatory cows, black as the pavement, dumb as hindsight. None of them even bother to lift their heads and watch me race past. Maybe reckless drivers come this way all the goddamn time. Maybe I'm as commonplace a sight out here as crows and copperheads. I can only partway believe that I ever belonged to this place, that vanished, wiped-away me, that fictionalized into nonexistence me. The pasture ends and the green shadows of forest take me back. And that's better. Not so much sky now. Somehow the sky feels like the phone call and the voice at the other end of the line. I can no more argue with the razor blue sky than I could have argued with the phone. I pass a tiny church and a tiny graveyard, a tiny plot of plastic flowers bleached pale by the sun, a few of those graves going all the way back to the Civil War, and my foot gets just a little heavier on the gas pedal. I have people buried there. And it occurs to me for the first time that maybe I'm trying to kill myself. It would be easier than going back. It would be easier than having to work past all the shit I'm going to have to work past. It would be easier, but almost anything would. It occurs to me that one of these hairpin curves will be just a little too tight, or I'll have a blow out, or I could take matters into my own hands and aim for the trunk of any one of these too convenient, thoughtful trees. And then there would be no more sky pressing down on me and no more phone call and no more feeling like a fool because I *should* have known, shouldn't I? The easy way out is the coward's way out, and right now who gives a rat's ass. But already the ugly fantasies of suicide are growing small and indistinct in my rearview mirror. Mind you, it's not that I lack the nerve or the resolve. It's not that I'm above that sort of thing, but, all the same, I'm easing back on the accelerator just a little, just a tad, as the road begins to ascend the next twisting incline, the next ridge dividing one narrow, stream-carved valley from another. My mouth is dry and tastes like aluminum foil or pennies or blood. My heart is John Henry's hammer pounding in my chest, and my head is filled up to bursting with telephone voices. "I wouldn't have *said* anything if I hadn't. If I hadn't thought you knew. Jesus, I'm so sorry, Ellie. I'm so, so, *so* sorry." *I'm sure you are. I'm sure that's exactly what you are.* And I might actually have said that, words tinged with acid and broken glass, or I might have said nothing at all. Only hung up. Only put the receiver back into its cradle and reached for my keys and the bottle of Jack I keep in a writing-desk drawer and...I honestly do not recall stopping the car, except now I have stopped, though the engine is still running. A dusty cloud of rust-brown, rust-red dust swirls about everything. I also don't remember putting the car into park or killing the engine or taking my foot off the brake, but those three things, too. I shut my eyes a moment, pushing back against the voices and all that momentum and all that cold, hard *fact.* When I open them again, I see the forest around me has burned, and not so very long ago. I don't remember the green trees and kudzu turning into this wasteland of scorch and soot and charcoal branches stark against the stark blue sky. I reach for the whiskey bottle, there on the seat next to me, as if more of the same will clear my drunken head. Drown and find sobriety. I screw off the cap and swallow a mouthful of fire. And that's when I see the kid, standing at the side of the road, only a few feet ahead of me. The dust and grit swirls about her, and she's staring straight at me. I screw the cap back on the bottle of Jack and set it in the floorboard, and I open the car door, and the whole world out there smells like the aftermath of conflagration. I almost gag on it, the smell is so dense, so all consuming, so complete. The car's engine pops and clicks, cooling down, metal contracting, and I squint through the dust at the girl. She's wearing jeans and a dirty yellow blouse with tiny blue flowers and her hair is the color of a rabbit. She isn't wearing shoes. She squints back at me and raises her left hand to shield her eyes from the bright afternoon sun.

And then everything *stops.*

The mad, pell-mell, headlong rush from the city through the suburbs to these woods, to the side of this mountain, it all *stops,* as if someone's slipped a monkey wrench into the conveyer belt of time and space, and for an instant I think maybe I'll tumble ass over tits, caught off guard, *me* still moving forward in a blur of blind fucking determination when the rest of everything has gone back to its normal, grinding pace. For an instant, I see myself lying in the terracotta dirt and grey limestone gravel, staring up at myself.

"You okay, lady?" the girl calls out to me.

"Yeah, I'm okay," I call back to her.

"For a second, I thought you was gonna run me over, you was going so fast. I thought maybe you was gonna run me down. You sure you're okay?" And the twang and the drawl in her voice, the bad grammar, that was me, thirty years ago, and so possibly she isn't anything more than a ghost, which means possibly she isn't anything more than a memory.

"I should be asking if *you're* okay," I tell her, and then I rub at my eyes while the dust settles around us, and I try not to choke on the burning smell.

"Oh, I'm just fine," she replies. "I'm right as rain."

"What happened here?" I ask her. "The fire, I mean." And I stop rubbing my eyes and stare at the devastation. She shrugs her thin shoulders, and I think how she can't be older than eight or nine, and I wonder how far away her house might be, how far she's walked from home so that I might have almost, as she's put it, run her over.

"I reckon it was lightning," she says. "But maybe it somebody set it on purpose. Maybe someone threw a cigarette butt out a car window. Sometimes people ain't careful. And sometimes they're just plain jackasses."

I wonder if I sounded that adult at only eight or nine years old. I wonder how long it's been now since I actually spoke to a child, so how would I know how they sound.

"But I'm betting it was lightning," she says.

The trees are still smoldering, the scorched upright trunks and the fallen logs, and I try to remember how long since there was a thunderstorm. Seems like ages ago.

"You wanna see something?" she asks me.

"I don't know," I say, suddenly feeling ill and self-conscious and all too aware of how drunk I am. "What sort of a something is it?"

"I'm not sure," she says. "Something the fire got at, something that got almost burnt up. At first I thought it was just a deer, but it ain't. You might know what it is, though. You might have seen one before."

"Is it an animal?" I ask her. "Is it some sort of animal," and then I spit because there's grit in my mouth, all that dust and grit stirred up by my tires, and there's also the harsh, dry taste of the fire.

"Maybe," says the girl. "Maybe it's an animal. It's sure something. Like I said already, I thought it was a deer, but it ain't."

"Well, I really don't know very much about animals," I say, wiping at my mouth, trying to walk in a straight line, walk like someone who doesn't have a bellyful of bourbon and grief and not much else, still trying to remember stopping and pulling over here and trying, too, not to smell what the fire has done to the side of the mountain.

"Well, I do," says the girl. "I know lots about the animals round here. This one time, I had a baby raccoon for a pet, but it got loose and run off. So, I know about animals. But this one, it's almost all burnt up, so whatever it is, I figure it don't look right no more. Whatever it was, I mean." A pause, a heartbeat, the dull pounding at my temples, and then she adds, "You been drinking."

I don't see any point trying to deny it.

"Yeah," I say, "I've been drinking."

"Yeah," says the girl. "I thought so."

She almost smiles then. It's *not* a smile, but I don't know what else to call the expression on her face. She impatiently waves me forward with her left hand, like she has someplace important to be today, and don't I know that, isn't that obvious? Do I think she can afford to squander the whole afternoon on me? I feel a little sick. Nauseous. My stomach rolls. I tell myself it's the bourbon and the smell of the burned woods, and then I follow her to the spot where she found the dead thing.

And then I wish that I hadn't.

Over here, the smell of the fire is compounded by the stink of rot, the sweet cloy of decay.

"You *see* what I mean," she says, not asking, telling me, because it's probably plain as day, just to look at me, that I have no idea what the creature in the shallow ditch at the side of road might have been, lying there cradled in wilted polk weed and seared blackberry briers. It's half curled into a ball that makes me think of a pillbug or an armadillo, like if maybe a pillbug or an armadillo tried to curl into its defensive position but only made it partway. Or, instead, I could say that the thing's curled fetal. Sure, that works, too. *Maybe it was the heat made it draw up like that,* I think.

"I was just walking along, minding my own business," the girl tells me, "and then there it was, and I was just standing here staring at it when you came along and almost run me over."

I start to say, *I wouldn't have hit you. I wasn't going that fast.* But I don't. I know that it would be a lie.

"It sure ain't no deer," she says.

"No," I agree. "It isn't a deer."

"That's what I thought it was at first. Probably 'cause it's so big and all, and there ain't nothing gets that big in these woods but a deer. Bobcats and coyotes don't get that big, and we don't have any bears left around here no more, and, besides, it ain't no bear neither."

No, but it looks a little bit more like a bear than a deer.

"I poked at it with a stick," she says, "but nothing happened."

"I'm pretty sure it's past minding if someone pokes it with a stick."

"I reckon you're probably right," says the girl in the dirty yellow blouse with the tiny blue flowers. Up close, I can see that most of the dirt is soot, that the flowers are embroidered. And that there's almost as much soot on her face as her clothes. Also, her bare feet are entirely black, as if she took a shortcut through the burned forest to reach the road and never mind if the ashes are still hot. As far as I know, that's exactly what she did.

I take another step towards the dead thing, and the briers snag at the legs of my pants and the ground is unexpectedly soft beneath my feet. The closer I get, the worse it smells.

"Lady, I don't know if I'd do that if I was you," says the girl.

"I just want a better look."

"I don't know about you, but I can see it just fine from here," she says.

"I'm pretty sure it's dead," I tell her.

"You never know. Sometimes they ain't. Like an ol' hognose snake, flipping over to show you its belly. Like a possum playing possum. Some things, they just pretend."

Whatever it is, there in the ditch, it's definitely not playing possum. There are maggots where its eyes should be and a hole in its gut big enough I could easily slip my fist inside. Hardly an inch of it isn't charred dark and crisp as a pork butt on an open-pit grill, and that mental image makes my stomach roll again.

"Why was you drinking, anyway?" the girl asks me.

If I hadn't thought you knew.

I wouldn't have said anything...

I shrug, but don't answer her. It's easier to stand here in the weeds and stare at the burned thing. I imagine it in agony, trying to escape the inferno, crawling as far as this ditch before it couldn't crawl any farther, lying here and cooking alive. It's covered in singed auburn hair, except where the hair seems to have been burned away entirely.

"Well, you must'a had a reason," the girl says.

"It *might* be a bear," I say.

"It ain't a bear, 'cause hunters killed all the bears round here a long time ago when my grandpa was still a boy, and, anyway, it ain't got no claws. It's just got fingers. So it ain't no bear."

And she's right. It doesn't have claws. It has fingers. It has fingers that almost look human. It doesn't have paws, either. I look down at my hands, then I look back at the dead thing.

"Mostly, I think people don't drink in the middle of the day unless they got a reason," she says, "unless they're just drunks. I got an uncle like that, and I got an aunt like that, too. They're married. To each other, I mean."

I turn my head and glance back at the girl. She's looking at my car, instead of at the creature in the ditch. She's scowling a scowl that would do any cartoon schoolmarm proud.

"I've had a rough day," I tell her, like it's any of her business. "That's why I've been drinking. I've had a rough day."

"Must'a been a pretty rough day," she says.

"Rough enough," I tell her, then look at the ditch again. The dead thing hasn't moved. Its lips were either burned away or have been eaten by scavengers, and I can see its teeth. They glisten wetly in the bright sun shining down from that razor blue sky.

"D'you get fired?" she asks.

"No," I reply.

"Well, then, did your boyfriend leave you? Or your husband?"

And I almost say, *No, not my boyfriend, my girlfriend. My girlfriend left me.*

"Something like that," I tell her, and there's a sudden, dull stab in my chest, a pointless dull pang of guilt or shame or regret or what-the-fuck-ever because I feel like I have to lie to this filthy hillbilly brat about my lover. About who and what I am. Because I'm not in the mood to try and explain. I'm not in the mood for her disapproval.

"I sorta thought that's what it was," she says, and for just a moment I want to strangle her and leave her corpse beside the corpse of the thing in the ditch.

"You from the city?" she asks.

"Yeah."

"I ain't never been to Birmingham. I figure I'll go someday, though."

"It's not that far from here," I tell her. I'm starting to think that I'm actually going to be sick. Even so, I look from the girl back at the dead thing. The smell is almost palpable.

"Did he hurt you?" she wants to know.

"Did who hurt me?"

"Your husband. Or boyfriend. Whichever he was. Did he hurt you?"

I squeeze the space between my nostrils and my upper lip between my left thumb and forefinger, because someone once told me it would keep you from puking. I squeeze so hard it makes my eyes water. But it doesn't do my stomach any good whatsoever.

"No," I tell the girl, and I stop squeezing. My lip feels numb now.

"Was it another woman?" she asks.

I wouldn't have said *anything if I hadn't. If I hadn't thought you knew. Jesus...*

I wouldn't have said anything.

"I'd rather not talk about it," I reply.

"My momma, she says it's good to talk about whatever's bothering us, whatever's paining us. She says she saw that on *The Oprah Winfrey Show.*"

"How long were you standing here before I came along?" I ask her.

"Not long," she says, "but I ain't got a watch, so I ain't exactly sure. Ten minutes. Maybe ten minutes. Just a little while. I poked it with a stick, then I threw the stick away, 'cause I thought maybe there might be germs, like rabies or something."

The thing in the ditch is at least as big as a black bear. Its teeth are sharp and look like antique ivory, like century-old piano keys. I peer up at the scorched trees, at the painfully blue and cloudless sky.

"You live close to here?" I ask the girl.

"Not far," she tells me. "Just over the ridge and down the holler. Not very far."

"Your parents know where you are?" I ask.

"They don't mind," she says, which isn't exactly an answer.

"I can give you a ride, if you need one." I glance back at her, and she's watching me, same way she was watching my car. Suspiciously.

"You been drinking," she says. "Not sure Momma would want me in the car with someone who's been drinking. But thank you all the same."

"Okay," I say. "I just thought I should offer."

And then she comes and stands next to me and we both stare at the thing in the ditch between the ribbon of asphalt and the burned woods. Its hands (not paws) are curled. Its fingers (not claws), those are curled, too. Its feet are hidden in a tangle of blackberry, so I'm not sure what they look like, if maybe the toes are curled, as well.

"I read this book one time about werewolfs," she says.

"Werewol*ves,*" I correct her.

"Werewolves," she says. "I read this book one time about them. My father has some books from when he was in the Navy, and one was about werewolfs. And my grandmama, she believes in ghosts and haints and witches and stuff. There's a cave up on the ridge where you can hear a woman crying when there's a full moon. That's what she told me. Not a real woman, but the ghost of a real woman."

"I ought to be going," I tell the girl. "If you're okay, if you can make it back home alone, I ought to be going."

"I'm fine," she says, "but you don't look so hot."

I'm about to tell her I'm fine, too, but then I'm vomiting into the brambles and polk weed, and I'm standing at the desk with the phone in my hand, and I'm racing along a winding mountain road. I'm being pressed between the earth and sky like a dead rose.

"See? That's what I thought," the girl says. "Well, better out than in."

I puke until I'm just dry heaving, and then I spit and wipe my mouth on the back of my hand.

"You feel better now?" she asks me.

I nod my head. "A little," I tell her, and at least that much isn't a lie. I wonder what I might have thrown up besides my breakfast and all that Jack Daniel's. "But I think maybe I should sit down a minute." I turn away from the dead thing and sit in the gravel at the side of the road. I realize there's red mud and soot on my shoes and beggar lice on my pants. I pick one off and flick it away. The girl leans over and picks a black-eyed Susan that escaped the fire, and then she hands it to me. She's not scowling anymore. She's doing that not-exactly-smiling trick, instead.

"Thank you," I say, and I sniff the flower, out of habit, to be polite, because I don't know what else I should do. At least it's something to smell besides the rot and ashes and my own vomit.

"You're welcome," she says. "I figured you could use some cheering up." Then she sits down next to me and starts tossing bits of gravel at the dead thing.

"If you're gonna drink some more," she says, "best wait till you get back home."

"Okay. But I don't think I'm gonna drink any more."

"I'm just saying, that's all," and she tosses another bit of gravel. "I seen some awful car wrecks up here because of people getting drunk and driving drunk. I seen cars just about wrapped all the way around trees, and I seen broken glass scattered all over the road like a thousand sparkling diamonds. I even saw a body, this one time. So I'm just saying."

"I should go," I tell her, and the girl nods.

"Me, too," she says. I realize she hasn't told me her name. I don't ask, because I haven't told her mine, either.

I stand up and dust off the seat of my jeans.

"You be careful," I tell her and look at the thing in the ditch one last time.

"I will," she says. "I always am."

And then I walk back to my car with the black-eyed Susan and open the door and get in. The windows were all rolled up, so it's gotten hot in there, just in the fifteen minutes or so I was standing with the girl. I twist the key in the ignition and switch on the AC, and when I look up and out through the windshield, the girl's already walking away, filthy black feet and that flowered blouse, already disappearing back into the burned woods, and I shift the car out of park and into drive. My mouth tastes like bile and whiskey, and I roll down the window and spit a couple more times before I pull away and continue on up the mountain. Overhead, the sky marks my every movement, my every smallest, most insignificant action. And I wonder if I'll sleep tonight, and I wonder, if I do, whether I'll dream about the phone call or you or the child and roasted monsters lying dead at the side of the road.

THE GREAT BLOODY AND BRUISED VEIL OF THE WORLD

This is a strange one, even for me. It almost feels to me like a Dancy Flammarion story in which Dancy never actually makes an appearance, where the barefoot girl who walks out of the burned forest stands in as her surrogate (and, for that matter, "Virginia Story" strikes me the same way, now that I think about it, only in "Virginia Story" Dancy's surrogate is the eight-fingered hitchhiker). Apparently, upon finishing "The Great Bloody and Bruised Veil of the World" I felt unusually insecure about the story, as evidenced by an email exchange with Sonya Taaffe. I'd asked her to read it, and she replied (4/27/20):

It's not stylistically or sensorily insubstantial at all; the inciting event of the conversation with the ex-girlfriend's sister is a lacuna ("I thought you knew"), but the details of the drive are crowdingly rich and immediate and so are the intrusive hints of the narrator's past and although it's a werewolf story, or maybe a werewolf story, the thing that's maybe a werewolf isn't a version you've written before (it's vivid for being dead) and the question of whether the girl by the side of the road really is some kind of echo of the narrator or just a girl who found a weird burned thing is irrelevant to the conversation and would probably diminish the story if cleared up either way. It's a good sideswipe of a wrong thing and it happens to a person who feels real in eleven pages. It reminded me a little of "Interstate Love Song," I think just because of the sense-of-place Southernness of it. If written in Rhode Island, this story would have been quite different.

The story is set along Mimosa Road in Dunnavant, Alabama, very near where my maternal grandparents lived when I was a kid, where I helped fight a terrible forest fire when I was fourteen years old (see "The Burning," *Cambrian Tales*). This is the first story I wrote after the beginning of the COVID-19 pandemic. It was written between April 19th and April 25th, 2020.

©LOCKE 2021

Untitled 41

1.

I open the red door and stand alone at the threshold, which may serve as a symbol for many things. And you lie alone in our bed, which is surely a metaphor for many, many more things yet. I am dreaming, or I am awake, and I know that, ultimately, it hardly matters which. Though, if I am awake, the logic of dreams has spilled out into the waking world, disgorged, coughed up by our unhelpful, unconscious selves. The air in the bedroom smells of the accumulated leaf litter of a hundred autumns, a hundred or a thousand, leaves that will crackle and crunch underfoot if I dare take one footstep towards you, which, of course, I will. The air is cool and dry, crisp as a ripe apple, and it smells of spices to which I cannot put names. The walls and the floors are golden and chocolate brown and the brilliant scarlet of swamp maples and the yellow-orange of dried tangerine peels. The high ceiling is the pale, bottomless blue of an October sky, dappled with only the scattered veils of cirrus clouds. Someone has taken great care in dressing this room, or it is only the doing of my sleeping mind. I've already said it does not matter which. There isn't a single piece of furniture in the room except the bed, as good as something from a child's tale of fairies and witches and dark forests that run on and on forever. The bed itself, I'll liken that to a funeral barge, beached here by some strange receded flood, washed up and stranded here in an autumn trapped between these walls. Four tall posts carved from cherry wood, carved with the images of hungry, writhing things and supporting the naked tester; there are no tasteful, concealing draperies hung on the canopy rails. That would be a mercy, and there is nothing here of mercy. The bedclothes are the colorless color of spider silk and cold spring water. My heart is racing, and I taste pennies or aluminum foil. I can smell my sweat, and I tell myself that I can turn around, even now, and simply walk away. I tell myself it was incautious, opening the door and looking inside the room. I tell myself that, if I turn away, this dream will become some other and less somber, less sorrowful dream. I tell myself that if I am, instead, awake, then the pantomime will end and you will scold me for ruining all our careful preparations – and that wouldn't be so bad, not really. But I don't turn away. I don't turn and shut the door again. Because there you are, nude and paler even than the colorless linen, tinted that way by death or only with skillfully applied greasepaint. I am thinking how I'm beginning to find more annoyance than comfort in not knowing if we are dreaming (or just I am dreaming or it's only you) or if this a game we've staged, when a third possibly occurs to me: the room may be exactly as I perceive it and no illusion of any sort, and you may be as dead as you appear to be. Every other scenario I conjure might be nothing more substantial than a defense against the truth I'm trying to hide from myself. I close my eyes, suddenly terribly afraid there might be some reason that I've forgotten for having opened the red door, for being here on autumn's threshold, some purpose that contained the only possibility of your salvation. What if Prince Charming forgot why he'd searched out Sleeping Beauty? What if the woodcutter forgot there was a living girl trapped in the belly of the wolf? What if, and what if, and what if, and what if, and what if? I open my eyes again and step, finally, into the room, and I pull the door shut behind me. Call that commitment or call it foolhardiness, six of one, half dozen of the other. The latch clicks, a sharp, insectile sound, and I take my hand off the brass knob. You haven't moved. You're as still as midwinter, here in this dreaming or waking temple to autumn, to all autumns that ever have been. I want to speak. I would say, "Open your eyes. This isn't funny anymore. It isn't clever, and we should stop it right now, whatever it is we're doing here." I want to tell you that I've had enough, and, if nothing else, that might at least wake me up. Or wake you, which would accomplish the same end. Maybe it should scare me to think that I may be nothing more than your dream of a woman and nothing at all flesh and blood and bone, but it doesn't. I think there are countless worse things than being only a dream in the mind of the one you love, especially when she seems to lie mute and dead before you. I want to say, "I've seen enough," but I don't. I don't say anything at all. Instead, I take another step nearer the bed, and all those leaves crunch loudly underfoot, and I disturb a small snake that slithers away beneath the bed, vanishing into the clusters of mushrooms that sprout unmolested in its shadow, great rubbery toadstools and the white-speckled caps of fly agaric, red as the door I've closed behind me. Also, there are woody bracket fungi growing from the footboard and from the vertical columns of the bed. I look down and kick at the blanket of fallen leaves, meaning to find the floorboards beneath, but finding only more leaves. I kick again, and now I've exposed dark, loamy soil and wriggling earthworms, or I only imagine that I have. I realize that I can hear birds, and I wonder if I've been hearing them all along. I wonder if tucked away beneath the leaves there is a machine playing recorded birdsongs. *Which of us ever thought this was a good idea?* I wonder to myself, but only to myself. I stop staring down at the leaves beneath my bare feet and look at the bed again. I look at you again.

2.

"The old, dark house," you said, and I said, "That's a movie, you know, a James Whale film. He was the same man who directed *Frankenstein* and *The Bride of Frankenstein.*" So then you wanted to know what I'd meant by that, *what* is a movie, and I replied "*The Old Dark House* is a movie. You've never seen it?" You frowned and glared at me through cigarette smoke, and you said, "I'm not going to tell it if you're going to be like that. If you're going to be like that, I'm better off just keeping it to myself." I should probably have apologized; instead, I asked you, "Be like what?" Even though I knew perfectly well what you meant. When you didn't answer me, I said, "No, no. Go on. I want to hear it. I really do. I promise I won't interrupt you again." Still no apology in there, but I have never much been one for apologies, not if they can be avoided. Too many people apologize too freely, I have always thought. Too many people make the most casual expressions of apologies. You took a drag on your cigarette, then set it down on the rim of the ceramic ashtray there on the table between us; lead-grey smoke leaked slowly from your nostrils, and I imagined you as a dragon trapped in human form. I imagined you as a steam automaton, but I kept these imaginings to myself and lit a cigarette of my own. You were drunk, and I was drunker, and I had just told you a ghost story – or something sort of like a ghost story – that my mother had told me when I was a girl. Afterwards, you'd said that once, when you were a teenager, you'd seen a ghost, or something that might have been a ghost. I'd wanted to hear the story, and "Sure," you'd said. "Sure, but only if you swear you won't laugh." So, I promised. I promised and even crossed my heart, a child's show of sincerity that seemed perfectly suited to this swapping of adolescent spook tales. "Go on," I prompted. "Well," you said, "that's just what we called it, the old, dark house. It had belonged to a woman whose name I can't remember. Shit, I probably forgot her name a decade ago. She'd taught tenth-grade English lit there in Charleston, but had died when I was still in elementary school, I think. Her husband was killed in France in World War II. Anyway, her house, it was this great, rambling affair, almost like something right out of a Charles Addams cartoon, and it was surrounded by a low stone wall and by four or five really enormous live oak trees. Those trees must have been at least two hundred years old, and their limbs bent almost down to the ground and were draped with Spanish moss and scabbed with resurrection ferns. Everywhere in the yard there were plaster animals, in the front and in the backyard, a plaster menagerie arranged all around the house. A whole Noah's ark of plaster animals. After she'd died, her children had let the house sit empty. Maybe they'd tried to sell it, but couldn't. Whatever the case, all those animals were left right where she'd put them." And even though I'd sworn not to interrupt again, sworn and crossed my heart, I said "That sounds plenty creepy enough, without a ghost in the bargain. I think those animals would have been enough to keep me away." You retrieved your cigarette from the ashtray and just sat quietly smoking for a moment, staring at the tabletop, so I wasn't sure if you were angry at me for cutting in or were just trying to recall some detail of the story. "Actually, I always sort of loved them," you said. "They seemed almost magical, the way very ordinary things can seem magical to a kid. It felt to me like they were guarding the house, keeping it safe from the world or whatever.

Amazingly, no one ever stole any of the plaster animals or smashed them or anything like that. Year after year, they went unmolested. Some of them had started crumbling from the rain, and their paint was faded and peeling, but no one messed with them." I asked if you wanted another beer, and you hesitated, rubbed your eyes, then said yeah, sure, you'd have maybe just one more, so I got up and went to the refrigerator. "Where's the ghost come in?" I wanted to know, and you answered, "You're really bad at this whole not-interrupting thing, has anyone ever told you that?" I agreed that I was, and I opened the two bottles of beer and returned to my chair. You took a long swallow, then went on. "One night," you said, "on a dare, I climbed over the wall, into the yard with all the plaster animals. I knew this boy who claimed he'd seen blue lights moving around in the house at night, and I'd called him a liar. Which is when he dared me to go see for myself if I was so sure he wasn't telling the truth. He bet me twenty-five bucks I was too scared to go up to the porch and look into a window. I doubt he actually had the twenty-five bucks, but I did it, anyway. We waited until after dark, and then he drove me over to the house – he was older and already had his license – and I scaled the wall, walked past a couple of plaster elephants and donkeys and a giraffe that had been painted pink with blue polka dots. I walked underneath those live oak trees and right up onto the front porch." Here, I set down my bottle, and I asked whether you'd been scared. "Maybe a little bit," you admitted. "But I did believe that he was lying about seeing the blue ghost lights. I thought it was just an empty, old house. The only thing to be afraid of was maybe stepping through a rotten porch board in the dark and breaking my ankle. I didn't even look back to see if he was watching me. I could hear his car engine idling, so I knew he hadn't driven off. I went up to the front door and I almost knocked. I don't know why, but I almost did. And then I looked through a window." You stop and take a final drag from your cigarette before crushing it out in the ashtray. "So, what did you see?" I ask, too impatient to let you get to it in your own good time and in your own way. You look at me, and then you look down at your hands, folded in your lap. "I saw a woman," you tell me. "I saw a dead woman lying on a bed, surrounded by fallen leaves."

3.

This next part *is* a dream, beyond any doubt, and I will take whatever stingy measure of comfort I can from that certainty. You and I are together in a boat, some small sort of rowboat. I don't know much about boats, neither awake nor asleep, so I don't know if there's a name for *this* sort of boat. The boat is wide and squared off at both ends, not narrow and sleek, like a canoe. There is a tangle of old fishnets at my feet and a rusty green tool box. The boat has oars and oarlocks, and with your strong arms you are rowing the boat, dragging it across the surface of a wide, still lake. Except for the disturbance from the oars dipping into the water and rising out again, faintly splashing, and except for the boat's faint wake, the lake is mirror smooth. It's so clear that, when I look over the side, I can see straight down to the bottom, twenty or fifty or a hundred feet below, a blue-green tinted world of drowned logs and boulders and the darting silver bodies of small fish. And all around the lake there is autumn. The colors of the trees are so bright that they might be a bonfire. I look up at the very blue sky, and there are hardly any clouds at all. The air isn't quite cold, but it's cool enough that I wish I had a sweater. Neither one of us says anything. You paddle. I watch you paddle, and I watch the autumn world spread out all around us. After a while, and not a very long while, we reach the shore, and

I follow you out of the boat and into the blazing forest, up a steep hill and another steep hill after that. "Where are we going?" I ask, and I think this is the first time that either one of us has spoken a word in the dream. You glance over your shoulder at me, frowning slightly that I can't be more patient, that I can't enjoy the not knowing, the waiting to see. I'm startled suddenly by how young you look. Just since we got out of the little rowboat, you seem to have grown younger, and seeing you so young, I feel like an old woman. "It's not what you think," you say. When I ask, "What's not what I think?" you reply, "None of it. None of it is what you think it might be." We are both barefoot, and the carpet of fallen leaves crackles and crunches loudly with our every step. The only other thing I hear besides the leaves is the cawing of crows. I can't see them, but I can hear them plainly enough. I have never liked crows, though I don't know if I could explain why. Maybe it's only because they eat carrion. "I want to know where you're taking me," I say, and as soon as I've said it I wish that I hadn't, because I sound frightened, and I hate sounding afraid. I hate letting anyone hear fear in my voice. I'm not as brave as you. I never have been. I've never been the sort of woman to take dares or risks or to gamble. I've never walked past plaster animals in the night and climbed the front steps of an old dark house. "Why is it that you've never liked the fall?" you ask me, instead of answering my question. I don't have to think very long on my reply. "It's always reminded me of dying," I tell you. "October and November are the dying months, aren't they? Aren't they the year's long, withering sigh, the terminal illness before the death of winter?" The land is growing rockier the higher we go, grey limestone boulders crusted with moss and lichens and the flat green scales of liverworts. I look back the way we've come, back through the tall trees to the lake, and the hills seem to have grown steeper, as if maybe they'd leveled off just a little to ease our passage, but, now that we've passed, are becoming their old precipitous selves again. "It isn't death," you say. "It's only sleep. You might as well be afraid of going to bed every night." And I tell you, "Well, maybe I am." Then you're not with me anymore. I'm climbing the hills alone, and I wonder if I was always alone. I wonder if it was me who rowed the boat across the still lake, and I only was pretending you were there with me, because I dislike being alone even worse than I dislike autumn. I walk a little faster, not wanting to be caught out after dark in these woods. *But,* I tell myself, *for all I know, these woods go on forever, and you'll never find the end of them, no matter how fast you walk.* The crows are louder now than before, and when I look up into the trees I can see them perched on the branches, dozens of them, black as pitch, their dark eyes gazing down at me. *It's only a dream,* I remind myself again. *And even if it weren't, they're only crows.* And then, to my surprise, I've come to the top of the hill, and way up there is a wide ring of live oaks where they have no right to be, draped in Spanish moss and resurrection ferns, the evergreen leaves of the trees like a blasphemy in the midst of all that autumn. I shut my eyes a moment, afraid of what I'll find at the center of the ring of trees, afraid that I'll find you, and your skin will be as grey as the bones of these hills, and your lips will be as blue as the waters of the sky above me. I don't want to see that, and I wonder to myself how long I can stand there, eyes shut, delaying, putting off, and haven't you told me time and again how good I am at procrastination? "It's not what you think," I hear you say again. "It hardly ever is," and I'm so glad to hear your voice, so glad you haven't been reduced to some mute imitation of death that I open my eyes. And no, it isn't what I thought it would be. And you are not there with me at the top of the autumn hills, standing before that incongruous ring of live oaks. The crows have come, though, to see whatever I have come so far to see, to find out if it's even half as important as I've imagined it must be, and to jeer at me and to scold and to taunt.

Eight for a wish, nine for a kiss.

Beneath the shaggy, low-slung boughs of the live oaks there is a tall red door with a tarnished brass knob. The door needs no walls to make sense of its being there. It needs no house to justify its existence. And I think that maybe no door ever has, that maybe houses are only things we build around doors so that we can fool ourselves into believing we've tamed and contained them and nullified all their terrifying possibility. I want to turn around and walk back down the autumn hills to the lake and get back into the boat. Maybe if I row back out onto that clear, deep water I would wake up. But I don't do that, because that isn't why you've led me here. And if I were to try, it would be the worst sort of insult to the memory of you. Instead, I step forward and I open the red door and stand alone at the threshold, which may serve as a symbol for many things.

UNTITLED 41

This story was written between September 30th and October 4th, 2018. I'd been reading Angela Carter and it probably shows more than I'd like it to, but...I've always worn my influences on my sleeve. The story began with a dream I had of a red door opening onto autumn, and I just let it lead me where it pleased, no questions asked.

Untitled Psychiatrist No. 4 (July 1987)

I dislike coming here. But that's no secret. Dr. Knowles is well enough aware exactly how much I dislike coming to see her, or at least she knows as much as I've told her. I've said, "I'd rather be doing almost anything else." I've said, "It was never my idea, starting this. I wouldn't have, not if I'd have had a choice." I've spent entire fifty-minute sessions staring out her office window at the parking lot, counting the cars that come and go instead of talking, noting their make and model and color and the faces of their drivers rather than puking up any more of my soul to this woman. And she sits there in her swivel chair, infuriatingly patient, watching me, watching me as if even when I'm intentionally doing nothing I'm inadvertently doing something, as if saying nothing is saying *everything* she wants to hear. And that makes this seem all the more like a trap. Inaction is action. Someone said that to me a long time ago, but I can no longer remember who. Someone I went to bed with. Someone I fucked because I had nothing better to do, so I forgot his face or her face and got on with my life and didn't look back. Except to not forget that line, *Inaction is action.* In one corner of Dr. Knowles's office there's a small Swiss cheese plant in a terra-cotta pot. And I've been staring at it for fifteen minutes now, not talking just staring at that damn plant, but I can tell that she's about to say something. I don't want her to be the first to speak. I'd rather that be me, if anyone has to say anything, I'd rather it be me. So, I say, "Did you know that the Latin name for that plant is *Monstera deliciosa?"*

"No," says Dr. Knowles, "I didn't know that." And she doesn't smile or frown or anything. Except she pretends to be interested in what I've asked her. I can always tell when she's only pretending.

"Well, it is," I say.

"How do you know that?" she asks.

Instead of answering the question, I shrug and I tell her that the name means *delicious monster.* Or *monstrous and delicious,* depending what order you translate it in.

"Did you study botany in college?" she wants to know.

"No," I tell her, and that's the truth. I've told Dr. Knowles a lot of lies, just to keep her happy and pass the time, but that isn't one of them. I stare at the strange glossy leaves, and I just say, "My mom had a big one when I was a kid. Lots bigger than that one," and that's enough about the stupid Swiss cheese plant. Dr. Knowles has gotten pretty good at being able to see when I just want to let something drop, and she doesn't push. She doesn't *push,* but she does *prod.*

I'm quiet again for almost five minutes, and then she decides to prod.

"What you told me about the attic," she says, "was that one of the true things?"

Yes, she knows that I lie to her sometimes. She's known that almost from the very beginning, almost from the first time I came here to this tiny office and had to sit in the waiting room and then had to sit on this sofa and watch the clock or the parking lot or the Swiss cheese plant until my time was up and I could leave.

"Mostly," I tell her, and mostly that's not a lie.

"Could we talk about that some more?" she asks. "We still have thirty-five minutes today. We won't if you don't feel like it, but I wanted to ask, just in case."

"We won't what?" I ask her, asking just to be difficult. "We won't what if I don't want to?"

"We won't talk about the attic. If you don't want to."

"It was just a goddamn attic. What's there to talk about?" And I decide to stare out the window at the parking lot for a little while instead of staring at the Swiss cheese plant. There's a white Volkswagen Bug, and I've always wanted one of those, even if they were invented by the Nazis. When I was a little girl, when I was in elementary school, my mom had one. It was the color of rust, because it mostly was rust, and in places the floorboard had rusted out and there were pieces of plywood covering the holes. And that's twice today my mom has come up, but I don't let myself pause to think about that. What could be more fucking cliché than thinking about your mother in a psychiatrist's office? Almost nothing, that's what. Almost nothing.

"Fine," I say. "We can talk about the attic, if that's what you want."

"Okay," says Dr. Knowles. "Can we talk about Mistral, too?"

And now I'm quiet again for a little while, because she's caught me off my guard, though I don't know why. Why did I think she'd want to talk about the attic if not because of Mistral? Otherwise, the attic was just an attic, just a place where people put things that were in their way and that they probably never wanted to see again. Never wanted to *have* to see again. Isn't that what attics are for?

"Mistral is one of the eight winds of the Mediterranean," I say. "It means *masterly* in French." That part's not true. *Mistral* means *masterly* in the Languedoc dialect of Occitan, which isn't the same as French at all. It's a Romance language, but it isn't French. Anyway, like I said already, sometimes I lie to Dr. Knowles. Sometimes I just tell her things I know are not true. "It's one of the eight winds," I say again. "It's cold and dry and blows on sunny, bright days. It almost drove Vincent Van Gogh insane. He had to battle the Mistral day after day after day when he was living at his yellow house in Arles."

"But that's not the Mistral I meant," says Dr. Knowles, as if I don't know. As if I don't know that she already knows that I know. "We were going to talk about the attic, because you said that was okay, so when I asked about Mistral –"

"I know what you were asking," I tell her, interrupting and not caring that I'm interrupting her.

"So, can we talk about *that* Mistral, the Mistral from the attic?"

"You really think we've got time left for that?" I ask her, still staring out the window at the white Volkswagen. I always thought if I could have one of my own I would want it to be green, grasshopper green.

"I think so," says Dr. Knowles. "I think we do."

I stare at the parking lot, the blacktop and white lines and yellow lines painted on the blacktop, and I close my eyes and imagine myself behind the wheel of a grasshopper-green Volkswagen Bug. I imagine myself driving far, far, far away from Dr. Knowles and this whole damn city and everything I have ever known and everything I ever have said. But it doesn't last, the pictures I'm making in my mind of the car and my getaway, of highways in places I've never been, because suddenly I'm thinking about the attic, instead. I'm thinking about the first night in the attic. Or the first day. I have trouble being sure, sometimes, maybe all the time, whether it was night or day. I've gone up the stairs again, the stairs leading to the narrow trap door, and I've pulled the bit of rope again, the bit of rope that opens the door. And then there's the smell of dust and mold and spiders and moths and all the stuff that people put in attics and to forget.

"Are you okay?" Dr. Knowles asks me, and I smile. I didn't mean to smile, I don't think, but I do smile, and I open my eyes.

"I'm fine," I tell her. "Why wouldn't I be fine."

"I was only asking," she replies.

"I'm fine," I say again.

"We don't have to talk about her today, not if you aren't feeling up to it."

"I said I was fine, didn't I?"

Dr. Knowles is quiet for a moment, and then she nods and says yes, yes, that's what I'd said, what I'd told her, that I was fine.

"I wouldn't have said it if it weren't true."

"I know," says Dr. Knowles, pretending she believes what she's saying, and I listen and pretend I believe it, too.

Dry, cold air that smells like the act of forgetting, the desire to forget.

The need.

I stop turn my head away from the window and the parking lot, deciding it's better if I look at Dr. Knowles and the Swiss cheese plant and the clock and the office. There's no grasshopper-green Volkswagen waiting for me down there or anywhere else. It's cruel to think how maybe there could be. It's masochistic.

"I go up the stairs and I open the door. I open the little white door and I climb up into the attic of my mother's house."

"Have you noticed that you always say that it was your mother's house? Wasn't it your house, too? You lived there."

"No," I reply. "I mean yes, I lived there, but it was my mother's house, and she never let me forget it. Not after I was out of high school. Do you want to talk about my mother or do you want me to talk about Mistral?"

"Well," says Dr. Knowles, "I want you to talk about what you need to talk about."

Liar, I think. *You are a filthy liar, even if I don't know why, even if I can't figure out what you have to gain from telling me lies, and you just want to hear the things I don't want to tell you.*

I stand in the attic, and now there's a rectangular hole in the floor at my feet. It would be easy to step into that hole by accident and fall and break my neck. My damn fool neck, my mother would say, but I don't tell Dr. Knowles that's what she'd say. I stand there looking at the hole in the floor, and I reach for the light cord. It's just a frayed length of kitchen twine, the light cord, leading up to a socket and a bare bulb. Nothing fancy in this old house. I find the cord, and when I pull it nothing happens. The bulb's blown out. It might have been blown a long time, because no one ever comes up into the attic. There's nothing up here that anyone wants, only things no wants anymore, only things that were put here so no one would ever have to think about them again.

"The light was burned out," I tell Dr. Knowles.

"I remember," she says.

"We didn't go up here. Mom didn't like for us to go up there. She always said she didn't like the sound of footsteps in the attic, so we didn't go up there very much, my dad and me. Not that there was any reason to."

I don't just pull the light cord once. I probably pull it two or three times, and then I think how I should go back down the stairs and get a new bulb out of the drawer in the pantry where we keep them. I don't do that, though. I can't say why, but I don't do that. I stand there with my hand on the length of twine, peering into the darkness. There's a little bit of light getting in from the tiny window all the way down at the other end of the attic. If I'm up there in the daytime, then it's sunlight sifting through dust and the heavy curtains hung over the window. If it's night, it's the streetlight on the corner, cold white light and not warm yellow light.

"Why did you go up there that day?" asks Dr. Knowles. "I don't think you've ever told me why."

"It was so long ago, I don't think I remember why anymore," I tell her, though that isn't true. But sometimes I have to hold a few scraps of the truth back for myself, even when I'm trying hard not to lie.

Liar. You are a filthy liar, even if I don't know why, even if I can't figure out what you have to gain...

"My mother wasn't home," I say. "She'd gone to the market for something. I don't remember what, but she'd gone out to the market, so – whyever I'd gone into the attic, whatever I was up there looking for – that was a good time, because she wouldn't hear my footsteps on the ceiling."

Standing there beside the hole in the floor and the steps leading back down from the attic, squinting into the gloom, I am surrounded by all those forgotten, castoff things, by cardboard boxes taped shut for decades, by stacks of newspapers from before I was born, by ratty furniture and things that were mine when I was a little kid, things that mattered a lot to me back then, but which I have not thought about in ages. Those things, they're nearest the attic door. Board games and broken toys, a rocking horse that my grandfather made, a tall can of Lincoln logs. Children's books in crooked stacks, and I think how they've probably been eaten at by silverfish and roaches and mice and whatever else lives in attics and feasts on children's books.

"You didn't see her right away," says Dr. Knowles, not *asking* but *telling* me, and I think how a lawyer or a judge on a TV show might say that's leading the witness, something like that. "I mean, that's what you've said before," she adds, so I think it must have also occurred to her that there was something untoward about *telling* me what I saw and when I saw it.

"No," I reply. "I was too busy wanting to go back downstairs. Or I was too busy looking around at all the junk up there. Or both maybe. So no, I didn't see her right away." I say these things to answer her question, but I'm still thinking how sitting on the sofa in Dr. Knowles' office isn't so very different than being in court, up on the witness stand, replying to the prosecution and the defense and the judge – but especially to the prosecution. I'm thinking how maybe the difference between lawyers and psychiatrists isn't as great as most people probably assume it to be (though, if I am to be honest, I can't claim to understand all that much about how anyone but me sees the world or anyone else but themselves).

I look out at the parking lot again, fringed in leafy-green mimosa and magnolia and whatever else, but even with the shade from the trees the day's gonna be so hot the asphalt will be soft long before sunset. And that makes me think about the La Brea tar pits and mammoths and ground sloths and whatever else getting mired in the tar and dragged down to their deaths. And that makes me think about Mistral. No, I mean *really* think about her for the first time since coming into Dr. Knowles' office today. I rub my eyes and turn away from the window again.

"Did I ever tell you about the time I saw the La Brea tar pits?" I ask her, and she looks confused and leans back in her chair and almost (but only almost) frowns at me.

"No," she says, apparently deciding to weather without complaint my so suddenly changing the subject like that. "No, you never did."

"I was ten years old. My dad moved to LA after the divorce, but you know that. He took me to see the tar pits and the museum next to the tar pits with all the bones they'd pulled out of them over the decades. I had nightmares about them for a while afterwards, about what it would be like to get stuck in the tar and slowly pulled down, strangling, suffocating. You know. It must be an awful way for anything to die, even if you are only a dire wolf or only a coyote."

Dr. Knowles nods her head, and I can see now that she gets the connection, that I hadn't actually changed the subject after all. She stops almost frowning and her expression goes all non-judgmentally neutral again.

"The first thing I remember in the attic," I tell her, "the first thing out of the ordinary, was a smell like the tar pits had smelled that day, the sticky, pungent melted tar smell. And the second thing I noticed that was out of the ordinary, or maybe it wasn't but it seemed that way to me, there was this tidy little pile of dead mice right next to the attic door. Like someone had stacked them there a long time ago. They were just husks, little mouse mummies, as if they'd been there so long they'd desiccated."

Or as if something had come along and sucked them all dry.

And maybe that's just what happens to evil little fucking mice that snack on old children's books.

"It was summer, right?" asks Dr. Knowles.

"Yeah, it was July. Like now. And that was the third strange thing," I say. "It should have been hot as blue blazes up there in the attic, but it wasn't. It was cold, like there was an air conditioner running full blast. We didn't even have AC downstairs, just box fans. But I swear, it was like a meat locker up there. I realized that I could see my breath fog."

And across all these years and everything that's happened since, I'm standing in the dark with the rectangle of light at my feet, and there's the tidy pile of mouse husks, and the tar smell burns my nostrils, and I really can see my breath fogging. *Don't you run,* I think. *Don't you dare fucking run. You'll just have to come back later on and spend all the time between now and then feeling foolish and dreading it.* And then I think, *Yeah, but I could come back with a fresh goddamn light bulb.*

"And that's when you realized you weren't alone?" asks Dr. Knowles.

I nod my head, and then I answer, "Yeah, that's when I saw her. She was sitting in an old armchair at the other end of the attic, sort of curled up in it, the way you do in armchairs, just sitting there watching me."

If it's night time, it's the streetlight on the corner, cold white light and not warm yellow light.

"How did that make you feel?"

"How do you *think* it made me feel?" And the words are out before I can think better of them or the annoyed tone in my voice, but Jesus, what a dumb goddamn question. I imagine Dr. Knowles, fifteen years younger sitting through some college lecture, learning how to ask perfectly idiotic questions once she got her own practice.

"I'm sorry," she says, a little too quickly. "I shouldn't have –"

But I interrupt her for the second time this session. "Like being stabbed in the gut with an icicle," I say, wondering if it actually did feel anything like that, what it would feel like to be stabbed in the belly with an icicle, if I'd feel the cold before I felt the pain or if I'd feel both right about the same time or what. "It should have scared the shit out me, especially since I was already jumpy and all. It didn't though. There was just this sharp coldness in my guts, and I stood there staring back at her. She had bright blue eyes. I could tell even from my end of the dark attic, how bright and blue her eyes were, and it's not like they were glowing or anything hokey like that, not like something from a monster movie."

And I can see Dr. Knowles wanting to ask me, *And then what happened? What happened next? And how did that make you feel?* Even though she's heard this all once or twice before and has it all written down somewhere. Or maybe it's just that she sees so many crazy women that she can't keep us straight or she forgets shit. I don't know. I'm not even sure if I'm telling this story exactly the same way that I've told it to her before, but that's okay. Dr. Knowles would probably be the first to tell me that any deviations are significant, that what did or did not actually happen that day or night is entirely irrelevant. It's what I remember, on this particular day, and how, on this particular day, it makes me feel. That's what's important. Or maybe I'm just being an asshole. I am my mother's daughter, after all, and I never rule out that possibility.

"Her eyes were bright and blue," I say again. "Like blue ice, the way ice is blue inside a glacier. That cold blue, like all that freezing air pressing in around me. And I just stood there staring at her, and she just sat there, curled into that old armchair watching me. I wanted to say something, but I couldn't, and I remember wondering if possibly my jaws and tongue had frozen solid. And then she smiled."

Dr. Knowles is chewing at her lower lip, and I wonder if she's aware that she's doing it. I wonder if she's aware that I've noticed.

"Her smile wasn't as bright as her eyes," I go on, "but it almost was, and I realized then I wasn't so much seeing a woman down there at the other end of my mother's attic. No, I was seeing nothing at all, a hole in reality, and maybe it was *shaped* like a woman, and maybe it actually had *been* a woman once, a long, long, long time ago, like how a long time ago all those bones from the tar pits had been parts of living animals. That's what I was seeing, this hole punched in the world, and only those bright blue eyes and that white smile was any more solid than nothingness."

And what happened next? Do you remember what happened next? Is that when she told you that her name was Mistral?

No, that's when she stood up…

That's when she came apart.

And what do you think you really saw?

I glance at the clock and am relieved that there's only fifteen minutes to go. Then I rub my eyes and remember that scene in *Ferris Bueller's Day Off* when the clock starts running backwards. At least, I think it was in *Ferris Bueller's Day Off;* it might have been in some other movie, that scene.

"She wasn't real," I say.

"What do you mean by that?" asks Dr. Knowles, and she stops chewing at her lip, and I think she's probably stopped just a second or two before drawing blood.

"I mean it was dark, and I don't know what I really saw."

…the most beautiful woman that I ever saw, ever, the most beautiful thing, the most awful thing, the most broken thing, the most utterly irredeemable thing, and she told me that her name was Mistral, and she had a French accent. Or I think it was a French accent. It might have been Occitan, lenga d'òc, *like the word Mistral, which is a cold, dry wind blowing through the attic of my mother's house.*

"I mean," I tell Dr. Knowles, "that I might have been imagining things. When I was a kid, my mother said I was bad about imagining things. Or just making things up to get attention, so maybe that's all I'm doing now."

Imagining that I saw a hole in the world that called itself Mistral and spoke with a voice like winter. Or lying and inventing her because I'm sick of my life and sick of how one day just keeps coming after another and sick of sitting on this sofa and telling you things I would rather keep to myself.

"I don't think you're making it up," Dr. Knowles says, in that phony way that's meant to be comforting, that's meant to assure me that she trusts me and believe every syllable that crosses my lips is gospel.

"But you don't *know* that I'm not, do you?"

"Are you a ghost?" I heard myself say, and the hole in the world with bright blue eyes and that guillotine smile replied, "No, dear. I'm not a ghost. I remember dying. In fact, I remember dying twice, but I'm not a ghost. Still, if it's easier that way, simpler for you to understand, I don't mind if you think of me as a ghost. Not if that makes it easier on you. I'm not here to cause you any pain."

"No," Dr. Knowles admits to me. "I can't ever be sure that you're telling me the truth. But I do think that what you're telling me means something, even if you're making it all up. Fiction takes the shape it does because there's something we need to get out, something we need to say, and that's as important as whatever might have actually happened. I think I told you that once before, when we were talking about your cousin."

And I almost tell her I think she's full of shit. But only almost.

I can stand another few minutes, so long as the clock hasn't started running backwards on me.

"I mean to tell the truth," I say, but that might just be the worst lie I've ever told.

"I know," says Dr. Knowles, as if she possibly could ever know a thing like that.

"I do mean to."

"I understand," she says, and then reaches for her day planner, and I breathe a sigh of relief. "Maybe this would be a good place to stop for the day. We can come back to it next time. Or we can talk about something else. Whatever you need."

A grasshopper-green Volkswagen Bug, that's all I need. All I need in the world.

"Okay," I tell her, and I reach for my purse on the table, and Dr. Knowles smiles and scribbles in her book.

UNTITLED PSYCHIATRIST NO. 4

There's not a lot to be said about the genesis of this one. Mistral occurred to me as a creature of shadow, a woman cursed to exist as negative space, something like that, and I stuck her in this vignette, another of my seemingly endless psychiatrist tales. I have spent far too much of my life in psychiatrists' offices, and it shows. This story was written between May 30th and June 3rd, 2020, two months after I began "self-isolation" due to COVID-19 (and I am now working on Month No. 9).

As Water is In Water

1.

Lying awake, listening to the metronomic, insect sound of the clock ticking on the chifforobe, lying awake and trying hard to think of anything but drowning, lying awake and waiting for whatever happens next. It's a rainy February night, a night of rain because it isn't quite cold enough for snow, and the sound of the rain against our bedroom window is a not inappropriate counterpoint to the ticking clock and the drowning thoughts I'm trying so hard to avoid. Try not to think of a polar bear, as Dostoyevsky suggested. Try not to think of any given thing, and I will surely think of nothing else. You're asleep beside me, and the gentle rhythm of your sleeping breath is another counterpoint. I lie on my back and stare up at the ceiling that is not quite lost in the darkness, envying you, because whatever nightmares I might have could not be half so bad as being alone in being awake at three forty-five in the morning, listening to the clock and the rain and the easy sounds you make when you sleep. Whatever dreams I might have would not be half so bad as waiting for the nightmares that come when I am fully awake. I could switch on the lamp on the table beside the bed and read a few pages of the novel I've been trying to finish for weeks now. I could get up and go downstairs and turn on the television. There are any number of things I could do besides lying here waiting. But I know that I won't do any of them. I know myself well enough to know that, and I have been through this enough times now to know the routine. I shut my eyes, and this time I manage to keep them shut almost a full five minutes. When I open them again, nothing at all has changed. I think about your prescription bottle of Ambien tablets in the bathroom medicine cabinet, and I pretend that I'll get up and take one, even though I know that I'll do nothing of the sort. Which makes me an accomplice in my insomnia. I roll over on my right side and stare at the window, instead of staring at the ceiling. The curtains are drawn shut, backlit by the garish blue-white LED glow from the street, new streetlights installed a year or so ago because LED is supposedly cheaper than incandescence, and so what if it turns the nights bright as an oncoming train, and so what if it disturbs the migratory patterns of birds. So what, because someone somewhere in the city government will see a net savings ten or fifteen years from now. I shut my eyes again, and I try not to think about wanting to be asleep. I try not to think about the smell of seawater and the sound of waves lapping against granite and against the decaying pilings of a sagging pier, and I might as well be trying not to think about a polar bear. I remind myself that I do not believe in ghosts, not in any traditional sense, not in the restless spirit trapped between life and death sense, because that would require, would presuppose, that I believe in souls and in life after death, and I remind myself that I am an atheist and believe nothing of the sort. I try not to think about the ocean and everything that swims under the ocean and crawls and wriggles across the silty bottoms of all the oceans of all the world. I tell myself that, and then I try to think of nothing that isn't tiresome and mundane and perfectly ordinary in every way – the ugly LED streetlights, how the car needs new tires, the doctor's appointment I have three days from now, a friend from college whom I have not seen in years, an article I read somewhere online about American-backed Kurdish rebels in Syria. But somehow everything circles back inevitably to the things I'm trying *not* to think about. Everything circles back to thoughts of drowning. Everything circles back to the sea. I glance again at the soft amber glow of the clock face, and now it's five minutes after four. Three hours left to sunrise, and three hours might as well be an eternity. I only very briefly think about making some or another noise and then pretending it was an accident that I've awakened you. But you have work in the morning, and I tell myself I'm not so great a coward that I can't face three more hours of this by myself. I shut my eyes, and I try not to think about the sea, and I begin counting quietly to myself, counting in my head, imagining myself standing in an empty classroom and writing the numeral one on the chalkboard, then carefully erasing it before I write the number two, and so on and on and on. It's a technique I taught myself a long time ago, because all my life I've had trouble sleeping. I didn't need the ghosts I don't believe in to keep me awake; I'm capable of that all on my own. I reach fifty-two, and I'm just about to wipe it away and write fifty-three, when I smell saltwater and seaweed and the muddy, fishy stink of low tide, and so I squeeze my eyes shut more tightly. But – try not to think of a polar bear and you will think of nothing else. And now my heart is racing and there's flop sweat to dampen the sheets as my own personal ocean leaks out through my pores. I can taste the sea bitter on my tongue. In a few moments more I can hear it, as well, and when I open my eyes again, there's a bright, restless motion washing across the drawn curtains and the walls and the bedroom ceiling, movement like coruscating sunlight reflected off the surface of water. Only it isn't sunlight at all. It isn't any sort of light. And I think, *If light cast a shadow, it would look like this. It would look like this exactly. What I am seeing is the shadow of light reflected off water.* I lie there as still as I can for as long as I can, watching the impossible shadow of light and smelling the sea and hearing gulls and the distant toll of bell buoys until I am able to endure it no more, and then I reach out and switch on the lamp on the table beside the bed. And then there is only the February night and the sound of rain against the window, the faint popping of the radiators along the baseboards, and the sound of you asleep.

2.

The psychologist's name is Keller. Imogen Keller. I have been seeing her now for almost six months, even though she's an expense I cannot actually afford. *She's not even a real doctor,* my mother would have said, when my mother was still alive. *Here you are wasting more than a hundred dollars every time you see this woman, and she isn't even a real doctor. She can't even prescribe drugs. All real doctors can write prescriptions.* Imogen Keller is a few years older than me, a few years past fifty, and her hair has gone almost entirely white. Her eyes are blue, and during our sessions she makes notes in a stenographer's pad in shorthand. Until I started seeing her, I had no idea that anyone still uses shorthand. When I asked her, she said it was something that she learned in high school, back in the seventies, back before computers, back when girls still took home economics and studied to be secretaries. Once a month, I make the drive from Providence down to her office in Cranston, and I talk, and she listens to me. I don't care that she's not a real doctor. If I were someone else, I might see a priest, instead. If I were someone else, I might be able to talk about these things with my lover or a friend or a family member. But I am who I am, and so I make my confessions to Imogen Keller. The walls of her office are painted the color of butter, a yellow so pale that it's almost white, a white that's turned a dingy hint of yellow. I talk, and she writes with a pencil in her stenographer's pad, and she listens. If I wanted a real doctor, if I wanted prescriptions, I'd see a psychiatrist.

We're talking about the day last summer when I almost drowned in the bay off Conanicut Island, just below the Beavertail Lighthouse. We're talking about the day when I might have tried to drown myself. This isn't the first time we've discussed that day, and I have no reason to believe it will be the last. I sometimes think that Imogen Keller suspects that I'm not being entirely truthful with her, and so we only rarely talk about anything once and only once. She gently encourages me to return again and again to traumatic events – or events that only seem traumatic because I've spent so many years worrying over them – because she's trying to catch me in a lie, waiting to see if I'll slip up and change some small but crucial detail. So far that hasn't happened, or if it has I haven't noticed and she's been kind enough not to point it out.

"But you're a strong swimmer," she says. "You've told me that."

"In high school, I was on the swim team," I reply, though this isn't anything I haven't told her before. "I was pretty good. I won a few medals. For a while, I thought maybe I'd go on to compete in college, too. I didn't, and I don't really know why I didn't. I just didn't."

"So that day on the island, what happened that day, it wasn't because you were in over your head," says Imogen Keller, and then she smiles at her pun. I return the smile, and I nod, and I tell her no, it wasn't that, though a place like Beavertail can be dicey even for a good swimmer, what with the rocks and the rip currents and the way the water gets very deep, very quickly.

"I got it in my head that I could swim out all the way out to Whale Rock and back, all the way across the west passage of the bay.

There used to be a sparkplug lighthouse on Whale Rock, but it was destroyed in the Hurricane of 1938. The foundation is still there, though, and you can see it from Beavertail, especially when the tide is out. I've sat with binoculars and watched cormorants perched there on what's left of the lighthouse, and once I saw a couple of seals basking on the rocks."

"How far would that be to swim," asks Imogen Keller.

"About a mile," I tell her. "A mile and a quarter, maybe."

"And you'd swum that far before? In the ocean, I mean? And, of course, you'd have had to swim back, so that would have been over two miles."

"It's been a long time," I say. "I mean, a long time since I swam that sort of distance in the sea. And swimming a couple of miles in the sea is an entirely different thing from swimming a couple of miles in a pool or in a lake. Sure, I'd done it, but I was a lot younger when I did."

"But that day, you thought that you could," she says. It isn't a question.

I shrug without meaning to shrug, and then I say, "Honestly, I'm not entirely sure I stopped to think about whether I was still that good a swimmer. I just wanted to make the swim. I remember sitting there on the rocks thinking how cool the water would be, that far out from shore. It was getting hot because it was July and there wasn't much of a breeze that day. Also, there were a lot of people, and the noise was wearing on my nerves, and I knew that out there in the bay, it would be quiet and the water would be cold."

"Isn't it more dangerous to swim in cold water?" asks Imogen Keller.

"It can be," I reply. "But this was summer, and the water was probably close to seventy degrees, at least up near the surface, so when I say I was thinking how the water would be cold, I don't mean that it would be cold enough to be dangerous."

"And your girlfriend, you told her you were going to try and swim that far?"

"No," I say. "I only told her I was going in. She was sunbathing and reading, and she told me to be careful. But I didn't tell her what I had in mind."

"Do you think she would have tried to stop you? Is that why you didn't tell her you were going to try and swim all the way out to Whale Rock?"

I don't answer her, but instead look down at my shoes and the carpeted floor, carpet almost the same color as the walls, only just a shade or two more yellow. If the walls look like butter then the carpet looks like margarine, and I wonder why anyone would ever think it was a good idea to cover an office floor, or any floor, for that matter, in carpet the color of margarine.

"Well," she says, after a minute or two of silence has passed between us, "maybe we'll pick up there next time."

"Sure," I say and nod again, and I almost add, *I was going to answer the question. I wasn't trying to be evasive. I was only trying to remember what I said that day.* But then I think better of it. Imogen Keller asks me if the second Monday in March is good for me, a Monday afternoon three weeks from now, and tell her sure, the second Monday in March works for me, and she writes the date and time down for me on an appointment card and closes her stenographer's pad.

3.

This is a true story, or it is as near to a true story as I will ever be able to tell:

Putting it here, it will feel like foreshadowing.

Or a belated sort of prologue.

When I was eleven years old, the week after my first period, I saw living fish fall from the sky. Not only fish, though, but also crabs and lobsters and starfish, sea urchins and squids and snail shells that bounced like hailstones. I have no idea if anyone else saw what I saw. And though I have just said this is a true story, I will also admit that I have no idea if this fall of fish *truly* did happen. But it is true that I *witnessed* it, or that I at least *believe* that I witnessed it. There are certainly other explanations, alternatives to the possibility that what I saw actually did occur in the world outside my perceptions of the world. Imogen Keller, and others over the years, have pointed this out to me, and I readily concede that possibility. I see nothing to be gained by doing otherwise.

A day late in spring, almost summer, and I think it might have been the first truly warm day in May. My mother was out running errands, away at the market or the post office or the library. My sister, who is three years older than me, was at a friend's birthday party. I remember that. We lived in an old house down in Kingston, not too far from the university. This was after my father left, after my parents' divorce. There was no one at home but me, and I was sitting at my desk in my bedroom, trying to finish my homework so that I could watch television after dinner and after the dishes were washed. I recall that it was math homework, and I've never been very good at math. I might have become a scientist, if I'd been better at math. I was sitting at my desk, looking out the window at our backyard and at the woods beyond our backyard, when it seemed as if a cloud passed over the sun, even though walking home from the bus stop I hadn't seen any clouds. All my life, the few times I have ever told this story to anyone, I have always stressed that it was a bright, sunny afternoon, that walking home from the bus stop I had not *seen* a single cloud in the sky. I have always pointed this out, though, honestly, I'm not at all sure why it matters. After all, a rain of fish is not a rain of water.

All the same, a shadow fell across our backyard.

There was a strong smell then, an acrid odor like a hot car engine or burning oil, and there was a rumbling, faraway sort of sound that came from everywhere all at once – from above me and below me, from *everywhere.* It wasn't thunder, or at least it wasn't like any thunder I'd ever heard before. There was something distinctly mechanical about the rumbling sound, and I had never heard anything like it, and I've never heard *anything* like it since. And as the rumbling faded away, the fish and all those other sea things began to fall, pelting the grass and the slate flagstone walkway leading from the back porch to the little shed behind the house, hitting the roof above me, hitting my bedroom window and leaving slimy, wet streaks on the glass. I should have been scared, but I wasn't. I thought, *Well, here is something I've never seen before,* or I thought something to that effect, and I closed my textbook and got up and went to the back door. I stood there and watched. It only lasted a few minutes, and then the sun came back, bright as before. The entire back yard was carpeted in flopping, squirming, dying creatures. I remember leaning out the back door and craning my neck, looking up into the sky, expecting maybe to see whatever had dropped them all, whatever had made the rumbling sound and the bad smell. But there was nothing there, just a clear blue May sky. And that's when I heard my mother drive up. I thought surely she'd know what was happening, surely she would have seen this before. I closed the back door and went to meet her, only to find there were no fish in the front yard or the street that ran past our house. And when I led my mother around the side of the house to the back, there were no longer any fish there, either. She frowned and wanted to know why in the world I'd make up such a ridiculous story. I didn't argue with her. I didn't insist that I wasn't lying, that it wasn't some sort of joke. I just let the matter drop. Neither of us ever brought it up again. I don't think she ever even told my sister. Sometimes I would pretend that I really had made it all up and that I'd been so delighted with the strange cleverness of my lie that I had half convinced myself it was true.

Only, after that day, every now and then I would find a snail shell in the backyard, when I'd never found any there before. I kept them all, hiding them in an old Whitman's Sampler box beneath my bed. There were whelks and periwinkles and moon shells. My mother had a book – *A Field Guide to the Atlantic Seashore from the Bay of Fundy to Cape Hatteras* – and all the sorts of snails I found were in it, so I knew what they were. I also found a crab claw once. And a single tiny starfish. I don't have them anymore. At some point, I stopped picking up the snails, and at some point after that, maybe a year or two later, the box went missing. I asked my mother if she'd seen it, and she said she hadn't, and I didn't press the matter. I didn't even bother asking my sister. I just let it go, the same way I'd let my mother think I'd lied about seeing fish falling from the sky.

4.

This is a dream. I will not say it is *only* a dream or that it is *merely* a dream. I think too many people rush to underestimate dreams:

I'm sitting in Imogen Keller's butter- and margarine-colored office, and we're talking about the day in 1981 when I saw fish falling from the sky. Her stenographer's pad is open. She's chewing her pencil, which she does sometimes, both in my dreams and awake. There's a window behind her, and I can see that it's a cloudy day. In that room's waking counterpart, there aren't any windows. But in my dream there are, and in my dream there are dark, roiling clouds, and I'm thinking there's going to be a thunderstorm soon. I'm thinking I'll get drenched when I leave the building and walk back to my car.

"It's not the fish that I find remarkable," Imogen Keller says to me. "After all, there are plenty of reports down through history of fish – and many other sorts of small animals – falling from the sky. What is remarkable about what you say happened to you is that they all suddenly vanished. That's the truly strange part of your story."

"It's what happened," I tell her. "Well, it's what I believe happened."

"Dear," she says (though waking she has never called me "dear"), "it isn't necessary that you qualify your experiences that way. Not to me. You say it happened, then I accept you're telling me the truth, as you perceive it."

"That seems awfully naive, especially for a psychologist. People tell lies. People tell lies all the time. I bet I've told ten thousand lies in my life."

There's a sharp crack of distant thunder, and Imogen Keller glances over her shoulder at the open window. I don't think that it was open only a minute before. She turns back to face me, and she says, "Well, then are you admitting you made the whole thing up?"

"No," I say. "No, I'm not saying that. I'm only saying I don't think it's wise to take my story at face value, as if there's no possibility I may be lying."

"You think it's unwise of me to trust you?" she asks.

"I think you should close that window," I tell her, but she ignores me and reaches for a book on her desk. It's bound in red cloth and looks very old. I can see that there's a fish on the cover, stamped into the book with black ink. She sets the book in her lap and opens it, and I can see that the pages are yellow and brittle. She turns them with exquisite care, the way I imagine someone would handle high explosives or a newborn baby (I've never held either). She finds the page she's looking for, or she settles on one at random. I can't say which.

"The window is fine," she says. "Don't you mind the window. Listen," and she begins reading to me accounts of fish and frogs and worms, spiders and snakes falling from the sky – Marksville, Louisiana in October 1947, Moose Jaw, Saskatchewan in 1903, Nepal in 1900, Singapore in 1861, and on and on and on. Finally, I interrupt her. Finally, I say that I get the point.

"These things happen," she says. "That's simply a fact. Though I will note that in none of these cases did the creatures that fell simply vanish afterwards. But, honestly, I think this is all beside the point, because what we're not talking about – not really – is your almost drowning yourself in Narragansett Bay. We're not talking about that, and we're not talking about the ghost."

And I almost ask, *What ghost?* But only almost.

I look down at the margarine-colored carpet, and it's covered now with tiny silver-blue fish, fingerlings, their iridescent scales glinting as they flip about, gasping for air. I reach down and try to pick one up, but they keep slipping through my fingers, as though they're no more substantial than water.

"Or maybe it's your hands that are insubstantial," suggests Imogen Keller.

"Where did you find that book?" I ask her.

"Frogs and fishes and worms," she says, "and these are the materials of our expression upon all things. Hops and flops and squirms, and these are the motions. Do you remember what happened when you opened the bedroom door?"

I give up trying to catch one of the little fish, and I look at her.

"I don't want to talk about that today," I say.

"Not today or not ever?"

"Not today," I answer.

"But that's really why you're seeing me, isn't it, dear? Not because of what happened when you were a kid, but because of what happened when you almost drowned, and because of what you saw when you opened the door, and because of what is still happening, every minute of every day."

I start to reply, but I'm no longer sitting on the sofa in Imogen Keller's office. I'm standing in the hallway outside our bedroom in our apartment on Federal Hill. The hallway is dark, and the air is heavy with the stink of fish. I reach out my left hand and press it flat against the door. The wood is damp and cold. I start to reach for the knob, but then I stop myself. I can hear something on the other side, and the sound makes me think of the sea. I know that if I were to take hold of the doorknob, it would be cold as ice, cold as the bottom of the Atlantic Ocean fifteen thousand feet down, the cold of endless bathypelagic nights.

"You're only delaying the inevitable," says Imogen Keller, closing the red book. "Sooner or later, you have to open that door, if only because you already *have* opened it."

I open my eyes (wondering when I shut them), and I find that I'm back in the psychologist's office (if I ever left), and for the first time ever I find the sight of those pale yellow-white walls comforting. I'm holding three of the tiny fish in my cupped hands.

I say, "That's exactly why I never have to open it again."

There's no longer an open window in the room. There's no longer any window at all, but I can still hear the distant rumble of thunder or of vast machineries in the sky.

5.

This is a Friday afternoon in early October, the autumn after the summer that I tried to drown. I've got the day off and so do you, and that's something that hardly ever happens, not weekdays. We spent the morning in bed, being lazy and sleeping late and then fucking until almost noon. Then we get lunch from the deli on Hudson Street. And now we're sitting on a park bench a little ways south of the bronze statue of Ebenezer Knight Dexter and well north of the towering yellow bricks and crenellated turrets of the Cranston Street Armory. The park is mostly empty, and I'm glad for that. It's a warm day, warmer really than it ought to be in early October in Rhode Island, and neither of us is wearing a sweater. I light a cigarette and smoke and listen while you lament the fate of the enormous hundred-plus-year-old chestnut tree that used to shade this spot, but was cut down a few months ago (before anyone had a chance to protest) because someone threatened to sue the city if it wasn't, because their child has a nut allergy and plays in the park. All that remains now is the stump, and you're telling me how you wish they'd had the decency to remove that, too, that it's an unsightly reminder of the butchered tree. There's not a single cloud in the sky laid out vast and bottomless blue overhead, and the only noises are the birds and squirrels and an occasional car passing along Parade Street. I think how this is an almost perfect day, how I want to *remember* it as an almost perfect day. We get so few of those anymore. You stop talking about the chestnut tree, and I finish my cigarette and deposit the butt in the cinnamon Altoids tin I carry with me for just that purpose. It's more than half full, and I think about walking over to a nearby trashcan and emptying it.

"The insomnia's back again, isn't it?" you ask me.

"It comes and goes," I reply.

"I can tell that you're not sleeping much."

I say that I'm sorry if I'm keeping you awake, and you say no, that I'm not, not keeping you awake, and that I shouldn't worry about that. You ask why I'm not taking the Ambien, and I tell you that I don't like how it makes me feel the next day, and you nod and tell me that's fair enough. You say you read something online somewhere about magnesium helping people sleep, and I say that maybe I'll give that a try. I glance past you, towards the statue on its grey granite pedestal, standing watch as it has silently stood watch and witness now since 1894, ringed about with black wrought iron. You've picked a stick up off the ground, and you're poking about at the dirt between our feet, at the barren patch of earth in front of the bench. Too many shoes linger here and stomp and grind and kick for the grass to take root, and the exposed dirt turns into a mud hole whenever there's rain or melting snow. We haven't had a good rain in weeks now, and the ground is dry as dry can be. You draw something in the dirt that looks sort of like a fish.

"If I could take it back, I would," you say, and there goes the perfect day, and here is the day that this will be, instead.

"That's not why I can't sleep," I tell you. "I've had insomnia almost all my life. I've told you that."

"Well, I would, all the same. If I could. I don't know the words to explain how much I regret it."

You're referring to the brief affair you had last winter with a woman you met at work, and I'm sitting here wishing that you hadn't brought it up. I'm sitting here wishing there were some way I could convince you that I'm not angry anymore, at least not about *that,* and that your infidelity has nothing to do with my inability to sleep and nothing to with what happened at Beavertail Lighthouse, nothing to do with my nightmares, that there are other reasons I see a psychologist than your affair. I feel the smallest twinge of resentment that you've brought it up and marred a perfect day, but I push those emotions back down into the deep black hole where they live.

"Sometimes," you say, "I wish that you'd cheat on me, just so we'd be even."

"I don't think it works like that," I tell you, and then I think about having another cigarette. I'm trying to stop, but I've been trying to stop for years. "Can we not talk about this today?"

"I just worry that's why you're not sleeping," you say again, and again I tell you that it isn't. I try harder to sound convincing, but I know all too well there's no dividing you from the holy burden of your guilt. So, I change the subject. I tell you that I've been thinking how we could head up to Maine next weekend, all the way up to Penobscot Bay, find a room at a bed and breakfast, spend the weekend beachcombing and eating seafood and poking around antique shops. The fall colors might still be bright, I say, not sure whether or not they've already peaked that far north.

"It would be a nice change of pace," I say, and you shrug and scrape at the ground with your stick.

"I thought you didn't like Maine," you tell me.

"I'm willing to give it another chance," I reply. "We should go."

And that's when you dig up the periwinkle shell. Only I don't realize what it is right away. At first I think that it's only an acorn. You lean down and pick it up and rub the dirt away with a thumb. And then you hand it to me, and I see exactly what it is.

"Maybe," you say. "Maybe it would be good for both of us. Anyway, we should be getting back home."

I don't say anything right away. I just sit there staring at the periwinkle shell and thinking about that day when I was eleven years old and fish fell from the sky and covered my backyard, fish that no one else but me would ever see. I think about the snail shells bouncing off the stone walkway behind our house, and I think about finding them in the grass for months afterward. I think about the yellow Whitman's Sampler box I kept beneath my bed. You get up off the bench, and I drop the periwinkle shell, letting it fall back into the furrows you've plowed, back into the dirt where you found it.

6.

It's the second Monday in March, a rainy afternoon, and once again I am sitting in Imogen Keller's butter- and margarine-colored office. I was five minutes late, because I took too long getting out of the house, and then there was traffic, but she said not to worry about it. Still, I've always despised being late for anything. I have already told the psychologist that I've decided this will be our last session. When she asked me why, I told her that I simply can't afford the luxury of seeing her, that I have to find a way to get through whatever it is that's happening all on my own. She asked if I thought I could do that, and I replied that I didn't think I have much choice in the matter, and I could tell she wasn't happy with my answer. I suspect she also knows that, regardless of my finances, I haven't decided to stop seeing her because of money. I don't like that I haven't told her the truth and admitted my cowardice, but for some reason I don't feel like trying to explain, I believe the lie is necessary. My life is filled, I think, with necessary lies, and it may be that all lives are.

"If this is our last session," she says, "don't you think we should talk about what happened that night? Don't you think we should address what's keeping you awake?" She crosses her legs and uncrosses them again. She's wearing a skirt that needs ironing, and I notice that there's cat hair on it.

I don't answer right away. I stare at the clock, instead. There's still forty minutes between now and the moment that I can stand up and leave the office knowing that I never have to come back here again.

"We don't have to, of course," says Imogen Keller. "It's your time, just like always, and we can talk about whatever you want."

Sitting here, I imagine all the things we might spend the next forty minutes discussing as a series of index cards. *Just pick one,* I think. *Just stop dithering and pick one and get it over with.*

The night I woke from especially bad dreams and vomited seawater.

The tiny patch of barnacles I found growing on the bathroom floor a few days later and that I had to scrape off the tiles with a putty knife before anyone else noticed them.

Or what I might have seen beneath the surface of Narragansett Bay, the day I tried to swim out to Whale Rock and very almost drowned.

Or – well, there are quite a few imaginary index cards lined up in front of me.

Pick one. Get it over with.

Make it count.

"The ghost," I say. "We can talk about the ghost."

"You're sure?" she asks.

"Be careful," I say, "or you'll talk me out of it."

I'm lying in our bed in the apartment we rent in the old house on Federal Hill. I was dreaming about the day I was eleven years old and saw fish fall from the sky, and then a noise woke me, a far off, rumbling noise that's really much more like machinery than thunder. It hasn't awakened you. You're still lying here asleep beside me, breathing softly, steadily, curled fetal and your back turned to me. It takes me a few moments to realize why the room isn't as dark as it ought to be, to find the source of soft bluish light playing across the walls and ceiling and bed and floor. And then it takes me a second or two longer to focus my eyes and realize exactly what it is I'm looking at, what I'm seeing. Someone else might have screamed. Another woman might have cried out or at least have shaken you awake. I just lie there, staring at the figure hanging in the air just beyond and above the foot of the bed. It's a young woman, hardly more than a girl, and the way her hair drifts about her face, the particular *way* she's floating, I understand that – even though I am seeing her here in our bedroom – she's underwater. Her eyes are closed, and she's entirely naked. She's giving off the pale blue glow. It leaks from her skin the way light leaks from the bioluminescent organs of deep-sea fish. The room is perfectly silent. I can't hear the clock ticking on the chifforobe. I can no longer hear you breathing next to me. For the moment, there is nothing in all the world but the sight of the floating girl. Her bare skin is scarred and dappled with barnacles and sea anemones. Very slowly, I sit up, and I realize that I'm crying. And maybe the sound of me crying is what gets the girl's attention. She opens her eyes and looks down at me. Her eyes are the color of dark green glass that has been tumbled in waves and sand for decades upon decades. Her lips part very slightly, and I think (or I am afraid) that she's about to speak. But then she's gone, taking the strange blue light away with her, and I sit there weeping until it finally wakes you.

"But you didn't tell her what you saw," says Imogen Keller.

"You already know that I didn't," I say.

"Because you were afraid she wouldn't believe you or because you were afraid that she would?"

"Maybe a little of both," I reply. "I'm honestly still not sure which would have been worse."

"And you think she was a ghost, the girl you saw that night?"

"I don't know what else she could be."

Imogen Keller nods and writes something in shorthand on a page of her stenographer's pad.

"You must have a lot of those," I say, and I point at the pad so she'll know what I mean. She shrugs, then nods.

"I suppose so. Everything gets transcribed, but I'm a packrat. You're sure you didn't recognize the girl?"

"Right now, I'm not sure of much of anything," I tell her. "Right now, you could probably convince me I'm mistaken about my own name."

Imogen Keller frowns what strikes me as a practiced sort of frown, and she says, "I wish you'd reconsider discontinuing our sessions. Perhaps I could work something out, maybe see you on a sliding scale, something more affordable. I don't mean to be pushy, but I worry about you."

Maybe she really does. Maybe she's only curious. I don't pretend to understand myself, much less anyone else.

"I'll think about it," I lie.

"And you've never seen her again?" asks the psychologist.

"I've already told you that I haven't. But no, I've never seen her again. Just that one time. I hope it stays that way."

There's another lie.

How many nights now have I lain awake, trying to get back to sleep, trying not to think of polar bears, trying not to wish she'd return? How many times now have I been teased by lesser hauntings – lying there in our bed and tasting saltwater, hearing waves crashing against granite boulders, smelling the sea, smelling saltmarshes and dead fish, glimpsing the shadow of light reflected off the sea? How many times have I been disappointed, and how many more times will I be disappointed before this ends?

"You can call me anytime," says Imogen Keller. "If something happens. If you change your mind."

"Thank you," I say, and then our last hour's up, and she puts away her stenographer's pad with all my ghost stories written down inside it, and I go back out into the rain.

AS WATER IS IN WATER

Oh, look. Another psychiatrist story! This one I can mostly blame on Charles Fort, whose fastidiously-documented ramblings will never cease to fascinate me. Also, all the times I went swimming in the cold, deep, choppy waters of Narragansett Bay off Conanicut Island. "As Water is In Water" was written between January 24th and February 2nd, 2018.

©Loek

The Green Abyss

There really is no putting it all into words, no accurate and conclusive act of reductionism that will describe the view from the bridge. Gazing out across the waters towards the low western cliffs, weathered beds of shelly Oligocene limestone as pale as snow, I watch the sun dance on the pool until the clouds return. It's easier when the sun is shining, not only because of the warmth but also because the reflecting gleam obscures any definite view of the depths and the things that swim there. I'm dreaming, or I'm not. Likely, it doesn't matter. This place exists beyond my imagination, or it doesn't. And that's another distinction that hardly matters. More possibly, I begin to suspect it's not a simple case of being wholly one thing or the other. Everything here on the bridge above the pool may be balanced forever upon a threshold. *Here* and *now* are eternally, perpetually, liminal. I am well out beyond the X and Y coordinates of time and space. The bridge, the pool, its denizens, those white western bluffs – it's not geography, and it's not trigonometry.

"Hold your breath," she tells me.

"Was that thunder?" I ask her, and she looks back at me with eyes the color of olivine crystals.

"I wasn't listening," she lies, then bends close and kisses me.

She tastes like wind off dandelions.

"Hold your breath," she says again, when our lips have parted.

And I think, I've missed my chance. I might have breathed her in and having done so I *could* have held my breath and never had need to breathe ever again.

She holds my breath in the palm of her left hand.

Again, I hear the sound from the sky that might be thunder.

I lean farther out over the pool. Below me, the waters writhe with life.

"You've been here all along," I say. My reflection watches me, superimposed on the glistening surface. A school of giant gar, arapaima, and paddlefish glide by. "I mean, before there was a bridge, before anyone needed there to be a bridge, before it was built to –"

She reaches out and lifts the nib of my pen off the paper; she whispers, reminding me of what I've only just written about time and its relationship to *here* and *now.*

"I *was* here," she whispers, "*when* they'll *be* ready to lay the first stone, I'm here."

"Does it frighten you as much as it frightens me?" I ask and motion towards the pool. She takes her hand off mine, then steps back from the writing desk and the candlelight and from the chair where I sit. Shadows embrace her.

"You cannot even begin to imagine," she tells me.

I glance up at the sun, shining razors down between the clouds, trying again to remember if the pool is familiar because I've been here before. That's how impossible it is to truly divorce my consciousness from the safe, familiar constraints of time. God stuck a finger through the blue, and the sun was born, and I try not to allow my mind to ponder how black this place was *before* the sun. My dread is sufficiently acute without lingering on thoughts of some pre-solar, pre-Hadean incarnation of the pool.

The pool.

"Like a fly in amber, you and time," she says.

"It's hard to live in more than three dimensions," I say.

Beneath the bridge, in the green pool that must be twenty-five, thirty-five, fifty feet deep, a half-blind albino alligator, pale as those rocks on that distant shore, slips through a forest of swaying tape grass. Its jaws slowly open, as if in a yawn, and then snap shut on an impossibly large crayfish.

"I drowned when I was eight," I tell the woman standing beside me on the bridge and also behind me in my study. "I was swimming, and my legs got tangled in the weeds."

"You mean, you *almost* drowned."

"No. I meant drowned. I stopped breathing. They said I was dead for a little while."

"I'm sure they were mistaken," she says. "I don't recall seeing you, so they were almost certainly mistaken. You only almost drowned."

"I remember how cold and quiet and green it all was, after my head went under, after I stopped struggling."

The gars make another pass, and their diamond-shaped scales catch the sunlight and flash it back at me. Somewhere in their lap around the pool, they lost the arapaima and the paddlefish.

"Well, I don't recall seeing you," she tells me again.

"It wasn't this pool," I reply. "It was another pool, somewhere else. Somewhere that *is* somewhere, if you know what I mean."

She smiles and holds my breath.

And she tells me a story about the porous, honeycombed rocks below the pool, out of which flow these waters, and she tells me, too, how this pool is connected to all the waters of the world. All the waters of all worlds. So, there's another darkness that I have to consider, the darkness of subterranean streams, rivers, lakes, seas, passages that will never glimpse the sky.

"So, you see," she says, "it's odd how I don't recall you."

The sky rumbles, and I've become quite sure it isn't thunder I'm hearing. I don't look up again. No matter how much dread I feel gazing into the pool, at least the green waters are comprehensible. Whatever or whoever is hammering the sky, I fear it isn't comprehensible at all.

Below the bridge, there are eels as long or longer than tall, tall trees, hungry black eels like the boles of oaks.

"My lungs filled with water, and I sank," I say. My childhood eyes stared up at a Heaven gone to mercury, until the garden of bladderwort and sago pondweed closed to hide all that was above. "But I don't recall feeling heavy. Not like a lead weight, not like an anchor. It tasted almost sweet as candy."

"What tasted sweet, love?"

"The river where I didn't drown," I reply. "The river in Florida."

Econlockhatchee, St. Mary's, St. John's, Loxahatchee, St. Sebastian, Wekiva, Indian names and Catholic saints for crystal waters and tannin-stained arteries and silty veins.

"Hold your breath," she says.

"Too late for that now, isn't it?"

"Let go," she says. "Let go of time and hold your breath."

The sinking child, always I've half-hidden from myself this memory of a hand about the child's ankle. So, not only the entangling weeds, not only *that* bright panic, but also a something *else.* A strong, strong grip, towing the suffocating child down towards the rocky bottom, through ice water and verdant, current-tossed mansions. A grip colder than the water.

On the bridge, I shut my eyes, finally I shut my eyes, realizing I'd forgotten that was an option. I breathe in deeply, and the clean, predatory scent of the pool invades my nostrils and races through my blood, invading every cell of my being. But at least my eyes are closed. There's presently no danger I'll succumb to the *visual* sirens of curiosity and turn my gaze skyward. And I don't, for a few seconds, have to watch the cold-blooded parade beneath me. Here is, I think, *my* Scylla and Charybdis, *my* rock and a hard place. Devil and the deep green pool. Suffer all my analogies. They're insufficient layers of scar tissue against epiphany, against her. I have my six-headed demon, and I have my whirlpool, and I am such a small, small boat. No one makes it through this strait alive. Even Odysseus was forced to make a blood sacrifice.

"You're rambling, love," she says.

Love.

I don't think she's actually capable of love. That's merely a euphemism she picked up somewhere, the way she picked up that human face she wears, and "her" sex, the mask that all but hides the truth of her, all but those vicious, soothing olivine eyes.

The child, all those years ago, dragged down through the weeds, the child felt no love. The hand about an ankle was insistent, firm, but in no way loving.

"I am," I admit. "I am rambling. It's hard to marshal my thoughts."

"The sky is clear," she says. "Clearer still is the water. Open your eyes, and you'll see. Do not blind yourself. That's a fool's game."

She's rambling, too, I think.

But I do as I'm told, and I open my eyes. I look back down at the pool just as something that isn't an alligator or a crocodile slithers past, its broad grey back breaking the surface and spreading a V-shaped wake. It's some manner of lizard that's gone evolutionarily backward, seeking anatomical recursion, a reunion with those Silurian ancestors that had not yet gained limbs and lungs. The beast must be at least forty feet long and almost as sinuous as a serpent, flippers – fore and hind – where it's forebears had legs and feet. Its tail has become a sculling hypocercal rudder, and the smaller upper lobe of that divided tail also breaks the surface, shark-like. Its body is scabbed with algae and barnacles and remoras.

"You know a lot of big words," she says, as I read back over what I've written. She speaks from the shadows, safe from the candle's reach. The candle's wrath. There's a hint of mockery in her voice, but also a hint of admiration.

"I do," I reply. "In another life…" But I trail off.

"You drowned. Or so you say."

"It's a mosasaur," I tell her – on the bridge, not in the room where she stands in shadows and I write by candlelight. "That's what it's called. They all died out a long, long time ago. Became extinct." But, I remind myself, the pool exists Outside.

Free of time.

"It's rather beautiful," she tells me. "A lizard that wanted to be a whale."

"Since mosasaurs evolved first," I say, "perhaps we should say that the progenitors of whales were mammals that wanted to be mosasaurs."

"Chickens and eggs," she laughs. This is the first time I have ever heard her laugh, and it's not a pleasant sound; it's the very last sound the drowning hear.

…in truth she is a dreadful monster and no one – not even a god – could face her without being terror struck.

"I was only eight," I say again.

"When that happens, try not to be frightened. Hold your breath. Try not to breathe. When that happens, I mean."

"When I drowned?"

The hand around my ankle dug sharp nails into my child's tender flesh. Nails or claws. I never saw that supposed hand. I never saw the face or even a shadowy intimation. I went down, my arms raised as if in prayer, air bubbles trailing glassy silver from my hemorrhaging lips and nostrils. I kicked, and I thrashed, and I clawed at the water, but to no avail.

The child kicked.

And thrashed.

"You should burn it," she whispers, and I don't have to ask to know she means the pages I've written since sunset. She sounds frightened, almost.

The child kicked, and my chest caught fire.

"I want to tell you a story," she says.

"Doesn't mean I want to hear it," I reply. The great lizard submerges, and in a few moments there's no sign it ever was. The water is still again. The gars and arapaima make another pass, in their own way as grotesque as a lizard trying to be a whale. The fish gulp in the pool, pushing water over the delicate, blood-engorged filaments of gills, trading carbon dioxide for oxygen.

"The tale of the sheep crab and a parasitic barnacle," she says.

The child, drowning, flails, wondering dimly, through fading panic, how deep, how far down am I, how much farther to the bottom? The child's ears ache with the increasing weight of the water pressing in upon them. A school of small fish swim by, darting, flashing bodies brushing the dying swimmer.

"I don't need to hear it," I say, but she ignores me.

"The barnacle infects the sheep crab. The barnacle's *larvae* infect the *male* sheep crab, and they castrate it. They create a womb inside the body of the living host. They feminize the sheep crab. As its pregnant abdomen widens, it even stops growing fighting claws. The sheep crab cares for the parasites, until they finally burst from its makeshift brood pouch by the thousands."

I stop writing.

I keep my eyes on the pool.

"Was that supposed to frighten me?"

"Did it?"

The child drowns, and the world goes out like a blown bulb.

"Hold your breath, dear."

Is that all she is? A parasite?

A sheep crab?

I stare over the edge, knowing that the edge of this bridge is *all edges,* just as this pool is *all pools,* the *urabgrund*. I stare through space and time, and here, I think, here is the story of a boy dragged down into a deep, deep river. Which was not, compared to this pool, very deep at all. Yes, I can see the stone-littered, weedy bottom, but I know all too well it's an illusion, a false-bottom trapdoor to the world's abyssopelagic, *hadopelagic* regions. If I fell, I would sink like a bar of lead forever and forever. Down, down there in perpetual night and cold and eleven thousand psi. Not gars and mosasaurs, not down there, only planktonic snow, brittle-star constellations, black swallowers, and anglerfish jaws, the seeking arms of *Architeuthis dux*. I would fall, and I would sink. Without saying so, she has promised me exactly that. And here is the story, as I have just said, of a boy who drowned. He only went for a swim. It is now, decades later, a struggle *not* to fall and join all those primordial shapes gliding and slithering through the olive-green depths.

Nostalgia for hypoxia, a few precious, fleeting moments of death.

"You are becoming lost in the words," she says to me, speaking from the corner where her shadows whirl and writhe. "You're losing the heart of it."

I do not tell her how much I disagree.

I have my quill, my fountain pen, my typewriter, my laptop, and they are my window from which I look out across myself standing with her upon the bridge spanning the pool. And I haven't lost the heart of it at all. She would have me do just that, slip and fall, surrender to a failed childhood drowning. She is jealous of having lost that first time. She's simply jealous. Isn't that what sirens are, jealous, and isn't that what she is, a siren?

"There's really no putting it all into words," I say to her again, and she stares back at me with eyes precisely like the pool, filled with cold and fish and monsters.

I lay down my pen, switch off the computer, step back from the precipice.

She frowns, and it's an expression of sorrow more than anything else, that downcast face, all regret and disappointment.

She opens her hand and gives my breath back to me.

I hear peals of what might be thunder.

The eight-year-old boy in a Florida river feels the hand about his ankle let go, just before he blacks out.

And the pool is so very calm, so very flat, and I look away, concentrating instead on the far white cliffs. Soon, I realize that I am alone. The dream fades, as she has faded. The boy is dragged from the river, and his breath is given back to him, as well.

THE GREEN ABYSS

That recurring dream I wrote about in the notes following "Theoretically Forbidden Morphology," well, here it is again. In fact, this is probably a more literal account of it, one based on an actual, specific instance of the dream, which I had in October 2014. A few days later, on October 19th, I sat down and started this story, then shelved it on the 22nd. That happens sometimes. I begin a story, then shelve it. Usually, I never come back to them, and they remain forever unfinished. But I did come back to "The Green Abyss" the very next month, and I finished it on November 20th. The title is borrowed from Aristide Sartorio's 1895 painting.

Copyright Information

"Introduction" first published in *Vile Affections,* Subterranean Press, 2021.

"Virginia Story," first published in *Sirenia Digest* #146, March 2018; reprinted in *The Weird Fiction Review* No. 9, S.T. Joshi ed., Centipede Press, Winter 2018.

"Theoretically Forbidden Morphologies (1988)," first published in *Sirenia Digest* #140, September 2017.

"The Line Between the Devil's Teeth (Murder Ballad No. 10)," first published in *Sirenia Digest* #130; reprinted in *The Best Science Fiction and Fantasy of the Year: Volume 11,* Jonathan Strahan, ed., Solaris, 2017.

"King Laugh (Four Scenes)," first published in *Sirenia Digest* #142, November 2017.

"The Lady and the Tiger Redux," first published in *Sirenia Digest* #156, January 2019; reprinted in *Borderlands 7,* Olivia F. and Thomas F. Monteleone, ed., Borderlands Press, 2021.

"A Chance of Frogs on Wednesday," first published in *Sirenia Digest* #149, June 2018.

"Which Describes a Looking-Glass and the Broken Fragments," first published in *Sirenia Digest* #158, March 2019.

"Metamorphosis C," first published in *Sirenia Digest* #159, April 2019.

"Day After Tomorrow, the Flood," first published in *Sirenia Digest* #147, April 2018.

"The Last Thing You Should Do," first published in *Sirenia Digest* #160, May 2019.

"The Tameness of Wolves," first published in *Sirenia Digest* #161, June 2019.

"Iodine and Iron," first published in *Sirenia Digest* #153, October 2018.

"Untitled 44," first published in *Sirenia Digest* #162, July 2019.

"The Surgeon's Photo (Murder Ballad No. 12)," first published in *Sirenia Digest* #163, August 2019.

"Wisteria," first published in *Sirenia Digest* #164, September 2019.

"Cherry Street Tango, Sweatbox Waltz," first published in *Sirenia Digest* #151, August 2018; reprinted in *Subterranean: Tales of Dark Fantasy 3*, William Schafer, ed., Subterranean Press, 2020.

"Mercy Brown," first published in *Sirenia Digest* #166, November 2019.

"The Great Bloody and Bruised Veil of the World," first published in *Sirenia Digest* #170, March 2020.

"Untitled 41," first published in *Sirenia Digest* #152, September 2018.

"Untitled Psychiatrist No. 4," first published in *Sirenia Digest* #171, April 2020.

"As Water is In Water," first published in *Sirenia Digest* #144, January 2018.

"The Green Abyss," first published in *Sirenia Digest* #106, November 2014.

About the Author

The New York Times has heralded Caitlín R. Kiernan as "one of our essential writers of dark fiction." Their novels include *Silk, Threshold, Low Red Moon, Daughter of Hounds, The Red Tree* (nominated for the Shirley Jackson and World Fantasy awards), and *The Drowning Girl: A Memoir* (winner of the James Tiptree, Jr. and Bram Stoker awards, nominated for the Nebula, World Fantasy, British Fantasy, Mythopoeic, Locus, and Shirley Jackson awards). To date, their short fiction has been collected in fifteen volumes, including *Tales of Pain and Wonder, From Weird and Distant Shores, Alabaster, A is for Alien, The Ammonite Violin & Others, Confessions of a Five-Chambered Heart, Two Worlds and In Between: The Best of Caitlín R. Kiernan (Volume One), Beneath an Oil-Dark Sea: The Best of Caitlín R. Kiernan (Volume Two),* the World Fantasy Award winning *The Ape's Wife and Other Stories, Dear Sweet Filthy World, Houses Under the Sea: Mythos Tales, The Very Best of Caitlín R. Kiernan, The Dinosaur Tourist,* and *Comes a Pale Rider.* Between 2017 and 2020, Tor.com released Kiernan's Lovecraftian spy-noir *Tinfoil Dossier* novellas – *Black Helicopters, Agents of Dreamland,* and *The Tindalos Asset.* They have also won a World Fantasy Award for Best Short Fiction for "The Prayer of Ninety Cats." During the 1990s, they wrote *The Dreaming* for DC Comics' Vertigo imprint and, more recently, scripted the three-volume *Alabaster* series for Dark Horse Comics. The first third, *Alabaster: Wolves,* received the Bram Stoker Award. In 2017, Brown University's John Hay Library established the Caitlín R. Kiernan Papers, archiving juvenilia, manuscripts, artwork, and other material related to their work.

Sometimes described as a polymath, Kiernan's accomplishments have not been limited to fiction. They studied paleontology, geology, and comparative zoology at both the University of Alabama in Birmingham and the University of Colorado. In 1988, they described a new genus and species of mosasaur, *Selmasaurus russelli,* from Alabama and ten years later discovered the first evidence of velociraptorine theropod dinosaurs ("raptors") from the southeastern United States. Their 2002 examination of Alabama mosasaur biostratigraphy remains a benchmark in the field. In 2019, Kiernan returned to paleontology after a long hiatus and is now a research associate and vertebrate fossil preparator at the McWane Science Center in Birmingham, Alabama. Recently, they coauthored *"Asmodochelys parhami, a new fossil marine turtle from the Campanian Demopolis Chalk and the stratigraphic congruence of competing marine turtle phylogenies"* (based in part on a specimen they discovered in 2002), and they are currently coauthoring three additional papers on fossil turtles as part of a major study of marine turtle evolution. They live with two cats, Selwyn and Lydia, and their partner, Kathryn A. Pollnac.